D1520045

A Matter of Destiny

A Matter of Destiny

A Story of Conflict in Love and War

Gene Baldwin

To order additional copies of this book, contact:
Xlibris
844-714-8691
www.Xlibris.com
Orders@Xlibris.com
832480

Contents

Chapter One 1

Chapter Two 23

Chapter Three 35

Chapter Four 65

Chapter Five 79

Chapter Six..99

Chapter Seven 121

Chapter Eight...137

Chapter Nine 159

Chapter Ten..171

Chapter Eleven 197

Chapter Twelve...209

Chapter Thirteen 223

Chapter Fourteen 251

Chapter Fifteen 281

Chapter Sixteen..295

Chapter Seventeen..323

Chapter Eighteen 343

The real test of a man is not how well he plays the role he has invented for himself, but how well he plays the role that destiny assigned him.

Jan Patocka (1907-1977) Czech philosopher

This book is dedicated to Pilot Training Class 52-A and to all fighter pilots who, everyday, push the envelope in meeting the challenges of their aircraft and mission. It's their camaraderie I tried to capture in this book.

CHAPTER ONE

THE LOUDEST WHISTLE Brian ever heard, pierced the air six feet from his head, shattering his turbid dreamlike state. "Okay, you Gooney Birds, off your butts and hit the deck runnin'. You've got ten minutes to impact with the asphalt in front of this building."

Brian rolled over, amid coughing, yawning, mumbling, and vocal sounds of muscles being stretched into action. He rubbed at his eyes, trying to get his bearings, and focus on a figure at the side of his bed. He could only see two legs and a belt. Easing his head out from under the upper bunk, slowly the body emerged into a tall Sergeant, standing there, his hands on his hips, a Boy Scout type hat centered one inch above his eyebrows. His eyes were penetrating, glancing side-to-side, scanning the room. The eyes stopped their search pattern and centered on the fellow in the bunk above Brian, who had made no effort to change his prone position. "What're you waiting for, Mister, a personal invitation?"

Groggily, a reddish face rose from the top bunk, looking at the face in the funny hat. "You must not have had a very good night, Sergeant. You seem a little cross this morning." He peered at him, almost eye-level from the upper bunk, a sheepish grin extended across his face.

"Let me tell you something right now, Mister." The Sergeant moved to within three inches of Joe's face. "You aren't funny and this program's no place for a goddamn comedian. Get your act together quick or you'll be on the next bus outta' here. You read me loud and clear?"

"Yeah!" The voice in the upper bunk responded with only slightly more humility than before.

"Yes Sir, Sergeant. Not 'yeah'. You ¼" He abruptly halted the remark, shaking his head as he spun in place and moved toward the door.

A large red glob of hair, with a face attached, suddenly leaned over the edge of the top bunk. "Hi there, I'm Joe Tanner. Welcome to Dog Patch Airport."

"Brian Brannon." He was startled by the encroachment while he was contemplating his new environment. "You don't sound too happy with this place," he responded, as he swiftly assessed the owner of the booming voice, who had now dropped down and was standing beside him. Joe Tanner was a commanding presence; standing six feet four, square -shouldered, topped with flaming red hair that hung loosely over a forehead dotted with more than a few indistinct freckles. His probing green eyes were mesmerizing.

A ready smile quickly disarmed any thoughts Brian had regarding the impertinent intrusion. "I've been here about ten hours and I'm already wondering what the hell I've done to myself." Joe was overemphasizing his disgust in his inflection. "Where're you from?"

"Ruston, Alabama. How 'bout you?"

As Joe explained details about beginning life somewhere in Sumpter, South Carolina, and a brief family history, Brian half listened as his thoughts skipped away to Ruston.

Ruston, Alabama was typical of most small towns, composed of two drug stores, three grocery stores, one bank, one theater, and three traffic lights. There were few diversions in a town of 2,230 people, where folks preferred front porch rocking to the more cosmopolitan goings-on in nearby Birmingham. There was nothing geographically to distinguish Ruston from any other small town. Its most distinctive characteristic was in its eclectic inhabitants and their imaginative array of personalities. A harmonic blending of unusual backgrounds and ideologies turned potential discord into a pleasing melody. Some of the more eccentric, found on the faculty of Agnes-Baines State College for Women, provided the counterbalance to the ordinary. The subtle merging of these complex personalities, surprisingly, afforded a bonding and cohesive loyalty to each other and their town. It was this viscose blending of its inhabitants that provided Ruston its unique quality. It was comfortable growing up in a town where he always felt in control of his environment. It was home.

"Alabama, huh? Another good 'ole Southern boy. Just talked with some 'I know everything type' from New Jersey." He laughed so hard the shock of red hair in front danced on his forehead. "That Yankee know-it-all was just as overcome with a terminal case of the gloomies as me. That made me feel a whole lot better." He chuckled at the thought.

"Things'll settle today when we process. Maybe everything'll fall in place." Brian emphasized by rolling up on one elbow and looking straight at Joe.

"I'd be damn happy if you're right, but I doubt it. My basic gut feelings don't usually lie to me. In fact, this is the same bad feeling I got the day I walked through those big 'ole castle gates at the Citadel." Brian raised straight up.

"If you went to Citadel, this'll seem like the Boy Scouts."

Joe broke out in another big laugh. "I *went* to the Citadel, but I didn't *stay* there. One semester was a damn grateful plenty of that military crap. I transferred to The University of South Carolina, and never ventured closer than three blocks to the ROTC building 'till graduation."

"Well," Brian tried to choose his words carefully, "I reckon' you're about to come across a lot of military crap startin' right about now."

"Damn if you don't have a marvelous grasp of the obvious. Exactly why I'm concerned." Joe shook his head. "If I hadn't been stupid, I'd have taken ROTC and be sacked out over in the Bachelor Officer's Quarters instead of in this place that has all ambience of a cow barn." He waved his arm around at the raw, sterile surroundings of the barracks.

"Another good rendition of hindsight." Brian terminated the conversation by rolling out of his bunk, standing beside Joe Tanner. "Better get with it – we've just got eight more minutes according to the Sergeant."

The Sergeant stood at parade rest, rigid as a statue, waiting for the new group of sixty Aviation Cadets to line up in front of the barracks as best that they could. The group wasn't a very military looking array of humanity. Most were still in civilian clothes, of every different type, and modicum of style. They stood there nervously waiting for the next instructions from the Sergeant. One or two straggled out late to the formation and Joe, of course, brought up the rear.

The Sergeant snapped to attention, his boots making a large thud as the heels hit together. He plodded back and forth in front of the cadets, his eyes taking in each face. "Listen up, Gooney Birds, I'm Staff Sergeant Hacker. I'll be one of your drill instructors during pre-flight, and if you're wondering, yes, this will probably be the worst three weeks of your life. I'm going to attempt to make you look like a Cadet in the United States Air Force, and by looking at this ungodly group of humanity, that might be a little too ambitious, even for me." He paused to let the statement soak in. "This morning, you're gonna' march -- and believe me, I use that term loosely -- to chow. Later, you gooney birds will draw your uniforms, get a checkup physical, get your immunizations, put on those beautiful fatigues you'll be issued, and then we will go to the Base Theater to get a welcome from the Base C.O. Any questions?" Two hands shot up. "Good, I didn't think you had any."

By 1030 hours, everyone had survived the intense physical, eight shots, and was dressed in very new-looking, olive drab, fatigue uniforms. Aviation Cadet Class 51-G marched, or something closely akin to marching, to the Base Theater. It was only a slightly more military looking formation than the previous one, the main difference being they were now dressed alike and moving in the same general direction. They filed into the theater, taking their seats quickly.

"**Ten hut,**" boomed Sergeant Hacker, and all rose from their seats.

Brian eased his head and eyes slightly to the left to see the processional of officers that were walking briskly down the isle.

"Straight ahead, Mister!" The words blared into his left ear as a blurred vision of the Sergeant moved into Brian's peripheral view. He quickly snapped his head forward.

"Take your seats, gentlemen." As the sound of shuffling into their seats subsided, he continued. "I'm Colonel Zwiecker, Commanding

Officer of the thirty-five, fifty-fifth Flying Training Wing. This is Lieutenant Colonel Flynn, who is the Tactical Officer in charge of Class fifty-one-G. The other officers here on the stage with me, you'll get to know, in a very personal way, very soon. I want to welcome you to Perrin Air Force base and the United States Air Force. You are about to embark upon an adventure that you'll remember the rest of your lives. Our job is to make you officers and pilots in the finest military service on earth. During Basic flight training, you'll be tested in every conceivable way as you begin to accomplish that goal. You'll complete basic flight training knowing that you've taken the first step in becoming one of the few who are privileged to wear the silver wings of an Air Force pilot. You'll join an elite fraternity of those who have been right where you are today, men who met the demands, the challenges, and self-discipline to become pilots in The United States Air Force.

Some of you will go on to multi-engine training, and some will be chosen to fly fighters in advanced training. In either case, you'll leave here fully prepared to enter that phase of the flight program. Look to either side of you. The cadet sitting on your left or right probably won't complete basic flight training, and some of you'll request elimination. A request for elimination will, in no way, be held against you. This program demands every ounce of you emotionally, mentally and physically. You'll be called upon to reach deep into your resolve for the very best you have to give. Sometimes *more* than you have to give. Some of you will not be able to adjust to these demands. Unfortunately, statistics tell us that approximately fifty percent of you won't complete this program. Those who do will feel a sense of pride and accomplishment unlike any other feelings in your life. Good luck to each of you!"

"Ten- hut!"

The officers filed out in the same order that they entered. A sense of doubt overwhelmed Brian for a split second, then slowly he felt a resolve take over his thought process. Colonel Zwiecker's speech instilled in him the idea that nothing; *nothing* was going to stop him from completing the program. At that instant, a visceral feeling of obstinate determination seized his entire being, replacing the apprehension that plagued him from yesterday. He had to make it.

He remembered his mother's opposition to his entering the Air Force's flight program. He could hear the subtle, but cutting, voice that offered her reasons for him not to apply. She skillfully created just the right space in her arguments for Brian to work in a solid case of guilt. He hated the feeling. Their conversations on the subject had been quite contentious and he never could make his views clear. He remembered the cross-examination waiting for him at breakfast each morning, complete with well-placed innuendo of indictments.

Brian pulled himself up to a plate of eggs and bacon, sharing space on the plate with a generous helping of grits. His mother pulled up a chair opposite him, positioning herself directly in front of his view. "You haven't told me how things went at Maxwell Field" she said softly. "When you came in last night, I was asleep and now this morning you've completely avoided the subject. Tell me all about it."

He looked up from breakfast. "I guess it went pretty well, but who knows?" He wiped his mouth with the napkin, pacing himself. "There're too many ways not to get accepted. They accept so few, just one out of four, you never really know until you get the results."

"Obviously, you still hope it went well." She fingered her coffee cup handle as she carefully phrased her thoughts. "We've been over this subject and agreed to let it drop, but I need to mention *one* other point because it's important to me ¼"

"Please! I've heard it all." Brian interrupted. "Let's not get into the subject of me going back to Auburn again." His stomach churned. "By now, I reckon I know all your reasons. I know how strongly you feel about me flying, how disappointed you are that I'm doing this." There was an abrupt gap in the conversation. He looked down, staring at his unfinished breakfast. "Besides, if I'm not accepted, this conversation's taking place for no reason."

"I admit it's been hard for me to understand." She picked up her plate. "But I won't say another word." She shoved her chair back and walked to the sink. She stood there, arms braced on the edge of the counter top, her head lowered, looking down blankly at the dishes piled there.

He wanted to say something. The words almost came but he yanked them back. He couldn't breach the lack of closeness built up through the years. It was too late.

Following her divorce from Brian's father, the depression and shortage of teacher jobs forced his mother to take a teaching position in another town. He was left with his grandparents at the age of five. She and Brian were both satisfied with this living arrangement. That decision, which he had no part in, was the best thing that happened in his life.

The stabilizing influence on his early life had clearly been his grandmother. She stood between him and those forces he perceived as harsh or unfair. The balance between his grandfather's discipline and the gentleness of his grandmother were the security he came to regard as his sanctuary. He loved his grandmother's patience and sensitiveness. He knew, beyond a doubt, she was the best woman God ever created. The death of his grandfather was a solemn loss, but the death of Molly Cartwright DeShaso surpassed any trauma he had ever felt. His mother returned to Ruston, to take a teaching position she loathed, in a town she thought she had escaped. Now, it was just the two of them in the large house that, at one time, seemed so full of people and life. They struggled to correlate their relationship, thrust upon them with so little preparation.

He remembered clearly the day he got the letter from the Air Force. He stood there in the Post Office and eased the words into view a little at a time, pacing himself in the reading. His heartbeat increased as he scanned past the salutation, getting to the critical paragraph on the first page:

"...This is to inform you of your acceptance to the United States Air Force Aviation Cadet Program, Class 51G. You will report to the Aviation Training Detachment Perrin AFB, Texas not later than midnight, 22 Oct. 1950. . . ."

He felt the blood pulsate in his temples. The chances had been one in four, and he'd made it.

The day came for him to leave. Brian and his mother were having their usual breakfast discussion he had come to dread. He sat, looking at his plate, wondering if the morning inquest would be served shortly. He didn't have to wait long for the next course to be served with his fresh toast.

"Brian, tell me what happens if you don't complete the flight training. Do you have to stay in the Air Force?" She asked. "It seems you're taking quite a gamble on your future."

He dropped the fork into his plate, both hands raised in surrender. "Is this the only subject we can discuss at breakfast these days? I'll tell you right now. I don't want to hear any more about the Air Force, school --." He didn't finish the sentence. His body tensed.

She straightened in her chair. "Tell me something. Why can't we talk anymore? I've always wondered why we've never been able to communicate like most mothers and sons do. There's a barrier between us we just can't seem to cross." She made eye contact, as he looked up. "I've always had a feeling you blamed me for getting a divorce?" She looked penetratingly, her eyes narrowed as she continued. "You've built this idealistic picture of your father over the years." She leaned forward, pushing the cup and saucer aside. "There're so many things you don't know."

Brian straightened, his face burning with the rush of blood. His mouth became dry as he swallowed back the words that almost flew out.

She recognized the change in his expression. "Do you think I'm somehow responsible for your father's death? Is that the ghost that's between us?" Brian made no reply. She stood silently looking at him for a response. He slid his chair back and walked quickly toward the door. "My God." she exclaimed

Later that night, Brian put the last few items in an overnight bag. The last was a small picture of his father he kept on the dresser. He slept fitfully through the night. Thoughts were churning in his brain in a montage of scenes, past, present, and future. Dawn took its time arriving. He dressed quickly and zipped the bag shut. He took one last look around his room, grabbed the small bag, and walked down the long hall. Dropping the car keys on the oak hat rack in the long entry, he hugged his mother goodbye. She started to say something but stopped short of expressing her feelings. There was an unspoken reconciliation of the inevitable.

Brian walked through the stained glass and oak door, stopped at the bottom of the steps, and glanced back for one last look at the white frame house. It had been his home as long as he could remember, but he was seeing features he'd never noticed before. He looked up at the high gables, then the long porch with the swing, and the shutters that needed painting, framing each window. The old house, passed down to his mother from her father, took on a different look this October morning. Its stately warmth held him fast to the spot, imposing its grip on his past, and showing him the security that was his youth. He knew his life was about to take a different direction. His boyhood had just ended.

Movement toward the theater exits by sixty cadets snapped his attention back to Perrin Air Force Base. The rest of the day disappeared in a haze of running, pushup, and instructions on everything from rolling socks to making square corners on a bed. Sixty totally spent cadets were finally dismissed. Even though exhausted, Brian took time to scribble a note to Anne on one of the several post cards he'd bought on the trip to Texas. He wrote a few innocuous words, jotted his address at the bottom of the card, and said he'd write later. He wrote a quick note to his mother, then scribbled a humorous note to Tyler on another card, and placed them beside his bunk for mailing.

It seemed the filament in the lights had just dimmed to black when Sergeant Hacker's whistle was an obscene invasion into the realm of dream-like sleep. Brian woke suddenly and swung out of bed, grabbing at his fatigue uniform, carefully positioned the previous night to save time. A buzz of activity took place in every direction as the thirty cadets on the first floor were obtaining their bearings, trying to organize their efforts to shave, dress in their fatigue uniforms, make their bunks, and be outside in formation in all of ten minutes. Brian shaved hurriedly and combed at his brown hair that had vanished into a flattop. He moved his face up and down, gawking at the image looking back. He wished he looked older. The newly acquired crew cut gave him a boyish look he didn't like.

"There's no way in hell that I'm ever gonna' get used to this kind of crap at oh-dark-thirty," blared Joe, standing at the next lavatory.

"I'd suggest you stop wasting time moanin'. You'd better get your butt moving."

"I *am* moving." Joe laughed. "You just can't tell it yet."

The day began with breakfast, then P.T. followed by a three-mile run, and capped with some classes on military custom and courtesies, and various other military topics. Brian spent most of the evening polishing brass until he removed all the lacquer down to base metal, allowing the brass to take on a high luster shine. Shoes required several hours of effort to put on a base shine so that the "spit shine," meticulously done with small concentric circles of water and polish, would be virtually as smooth as glass. He was exhausted enough that sleep was instantaneous.

The days passed rapidly during pre-flight due to the closely scheduled events. Letters from home were blessed respites from the rigors of training. Letters from his mother kept him informed of all the happenings in Ruston, and her latest reports from Dr. Goldstein. She left out no details of her latest bout with bronchitis, which according to her was almost pneumonia. Brian clutched the blue envelope he had read three times, rolled back on his bunk and thought back on his last three weeks in Ruston

Those last three weeks in Ruston with the kaleidoscopic Anne had given little enough time to know each other. In spite of the urgency, at the end of those rapidly moving three weeks they were still fumbling through the camouflage that goes with getting to understand a person. They delved deep in the short relationship to get down under those personality facades that give way only to trust.

Brian found contentment in remembering the first time he had seen Anne. He wrapped the feelings around him until he was sitting there in The Grill, with his best friend Tyler Dugan, watching people come and go.

Tyler Dugan and Brian had been inseparable since their first day in Mrs. Hood's kindergarten class. Their mercurial personalities blended with nonchalant loyalty. Tyler was easygoing, liked by everyone, and completely at ease with anyone. He was the catalyst that fused a group together for any venture. His voice wasn't animated with infective enthusiasm. It was deliberate, impassive, sounding about one octave lower than his slim frame denoted. He always assumed his role of informal leader modestly. Whatever Tyler decided to do, or wherever he decided to go, others automatically followed without the slightest encouragement from him.

Suddenly, the door opened. With no warning, he was staring at a radiance he'd never seen before. His eyes darted to the other girls standing beside her, hoping he knew them. One was vaguely familiar, but the name, the name was not attached to his memory. Every part of him was snatched back to the girl in the middle and Brian couldn't avert his stare.

Her chiseled features had a certain softness, accentuated by her smile. Shoulder-length dark brown hair was parted on the right side pulled back to the left, and held loosely with a barrette so it framed her face. With each movement of her head there was a discernable glow as the light reflected from her mahogany eyes.

Risking a glance at the rest of her, he locked onto the way she filled out the blouse and skirt in just the right places. He took in a deep breath and deliberately absorbed the entire picture of her. His feelings rose like the inevitable toss of the tide that shoved him toward her. There was no choice, knew he had to meet her. He moved quickly to the girl he thought he knew. "Hi. I'm Brian Brannon, uh ¼I think we met at a party at Auburn last year."

Her questioning look indicated she didn't remember, yet didn't want to state it too bluntly. "I'm a little fuzzy¼I guess we did." She said. "Was it at the K A house?"

"Nope. It was at the Delta Tau Delta house."

"Sure. I should have remembered. I'm Carol, this is¼" He completely tuned out the voice, staring at the brunette, waiting impatiently to hear her name. "¼and this is my cousin Anne Merrill." The words rang in his head as he mentally repeated it. *Anne. Anne Merrill.*

The next afternoon he slowly dialed the number for Main Dormitory as his fingers deliberately found each hole. He leaned back and waited to hear her voice on the other end. "Hello."

"Hi, this is Brian Brannon. We met last night at the Grill – remember – with your cousin Carol?"

"Sure. You knew each other."

"Well we met briefly at Auburn. We really didn't get to know each other." He cleared his throat. "I wondered if you'd like to go have a burger and take in a movie tonight?"

"I can't." She protested. I'm going with someone from back home in Collinwood and I don't think it would be such a good idea."

"That's okay. Maybe we'll see each other again – accidentally."

Two days later, he hesitated, mentally arguing with himself, but knowing he really had no choice. He called again. The only encouragement this time was the length of conversation following that first unsuccessful encounter. They talked for several minutes, getting past the coldness he felt the first time. He seemed to break through the friendly but distant rationale that she was going with someone, only to be told "no" yet again.

When a girl said no, even once, Brian usually shrugged it off and forgot about it. But that radiance, burned indelibly in his memory of her face kept encouraging him to make that next call. He couldn't understand the constant awareness he had about this girl he'd seen only once. She leaped into his thoughts when least expected. He found her there in his head, a vision he couldn't shake. He was powerless to obliterate the image and yet had no desire to erase the pleasure of seeing her in his every waking thought. After three phone calls he made himself realize his efforts to get a date with Anne Merrill were not going to pay off. He reluctantly admitted defeat.

"Hey." Joe was shaking him, "Hey, put those letters away and get your butt up. You've got to get ready for inspection, and you're laying there daydreaming about Alabama or something worse – naw, there's nothing worse than that."

"Bite me." Brian stated as he rolled out of the bunk. He quickly placed the letters in his footlocker and took out the shoe polish. He picked up one shoe and began making small concentric circles with the cloth. He continued dipping the cloth into the polish and making circles until the shoe took on a high luster. He reached down for the other shoe.

The makeup of Aviation Cadet Class 51-G was a complete cross-section of America. This blend of Americanism, merged into a common purpose, placed little emphasis on cultural differences. They were bonded together to outwit the system, Sergeant Hacker and the other TAC NCOs. Each of them was fighting to survive the rigors of pre-flight. Four cadets left the program by the end of the second week, unable or unwilling to adapt to the demands placed on their mind and body. Pre-flight tested their mental and physical being to the limits of endurance. It became the catalyst that bound the survivors together.

Joe's acidic wit played well off of Brian's tenaciousness. A clique began to emerge of those who grasped the intricacies of the training and felt superior in the way they achieved the myriad of requirements. Scott Jeter, from Thomasville, Georgia, was exceedingly lank, narrow shoulders, long arms and legs. His hands dangled loosely at his sides. He had a well-honed sense of humor that offset the occasional cynicism of Joe Tanner. Scott inadvertently became the third member of this informal group when he and Joe were comparing notes on Sherman's "March to the Sea." Scott was Southern from his slow drawl to his favorite expression: "That's worse than a suck-face mule." He graduated from the University of Georgia and completed one year of law school. Scott told the story with animation about being expected to join the rather stifling family law firm, in Thomasville, after graduation. The frustration of his announcing he was leaving for the Aviation Cadet program, by Scott's account, left his father with "his greatest disappointment in life."

"I was bound to disappoint my father sooner or later, so I figured I may as well get it over with."

Then there was Ellis Siegal, who was always around. Anytime there was a gathering of the other three, he appeared as if by magic, becoming a member of the group by default. Quickly, and rather naturally, he took on his nickname of Bugsy. His Ohio accent was strenuous on the ears of Southerners and it took a fair amount of time to decode some of his thoughts. Bugsy didn't exude confidence. He was downright cocky. His five-eight frame pushed the lower limits of the physical qualifications for pilot training. The walking, breathing evidence of the short man syndrome, Bugsy would draw himself up to his full height when engaged in conversation. An additional half-inch seemed added by his tenacious personality. Bugsy possessed a keen sense of his environment, very adept at knowing when to mute his cockiness, especially in the presence of Sergeant Hacker or the other Tactical Non-Commissioned Officers. The others knew his outward humility was only an adept display for his tormentors. It was a game he played masterfully.

The group was rounded out by Boyce Hollinger, the epitome of an Ivy Leaguer, and obviously well versed in all phases of proper etiquette and charm that comes from an "old money" background. His chiseled features and incomparable grooming made him stand out among the other cadets. Boyce reported to the base wearing a camel hair top coat, grey pin-striped suit, silk tie, and black wingtip shoes. When they lined up the first morning to draw their uniforms, he stood out extremely well in the formation. Sergeant Hacker walked back and forth, slowly contemplating the figure in front of him, as if forming words to go with his thoughts. Finally, shaking his head without comment, he moved on down the line. Boyce was the most likeable, easy-going of the group. He rolled with the punches, radiating undeviating optimism as the others groused constantly about assaults on their dignity. He was the placating influence on the other three. Boyce could create calm out of chaos. The group was welded together by an imperceptible bond that only they understood. The cohesiveness of the group defied the rigid requirements placed on mind and body. It made the three weeks move in a blur as days merged quickly into night with the rigors of a compact schedule. It was then that Brian could lay back on his bunk and contemplate the night things changed drastically with Anne.

It was a boring Saturday night when he agreed to meet Tyler at The Grill. They sipped their cokes and made comments about some of the other patrons in The Grill. For them, people watching was a pastime in and of itself. Brian instinctively glanced up at the sound of the door opening, watching several Agnes-Baines girls come through the door, looking about for a vacant booth. He suddenly noticed Anne in the group and jerked his eyes the other way. He felt uncomfortable.

He looked deliberately at Tyler, focusing his gaze so as not to be tempted to look at Anne. His first impulse was to suggest they leave. Instead, he casually cut his peripheral gaze back toward Anne. As the girls began arranging themselves in a booth, Anne's scrutiny turned to Brian and Tyler. She looked their way with a half-smile, as if measuring the distance to their booth and taking note of their behavior. Instead of sitting with the others, she moved directly toward them, wending her way through the maze of tables, and stood at the edge of their booth.

"Hey there" she exclaimed.

"Hi, how's school?" Brian inquired matter-of-factly, making himself look straight at her.

Without acknowledging his question, or looking at Tyler, Anne asked, "You probably weren't going to call me again, were you?"

"Hell no, I can be a little slow at times, but I finally got the point." Brian felt his face turning a slight salmon color.

She studied him for a moment. "I can see you're a little put-out with me." Her hands snapped to her hips and she leaned toward Brian. "What I wanted to tell you was; if you'd call me again, I'd like to go out with you some time."

Swiftly, Tyler scooted to the end of the bench and nervously cleared his throat. "Excuse me, I think I see somebody I need to talk to." He glanced back quizzically at Brian, hunching his shoulders at his incredulity of her offer. Brian frowned back his comment as Tyler ambled off toward another booth.

Anne quickly sat down opposite Brian, placed both arms on the table, and looked directly at him. "Your expression tells me you're a little confused. I seem to be good at confusing people."

"No joke? Tell me what caused this sudden change of attitude."

"Well, being new at A-B and sorta' naive about everything, I was told that you and your friend had a reputation for dating quite a few girls at A-B and that I'd be smart not to get involved. I've learned it's best to make your own judgments about people." She chuckled. "Besides, I like your persistence."

As he listened, he was captivated by her voice, sheathed in the softness of the more pronounced accent of south Alabama, yet enthusiastic in its inflection. The sound of her voice and the hypnotic effect of her presence were intoxicating. He accepted his silence was awkward. "What're you doing right now?" He nodded toward the table of girls she just left. "Do you have to stay with them?"

"Goodness no. I doubt they've even noticed I'm gone."

Brian slid to the end of the booth. "C'mon, let's go for a walk? Its gotta' be less crowded than this place."

"Okay." She said, sliding out of the booth.

Outside, they strolled along slowly, making mundane conversation about school, classes, and dorm life in Old Main. The usual first-date clumsiness was not there and he felt himself relax as they walked down the nearly deserted street, glancing occasionally at this person beside him. The lemony smell of her hair engulfed him as it swung loosely with her movements. Brian brushed her hand, causing her to look quickly at him. "I think I understand what you said back there about the advice you got. But on the phone, you told me you were involved with someone." He looked at her for an answer, but she didn't respond immediately. "Sounded serious," he added, urging a reply.

"Oh, that's another story entirely. Don't worry about it. I decided there's absolutely nothing wrong with going out and enjoying being with someone else occasionally." She glanced up. "One of the girls who gave me such free and easy advice said you and your friend went to Auburn. Registration's next week isn't."

"No." He laughed. "I mean yes; registration's next week, but I'm not going back. I'm going to flight training in the Air Force. I've got three weeks before I leave."

"Three weeks?" She paused briefly as if analyzing the statement then walked on.

As they entered the campus, they walked beneath the hundred-year-old oaks that extended their branches, rising fountain-like from their enormous trunks, forming a solid canopy of foliage. The front campus of Agnes Baines State College for Women was situated on Ruston's highest point. The campus was compact, with the new buildings in architectural harmony with those of historic note. The predominant building was Ole Main, largest girls' dormitory in the country. The streets, as well as the walks, were all brick, laid out in a symmetrical herringbone pattern. The bricks were old, uneven, rutted, and walking on them in high heels one of the true challenges for new students. But it was the classic feature most remembered by all past students. As they approached the Tea House entrance, Anne turned and pointed toward Old Main and to her room's window on the second floor. "That's our room, the one with the pathetic looking plant in the window. It gives us a bird's eye view of everyone coming and going to the Tea House and it's close to the Post Office."

"Good planning, or good luck. Hey, why not go to the Tea House and grab a coke?"

Brian brought the drinks over to the booth, turned and strolled over to the large multi-lighted jukebox. Carefully looking over the list, he put in a quarter and selected five songs. As they talked, the first song, *La Vie En Rose,* began. He examined her face as she talked, intrigued by the sensual movement of her mouth. Her effervescent, outgoing personality was refreshing. She explained the reason for her transfer to Agnes-Baines was not because of wanting to be with her cousin Carol, and roommate Lori that he'd met during their first introduction. It was simply because of a scholarship offered at A-B. The financial help was required to help her mother meet the cost of college. There was absolutely no pretense to her. Her easygoing confidence stated the obvious: accept me as I am.

The rest of the evening seemed to evaporate as they laughed and talked. The lights blinked twice to announce there were ten minutes before girls had to be in the dorm.

"Gotta' go. There go the lights." Anne said.

"How about tomorrow? We could take in the movie or something?" Brian inquired.

She hesitated for a few seconds, as if mulling over the thought. "Sure. A movie sounds great. What time?"

"How 'bout eight? That'd give us plenty of time to get there."

"Okay, I'll meet you in the lobby at eight."

He held the door open and watched her disappear up the side stairs, taking in every last movement. He whistled *La Vie En Rose* as he ambled lazily toward the gate.

CHAPTER TWO

THE SUN EMERGED sluggishly from behind the dark, unruly clouds as the rain stopped its intrusion on an otherwise perfect Saturday morning. The significance of this particular day was its marking the completion of pre-flight. The formation of cadets dressed in their new khaki's with blue shoulder boards, brightened silver US insignia on each collar, and shoes that reflected hours of buffing was an impressive sight. Brian glanced around at the imposing formation, and a sense of accomplishment prematurely overtook him. He winked at Joe and quickly looked back at Sergeant Hacker.

Sergeant Hacker walked up to Brian, his nose almost touching his. "You Wanna' buy this place, mister?" He screamed.

"No Sir, Sergeant." Brian worked at removing his smile.

"Then what the hell are you looking around for, Mister Brannon? You think you've got preflight made?"

"No Sir, Sergeant." Brian shouted.

"That'd be a large miscalculation on your part, Mister Brannon.

If you think you've got preflight knocked, make one more wrong move. I'll be damned if I don't roll you back to the next class. Maybe you need a second time through."

Brian tensed at the words. He knew the Sergeant meant it. He learned early in the program that this man always meant what he said. He never bluffed. He swallowed hard as he formed the words, "Yes Sir, Sergeant."

The formation moved out smartly for their march to the cadet area, counting cadence like orchestrated thunder. When he halted the formation in front of the administration building, he was smiling at Class 51-G for the first time. "Good luck to each of you."

"Yes Sir, Sergeant," came the chorus of voices.

Brian hustled next door to the supply room, where he acquired books, flight suits, flight jacket, brief case with all sorts of devices, along with a pair of coveted Air Force pilot sunglasses to add to the weight of his full duffel bag of uniforms. He trudged toward his barracks assignment, gear in tow, walking haltingly under the weight of the recently issued equipment.

"Hold it there, Mister." Two cadets materialized from nowhere, each with several white stripes on their shoulder boards. They moved directly in front of him. "Do you have any remote idea of where you're going, or what the hell you're doing, Mister?" You passed an officer and didn't salute!"

"Where?" asked Brian, looking past them.

"Keep those eyes front and center, Mister," shouted the tallest cadet. "You'd better develop your peripheral vision, Mister, because if an officer passes within a block of you, you'd better snap your head in that direction and salute. In the mean time, keep those eyeballs caged like a gyro. You understand, Mister? And, if you get asked a question in the future, you answer 'No excuse sir.' Got that, Mister?"

"Yes Sir." Snapped Brian, in his loudest voice.

"I doubt you're gonna' make it here. You don't look like a pilot to me." There was a slight pause, then, "Very well, carry on, Mister."

He caught a glimpse out of the corner of his eye of a large number 320 affixed to a building to his right, and made a sudden turn to get into the safety of the structure as soon as possible. Immediately to the right was room number two. The corner room permitted a view of the entire area including the mess hall diagonally across the street. He released the gear, letting it fall on the floor, and fell across the bunk, relieved to be alone.

"Damn, this crap's heavy. Stand clear so I can drop this load." Joe roared as he entered the room.

Brian eased into a broad grin to see who his roommate was going to be. "I knew it was you. The first thing I heard was bitchin' and moanin'."

"Hey, this is great. Sleeping in a room with twenty-nine other guys is a bit too much togetherness for me. Let's get this place straight and slip over to the cadet club for a coke. Christ, I almost feel free."

Joe's announcement was short lived. One loud knock on the wall announced two upper classmen, who popped into the room. "Hit a brace, Misters. Mister Mullen and I are here to give you two a little guidance. First let me make it clear; you'll hit a brace anytime an upper classman enters this room. When you're outside you'll square all corners wherever you're going, and not in a formation. You'll keep your eyeballs caged at all times. You'll 'fall out' five minutes before first call for all formations. I'm Mister Low, and you'll probably remember that name on your deathbed. Mister Mullen and I live right across the hall, in room one. You'll be lucky enough to have us in your knickers every minute of every day." He moved around the room, kicking the items of issue across the floor. "I'm giving you one hour to get this room in inspection order, all hangers exactly one inch apart, shoes aligned under the bed with spit shines, and a white collar bed that I can bounce a quarter on." They both disappeared as quickly as they came.

"Is that sonofabitch for real, or did I just have a bad dream?" Joe shook his head.

"Let's get him off our back." Brian responded.

Exactly fifty-nine minutes later, Mister Low made the customary one knock, as he lunged through the door. Brian and Joe hit a brace in front of their bunks, waiting for and expecting the worst. Unfortunately for Mister Low, there were no glaring errors to be used to admonish his captive underclassmen. Frank Low stood there glaring at his captive audience. "You two have a long hard road ahead. I'm gonna' see if you have what it takes to stay in this program, and I doubt you do. I'm gonna' be the one that breaks the both of you."

As the door banged close, Joe fell into the chair. "God a'mighty, we fell into it this time." Brian made no comment on the situation. He was thinking about what Low had said.

Joe reached over and took the picture of Brian's father off the desk. He held it out studying every feature. "Your Dad?"

"Yeah." Brian reached for the picture.

"Little unusual to have a picture of your Dad on the desk. You do like girls, don't you?"

"Not really. I'm a queer, and I've had my eye on you from the start." Brian said.

Joe instinctively moved back a step. He smiled slowly, watching Brian's face. "Damn, Man, don't do that. You had me about ready to holler for help."

"Now, you've gotta' wonder. Better sleep with one eye open."

"Nope. I can spot one from a block away. You aint prissy enough."

Sunday was a day off for the new cadet class. It was the first they'd enjoyed since their arrival at Perrin. When they met at the Cadet Club, Brian and Joe learned that Scott, Boyce and Bugsy were assigned to the other three flights. The Group kicked back and relaxed while they enjoyed sharing "horror stories" of surviving the worst that could be thrown at them. Scott finished a colorful harangue about the upperclassmen in his barracks. "These miserable sonsabitches take it to the extreme. They're worse than --."

Bugsy barged in and cut him short in mid-sentence. "Yeah, we know. Worse than that silly-ass mule you talk about." Laughter spotlighted Scott's exasperation.

Scott slid forward in his chair, squinted as if looking into the sun. He leaned toward the source of the mockery. "You know, Bugsy, in Georgia you're what's known as a 'piss-ant'. Small, unnecessary, and aggravating as hell." Laughter indicated who won that contention of wits.

Boyce scrooched up his face, with a look that indicated his puzzlement. "What kind of ant, Scott?" The laughter now was uncontrollable.

That night Brian lay there contemplating the fact he was actually into Basic Training and tomorrow would be his first flight. He would finally be in the air. The anticipation was not conducive to sleep. He rolled and tossed until his mind wandered back and forth between the past and present. He moved the pillow under his head to a more comfortable position. He ignored the sounds of Joe's deep breathing, losing himself in shifting visions of Anne. His scrutiny of the scenes settled down to that first date with Anne, after their brief walk back to her dorm the night before. His thoughts swirled with flashes of that night.

He could almost feel the movie theater's armrest, hard and cold against his rib cage. It dug into his side as he moved as close as he could get. The wood and metal would permit his body to be only so close to her in the darkened theater. He didn't watch much of the movie. He'd get fully engrossed in the flickering frames for a few minutes, and then glance at her. When he looked over at her, the dialogue became only a background buzz of incoherent conversation. He watched the shimmering lights from the screen illuminate her face when she turned toward him. There was a feeling, completely new to him, gripping his insides as he contemplated the beauty of her face. The mood was snatched away when the credits suddenly appeared on the screen. The glare of the house lights coming up slowly discontinued the atmosphere he was enjoying.

During the walk back, the cool of the evening glided over them. The oppressive heat of the day had been cooled by the shroud of night. There was just enough breeze moving the sultry air to make it more friendly. The clock at the bank boomed the half-hour as they walked by, a subtle announcement the evening was almost over. Brian glanced at his watch, confirming the Bank clock's accuracy. He had no desire for the evening to end.

As they reached the front campus, he motioned to one of the wrought iron and wooden copies of the Charleston Battery Benches. "We've got a few more minutes yet." She answered by turning so swiftly her skirt swirled around as she plopped on the bench. He looked at the girl beside him, and then out over the large open grassed area of the front campus, crisscrossed with brick walks, their intersection marked prominently with a sundial. The chirping of crickets punctuated the night. Sporadic distant laughter and chatter emanated from open dorm windows. An occasional car's lights danced across the grass expanse, popping in and out of view as it passed behind the huge oaks forming the boundary between the college and town. The leaves moved casually overhead with each muffled breeze. The stillness of the night accentuated their silence as they sat there. Sliding his arm along the top of the bench, he closed his fingers lightly round her shoulder. "Tell me about Collinwood. What's it like down there in South Alabama?"

"Oh, I reckon you'd call Collinwood's just another small sleepy town." She stopped and looked at Brian, a half-smile indicated her reservation. "You aren't really asking about the town, are you?"

"Actually I wanted to hear the sound of your voice." He chuckled. "Okay, guess I was interested in the story that was too long to get into last night. Who's the mysterious guy you said you were going with?"

"It's certainly no mystery and I doubt you're really interested in this story, but I'll make it short. When my father died, I was only eight, and Judge McBride took the place of my father in lots of ways. That's Justin's father. Justin's the fellow you seem so interested in." She looked at him for a reaction. There was none. He sat staring into her eyes, waiting for the rest of the story to unfold.

"I probably spent as much time over at their house as mine."

"The Judge, being a good friend of my Dad's, obviously felt some responsibility toward me after he died. Justin and I were friends all through grade school and just as expected started going together in high school." She glanced directly at Brian again for emphasis. "Justin probably understands me better than anyone else."

"Well now, tell me something. Is 'ole Justin your best friend, a brother figure, or your boy friend?"

"I guess that was meant to be about as sarcastic as it sounded." She snapped. Her gaze dropped, then shot back toward him. "Just for your information, you happen to be right on all three counts."

"It wasn't all that sarcastic. You just seem a little touchy about 'ole Justin."

She sat there glaring at him, as if thinking of something to say or getting ready to jump up and bolt away. There was a period of silence that seemed much longer than it actually was. He looked out across the campus, then back at her. He cleared his throat as the tightness closed its grip.

Brian laughed. "Okay, I'm a horse's ass. I didn't mean to get into your relationship with some guy I don't even know. You're so easy to talk to, it sorta' slipped out." He stopped momentarily. "There's nothing I hate more than first dates when you have to make conversation and find some mutual point of interest to talk about. With you, I don't have to do that."

She touched his arm. "Don't worry. I'm not mad at your blasted question, even if you did sound like a horse's patoot. It takes a lot more than that." Anne looked at him, her head tilted slightly, smiling. He leaned toward her, slowly bringing his face closer until their lips met. She didn't turn away and there was no protest. He placed his hands on her shoulders, pulled her close and kissed her again with more intensity. He could feel his heart beating against his shirt. She moved her head back, looking into his eyes, as if searching there for an explanation. Neither spoke. They looked intently at each other, neither noticing the lights were blinking their announcement that this evening was almost history. They were absorbed, measuring the extent of the other's reaction. Their eyes were locked in evaluation of the energy that shot between them in that one volatile moment.

She looked over his shoulder, then back at him. "Geez, It's time to go." She said.

He stood up, taking her hand, pulling her to her feet. They strolled toward the side entrance in no particular hurry. As they reached the door, Brian took her hand and forcefully turned her toward him. "How 'bout tomorrow?"

"I really need to study and, besides, I told you I was going with someone." She said.

"That sure didn't stop you from going tonight." He searched her face for a reaction.

Her smile left suddenly. "Yep, and look what happened." She smiled. "Reckon it was a little bit my fault too."

Brian wasn't going to let it go that quickly. "It doesn't matter whose fault. It happened." He took her hand. "Tell you what. Study till nine o'clock tomorrow night, then I'll meet you right here, we'll amble over there to the Tea House, get a coke, and just talk for a while. There's certainly no harm in that."

She smiled again. "Okay, tomorrow night at nine, but I won't be able to stay long. Hey, thanks, I enjoyed the movie." She turned and ran up the steps.

The next evening he leaned against the lamppost near the street waiting nervously for her to come down. The night was sultry. The humidity clung to him like his impatience, making the waiting more intolerable. He glanced at the door, as two girls emerged talking in muffled tones. Glancing at his watch, he saw it was sixteen minutes after. Bitterness swept through him. *She's not coming after all.* He turned to leave.

"Hi. Sorry I'm late." His insides warmed with the sound of her voice. He spun around and walked to her. "I thought you'd changed your mind."

She gave no explanation and made no attempt to remove her hand as he gently took it. He looked up at the sky as they walked across the street to the Tea House. "It's still hot but look at that sky up there. Great night." She glanced up, then back at him, smiled but still made no comment. He stopped abruptly, turning her toward him. "Hey, just a minute. Are you sorry you met me tonight? Is that why you're so quiet?"

"I'm a little concerned about where this may be going. I thought about last night and felt a little guilty all day." She said.

"The only place this is going is over there to The Tea House and talk a while. Nothing more."

"Then let's go." She pulled him along as she bolted toward the Tea House door.

As they sipped their bottles of coke, he watched her face intently as it became animated with descriptions of the people and events in her life. Her sense of humor was sporadic, quickly punctuating her conversation. She suddenly became silent, searching his eyes.

"Why do you have this burning desire to fly?"

"Now, how in the world do I explain something like that? I can't remember a time I didn't want to fly. Just looking at an airplane turns me on." He hesitated. "My mother, on the other hand, thinks it's rather stupid. It's like she thinks I'm about to join the French Foreign Legion."

"Brian, it just occurred to me. You've never mentioned your father except to tell me he died when you were young."

He looked down at his coke, turning it slowly in his hand. He glanced up abruptly. "My father's not something I talk about much. Things like that we shove somewhere in the back of our minds. There it doesn't bother us too much."

"I'm sorry I made you dredge it up. Really sorry."

He looked at her intently, fidgeting with his coke. Clearing his throat, "It's just that -." He stopped. Looked at her expression of anticipation and lowered his guard. "The memories of him are pretty scarce." He looked away nervously.

She touched his hand gently. "How old were you when he died?"

"Nine. We never had a chance to spend much time together. They divorced when I was five. There was a lot of animosity between them." He took a swig of coke. "My father was an alcoholic."

"What was he like?" She asked.

"He was – I'll tell you about him later." He cleared his throat. "How about another coke?"

"No thanks." She looked at him, analyzing what she had heard, then squeezed his hand. "I'm glad you felt you could tell me that."

Later, he walked her to the dorm door, took her in his arms and pulled her close. He kissed her cheek, and then pulled her close. Their eyes locked. He bent down and kissed her, feeling the closeness of her body. "I'll call you tomorrow."

She smiled. "Okay."

Lori, Anne's roommate, bounded down the steps to tell Brian that Anne was running a little late for their date. She and Brian spent the time talking about people, the latest jokes, and amusing things happening on campus. He had been immediately attracted to her quick wit, which she used flawlessly. She could find humor in the most awkward situation, rendering it completely innocuous. Her bubbly disposition that never subsided, highlighted her eternal optimism.

Lori Barnes was five feet, maybe a tad more, weighed slightly more than one hundred pounds, with a delicate neck and eyes, and a milky white complexion. Her dark brown hair framed a pixie face, and expressive, flashing green eyes. She was definitely petite in every respect except her personality. Their friendship had blossomed quickly and naturally over the last few days. Anne joked about the animated conversation they were having as she came up unnoticed by either of them. "Don't let me intrude. I can always go back up and give you two more time."

"Hey, that's not a bad idea." Lori glanced at her watch. "Come back in a couple of days."

"Let's go, Brian." Anne announced. "My roommate's fickle anyway. It wouldn't last."

Brian glanced back and realized this was the first time he'd ever had a female friend, a buddy of the opposite sex. He enjoyed the alliance and didn't jeopardize the rapport by using it for insights into his and Anne's relationship. There was a comfortable feeling when he was with Lori, a release of energy and an unhesitating knowledge that his lowered defenses were protected.

It was obvious Anne came to accept the time spent with Brian as something prosaic, to be kept in its proper perspective. Her interpretation of the meaning of their time together was clearly expressed in her actions, maintaining that narrow margin of safety in their emotions. Because of this, there was no protest when Brian called and suggested going somewhere for a burger, a movie, or an afternoon walk in the woods. He enjoyed her company and relaxed completely when he was with her. There were a sincerity and openness about her that intensified her personality but never completely uncovering the enigma of her temperament. There was a veil he couldn't penetrate in getting to her innermost thoughts. He kept the relationship up beat and free of any demands that could jeopardize the rapport they so easily established.

He had never known a person like Anne Hunter Merrill. The mystery of her was invigorating, a challenge eagerly accepted. Slowly, closeness developed that Brian had never experienced before. He had to face feelings that manifested uneasiness in his analysis of these days with Anne. A chance encounter had abruptly become a turning point in his life and something had begun he never expected. It churned uneasily in his brain.

CHAPTER THREE

MONDAY HIT LIKE a small jolt of electricity. Brian found himself standing in formation, in a tight brace, chin buried in his chest, elbows tucked tight against his side, stomach sucked almost to his backbone, chest expanded, spewing answers to questions about checklists, and operating limitations of the AT-6 aircraft. Mister Low seemed to have taken on a special mission in life, seeing how hard he could ride Brian and Joe. He'd singled them out for his most ambitious hazing and never let up. Joe withstood the taunting ridicule amazingly well, even though the pressure was steady and unrelenting. He swore silently under his breath and waited until the formation broke to let out his enormous vocabulary of invectives. As the colors sounded, Brian relaxed his mind for a coveted lull in the diatribe. The National Anthem and the raising of the flag were his only moments of peace.

Breakfast was only a glimpse of the juicy sausage links, eggs-over-easy and sweet roll on his tray. The unabridged harassment by the cadet officers permitted, at most, two bites. Brian left the table hungry, but excited that this very morning would be his first flight in an AT-6, the "dollar ride" as it was called. "May I be excused, Sir?"

The march to the flight line was swift, periodically picking up the pace with double time. Brian gulped in the frosty air as he sang out the cadence in unison with the others. The excitement of the day, coupled with the bite of the frigid autumn air, filled his brain with anticipation. The moment was invigorating. A tingle shot up his spine as he heard the roar of aircraft engines in the distance. He smiled at the idea he'd soon be in one of those silver machines and in the air. This was why he was here but it was almost too much to assimilate. The flight was called to a halt in front of two large briefing rooms called stages. They marched in, single file to a huge room on the right. Across the front of the massive room was two long chalk boards for diagraming turns and aircraft attitudes for students. He could visualize the scene of students gathered around their instructor who would be diagraming maneuvers on the board, then talking with his hands, gesturing briskly imaginary aircraft through the air. He heard reports that pilots are unable to communicate with each other without using hand gestures.

Brian spotted the solid row of windows on the right side of the room that looked out on the flight line. He walked over and sucked in a breath. There they were, row after row of graceful, silver AT-6 aircraft, the sun gleaming off the aluminum skin, waiting to be brought to life. The low wing, sleek machines were lined up in organized rows, as if each craft was standing inspection. They appeared larger than photos he'd seen. The massive radial engine's cowling were painted different colors, indicating the assigned flight. The Plexiglas canopies were open, waiting for their masters. The flight line was a syncopated roar of engines being revved up in the morning preflight by the mechanics.

Hearing the sudden shuffling of feet over the outside noise, he looked back as everyone was taking a seat, and lurched for the one on the very end. He could still keep his view of the flight line.

"**Ten-Hut.**"

Every cadet snapped to attention, eyes riveted on the group of officers entering the room. Brian counted fifteen instructors in flight suits, and two other officers in Blues. One of the officers, not wearing a flight suit, stepped forward.

"Take your seats, Gentlemen. I'm Major Garner, Stage Commander, and this is Captain Grissom, Assistant Stage Commander. The officers you see lined up here will be your instructors during the flying portion of basic training."

Brian scrutinized the line-up trying to see which one of this group would most likely be his instructor, as the Major continued. "This is the most comprehensive pilot program in the world. For those of you who end up in combat, you'll be damn glad it is. Even after the best screening devices, and a battery of psychological tests, there are those sitting among you who weren't meant fly military aircraft. I want each of you to assume this doesn't apply to you. We know this program is demanding, but give it your very best, and it'll be the most rewarding experience in your life. Instructors will call your names. Good flying, Gentlemen."

The instructors stepped forward, one by one, calling out two names. The cadets proceeded to follow their assigned instructor to various corners of the briefing room to get acquainted. A short, serious looking instructor called out two names, while Brian sized up his mentor. The first impression was not one to instill confidence in the assignment.

"Mister Beatty, and Mister Brannon." He announced as he moved toward the seated cadets. Brian and Ed Beatty jumped from their seats. "Gentlemen, I'm Lieutenant Browne. I want to brief you on the procedures that I insist upon." He threw his foot onto the seat of the chair in front of them, leaning on his knee. His eyes narrowed. "I'll alternate which one of you I fly with first. Always be prepared for the flight. Know your checklists cold. I'll ask questions here in the briefing room before we go out to the flight line. I'll expect succinct and correct answers everyday. Any questions?"

Brian had several, but thought it best to hold them until a later time. He quickly responded. "No Sir," almost in unison with Ed Beatty.

"Mister Brannon, I'll fly with you first today. Go draw your chute. The tail number is eight thirty-one on row twenty-seven. Mister Beatty, be waiting for us when we taxi in."

Brian put his chute on and walked beside his instructor as the chute bounced against his legs, looking constantly for the correct row. Lieutenant Browne broke the uneasy silence: "Where're you from, Mister Brannon?"

"Alabama, Sir." He snapped out his answer.

"I was stationed at Maxwell Air Force Base for a short time. What part of Alabama?" Lt. Browne asked.

"Near the center of the state about sixty-five miles from Montgomery, as the crow flies." There was no additional response from Lt. Browne. *Here's a man of very few words.*

As they approached the AT-6, Lt. Browne jumped on the wing and placed his chute in the back cockpit. He jumped down and stared coldly at Brian. "Put your chute on the wing and follow me around on the preflight inspection." Brian tossed the chute quickly and followed closely behind Lt. Browne. He meticulously pointed out each part of the aircraft being inspected and what should be looked for. Brian watched, listened intently, touching, feeling, assimilating this majestic piece of machinery. It was awesome.

"Get your chute on, get in the front cockpit, and strap in. Today I'll explain what I'm doing. Follow through with me on the controls to get a feel of the control pressures on takeoff. After today, I'll expect you to do everything, from engine start to takeoff. Okay, let's do it!"

Brian snapped the fasteners on his chute, swung over into the cockpit and snapped the shoulder harness and lap belt together. He began looking around the cockpit, dazzled by the massive array of instruments and gauges. He was still fascinated by this strange environment when he heard Lt. Browne yelling from the rear, and pointing to his head. He heard the shouts from the rear. "Get your damn headset on."

Brian grabbed the headset and snapped it on his head as fast as possible, feeling foolish, and thinking about the impression he was making on his instructor for this first flight.

"You should already know your starting procedure, but just watch this first time, and know what indications you're looking for on the instrument panel." Lt. Browne's voice crackled into the headset.

There was a siren type sound as the energizer increased its RPM's, wailing at a higher and higher pitch, screaming in anticipating of engaging the starter. There was a strained chugging of the engine as the energizer engaged the starter, the mixture was rammed forward, a cough, then the smooth resonance of power as five hundred-fifty horsepower came to life. Brian glanced up at the puffy, cumulus clouds spaced irregularly around the horizon. Excitement surged through him, as he inhaled deeply the different smells in the cockpit.

They taxied onto the runway, as tower clearance came through the headset as jumbled cryptographic instructions. The engine began its throaty roar as the throttle was advanced to maximum power. The aircraft shuddered under its own power, weaving slightly from side to side with every action of the rudder, as it accelerated down the runway. The wind from the open cockpit swept by Brian's face, as he watched the earth move away in a graceful detachment. His new domain energized his very being.

"See how much rudder it takes to counteract the torque of the engine. Feel me letting off pressure as the rudder becomes more effective with increased airspeed? Now, hit the hydraulic actuator, and retract the gear. Make the first power reduction here to climb power, and clear the area behind us as we turn out of traffic. Any questions?"

Brian had about fifty, but decided this instructor wasn't really asking for any. He grasped immediately that his instructor expected everything to be understood the first time. Lt. Browne, not only appeared demanding in what he expected, but obviously was not blessed with an ounce of patience. It was extremely clear that this man expected maximum performance, not just maximum effort.

As they passed through three thousand feet, Brian saw the mixture knob move back from auto-rich. "Close the your canopy." Brian slammed the canopy forward to the closed position. There was an immediate decrease in the wind and noise. Brian felt a wiggle in the stick from side to side. "You've got it, now make some coordinated turns, about ninety degrees in each direction."

Brian eagerly gripped the controls and banked the T-6 to the right. The voice of Lt. Browne blasted into the headset. "Easy on the stick movement, use pressure, not sudden movements. Those pedals on the floor are rudders. Use 'em! Look at the ball in the turn indicator. You're in a slip to the right. You've gotta' make a coordinated movement of the ailerons and rudder. Fly the damn airplane, Mister, don't let it fly you!"

Brian clenched his teeth at the rude indoctrination of being Lt. Browne's student. He made a turn to the left, easing pressure on the stick and pressing left rudder. The ball still varied slightly from the center position as he felt the movement of the aircraft through his body. The voice in the rear bellowed again. "My God, Mister. I wonder what makes you think you're gonna' be a pilot in this man's Air Force. You can't even coordinate your feet and hands. Now, get with it fast, Mister Brannon, or we'll land now. I'm tired of watching this aircraft wallow all over the sky."

Brian rolled into another turn, then another, and still another, as the voice in the rear screamed corrections. Sweat began to run down Brian's forehead, stinging his eyes, and his head buzzed with the condemnation. He unconsciously tightened his grip on the stick instead of relaxing. Finally, the turn and bank indicators were almost in agreement of their analysis of the aircraft attitude. The voice in the rear was silent. Momentarily.

That evening he couldn't wait to write Anne, to share with her the feeling that overtook him that morning in the air. He wanted her feel his enthusiasm. As he took up the pen, he suddenly realized this wasn't something he could define, especially on paper. It's visceral. He wrote that he'd finally made his first flight and he was as excited about flying as he had thought he would be. Then he told her of the lonely feeling that seemed to overtake him about this time of the evening. He tried to find a discriminating way to say how he felt. It should be a simple assertion, yet the feelings were elusive when he reached into his mind for the words. He signed the letter and placed it in his flight suit for mailing. He ran his hand over the letter and fell back on the bunk and thought of the time when he began to have uncertainties of the relationship.

Each day brought an unwelcome awareness of the limited time he had left in Ruston. Eight days remained and he knew there was much to be said, felt, and experienced with Anne. As they sat on their bench, the evening chill signaled the first signs of autumn. A crisp breeze swept over them; making the few fallen leaves rustle in a muffled burst of sound. Anne gave a shudder and moved closer. She tilted her head up, and with her breath warm against his ear, whispered, "Are you sure you want to leave? Just tell the Air Force you've changed your mind."

"Don't be so blasted tempting with those kinds of ideas. Looking at me that way sure doesn't help."

"Well, I have to admit I don't know much about the military. Not to mention there's a war going on over there. I heard you could actually get hurt in one of those." She became quiet. "I don't understand all the things that have been happening with us these last few days."

"The only thing you have to understand right now is – 'I love you'." It came out effortlessly. It was out there, exposed, disclosed as if he had no control over it. He never intended on stating it so conspicuously but there was no way to suck back the words. He understood the feeling just expressed was at risk and the suddenness of it didn't help. He wished to God he hadn't said it.

She looked stunned at the declaration. "Brian, you come barging into my life like a tornado and turn my life upside down. I didn't expect any of this to happen when we walked up to the Tea House that night. There're things about me you can't begin to understand. For right now, let's leave things as they are."

"You make it sound like there's something mysterious you want to tell me about. Is there?" She turned away without responding. The silence was ominous. "It wasn't just what I said. Anne, what's really bothering you?"

"Nothing. It's really nothing." She said. Later, as they reached the side door of the dorm, Anne turned to face Brian. "I've hesitated to mention this, but Justin called tonight and he's coming up tomorrow. He said he hasn't seen me since school started and is bothered that he hasn't even had a letter. I told him how busy I am but he wouldn't take 'no' for an answer." "Dammit, I thought by now you'd told him about us." Brian's anger showed itself for the first time. He glared at her. Her stubborn and intractable attitude about seeing Justin caused anger to well up inside his head. His gut felt like it flipped. He tried not to let her know how upset he was, but he couldn't cap his emotions. "Anne, why the devil haven't you told him about these last couple of weeks?"

"There was really no reason to tell Justin."

"Well, now that tells me a bunch."

"Brian," her eyes glared as she moved closer. "Be reasonable..."

"My God, there're only a few days left before I leave." He cut off her statement in mid-sentence. "Didn't you give that some thought when you decided to spend time with him?" He shook his head. "He could have waited." He turned away abruptly, looking toward the trees.

"Now, when you unflair your nostrils, maybe I can give you an explanation. I just told you how I feel, but you're not going to be the least bit understanding about it, are you? Listen. Justin and a friend are coming through on their way to Birmingham. Justin's important to ..." She stopped, looking intently at Brian. "Don't put pressure on me, Brian. We've had a great time together. I..." She stopped, glanced down, and then back at Brian. "Do you think I'm not going to see

Justin after you leave?" She hesitated, "If you do, you really haven't heard a blasted thing I've been saying. I think *you're* the one who has a decision to make."

She glared at him. "Call me later, if you want to." She turned, reached for the door and went in without waiting for a reply.

Brian felt a knot in his stomach as if he'd just taken a blow to his gut. Walking rapidly to his car, he smacked his fist into the door, shook his hand with the pain, and opened the door. He sat there staring into the night. The image of her with someone else slammed into his brain. It had never occurred to him she could make him feel so threatened. The realization stunned him. He was disappointed she hadn't told Justin, felt hurt she'd allow his intrusion on the little time they had remaining together, and dismayed at the statement given very matter-of-factly that she intended to see Justin after he left. *What the hell's she thinking, feeling?* Uncertainty grabbed at him. He tried to analyze what she had meant by what was said. The only thing he was sure of was the difficulty he had in understanding her emotions. Yet enigma was definitely part of her magnetism.

The next day was Friday. He looked at the phone, wanting desperately to pick it up and call her, just as she suggested. Pride suddenly over ruled the desire. The decision not to call ate at him, and even though he knew he'd later regret it, he was powerless to do anything else. He knew she would be with Justin tonight. There was no changing that.

Saturday was worse. Thoughts of Anne seemed to consume his thinking. But he still couldn't do the one thing he wanted most to do. He couldn't swallow his pride. It was like an anchor dragging him toward the depths and he wouldn't let go. He moved through the day in a robotic daze, finally settling on going to The Grill. He reluctantly opened the door. Immediately wondering why he even came in, he spun quickly to leave rather than hang around with some of the guys. He was in no mood for making small talk.

"Brian, wait!" He pivoted at the sound of the familiar voice. Glancing around, he saw Lori sliding out of a booth to his left. She ran toward him, took his hand, and led him back into The Grill.

He stopped, pulling her back. "Hey, wait a minute. Let's don't go back in there. How would you like some of the best blasted barbecue in all of Alabama?"

"You just said the magic words. I love barbecue." She responded with a grin.

As he opened the car door, he immediately realized he'd lost most of those feelings of despondency and frustration. He was with someone with whom he could totally relax and it lifted his spirit. He smiled for the first time in two days. "I'm gonna' take you to one of my favorite spots. It's about ten miles down Highway twenty-five here. It's called The Oaks. It sets smack dab in the middle of an oak tree grove. Wonder if that had anything to do with its name?" He chuckled at the rhetorical question, and then continued. "Not much atmosphere but, believe me, you're gonna' love Miss Hestor's 'que."

"Anne's told me about The Oaks and your trips down there. My mouth's watering already." She smacked her lips for emphasis. Brian started the engine and automatically reached for the radio dial. As he pulled away toward the street, he tuned the radio. Lori settled back into the well-worn seat and listened to the music. It wasn't necessary to say anything. The silence was comfortable and in harmony with the music. The next song, *Ballerina*, brought an immediate reaction from Brian. Leaning forward to listen more intently, he looked at the radio as if he could see the band playing.

Lori sat up, turned toward him, then asked: "well now, does

that song ever strike a chord! What about *Ballerina* that got your attention?"

"Doesn't music do that to you?"

"Well, sure. I'm a music major. But there're few, if any, that put me in never-never land when I hear it."

"C'mon, I wasn't that obvious. I just happen to associate things with songs, like a particular time, a girl, or a place. There was something I heard once that made a lot of sense. They said music is the sound track of your life. *Ballerina* happened to remind me of a girl I knew. Her name was Kay."

"She must've made an impression on you. There was something there – right?"

Brian kept looking down the road, thinking of an answer that would end this unwanted interrogation. The glare of an oncoming car's lights reacted with the mental flash of remembering the last time he saw Kay. Thinking about that night made him realize he couldn't provide a succinct explanation – not now. "Let's just say it didn't work out." He glanced her way. "Okay?"

"I learn something new about you all the time, Mister Brannon."

"Yeah, like I once knew a girl named Kay and like music." He guffawed.

"Brian, don't pass that off with some cute, sarcastic remark. I think it's great you have those kinds of feelings. It's not a weakness, you know. Loosen up a bit. I like knowing how you feel about things." She touched his hand. "However, you do surprise me sometimes."

He looked at her, smiled and nodded. "You're right. I've probably developed a bad habit of holding back feelings when I shouldn't. It comes from going out with too many gals who you wouldn't dare tell too much.

Hey, here we are. Look into the trees up ahead?"

He slowed up and pulled in as the tires crunched on the gravel drive, stopping near the front door of the rustic building. The converted country store had a wide covered front porch with brick pillars framing its entry. There was evidence of gas pumps removed long ago. The well-weathered wood siding was mute testimony to the years of shielding the seasoned building. There was hominess in the setting among the large oak trees that was inviting. The facade beckoned them to come in.

The screen door screeched its welcome as they walked in and looked around the narrow, elongated room. Two tables had customers already enjoying their food, too engaged in their food and conversation to notice the new arrivals. Brian pointed to a table in the front corner of the room. "Let's sit over here. That's my usual spot."

Lori stopped and surveyed the old building. "I like this." She stood there as if taking visual pictures of the old weathered room. Her eyes stopped at the old cash register. "It still looks like an old country store. Hey, look at that old curved-glass counter over there with the cash register. Haven't seen one of those in years."

Brian feigned impatience as he directed her to the table and pulled out her chair. A lady was quickly approaching. She smiled, looking like someone's grandmother who was about to welcome you to her home. Brian stood up as she reached the table. She hugged him then held him out at arms' length. She glanced questionably at Lori.

"Miss Hestor, I want you to meet Lori Barnes. She's a very good friend of mine."

"Oh!"

"No, Miss Hestor, she's a *friend*."

Lori smiled, nodded her head and said, "Brian won't quit bragging about your barbecue. In fact, he makes a point of telling everyone it's the best in Alabama."

"It's pretty darned good if I do say so myself. Now, what'll you folks be having tonight?"

"I just want one of those barbecue sandwiches I've heard about." Lori stated.

"Make that two, Miss Hestor, and two cokes. A coke okay with you, Missy?"

"Sure, that's fine." She said.

As they waited, Lori leaned forward. "What's with the 'Missy' all of a sudden?"

"I don't know. It just popped out. Seems to fit though."

"Never had anyone call me anything but Lori." She shook her head. "Missy's fine."

"Glad you don't object. Not that it was gonna' change things."

She reached across slapping him on the back of the hand. "You need more training." The smile vanished abruptly from her face, replaced by a look he'd never seen before. "I reckon you know pride has a pretty heavy price." She said.

Brian raised his hand, indicating for her to stop.

"No way. Just take your hand down and listen to me for a minute." She pushed his hand down to the table. "I'm friend enough to tell you like it is. Just call her. You're dying to do it. So do it."

"It's not that easy. I sure as hell don't understand how she feels about us. It's not easy getting inside her head sometimes. There's probably not much of a future to this relationship anyway.

Before Lori could respond, a young girl brought the tray of food to the table. "Miss Hestor says for y'all to enjoy."

The drive back seemed much too short for the depth of conversation. Lori was not her usual witty self, injecting little humor into her advice. "You sure don't have much time left. Now tell me why the devil you're willing to waste it like this?"

He rebounded. "Okay! Geez, I may end up looking pretty damn stupid after this, but I'm gonna' take your advice." He shook his head as if he wasn't sure. "I hope you're right."

Brian opened the door and Lori jumped out quickly, stood on her tiptoes and kissed his cheek. "Had a great time. Wait here. I'm going to wake someone up and save you that call, if you know what I mean."

The time seemed to drag on for much longer than the fifteen minutes it took for Anne to come through the door smiling, and looking more radiant than ever. No words were spoken. She walked slowly toward Brian, looking intently into his eyes. As she got close, she put her arms around his neck. They held each other for several minutes and neither spoke. She slowly lifted her head, and looked into his eyes. "I don't always understand you. And I don't really know what we have going here. But whatever it is, there's no need to waste these last few days playing some stupid game. There's not much time left, is there?" He knew there was indeed little of that left.

The loud knock at the door immediately snapped Brian back to the present. Mister Low was already through the door, standing with hands on his hips, glaring at his prey. Joe jumped up as Brian rolled off the bed to greet their intruder. Both hit a brace. Low walked slowly around the two, increasing their anxiety and anticipation of what was going to follow this unexpected visit. Low stopped, as something obviously grabbed his attention. His gaze fixed suddenly on the desk. His hand leisurely reached down for Brian's father's picture. He picked it up, carefully turning it side to side assessing the image. "Who the hell is this fairy?"

Brian tensed. Joe sensed his movement toward Low, and quickly

49

put his hand out holding him back. Thankfully, Low never saw Joe's instinctive movement to restrain Brian. Brian sensed the mistake he was about to make, and resumed the brace. "That's my father, Sir. Put the picture back on the desk, Sir."

"Why do you have a fairy's picture on the desk, Mister Brannon? Speak up."

"I'll ask you one more time. Put the picture back, *Sir.*"

"Or *what*, Mister Brannon?"

"Or I'll ..." The loudspeaker blared its interruption as the bugle sounded the call for the next formation. The penetrating notes reverberated through the room, as the tension hit its peak.

Mr. Low dropped the picture face down on the desk. "We'll talk about this later, Mister Brannon." They stared at each other, the air charged with electrified energy. Low spun around and left the room.

Joe walked over, looking questionably at Brian. "You're pretty touchy about your Dad. You've never mentioned him. What's the story?"

"It's just that ..." He stopped. Looked at Joe's expression of anticipation and lowered his guard. "the worst part is I never knew him that well. I've got memories of him like snapshots in time. Scarce memories at that." He looked away nervously.

"I take it he's dead. How old were you when he died?" Joe asked.

"Nine. They divorced when I was five. After that, I saw him on rare occasions when he'd stop by for an hour or two. We didn't have a chance to spend much time together. There was a lot of animosity between him and Mom and he knew it." He placed the picture back on the desk. "My father was an alcoholic." He paused a moment to watch Joe's reaction. He showed no shock at the statement and Brian suddenly realized how easily he was talking about this.

"What was he like?" Joe pressed the issue.

"He was an engineer. He had a brilliant mind and great personality. He was a man's man, not quite as tall as I am, but strong as an ox. I've been told he was a caring person, easygoing, except when he drank. My grandmother told me he was the only perfect gentleman she'd ever known. I think about that often. That's the way I remember him, even though I've been told he had one helluva' temper when he was drinking." He chuckled as he continued. "This probably isn't funny to anyone but me. Uncle Gus told me of a time in New York when they took a cab together to their hotel. My Dad had a few drinks that night. Probably more than a few. As he paid the taxi driver, the guy made some offhand remark about the south and, without a word, my father hit him so hard he flew over the hood of the taxi."

"Great." Joe exclaimed. "That Yankee got exactly what he deserved."

Brian paused, pondering the subject. He stared out the window, suddenly feeling awkward at what he was about to say. He looked up at Joe and half whispered, "You know." He cleared his throat. "He never even raised his voice to me, much less raise a hand." Joe looked at him, nodding his understanding. "Let's get moving. Enough of this show-and-tell crap."

The days passed swiftly in a flurry of classes, physical training, and flying with no let up. At evening chow, after a particularly bad day of classes and flying, Joe was trying to get a sufficient amount of food to withstand the onslaught of harassment.

"Whistle, Mister Tanner. That bite looked a little too large for you to whistle. Let's see you pucker for the group. Go on, make some kind of sound, Mister Tanner." Mister Low growled with a wide grin being formed, enjoying the obvious distress Joe was experiencing.

Blood rushed to Joe's face in obvious notation of his anger. There was no demarcation between his red hair and his face as it turned vermilion with his iridescent ire. The veins in his neck, perceptible at the end of the table, indicated the outrage that was physically boiling over. Both fists slammed against the table hard enough to rattle the glasses at the other end. He stared piercingly at Low. "Goddamn it, you sorry sonofabitch; I've had all I'm gonna' take of you!"

The words hung in the air like ice crystals, cold and hard, then quickly reverberated through the mess hall. Abruptly there was absolute silence and Cadets at the nearby tables stared at Joe. With shocked expressions, they watched to see the results of the confrontation unfold.

Mister Low was so shaken by the outburst that he just sat there slack-jawed, beginning to pale as color drained from his face. He stared skeptically at the originator of the outrage, his mouth slightly open as if he wanted to respond. Mr. Mullen rescued the silence and snapped the atmosphere of tension. "Easy, Mister Tanner, just calm down a bit." His voice was composed and measured. "It might be better if you were excused and went to your room to get control."

Joe never broke his loathsome stare at Mister Low, but stood up rapidly, slamming the chair straight back with his legs. Without comment, Joe turned and left the mess hall.

Brian enjoyed the expression of shock, now diminishing, on Low's face. He glared at him with pure hate, and then quickly snapped his head straight ahead as their eyes made contact.

"What the bloody hell are you gaping at Mister Brannon?" Low yelled from across the table, then turned back toward his roommate. "That cadet's history!" He blustered.

"For Christ's sake, Frank, ease off. You don't need to take this any further right now. I'll see you back at the room." Mister Mullen injected himself into the tenseness.

When Brian entered the room, Joe was sitting at the desk with his head in his hands. He made no effort to acknowledge Brian's entry.

"Well, that damn temper of yours may have ripped it. I hope Mister Mullen can reason with that SOB. He's wanted both our butts since Day One. You had to be the one to hand it to him on a platter." Brian couldn't keep the sarcasm and disgust out of his voice.

Joe showed no emotion. He sat erect and responded matter-of-factly. "I really don't give a good Goddamn. They can take this program and shove it. I can assure you I won't take another minute of Low's crap. God Almighty, it was the Citadel all over again." He clinched his jaw as he remembered, looked over at Brian, and then began again. "I didn't tell you before, but I took a swing at a sophomore weeny who thought he was put on this earth to break me. It was *he* who got broke."

"I never asked why you left the Citadel. Figured you'd tell me in your own good time. I don't give a rat's ass about what happened back there." Brian bent down close to Joe. "Sooner or later you're going to have to deal with losing it like that. You stopped me the other day from blowing it and tonight there wasn't a damn thing I could do to help you."

Joe looked up, ready to respond, but before he could comment, Mister Mullen appeared in the doorway, making the customary one knock. He slowly closed the door and stood there for a moment, scrutinizing Joe. "At ease. Both of you." It was a moot point since Joe hadn't moved at all. He continued, "Do you have any idea how completely out of line you were tonight Mister Tanner?" He didn't wait for a reply as he continued. "I expected to come in here and tell you when you were meeting the board. But instead I'm gonna' say something that happens very rarely. Most of the guys in my class realize why you took off on Frank. He's been riding you hard from the time you checked in. It's as if he has a personal grudge of some kind. Like he's singled you two out to see if he can make something like this happen. Some people can't handle authority without abusing the responsibility that goes with it."

He looked hard at Joe, making sure that he felt the impact of his assertion before he continued. "Several of us have convinced him not to press the issue." He pointed his finger at Joe, his jaw muscles flexing as he spoke. "Mister Tanner, you're getting a very, very rare second chance, use it well." As he was leaving, he spun around. "One false move by either of you, and Mister Low will make damn sure you aren't a part of this program before the sun sinks. Frankly, I figure he'll still find a way to get you two."

The door closed behind Mister Mullen as he left both of them to consider what had been said. A surge of relief swept through Brian, as he glanced at Joe for a response. Joe sat there, looking straight ahead for a period that seemed like minutes instead of a few seconds. A grin expanded slowly across his face. He looked up at Brian and winked. "What the hell, I came here to fly airplanes. I won't let one hawk-faced, pea-brained, Yankee, sonofabitch make me quit."

The door sprang open again. Boyce, dressed in his suit, silk tie, wingtip shoes, and his overcoat slung loosely over his arm stood there smiling. "I came to say goodbye, guys. I've already told Bugsy and Scott..."

Joe shook his head as he interrupted Boyce. "What a screwed up day this has been. What the hell are you trying to say, Boyce?"

"I think he's about to pose for Esquire. Right?" Brian chimed in.

"I just eliminated myself from Aviation Cadet Class fifty-one G. Now, I think I'll go have a drink in beautiful downtown Sherman while I wait for the bus to Dallas. I'll think about you poor bastards when I sleep 'till ten every morning, have a leisurely breakfast, then plan my evening out with a damn good looking girl."

"Cut the crap." All the time looking him up and down, and shaking his head in disgust, Brian stated. "You didn't really do this thing, did you? Why, Boyce?"

"Hey, seriously, guys." He hesitated a moment, as if wanting to choose his words carefully. "Academics are a snap but I never got that comfortable feeling in the cockpit. I'd tense up the minute I touched that stick. I'd break out in a cold sweat and feel my gut tighten so I could hardly breathe. Fear, I guess. Hell, I got sick every flight – enough to puke twice. I see how you guys react to flying. You eat this stuff up and I don't. Taking that thing up alone was out of the question. I'd never solo." Boyce faltered, searching for words. "I found out I'm not cut out to be a pilot and I have the common sense to realize it. That's not the worst thing in the world that can happen to you, in spite of what you guys think."

Brian extended his hand. "I'm sorry, Boyce, really sorry. We're gonna miss your Ivy League ass around here. I'm glad I had a chance to know you." He squeezed his hand harder. "Good luck."

Joe stood up, and shook Boyce's hand: "I know you did the right thing if that's the way you feel. Take care, and give us a holler once in a while."

"Y'all keep the greasy side down, you heah," Boyce's stated in his best imitation of a southern dialect.

There was silence as Boyce disappeared through the door. Brian shrugged his shoulders and looked at Joe. "It's been one helluva' night, hasn't it?"

The weather turned colder in the middle of November. Biting, nasty, damp cold. The wintry winds wailing across the early morning formations created added misery of being chilled to the bone while being hazed by senior cadets. Brian almost became acclimated to the constant verbal barrage thrown at him each day, but could barely stand the cold that permeated his spirit. The more he shouted out correct check lists and operating limitations of instruments, the more ridiculous the questions became, and the more he shivered. The interrogation bounced off his numbed thought processes as he shouted out answers. Mr. Low was now putting his best efforts into breaking Brian. He came down even harder as he noticed a chink in Brian's armor. Low was getting to him, and Low knew it. The glint in his eyes indicated Low was enjoying the merciless persecution. Brian was powerless to stop the onslaught. He endured it as best he could, knowing it was pushing his limitation.

Just as the bugle sounded the preface to colors, Low leaned close to Brian's ear, not wanting others to hear. "You aren't gonna' make it, Mister Brannon. Believe me. I'm gonna' enjoy watching you walk out that gate."

The days merged into a tedious composite of military and academic classes, and flying. Brian was able to silence the shouting of Lt. Browne for short periods of time. Although some students were apprehensive of the basic acrobatic phase, Brian relished the adrenalin that surged as he pulled the nose straight up, chopped the throttle, waited for the last shudder of the stall, then just as it quit flying snapped the stick into his gut, kicking full left rudder, and feeling the aircraft lazily flip over into a spin.

It was becoming evident to each cadet who had "it" and who didn't have that special attribute commonly referred to as "The Right Stuff." Those who had it were confident in their ability, had the right reflexes, and were cool under pressure. It was something felt, never talked about. More and more students were being scheduled for check rides with Major Garner and Captain Grissom, and more empty seats were showing up in the mess hall. It was soon evident who was becoming an initiate in that tightly knit fraternity known as pilots, and who was returning as a member of the rest of the world. The system was unmerciful in deciding who had "it," and who would be left behind. As Mr. Low continued his harassment, Brian watched the demerits add up. Almost daily, he had flashes of doubt. He fought to subdue the apprehension. There was something he had to prove to himself. He *had* to complete this program. He knew he was doing this to prove something to himself, but he finally realized he was living it for his father too. He couldn't wash out now. Not now.

Tuesday, before Thanksgiving, found Brian in an exceptionally good mood, as he thought of only one more day before the break. Receiving a letter from Anne and one from Lori also elevated his spirits. He dropped the chute beside the chair in the ready room and proceeded to read Anne's letter. He barely caught the figure of Lt. Browne approaching from his right. Brian and Ed snapped to attention as Brian slipped the letter back into his flight suit.

"I'll fly with you first today, Mister Brannon."

The flight progressed fairly well, but not one of Brian's best. On the second landing the head set crackled with Lt. Browne's distinctive voice: "Taxi over to the mobil control and hold the brakes."

Puzzled, Brian didn't question his instructor, who he'd learned to respect, as well as regard in awe. He swung the tail around at mobil control facing out toward the grass strip and mashed hard with his toes on top of the rudder pedal to hold the brakes. Lt. Browne climbed out on the wing, reached into the rear cockpit, and fastened the seat belt and shoulder harness together. Abruptly, the realization of what was about to happen numbed Brian's thinking. The belts in the rear were being secured for a solo flight. The adrenalin rush was barely tolerable.

Browne leaned into Brian's ear, and cupped his hands against the noise of the engine. "I think you're ready to solo, Mister Brannon. The question is, do *you* think you're ready?"

Brian nodded in the affirmative and shouted above the roar of the idling engine. "Yessir!" He was apprehensive, even slightly afraid, but knew if he presented a glimmer of doubt about soloing, it would be the kiss of death from Lt. Browne. Any reticence would be interpreted as personal doubt. An element totally unacceptable for those who had "it."

"Shoot three full-stop landings and then taxi back over here and pick me up."

Brian watched his instructor jump off the wing, then reached down and switched the radio from intercom to the VHF frequency of mobil control. He taxied to the edge of the strip, received clearance for takeoff and slowly advanced the throttle to maximum power. The T-6 roared down the strip, the tail lifted slightly, and Brian eased a little backpressure on the stick. He was in the air, alone. The excitement was tempered by his concentration on procedures, *Gear coming up, climb power, adjust manifold pressure, now RPM's, level off at traffic pattern altitude, start the turn to remain in a closed traffic pattern. Think. Stay ahead of this aircraft. Before landing, GUMPS check: gas on fullest tank, undercarriage down and locked, mixture full rich, propeller two-thousand RPM, manifold pressure twenty-five inches and shoulder harness locked.*

He turned onto final approach, lowered more flaps, and reduced power. He dropped the nose, sighted the runway through the spinning propeller as the adrenalin pumped harder. At that precise moment the cold hard fact hit home that there was no one in the back to take the controls if he screwed up. Easing back on the stick, he reduced his rate of descent as the T-6 approached touchdown. He rounded out, held it off, held it off, and then he felt aircraft mush into the sod as all three wheels hit the ground. The aircraft bounced back into the air slightly, then settled back onto the strip. A keen sense of accomplishment engulfed him. Two more landings and he taxied back to pick up Lt. Browne.

"Good job, Mister Brannon." An ever faint, but distinguishable smile crossed the Lieutenant's face.

As Brian traded places with Ed, and jumped off of the wing, he saw several cadets coming in his direction, unaware that the mobile control tower always called back to the stage when someone soloed. The first four grabbed a leg and an arm each, and proceeded to the Ready Room's showers, carrying on the long tradition, Brian was thrown into the stinging cold water.

Brian felt someone watching him and spun around toward the door. Mr. Low was standing there with a smirk washed across his face. Brian snapped to attention as Low moved to his left side, silently, tediously, like a stalking cat. The air was electrified. Brian could only see the vague outline of his face in his peripheral view. Low moved behind him, lingering just out of view. Brian smelled his pungent breath as he spoke deliberately in his right ear.

"You think because you soloed today you've got it knocked." His lips almost touched Brian's ear. "Oh, yeah, you do, you smug SOB." His voice reverberated with tautness. "Listen up Mister. You're still my meat. No way in hell are you gonna' make it through this program. Think about that every minute of every day. You need only ten more demerits before you meet the board. I'll see that you get every one of 'em."

Suddenly he was gone.

Brian wolfed down the evening meal, glancing occasionally at Low. The cold, withering stare down the table left no doubt about Low's acceptance of his solo. Brian finished hurriedly, then ran to the cadet club's pay phone before returning to the room. He had to share this day's event with Anne. Joe caught up with him as he was stacking quarters at the phone booth. Joe silently fumbled through his pockets, pooling all he had. Brian recounted and looked at Joe. "I'm gonna' need more than this."

"Stay here and make the call. I'll go get more from the cashier. Now, get on with it before you bust a gut."

He dialed the operator, and placed a person-to-person call to Anne. The anticipation of hearing her voice again made his mouth dry, and awakened a few hibernating butterflies. He listened closely as the operator stated she had a long distance call for Miss Anne Merrill, and the slightly disappointed voice on the other end say, "Just a minute, Operator." Minutes later, he heard Lori's voice on the other end tell the operator that Anne was in the library, placing emphasis on the location to make sure that Brian knew where she was.

"I'll speak to *this* party, Operator."

"Please deposit four seventy-five for the first three minutes."

"Hi, Lori. Thought I'd call to see how everything's going in Ruston. How've you been doing?"

"Just great. It's so good to hear your voice. Anne'll be disappointed when she gets back and knows she missed your call. Is there anything you want me to tell her?"

"Just tell her that I miss her. I guess you're both are getting ready to go home for Thanksgiving tomorrow. Wish I could be there with you. Oh yeah, tell Anne we'll be getting a short Christmas leave. It was sorta' doubtful for a while because of Korea, but I'll see both of you in a few weeks."

"That's terrific! You'd *better* come see me while you're home. Birmingham is right up the road."

"You can count on it. Tell Anne." He paused.

"Tell her what, Brian?"

"Nothing really. Just that I miss her. I'll see y'all soon. Goodbye, Lori."

"Bye."

The disappointment was overwhelming. He anticipated hearing Anne's voice and sharing a special moment. He discovered, rather abruptly, that an unshared event loses some of its luster, yet he knew it was still an event he'd recall years later with extreme alacrity.

Even though most of the Cadets had soloed by now, there was a further decrease in the number who remained in Pilot Training Class 51-G. That final number of those who obviously had "it" was rapidly approaching the fifty percent figure stated so coldly by the Wing Commander the first day. In spite of the pitfalls still looming out there, waiting, ready to take him down in a second, Brian was constantly building his confidence. Those still in the program were beginning to take on the first attribute of those who fly military aircraft; larger than normal egos. He was no exception.

December twenty-second took on particular importance. This signaled that magic day they became upperclassmen. He could finally escape the torment initiated by Mister Low. Brian packed for the ten-day Christmas leave. He was preoccupied with anticipation as he folded clothes in the B-4 bag. Low bounded through the door and Brian instinctively snapped to attention.

"Easy there. You're now an upper classman and you're still jumping all over the place."

Brian slumped against the wall. "You don't give up do you?"

"Okay, I admit defeat. It happens so rarely I'm just not used to it. I got you eight of those last ten demerits. You stiffed me out the last two."

"You never knew my determination. You weren't about to get me."

Low's hand shot out. "I tried. No hard feelings?"

"You're some piece of work. I won't forget it." Brian fired back.

"Well, you've still got a lotta' program to go yet, Mister Brannon -- keep looking behind you."

Brian hurriedly finished packing and tossed the B-4 bag toward the end of his bunk. He was definitely ready for this break. Ready to get home. For a short time, his mind could relax and forget Mister low. Maybe he and Anne could start again just as he left her that last night. Most of all, he'd try to recapture the feelings of those autumn evenings on a bench in front of Old Main. He dropped the B-4 bag on the floor and remembered that last night with her.

Friday, October 20, 1950, arrived just as foreseen, and dreaded. Brian met Anne at the usual spot. Lori came down with her to tell Brian goodbye. She gave him a hug. "Take care, and drop us a line once in a while. Good luck!" He heard her voice trail off as the door banged shut.

Brian turned down the highway toward The Oaks without asking. It had become their favorite place to be alone and also for the absolute enjoyment of the food. The drive was slow and the music was good. As he was about to share his thoughts with her, he stopped. The right words were elusive.

Anne turned and moved closer. "I can't imagine you not being here." She said. "I met you right after getting to Ruston and we've been together constantly. Nothing's gonna' seem quite right after tomorrow."

"You know these last few weeks have made one helluva' difference in my life. I hate the fact that I'm leaving when we need more time. Three weeks weren't enough. We only scratched the surface of something that could be significant in our lives."

Anne nodded and turned toward the window.

On the way back to Ruston, they said very little. He wasn't anxious to talk about the inevitable. He braked to a stop under a large oak tree just outside the lighted area of the dorm, turned off the engine and adjusted the radio volume. A low background of subtle music was the only sound as they stared at each other. He reached over and gently pulled her close to him. She put her arms around him and they held each other, neither speaking. Their contact was communication enough.

Brian pulled his arm loose and glanced at his watch to see how little time was left. Anne placed her hand over the watch. "That's not going to slow down time one bit. Now, don't look at it again."

"You already know what I'm thinking, so it's no use to spell it out. I wouldn't do it justice anyway." He stopped abruptly, as the lights of Old Main began blinking its notice through the trees, interrupting the statement. "God, I wish we had more time."

Easing out of the car, he walked around to her side. His hand hesitated, holding the cold metal, not wanting to open the door. Turning the handle, he reached in and took her hand and pulled her to him. He held her there for momentarily, and then began walking slowly toward the dorm.

"Write as soon as you get there and tell me all about it. And be careful. I know you love airplanes but they can crash, you know."

"Don't worry 'bout that. Just be waiting right here when I get back. We've got a lot more to talk about yet."

"I will." She smiled. "Now go do your thing. I know you were meant to do it."

He pulled her close, his mouth close to her ear. "I love you, Anne Hunter Merrill." He whispered.

She pushed back suddenly. Standing perfectly still, she looked into his eyes. "I tried not to love you, Brian. I really did. But it seems you may have made that impossible." She spun around, disappearing up the stairs.

Impossible? He loved the sound of that word. Turning over in the bunk, it continued to reverberate in his head as he contemplated the implications.

CHAPTER FOUR

T HE FIRE BURNED fiercely in the fireplace, fighting to take the chill out of the air. He rubbed his hands together in front of the glowing embers, admiring the dancing, crackling flames. He leaned closer to the cedar boughs arranged loosely across the living room mantle and smelled the familiar fragrance of Christmas' he'd grown up with. He turned to warm the other side as he stared at the lights reflecting in the windowpanes. The Christmas tree was, as in every year, covered in luminous ornaments, multicolored lights, and tinsel draped on every available branch. He inhaled the fragrance of cedar hanging heavily in the room.

His mother rubbed his arm. "It's so good to have you home. You don't know how quiet it's been around here with just me rambling around in this big old house."

"It wasn't any different from when I was at school. I wasn't here then."

"I knew you'd be bouncing in some weekends. Now, you're

virtually gone for good." She looked away momentarily. "Why don't you take your bag to your room while I put on a pot of coffee? It'll only take a minute and we can have a piece of chocolate cake and talk a while," she said, as she left the room.

He didn't take time to tell her it was too late for coffee and cake. He knew it would be no use to protest, as he picked up his bag and walked back to his room. He tossed the bag toward the foot of the bed and flopped down hard across the soft quilt. Stretching to loosen tired muscles, he began to relax in the familiar environment. He closed his eyes, thinking how long it seemed since this was his room. All he'd concentrated on for the last few months was his new world, the intenseness of the flight program.

She called to him as she passed his room, carrying a tray, balancing two cups of coffee, cream and sugar, and two pieces of cake. Brian ambled into the living room, smiling at the large piece of cake she placed in front of him on the coffee table. On second thought, maybe it *wasn't* too late for cake.

They talked until the early morning hours. Brian listened intently as he was brought up to date of those in Ruston who had passed on, those who were ailing, and all the latest gossip. As he tried to explain the last few months of his life to her, there was realization of a different communication gap. Her look of detachment told him she couldn't put his experiences into the context of her life in Ruston. He became quiet while he listened to her explain the new extension to the Post Office, the additional traffic light, and new ownership of the Five and Dime store. He watched her intently, looking at a face he never observed as closely before. The wrinkles etched its surface, and the years had crept upon her, unnoticed by him. He saw how much the gray had begun to send shards through her dark brown hair and felt sadness that he hadn't been more attentive to the changes.

He continued to look deep into her eyes as they talked, realizing his mother's world didn't expand at the same relative rate as his. For the time being, things were better kept in the context of her life.

His gaze shifted like a shot to the flickering blaze of the fireplace. The multicolored flames were mesmerizing. As he watched the coals suddenly shift in the fire and small sparks rise toward the chimney, his mind saw other images. Various family members faces seemed to appear in the dancing flames. Images of another brightly lighted Christmas tree flickered into the apparition. In the soothing warm glow the fire gave off, he could hear the laughter of those no longer with them. As the heat warmed his face, he unconsciously drifted among other Christmases in this old house.

"Brian." His mother tugged on his sleeve, breaking his trance, bringing him back to the coffee and cake before him. "You seemed a bit preoccupied, staring into the fire there."

"Sorry, Mom. I was just thinking about how good it was to be home, you know, Christmas and everything."

"It's late, get some sleep and we'll catch up on the conversations tomorrow. Goodnight." She said as she disappeared through the door.

Tyler was shaking him awake as he tried to focus on the room and the intruder. "You gonna' stay in bed all day? C'mon, get up and tell me what's been going on."

Brian rubbed his eyes trying to get his bearings: "God. I might've known." He sat on the edge of the bed, running his hands through his hair. "Let me get dressed, a cup of coffee and then maybe I can at least focus." He glanced down at his watch. "Damn, do you realize I got a little over three hours sleep?"

"You can catch up later. Getcha' butt up. You're wasting time sitting' there – get dressed."

They tried to catch up on each other's life for the past few months as Brian hastily threw on his clothes. He was tugging on his pants, looking around for a shirt.

"Let's go to the Grill and get a cup of coffee and some of those cheese-eggs. I'll tell Mom not to fix me anything." Brian said, as he buttoned his shirt.

Brian and Tyler took their usual booth and ordered. They ate slowly, interspersing conversation with food. An hour and fifteen minutes and three cups of coffee gave them the time to complete the catch-up on each other's lives. It was obvious changes were taking them in different directions.

Tyler looked around The Grill, then back at Brian as seriousness replaced the good-natured banter. He ran his hands over the top of his crew cut several times, signaling he was ill at ease with something. It'd always been a dead give away when he rubbed his hand rapidly across his flat top, feeling the bristles. Brian read the signal quickly, wondering what was bothering Tyler.

"There's something I need to tell you." His hand shot through his crew cut again. "I met a couple of guys from Collinwood last quarter and asked about Anne." There was hesitancy in his voice. "They knew her, grew up with her. They told me some weird things about her relationship with this guy and his family. I don't know ..." His face showed concern as he hesitated. "Look, the only reason I'm telling you this is ..." He hesitated again, searching Brian's reaction.

"You can stop right there. I don't need to hear some demented rumor you heard from a couple of morons from Collinwood. It was pretty damn obvious you didn't like Anne from the get-go. So don't hand me this crap about some crazy rendition of deep dark family secrets. Got that?"

"Yeah, I got that. Forget what I just said." He slammed his coffee cup on the table. "You know, Fella', there was a time I could talk to you. But that was a long time ago. It sure as hell wasn't with the guy sitting across from me right now." Hurt, more than anger was evident in his inflection.

There was a hollow in the pit of his stomach as Tyler's words echoed in his brain. He didn't want to hear what Tyler was trying to tell him. No need to heap doubts where there was an ample store of it. He gave no outward indication of what he was feeling. The knot in his stomach slowly loosened but wouldn't completely disappear. "I'm sorry for comin' at you like that. I know you weren't going to tell me something unless you thought it was for my own good."

A smile slowly crept across Tyler's face. "Forget it. You've said worse, and I have too." He leaned closer. "And one more damn thing. Where do you come off telling me I didn't like Anne? If I didn't, you'd really know it." He leaned back, turned his head toward the door, then back to face Brian. "This whole conversation is absurd."

As he waited for Anne to come to the phone, he thought about how different it felt from last October. "Merry Christmas."

"Brian, what a surprise. When did you get there?" she said softly.

"Late last night. Can't wait to see you. God, it seems like a year already. What're your plans during Christmas?" He asked.

"Well..." She hesitated. "I don't know for sure. Are you planning on coming down?" She didn't wait for an answer. "If you'd like, why don't you plan to come down Wednesday? Aunt Lucy will be visiting her daughter and you can stay there. The house will be all yours if you wanna' spend the night."

"Sure. That sounds great. Can't wait to see you." He said.

"See you then. Merry Christmas." She said, as he heard the click of the receiver.

The drive to Collinwood was too long for his unrestrained imagination. He remembered the time Anne stressed the fact there were things about her he didn't know. Tyler's comments caused a profusion of doubts about the mystery, the enigma that was Anne. He had ample time to think about it, to try to analyze what significance any of this had. He'd have to wait.

He pulled up at the front of the house that was exactly as Anne had described so many times before. The large, white cottage was framed by a wide porch, its cluster of three square columns rising from white brick pillars, supported the porch roof. The front yard was dotted with large old camellia bushes in full bloom. He approached the two steps with anticipation and a feeling of apprehension. Just as he reached for the doorbell, the door opened.

"Hi there!" Anne reached out and took his hand. "I saw you coming up the walk. Come in, I want you to meet my mother."

"Hold it a minute." He leaned forward to kiss her. She turned slightly and pointed to the living room.

"I want you to meet Mama."

Mrs. Merrill was a tall attractive woman. More than a few gray hairs highlighted her dark brown hair and gave her a look older than her years. It was pulled tucked back tightly, accentuating the finely constructed features of her face. Her parchment white skin was pulled taught over prominent cheekbones. The resemblance to her daughter was immediately apparent. She took Brian's hand warmly. "I've heard quite a bit about you, Brian, and so glad to finally meet you. Anne told me about you being in the Air Force and that you met at school just after she got there.

"Nice meeting you, too, Misses Merrill. That's right, we met a few days after Anne got to Ruston." He glanced at Anne. "I've looked forward to coming down here to Collinwood since she first described it to me."

"Mama, I think I'll take Brian over to Aunt Lucy's so he can freshen up for dinner. We won't be gone long." Anne interrupted their initial conversation.

Once inside the car, Anne leaned against the door. Not the closeness he'd hoped for. The conversation was awkward, as she talked rapidly about all the activities at Agnes Baines, Lori, Carol, and the other girls Brian had met before leaving for Texas. She asked about the rigors of pilot training with a detachment of just making conversation. He only listened, knowing the tone of this conversation had to change quickly.

As they pulled into the drive and stopped, Anne opened the car door and walked rapidly toward the front entrance. She fumbled for the key, then opened the door without saying a word. Brian followed her into the entry of the small brick house, stopped, took her arm and turned her forcefully toward him, and kissed her long and hard. There was no protest, yet he didn't sense the response of a few months ago. They looked at each other for several seconds, searching the eyes of the other, neither saying a word.

Anne pushed back. "Brian." She hesitated for a while, and then motioned to the living room sofa. "Let's talk for a minute, about us."

"A very good subject." He followed her to the sofa and sat down. "Obviously, you've got something to say."

"Okay." She hesitated, as if searching for just the right words, then continued, "Those three weeks we had before you left were pretty fast-paced. I wasn't used to that. I told you then I felt confused at what was happening. I told Justin about us."

"Well now, I figured the problem just might be 'ole Justin." He cut into her statement.

"Hold it right there. Justin isn't the *problem* as you put it. When I came home at Thanksgiving, things seemed to close in on me. I was confused about my feelings for you, for Justin. Everything about my life was one big question mark. I had a long talk with the Judge about some things bothering me. There were questions – whatever, that I wouldn't discuss with him. I couldn't. This goes deeper than you think, and for good reasons. There are things I haven't told you." She hesitated. "The Judge gave me some good advice." There was a moment when she looked as if she wanted to explain, but stopped.

Brian began thinking about what Tyler started to tell him, but pushed it out of his mind instantly. He looked directly into her eyes. "I don't really give a damn what point the Judge was trying to make. If that sounds insensitive, so be it. The Judge succeeded in doing a number on you. And that's exactly what he had in mind with his *advice*." He tensed his jaw muscles. "Just tell me this. Didn't those three weeks we had mean *something* to you, or was I that screwed up in my thinking?" She turned toward the door. He took her by the shoulders, turning her back toward him. "Look at me. Look at me and tell me that last night in Ruston never happened."

"When you're right here, looking at me that way, it makes it difficult. You're different from anyone I've known. My God, Brian, I've got feelings for you, but I can't or won't put a name on it."

"These don't sound much like the things we were telling each other the night I left." Anger wasn't the way he wanted to react. He knew it would be one more barrier at a time he needed none. He looked at Anne, trying to garner some real understanding of what had happened since he left. His answer was there. He saw the doubts surface in her eyes.

She pulled back. "Why don't you get ready for supper? We can talk about this later." She frowned. "We're not really solving anything like this, and I think Mama's expecting us about now."

Brian stood up, still looking at Anne quizzically. He was on the verge of telling her about the anger building, stopped before he said something he knew he'd regret. "I'll change. Give me a minute."

The meal was somewhat awkward at first, considering the unresolved emotions at hand. In spite of the uncomfortable situation, Brian and Mrs. Merrill quickly found common ground in their conversation and the stiffness of their first meeting evaporated. They found a prompt rapport. They lingered at the table long after the meal was over. Brian was enjoying getting to know this unique woman, who piqued his interest and commanded his immediate admiration. She was obviously a true Southern lady, who'd been thrust into the role of matriarch, and bore the obligation well. He was also gaining insight into Anne's life by the way she and her mother related to each other. He watched their reaction to each other, without being obvious. Evidently, she and Anne were close but there was something lying underneath their discernable relationship that he couldn't quite understand. There was a formality he couldn't grasp.

"Dinner was delicious, Misses Merrill. Thanks."

"Well, Brian I expect you for breakfast tomorrow, and I'm sure you want to get better acquainted with Collinwood. Anne must have a hundred places she wants you to see."

Brian glanced at Anne, then at Mrs. Merrill. "I'm afraid not. I've got to get back to Ruston and spend a little more time with my mother. So, I'll be leaving very early tomorrow, but thanks for the invitation, and again, thanks for having me tonight."

"You're certainly welcome anytime, Brian."

Anne and Brian walked outside, down the walk, and sat on the concrete wall at the edge of the yard. There was no conversation. Each seemed to be waiting for the other to begin. Finally, Anne reached over and placed her hand on his. He turned to look at her.

He looked at the reflection of the street lamp on her hair and the way the light illuminated her face as he had remembered. His outward demeanor belied what he was feeling. He was content, just for this fleeting moment, to be there beside her. He knew it was about to end.

She glanced up. "Be realistic for a minute. We've only really known each other for those three weeks and we don't really know each other. You don't understand me. Not really. I'm not the person you should fall in love with. You probably know that too."

"Don't go making those kinds of decisions for me. I believe I can handle that myself. But, you're right on one count, we *don't* know each other."

"Brian, we were caught up in the excitement of the moment. You were leaving and ..." She stopped there, as if there was no need to finish the statement.

Brian looked out into the night, and shook his head at the hopelessness of the situation. He slowly withdrew his hand and stood up. Anne stood quickly, reaching for his hand again, as if to say something she had been reluctant to put into words. He looked at her for several seconds wanting to take her in his arms, hold her close once again, and make all of her doubts disappear. The reality of the moment quickly came into focus. "I really thought something special happened last September. It's damn obvious I was wrong. Goodbye, Anne." He turned and walked toward the car.

"Brian, Brian..." He didn't respond. He opened the door, started the engine and drove off into the night. He stopped long enough to pick up his things at Aunt Lucy's and began the drive back to Ruston. Staring into the empty highway, its centerline created a hypnotic effect that allowed his thoughts to hurl around in his head. Events, mingled with emotions, flashed through his reflections. He let his contemplations have free rein, with no effort at sorting out any pattern or direction to them. They varied between anger, dismay, and regret.

Sleep was a magic elixir for his psyche, and Thursday morning provided a more optimistic view of life in general. Brian relaxed at the table, as his mother prepared breakfast. The sound of sizzling bacon and smells of coffee brewing brought back memories of last summer. She spun around, facing him. He instinctively tensed. "Gosh, it's great having you home. Soon as the bacon browns, I'm going to fix you a batch of cream gravy. The biscuits are already in the oven. You didn't even get a whiff of those, did you." The rancor and defensiveness were gone. They both avoided any mention of his father or the divorce. Questions about the Air force were instigated because of genuine interest. She watched admiringly as Brian consumed breakfast. He relaxed. His defenses melted away with each helping of gravy, ladled generously over a biscuit.

He and Tyler spent more time together talking about old times, yet the subject of Anne and Collinwood never came up again. Tyler described the social life of Delta Tau Delta with great detail, including his latest adventures with his new interest, Barbara. She was the main attraction for this quarter. Their divergent experiences were replacing their previous commonality of thought and conversation. It was becoming more noticeable to both, but friendship still held its bond.

With time moving rapidly, he realized he needed to call Lori. He grabbed the phone, dropped back on the bed and dialed quickly. There was that softness of her voice as she answered. "I know it's late in the week, but do you have any definite plans for Friday night. How about a bite to eat and take in a movie at the Alabama Theater?"

"No plans. Gosh darn, it'll be great seeing you again. That sounds like fun, but come as early as you can so that we'll have plenty of time to talk. See ya' Friday."

Brian rang the doorbell, while admiring the neat, well-kept, brick home, and wondered how different it would be growing up in Birmingham instead of a very small town like Ruston. The door opened, and Lori threw her arms around his neck and squeezed painfully hard.

"It's hard to believe you're really here. Come on in and tell me all about flight training, and everything else going on. Mom had to go over to a friend's house to help out with someone who's ill. I hope she'll get back before we go downtown. I want her to meet you 'cause she hears me talk about you all the time."

"Hey, slow down and take a breath. I don't know if I should meet your mother now after she's heard all of the things you might've told her. My reputation's probably shot."

"Yeah, sure." She patted the sofa beside her. "Come sit over here and tell me about everything happening in your busy life these days. I know you've seen Anne during the holidays?"

Brian plopped down on the sofa, leaning back against the large pillows piled at the end. He frowned as he responded. "The way you ask that question makes me realize you already know how that visit went. You're her roommate, so don't play dumb with me, Missy."

"I really don't know what the devil you're talking about. You know I wouldn't set you up with a question like that, don't you? Well, don't you?" She glared at him, not waiting for an answer, as she continued, "You know, that'd really hurt my feelings if you thought for one cotton-pickin' minute I'd play games like that." She lowered her voice to almost a whisper. "Now, tell me what's wrong."

"Sorry. Let's forget this conversation and go to that place in Homewood, The Green Lantern, and get a bite."

"Sounds like we need a quick change of conversation. Let me grab my coat." She said.

"Now that you've had a glass of wine, maybe you'd like to tell me about your visit with Anne?" She inquired.

"Oh, so the wine's supposed to mellow me out. Not quite, Missy. But, since you're so insistent about my visit, I'll tell you this much: I reckon I got blind-sided by events I didn't see coming." He smiled as he raised his glass toward her. "Here's to friends, tonight, and enough of that situation."

She tapped her glass against his. "Yep, here's to us. Now quit changing the subject. Tell me what you're talking about with Anne. Enough riddles."

"God, you're insistent. Frankly, I still think you should've known something was wrong with the way Anne was feeling about me. After all, you can't live with someone and not have an inkling of what's going on in their head." He insisted.

"There were things bothering Anne. She became moody and despondent right before Thanksgiving. Anne didn't talk to me about everything." She touched his glass. "Maybe you need another. You aren't mellow yet." She smiled back roguishly as she continued. "She seemed different after Thanksgiving. She seemed to be preoccupied with school, exams and all. I just assumed she might be worried about school. You obviously think it was Justin."

"Justin, the Judge, and a lot of Collinwood. It appears the combination bent her mind a little. I can't believe a person can turn emotions on and off that easily. Tell me something. Was I that damn stupid last September?"

"No. Don't think like that." She looked troubled. "Talk to Anne. There may be something she still needs to tell you."

Brian glanced down at his watch. "I suggest we forget this topic, and get a move-on, so we can make the movie. Let's just enjoy the evening." He looked intently into her eyes. "I want you to know I appreciate your friendship. Just being able to talk to you always makes things take on a different perspective. Thanks, Missy."

The movie was enjoyable and the ride back to Lori's was filled with conversation, accentuated by frequent laughter at the way each told of the amusing, sometimes ridiculous actions around them. Lori was a sparkle that always brightened Brian's outlook. No matter what events tempted cynicism to creep into his thinking, her wit erased any pessimism. Her sense of humor was as spontaneous as the rest of her personality.

As she opened the door, Lori took his arm. "The evening went by way too fast. We need to sip a little coffee and talk some more. I can have a pot going in no time. You know how long it's gonna' be before I see you again?" She pleaded.

"Thanks, but I really need to start back. I still have a thousand things to do before I leave tomorrow to go back to Texas. If you find time, drop me a line or two and tell me how everything's going back here in Alabama."

"You know I'll write, probably more than you want to read. Be careful." Lori hugged him tightly and gave him a kiss on the cheek.

"Bye, Missy. You're something else." He gave her one more squeeze and turned to leave.

As he reached the car, he looked back and saw her still standing at the door. She gave a wave, then turned and went inside. As he sat there watching her, with feelings he couldn't identify, confusing, disturbing. He shook his head to clear the cobwebs, put the car in gear and drove away.

CHAPTER FIVE

B RIAN HATED INSTRUMENT flying. Being under the hood, flying strictly by the gauges was a confined, claustrophobic feeling. No references of horizon or ground exaggerated the criticism by Lt. Browne. The slashing condemnation accentuated Brian's mistakes and compounded the frustration of his miscalculations. He maneuvered the aircraft down final approach, working to stay on the glide path, watching needles point to erroneous indications. He tried futilely to keep ahead of the instrument readings. Lt. Browne screamed at him to come out from under the hood.

"Look up ahead, do you think you're lined up for an instrument approach to that runway? You're closer to Highway seventy-five than the runway. I've got the controls."

Brian knew he'd busted it. He'd just completed the worst flight since he'd been in the program. Some of his enthusiasm for flying diminished for the moment. He was depressed at his performance, wanting to erase the last two hours of blunders and miscalculations.

As they taxied up to shut down, he was thankful to be on the ground, and able to release some of the pent up tension, but terrified of what Lt. Browne was going to say. He figured it couldn't be much worse than what had just happened in the air. He sat there waiting for the worse. It soon came.

"Mister Brannon, I should give you a "pink slip" today but I've decided to wait 'till tomorrow. If you can get it together tomorrow, we'll let this one slide. If you foul up again, I'm writing both of these up for "pink slips." You understand that means a check ride?"

"Yessir." Brian answered.

Brian felt his head spinning while trying to figure out what was happening to him. He was in a stupor as he marched back from the flight line, his eyes glassed over as if he were dazed. Tomorrow was going to be critical. It could mean that check ride so few survived. The sight of the T-6 with the checkered nose cowling caused most to turn weak in the knees at sight of that aircraft. He knew the odds were against him; he sensed the doubt he worked so hard to defeat. It was still there.

Brian sat quietly during the evening get-together. The talk was on Korea, the war, and flying. No one seemed to notice Brian's absence from the discussion except Joe. Brian picked up on the scrutiny by his roommate and tried to enter the conversation, but not successfully. The Group broke up for the evening and Brian sat there staring blankly at his coke. Joe stayed behind, looking intently at Brian. They sat there for a few minutes without a word being spoken. Finally, Joe broke the silence that was becoming noticeable. "What th' bloody hell's wrong with you? Something must have messed with your thinking while you were on leave. It's damn obvious you're not acting right." Getting no reaction from Brian, he added, "C'mon, talk to me."

"There's really not that much to talk about. Let it go, okay?"

"Negative on the 'okay'. There's very little I'd be reluctant to talk to you about, and I figured that held true for you too. The only reason I'm bringing this up at all is to make sure you have your head screwed on straight. We know you don't have to be too distracted to make strange things happen up there." Joe indicated by pointing toward the ceiling.

"There's not a damn thing wrong with my thinking, at least not to that degree." He took in a deep breath, relaxing his thoughts as well as his body. "All right?" Brian looked quickly at Joe. "Guess I'm a little 'spooked' or something. I nearly got a 'pink slip' today."

"Bullshit, not you! What the hell's happening?" Joe asked.

"He didn't give me one today, but if I 'screw the pooch' tomorrow, I get *two*-- and a check ride." Brian lowered his voice at the end of the sentence.

"Christ, you're walking the thin line here. I don't get it. I damn well don't understand you're attitude since you got back from Christmas."

Brian laughed sarcastically. "Want to know the worst four words in the English language? 'We have to talk.' That usually has unhappy consequences. Seems her thinking changed since last October. Reckon I misread what was happening those three weeks we had together." He looked down at the tabletop, averting eye contact. "Why was I that damn stupid?" The question was purely rhetorical, he expected no answer and certainly didn't want one.

Joe slouched back in his chair, a disgusted sneer on his face. "Oh, now I'm beginning to see the big picture take shape. You're gettin' your mind screwed up by some goddamn southern belle when you should be thinking about flying airplanes. I thought you wanted this program, and nothing, short of the devil himself, would stand in your way. Damn." Joe banged his hand on the table, glaring at Brian. "For God's sake, forget her. She doesn't exist for you right now."

"Get off your freakin' pulpit. I don't need your preachin' right about now." Brian stared back at Joe.

"What you really need is somebody to knock some sense into that messed up head of yours. Maybe I could knock that damn female outta' your brain for you." Joe stated.

"Get up and give it your best shot." Brian fired back, as he vaulted from his chair.

"Sit down." Joe's voice lowered. "Maybe I've got your attention. C'mon, Brian, don't screw up now. Not because of some blasted woman."

Brian kept eye contact, his face still crimson. He lowered himself into the chair. "The hell of it is; you're right." He shook his head and smiled. "That speaks volumes when *you've* gotta' be the stabilizing force around here. Geez, that's a new twist." Both began to laugh.

"Cut it loose from your thinking for a while. Give it a rest." Joe stated. "You've got enough to think about the next nine months. Don't get your priorities messed up."

"Sage advice once again from the master, and I damn well know what my priorities are right now."

The next morning, Brian strapped into the seat, adjusted his headset, pulled the hood up and blocked out the world. In the air, he focused intently on the gauges, cross-checking heading, altitude, rate of descent, and the localizer needle that pointed to the field. He lowered flaps, and established a five hundred foot per minute descent, reduced power and forced the aircraft toward the runway. His body tensed as he applied pressure to the stick and rudders to maintain course. He knew there was no room for error. This one had to be on the money. Sweat poured down beside his headset, running into his ears. He maneuvered the aircraft toward the runway, his eyes darting quickly from instrument to instrument.

"I've got it. Pop the hood and take a look." Lt. Browne said.

Brian snapped the hood back and glanced up through the spinning propeller at the centerline of the approach end of the runway -- right on the money.

"Very good job." Lt. Browne looked over his shoulder with a slight smile.

Brian was taking his five-minute break to look over the mail before hitting the formation for lunch. Time dictated that he scan paragraphs, getting the gist of the letter, then he could completely digest and fully enjoy the contents on the flight line as time permitted. Joe rushing through the door broke his concentration suddenly. Brian assumed Joe always pushed the time factor for every formation, so he scarcely looked up when he blasted through the door. He tried to focus again on the letter. But Joe, not getting the attention he wanted, pulled his chair directly in front of Brian.

"We just lost one. I just heard about it. They augured in south of the field about an hour ago."

Brian dropped the letter on the desk and looked up at Joe, trying to grasp what he had heard. "What happened? Who the hell was it?"

"Bill Franklin and his instructor. They lost it doing acrobatics and couldn't recover in time. They bought the farm, but good."

Brian sat silently as Joe got up to get ready for "first call." The shock was beginning to take shape in his thinking. This first encounter with the occupational hazards of flying military aircraft was unsettling. There had been an unconscious belief they all led charmed lives in the air. He understood these things happen, but not to people he knew. Neither discussed what they were feeling at the moment. They quietly dressed for lunch.

The atmosphere was more subdued in the briefing room than usual. The flight ready room buzzed with conversation, centered on the accident. Brian, however, eased into his usual chair and fumbled in his pocket for the letter from Lori. He was hoping Lt. Browne would fly with Ed first, so he could read his mail. It just might give him time to sort through his feelings about Bill Franklin. He hardly knew the guy. They weren't in the same stage for flying and had no classes together, but he knew it was necessary to put the accident in perspective.

"Mister Brannon, I'll fly with you first today. We're going to do some more work on acrobatics today. You can do a couple of spins, chandelles, and then I'll let you do a few slow rolls for the first time. You have any questions on the procedures for the slow roll maneuvers?"

Brian slowly folded the letter. "No, Sir. No questions."

The flight proceeded normally with Lt. Browne's voice vibrating an eardrum occasionally at minor transgression in the cockpit. They climbed out to the acrobatic area south of the field and reached the briefed altitude of 7,000 feet. Two spins, one in each direction, went okay. Brian waited for the next instruction with some apprehension. Lt. Browne was in one of his more contentious moods.

"All right, Mister Brannon, clear the area below, place the nose on a cardinal heading, and let's see a slow roll to the right. Make sure you roll out on the same heading, and altitude. Remember to keep forward pressure on the stick as you reach the hundred and eighty degree point so it doesn't dish-out on you while you're upside down. You've got it, let's do it."

Brian increased his grip on the stick and rolled the aircraft to the right. Instead of instinct, his mind was translating movements to his feet and hands. This was not the way to fly acrobatics. The aircraft slowly rolled upside down and the nose fell below the horizon. Brian couldn't put enough forward pressure on the stick to get the nose back up. The nose continued to drop. He didn't want to fight the airplane, quickly deciding it was best to start over rather than try to salvage this maneuver. He hurriedly rolled the aircraft back to the upright position and pulled the nose level with the horizon. Lt. Browne shook the stick vigorously, "I've got it."

"What the hell's wrong with you? He screamed into Brian's headset. "Are you afraid of this airplane, Mister?"

"No, Sir." He shouted back.

During the next few minutes Brian wasn't sure what maneuvers he was experiencing. Lt. Browne snatched the nose up toward a wisp of clouds and did two snap rolls, followed by a violent hammerhead stall. He did every acrobatic gyration in his repertoire that the plane could withstand. Brian's headset flew off, his head snapped from left to right, his arms left his lap with the negative "G" forces, and then his entire body slammed back hard into the seat. After five minutes of violent maneuvers, the aircraft returned to straight and level flight. Brian fumbled around to get his headset back on. He had no idea what had brought on this illogical episode, but he definitely wanted to hear what Browne would say next.

"Did that bother you?" Lt. Browne asked.

"No Sir. Enjoyed the whole thing." Brian shot back his answer.

"Okay, now give me that slow roll to the right." His instructor stated in a quieter voice.

Brian rolled the aircraft through a slow roll, not the best roll ever done, but good enough to keep the intercom quiet. After a few moments of silence, Brian smiled and felt relieved, but still puzzled by Lt. Browne's actions.

"If you're wondering, Mister Brannon, I thought there for a minute you were a little apprehensive about going into that roll. I wondered if you're beginning to show a little fear of the aircraft. The accident this morning could've affected your confidence level. I needed to know -- obviously it didn't." There was a momentary pause before he continued. "Just remember one thing about this profession: not everyone has the ability, the coordination, or the right stuff that's required in the air. Only those who can handle *any* situation up here are the ones who grow old as pilots. Remember that. Fix it firmly in your brain."

Brian was impressed. This was the first time Lt. Browne had philosophized about any phase of flying. He had found him worthy to share this thought. Without stating it, Lt. Browne indicated the accident happened because two pilots were put in a position that exceeded their ability. Lt. Browne, in his candid manner, had provided the perspective that Brian was looking for. Flying placed people in one of three categories: washed out, dead, or having the right stuff. The alternative was all of those sleepwalking souls below that would never experience the challenge or exhilaration of flying. He looked over the side of the aircraft and felt sorry for them.

That evening he had time to read Lori's letter. She started with all of the news at Agnes Baines, including minute details of who was doing what, at what time. Lori was never brief on her descriptive explanations of events. She never failed to relate some news of Anne, always relayed in her casual oh-by-the-way style. Brian never mentioned Anne in his letters, nor commented on that part of Lori's letters. Lori casually mentioned the fact she'd met a Lieutenant, who was in advanced pilot training at Craig Air Force Base:

"...he's a very interesting guy and quite charming. He said he wanted to come up to Ruston some weekend to see me. I put him off by telling him how very busy I've been with work at school. Don seems persistent, however. Who knows how long a lonely gal can withstand the charm and persistence of a flyer!"

Somehow, this dismayed Brian. He should be there to check this Don guy out. His protective instincts were at work. A word or two of caution to Lori was definitely in order. "Cadet widows" were well known at all the pilot training bases. The tendency to occupy time while at that base, dallying with the feelings of a local girl, then moving on to other encounters wasn't uncommon. Lori wasn't aware of this character flaw, found in too many cadets and probably in just as many Lieutenant student officers. Brian folded Lori's letter, placed it carefully back into the envelope. He needed to think about a reply for a while.

The only major phase of flying that remained was a night cross-country flight. There was a buzz of activity, everyone was busy checking their equipment for the night navigation flight that would take them from Perrin AFB west to Gainesville, south to Denton, east to Greenville, northeast to Paris, then home to Sherman, a flight of one hour and thirty-five minutes. Student pilots checked flashlights, rechecked lines drawn on map, their log of headings and estimated times en route. Brian was sure these flights were deliberately planned for moonless nights. The briefing was concise and the Major explained takeoff' intervals would be five 103minutes.

"Just enough distance to make sure the navigation lights of the aircraft in front can't be used in navigating the course." Joe mused.

"I don't see anybody in this motley group I'd follow anyway. Take 'ole Larson there – he'll probably end up in downtown Fort Worth."

The aircraft lined up, nose into the wind to keep engine temperatures down, and waited for darkness. Brian was number three in line, followed by Ed, then Joe in the number five slot. The sun, barely in evidence over the horizon, leisurely disappeared. The orange-tinged twilight unhurriedly turned to solid ebony. It was time.

The tower barked out clearance for Number One aircraft to take the active runway for takeoff. "Blue one, you're cleared into position for an immediate departure, recheck altimeter setting, two niner niner six, winds southwest at six to eight knots. Blue two, you'll be cleared in five minutes. All aircraft are advised to clear your engines, and recheck your mags. before takeoff."

"Blue one, Roger. Rolling."

Brian waited the long ten minutes, rechecking maps and headings. At last, he was moving down the runway, cross-checking gauges as the T-6 lifted into the air. He retracted the gear, turned to his first heading, and peered into blackness. He quickly went on instruments until he regained sight of lights dividing the sky from the ground. He welcomed the horizon of dimly lit farms, as he climbed on course for Gainesville. He rechecked his power settings as he scanned the horizon for the lights of three small Texas towns to make sure they were in their relative positions in the dark sky that surrounded him. He leveled out, set cruise power as he heard Ed's voice crackle in his ear, announcing his takeoff roll. Later he heard Joe tell the tower he was "on the go." Brian smiled. *Joe just can't use standard terminology; he has to make sure he puts his own twist on it.*

Brian looked around the dim horizon, then up at thousands of stars flecking the dark sky. The beauty of the night was reassuring. He listened to the assured drone of the engine as he watched the twinkling lights of the small towns and farms. Occasionally he glanced over the side, seeing the procession of lights along roads, as cars moved at their snail's pace. He smiled as he spotted the lights of Gainesville on the horizon, double-checked his next estimated time en route and new compass heading. His deliberations were interrupted by a troubled voice shouting into his mike.

"Mayday, Mayday, Mayday. I've got engine failure. Losing altitude."

There was no mistaking Joe's voice. Brian sat bolt upright waiting for the next transmission, wondering what was going through Joe's mind. It better be right, 'cause the only one who could help Joe, right now, was Joe himself.

"Aircraft with engine failure, give your call sign and position." The tower operator barked.

"Roger, Roger, Blue five over lake Texhoma, going down."

"Roger, Blue five, slow down, keep cool, check mixture rich, check fuel on main tank, and hit your fuel boost. If you can't get some power quickly, bail out. Do you copy?'

Silence. Seconds stretched into eternity. Brian was thinking to himself, Get *with it, Joe. Tell us what's happening.*

"Tower. I've got partial power now. Heading for the field, but still losing altitude."

"Roger, Blue five, if you have any doubts about making the field, bail out now while you have altitude. Don't attempt to put it down at night. You copy Blue five?"

More silence.

"Tower. I've got the runway dead ahead. I'm low but think I'm gonna' make it."

"Blue five, got you in sight about two miles out. Your approach is too steep. Level off. Try to save some altitude." There was no acknowledgment by Joe. "Turn on your landing lights Blue five. Get those lights on! Okay, just hold what you've got." The instructor in the tower continued nonstop with his instructions and reassurance of Joe. "Okay, looking good, looking good. You're over the field boundary. Okay, put it down anywhere, you've got it made."

Brian released the built up tension. "Way to go, Joe." He shouted over the radio without thinking, and afterward was embarrassed at the loss of control. The tower operator provided no admonishment for the violation of radio procedure. It wasn't important at that moment.

Brian concentrated on his navigation, rechecking each checkpoint, adjusting for wind, and finally spotted the rotating beacon of the base on the horizon. A smooth landing and engine shutdown marked the end of an imposing flight. He was eager to see Joe, and give him a little static about his slightly quivering voice as he called out "Mayday." *No, maybe I'd better let ole' Joe settle down a bit before any hassles.*

Brian slipped off his boots, and sank onto his bunk, glad to have this phase of night flying over. He was waiting for Joe to come in smiling ear-to-ear, to give his rendition of the night's events. It was more than an hour before Joe came through the door. He wasn't smiling as he walked slowly over to the desk, sat down, and said nothing. Brian rose up on one elbow and looked over for Joe's reaction. Instead, Joe continued to sit, staring blankly out the window.

"Well, let's hear about this engine failure of yours. Let's see now, how do we start these fearless tales of daring-do? Oh yes, there I was seven thousand feet ..." He stopped, realizing something was wrong.

Joe made no comment or acknowledgment of Brian's attempt at sardonic humor. He stood up and took off his flight suit, dropped it on the floor, took his towel from the hook and headed for the shower. Brian felt a bit awkward about the comment and completely puzzled at Joe's actions.

Joe reappeared in the room, threw his towel toward the locker, flopped down across his bed, and turned toward the wall. Brian got up and walked over to the foot of the bed and waited a moment before speaking.

"What the bloody hell's wrong? Good God, man, you just handled a difficult emergency in great form, and now you act as if your world just collapsed. Damnation, talk to me."

Joe rolled over slowly to face Brian. He just shook his head as if he couldn't find the words. Then he slammed his fist into the wall with a thud that had to hurt. "I just learned I don't belong here! I was scared shitless up there, wondering what to do. My hand was trying to find the mixture, then the boost pump; my butt was puckering, my mind going blank. And I couldn't even decide whether to jump or not. It was pure-ass luck that I got it back on the ground. Just pure goddamn luck."

"Bullshit, you got it back because you made it happen. You knew what you had to do, and you did it. Dammit, Joe, your instinct, reactions, your skill. That's what took over when the crunch was on. Tomorrow you're gonna' laugh about it."

"No, hell, you don't understand." He shook his head emphatically. "When I got the damn thing stopped, I just sat there, shaking. I was shaking, Brian. Then the tower told me my replacement aircraft number." He glanced up again. "Christ, they didn't tell me 'good job', 'kiss my ass', or nothing. They just gave me another aircraft number. I told 'em to forget it. I was through for *this* night. Then, some jaybird in the tower tells me to report to my instructor in the briefing room.

The stage commander was there too. They proceeded to chew my ass out for a bad attitude and told me to get out to the aircraft and get on with the cross-country. I just shook my head and told them 'no way, not tonight.' I couldn't do it again. I couldn't climb back in another bird and do it again."

Brian stared at Joe incredulously. He knew he was watching someone who'd been pushed past his limitations and it smacked him right in his ego. He knew whatever he said wouldn't substantially change what Joe was feeling. He was looking at a friend who was encountering the hard cold fact that maybe he didn't have that essential something, that never-talked-about ingredient. He felt a fist knot in his stomach. He reached over and placed a hand on Joe's shoulder. "Hey, let's get some sleep and talk about this tomorrow. Things will look different tomorrow. They take on a different perspective in the daylight, believe me."

"Yeah, sure." Joe rolled back on the bunk again and stared at the wall.

The next day Joe looked at his watch, slowly slid out of his seat and left class. At 0900 a board of officers would meet to discuss and decide his future in the Aviation Cadet Program. Brian found difficulty in concentrating on anything being discussed in class. His thoughts were several blocks away at a meeting, taking place around a large mahogany table in the Wing conference room. He scrutinized the reason for Joe's predicament. They were at a point in basic training where those who didn't have "it" were already washed out. *How the hell was this happening to Joe? But, why worry? That silver-tongued sonofagun can talk his way out of anything.* He tuned back in to the instructor.

Finally, the break for lunch formation came. Brian ran into the barracks, actually stumbling into his room. Joe was sitting with his feet up on the desk, expressionless.

"Well, what happened?"

"Typical Elimination Board. Except, they were willing to give me another chance based on my record, and a damn fine recommendation from my instructor."

"Fandamntastic." Brian shouted.

"Take it easy. I haven't finished. I didn't take 'em up on the offer..."

"What the hell are you telling me?" Brian cut him short.

"Damn, will you just wait a minute? What happened to me up there last night was a feeling I've never had before, and never want again. I lost something last night I'd always taken for granted. It's not a macho thing. But it's a total loss of my confidence level. That magic ingredient, that burning damn desire to be a military pilot isn't there anymore. I've been fooling myself a long time. Now, I'm gonna' do the smart thing."

"Then you fooled a helluva' lot of people, including me. I thought you were a natural, the guy who had all the confidence in the world. I can't buy this 'I don't have it crap'. Not from you. Think of what you did last night. Damn few cadets in this class could have done it, but you did. Now, go back and tell 'em you've changed your mind. For Christ's sake, don't self-eliminate now."

"It's done. There's no going back now. Look, let's say goodbye now. I'll be packed and out of here when you get back from the flight line this afternoon. Don't make it any harder."

"Then there's not much left to say is there?" Brian said in a lowered voice.

"Nope, not really." Joe stepped closer. "You know how I feel about you, fella'. I've only known two people I could count on anytime, anywhere, and you're one of 'em. We had some hellatious times here at ole' Perrin Air Force Base. I won't soon forget 'em."

Brian had to compose himself a bit. He blinked back the moisture starting to fill the corner of his eyes. He forced a smile, took Joe's hand, and squeezed a handshake that said it all.

"Take care. I don't have to tell you how much I'm gonna' miss your bitchin' and moanin'. It's gonna' seem really tranquil around here. Now, I can probably get some peace and quiet." It was impossible for Brian to keep the jocularity going any longer. He turned serious. "Damn, I'm gonna' miss your butt. He stuck out his hand again. "Lotsa' luck, Joe."

"You too, and keep the greasy side down, you heah?"

He had a bad feeling he was looking at his friend for the last time. He cursed under his breath that life had a habit of doing this to friends far too often. Joe had made an impact on his life in the few short months they were together, and he was sure the hollow feeling in his gut would be there for a long, long time. Boyce leaving was one thing, he could accept that, but not Joe.

That evening at the cadet club, Scott, Bugsy and Brian sat around a table with very little discourse about the loss of Joe. Interruptions by others were cut short. Occasionally, each in turn, would look up and shake his head in disbelief that Joe was no longer with the group. There was no need to try to put feelings into words. Their feelings were understood. It was a characteristic of the closeness that had prevailed within "The Group."

Scott took it upon himself to break the silence. "I'm gonna' miss that redheaded peckerwood. There was only one Joe. He kept me laughing with his bitching about the program. I bet he's already teed off on some unsuspecting soul in Sherman by now."

"That's for damn sure." Echoed Bugsy. "I'm sure as hell gonna' miss him. But let's get real about this. If he didn't have it, then he shouldn't be up there."

Brian slammed his fist on the table and glared at Bugsy with total contempt. "You stupid sonafabitch. You never really knew Joe. As far as having it, you aren't in the same damn league with that guy, in flying or being a human being."

"C'mon, Brian, ease up. Bugsy didn't mean it the way you took it." Scott was doing his best to soothe the situation. "Christ, we know how you feel about Joe."

Brian shoved his glass back and stood up. "I'm sorry, Bugsy. Really sorry." He placed his hand on Bugsy's shoulder, squeezing gently. "You didn't deserve that." He turned and left the Club.

The first thing to catch his attention as he entered his room was an unmade bunk. He glanced around the room at the empty clothes rack and a semi-cleared desk. He slammed his hat down on the floor, and sat on his bunk. He cursed under his breath as he felt the warmth of a tear run down his face. He felt someone looking at him. Low was leaning against the doorframe.

"I'm sorry about Tanner. He had more moxie than anyone I've come across in this program. I know I couldn't break him. He sure as hell earned my respect."

"Yeah, he survived you, but couldn't survive himself." Brian answered.

"I'll be leaving tomorrow for Willy Air Patch. I got jets." Low said. "Before I leave, I just wanted you to know how I felt about Tanner. Hang in there."

"Yeah." Brian replied.

Low turned and was gone.

The surviving cadets of class 51-G gathered in the cadet club for a briefing and their assignments for advanced training. All stood at attention, automatically, as the parade of TAC Officers walked to the front of the room.

"Take your seats, Gentlemen. I know you're anxious to hear where you'll be going for Advanced, and to what type aircraft you've been assigned. This is normally based on your preference cards, grades, and of particular importance, your instructor's recommendation. This time we have a very different situation."

With that, every cadet sat a little straighter in his chair. Something didn't sound right. The murmuring was audible enough for the Major to clear his throat to regain attention. The Major continued, "The entire Aviation Cadet Program, at single-engine training bases, has been filled with students from our NATO allies. These students *must* go to fighters based on our host agreement with their country to provide pilot training."

Cadets began looking at one another. Bugsy leaned over to Brian. "Somebody's about to get the shaft, and the Major has put a little grease on it first." They looked back toward the front and listened, as a hush fell on the room.

"What I'm about to tell you won't be easy for some of you to accept. Those who had counted on fighters, jets, will have to wait until graduation. Then, those who are accepted can transition into fighters. For now, everyone in this class will be assigned multi-engine advanced, at either Reese Air Force Base, Texas, or Vance Air Force Base, Oklahoma."

There was a dull undercurrent of cadets mumbling invectives, and not too subtly. It sounded like a beehive swatted into action. It had to be perceptible to the officers in front of the group of Cadets.

"Gentlemen, I'm sorry I had to be the one to bring you this kind of news. I wish all of you luck. Base assignments are posted in the back of the room. Carry on."

The room stood at attention for the departure of the officers.

Bugsy grabbed Brian's arm. "Well, let's go see where the hell we're going. Maybe the three of us got the same base."

Brian turned toward him. "As if it makes any difference now. Is there a helluva' difference between sitting in the panhandle of Texas or on the mesa's of Oklahoma? Damn I didn't want multi-engine. I never counted on this."

"Aw, come on, Brian. Shake it off. Let's go take a look. At least we made it to advance. There's a long list of those who aren't going with us to any base. Think about that one for a while." Bugsy said.

Scott ran his finger down the line of names. "Hey, all right! Brian, we got Vance. Enid, Oklahoma beats that constant wind wailing across the Texas Panhandle." Scott's finger stopped at a spot on the list. "Damn, I'm sorry, Bugsy. You got Lubbock, Texas. You better hold a rock in both hands so you don't blow over into New Mexico."

"You're really funny, Scott." Bugsy looked at Brian. "See. That's what happens when cousins marry." He broke into a large grin. "Well, what th' hell! Let's go to town tonight and say goodbye to Sherman so they won't forget us too soon."

No one cared about being written up for being intoxicated, or conduct unbecoming a future officer. With little thought of the consequences, the three of them painted the town red, though Sherman, Texas didn't require too much paint. The night ended in a blur as they returned to base and hit the sack to sleep off their indiscretions.

As he finished packing, Brian sat down to write a last letter to Lori. He explained the lack of travel time they were given between bases. He told her he'd counted on a few days in Ruston between Basic and Advanced, a deserved breather, but it wasn't to be. He asked the obligatory questions regarding this guy Don. The subject of Don's sincerity had never been mentioned and Brian still avoided this subject. The one thing he never told Lori, was about Joe's leaving. He couldn't explain such things in a letter. His thoughts this night were hard to put on paper. He'd just completed a comprehensive and difficult part of the program that left friends behind. Experiences of the last seven months surpassed the previous twenty years of his life in shaping certain emotions, awareness of individual imperfections, along with a much keener sense of his own weaknesses. These thoughts were not to be shared. They took residence in some deep reclusive part of his reasoning. His thoughts abruptly returned to the letter. He closed, "I'll write as soon as I get to Enid."

He lay back on the bunk, closing his eyes, as thoughts drifted into a hazy collage of all the things that had transpired the last few months. A parade of faces and events flashed past. Some caused momentary stopping points in his reflections, briefly reliving some exploit, shared laughter, a somber moment. Emotions he couldn't quite bring to the surface nudged at his consciousness, always just out of reach. Sleep mercifully overtook the process.

CHAPTER SIX

THE SETTING SUN cast a pinkish glow on the white two-story barracks, as Brian moved through the neatly marked streets. The typical military structures were the same here at Vance, assuring him he was on another Air Force Base. Aircraft engines roaring in the background confirmed the observation. He eagerly bounded up the steps of the barracks, stood in the door and observed his new surroundings. The room was a replica of those at Perrin. It was sparsely furnished, void of color, but still providing the necessities. At least according to United States Air Force standards concerning the needs of an Aviation Cadet. It was obvious that whoever was going to share the room had already settled in. There in the corner was a B-4 bag with the initials VMG stenciled indelibly on the nameplate. Uniforms and civilian clothes were hung neatly in the locker. Brian fingered the bright blue and yellow plaid of a shirt, admiring anyone with gumption enough to wear something this hideous.

"If you like it, I'll let you wear it sometimes." A voice sounded.

Brian embarrassingly dropped the sleeve of the shirt. "Nice shirt." He walked over with hand extended. "Brian Brannon."

"Vince Giacano. Looks like we're gonna' be roommates."

"I see you're all settled in." Brian scanned around the room. "Where's home?"

"New Jersey, and I'll go ahead and tell you right up front. No, my family's not in the Mafia."

"I didn't think so." Brian responded. "You look too harmless."

Vince broke up with laughter, as he took Brian's hand in a vice like grip. "Guess I didn't inherit the volatile Italian personality. I just got all the good-looking genes. By the way, which Base did you come from?"

"Perrin, and you?"

"Randolph, West Point of the Air, and they never let us forget it. Their motto was: 'Tradition, Unhampered by Progress'."

Brian was six feet, one inch tall, but had to look up at his new roommate. He always assumed Italians were short. Vince dispelled that theory. His smile was locked into place, hair the color of ink, constantly being shoved back from his eyes, and hands that were in perpetual motion. Brian had a good feeling about Vince and enjoyed his sense of humor, even for a "Damn Yankee," a New Jersey Yankee at that. It wasn't going to be dull.

"Brian, where the hell have you been?" Scott's unmistakable southern accent invaded the conversation like molasses. "I thought I greased the skids for us to get a room together but my planning and that of the Air Force somehow manages to stay at odds. Some pin head with three stripes went ahead and assigned somebody else. Anyway, I'm right across the hall there." He motioned behind him with his thumb.

"Vince, meet an old buddy from Perrin, Scott Jeter." Brian stated.

"Just remember you're now surrounded by Rebels, and we still haven't forgotten."

"Hi ya' doin, Scott." Vince put his hand out, while scrutinizing the author of the intrusion. "Don't tell me you characters are still fighting the Civil War?" He glanced back at Brian. "I had to live with that Texas Alamo crap for six and a half months. I don't need the Civil War as a replacement."

"The recent unpleasantness to which you refer, Suh, wasn't the Civil Wah." Scott added in an exaggerated Southern drawl. "It was the Wah of Nawthen Aggression."

"Christ, my ancestors were still stomping grapes in Sicily when your great grand pappys were trying to change the map here. Never have understood why that war never ends with you Rebels. So, youse guys, let's call a cease-fire and go over to the Club. Let's meet some of the others who were lucky enough to get assigned to dear old Vance."

Brian and Scott looked quizzically at each other, and in unison said; *"Youse guys?"*

"Lord, do we have our work cut out for us!" Scott added emphatically.

Monday launched the last phase of the flight program for Vance's newest Aviation Cadet Class. Their new shoulder boards, with a large white stripe running lengthwise, denoted an Advanced Phase Cadet. Brian felt the eagerness surge within him once again as they marched to the flight line. They used all the cadence-counting ditties they knew and some that were invented on the spot. The flight-suited cadets filed in and quickly took places around the tables, waiting restlessly for the customary briefing on what was to be expected. A Major stepped into the room and proceeded to the front.

"Welcome, Gentlemen. I'm Major Nelson, Flying Training

Officer. I'm well aware of the reasons for your entire class going to Multi-engine Advanced, and understand some of your frustration. I know some of you think you're destined to fly fighters. Your chance will come." He looked out over his audience, and then continued, "In the meantime, you have the opportunity to learn more about instrument flying than any fighter pilot ever gets exposed to. Take a look out there at those B-twenty-fives. That'll be the classroom that'll teach you the confidence and the satisfaction that goes with flying multi-engine aircraft. The washout rate here won't approach that which you've just experienced, but don't be misled. The next six months will be more comprehensive and intensive in both the classroom and flying. Good luck. Your instructors will be out to call off your names. Good flying, Gentlemen."

Brian waited, anxiously, looking around the room, anticipating his new instructor. He hoped for a more laid-back personality to fly with than Lt. Browne. His wish seemed to be granted in the persona of one Capt. William Dodson. He filled the door as he entered the room. Ed Beatty reached over and punched Brian. "Now that's a big man. In fact, tight end big." His massive frame was enhanced by a pleasant-looking smile. As it turned out, Bill Dodson was a second-team All American linebacker at Kansas State. And the soft-at-the-edges smile belied a tough taskmaster.

Dodson called out the names of Cadets Beatty, Brady, and Brannon. Brian slapped Ed's arm. "It must be fate, or somebody still knows how to use those alphabetical listings."

"Naw, they wouldn't be so obvious. They looked at us and realized we just make a helluva' team." Ed quipped.

As the third student ambled over to join them, Ed and Brian introduced themselves. Walt Brady was from Washington State. He was a dimmer image of most of the cadets. His reddish-blonde hair, crew cut short, gave him a look that belied his age. When he slouched in the chair, he had the appearance of a high schooler. Walt's personality was lacking in exuberance, but he seemed to have a likeable, easygoing temperament. Brian and Ed looked at each other knowingly. Capt Dodson approached the three and introductions resumed. He was precise in how the flying schedule would work.

The initial flight was an introductory and supposedly a motivational flight. Each had a shot at some control time and basic air work and their first and last sightseeing flight over Oklahoma. Brian was impressed with the size and complexity of the B-25 but didn't feel comfortable with the handling characteristics. "This thing handles like a semi without brakes." Dodson glanced a frown in his direction. Brian felt embarrassed at his attempt at humor. There was none of the exuberance he experienced in the cockpit of the T-6 and it showed in his performance that day. Even though he disliked being in multi-engine advanced, he knew his attitude had to change, and quickly, or he would never complete the program.

From that first day in the air, things were totally different in the expectations of Capt. Dodson. The constant smile was no indication of his demands in the air. It was patently obvious that multi-engine instructors were a precise breed, not overly endowed with humor, and embodied with little patience toward minor miscalculations. Precision was their byword.

Immediately after classes Brian, Scott and Vince headed for the club. Ed joined them at a table already loaded with glasses. The stag bar hummed with activity, as story-swapping about flying, foibles of the classroom, and occasionally women, not necessarily in that order, was the main fare for discussion. Scott and Vince were engrossed in an argument about the critical airspeed for single-engine flight, as Ed slid his chair closer to Brian, leaning in his direction.

"What's your take on Walt Brady?"

"He seems okay." Brian answered. "Maybe a little too laid back."

"Laid back? Comatose would be more like it. The guy worries me." Ed added.

"No sweat. We've got him outnumbered." Brian laughed.

A new Group was formed. It wasn't a conscious decision, the four just seemed to gravitate to the same table or corner of the bar at the Club. Brian, Scott, Vince, and Ed enjoyed each other's company. It wasn't because of a common background, geographical area, or even sharing a similar personality. Each brought something different to the group, but there was an unidentifiable common bond, a concurrence of thought. Vince, the newcomer to the team, loved laughter and caused his share. He was the wildest, funniest, and most entertaining. He filled any room with his personality.

The weeks tended to move swiftly in Advanced, totally unlike Basic where every action seemed to be under constant scrutiny. It was easy to get into the required routine of classes, flying, Cadet Club, and weekend relaxation. The air work was more exacting than Basic and held less enjoyment. The flights were three hours, sometimes close to four, making the time excruciatingly long when you weren't in the left seat at the controls. Wild Bill, as Ed quickly tagged him, was noted for stressing single-engine procedures. He'd pull a throttle back to simulate an engine out at takeoff, right after 'gear up', and minimum single-engine control speed barely attained. The cadet in the left seat was fighting control of the aircraft, identifying which engine was out, literally standing on the rudder pedal to maintain directional control, then completing the emergency checklist. It was a common occurrence for one of them to get out of the seat with flight suit stained with perspiration from the ordeal of handling in-flight emergencies. Wild Bill was most creative with the simulation of lost generators, no hydraulic pressure, popped circuit breakers, and numerous single-engine landings.

Brian seemed hard-pressed to find time to correspond with Lori, and sometimes went a couple of weeks without writing. Lori, on the other hand, never failed to write at least once a week. Nothing could have the morale-boosting effect of Lori's letters, especially during the week's long routine. The closeness he felt for Lori didn't diminish during the long separation. She filled a void experienced by the lack of communication with Anne. Letter writing was an art form with Lori and her letters were like conversations. Her thoughts poured out as if she was sitting right there. He always read her letters with anticipation, particularly pleased when they included some mention of Anne. She rarely disappointed him. Several times, Anne sent a brief message through Lori, hoping everything was going well for Brian. Now, Agnes Baines was out for the summer, eliminating all references to Anne in Lori's letters.

The heat came on suddenly as if spring bowed out to summer with no warning. The gleaming metal of the aircraft was like touching a hot iron and the concrete radiated the sun in shimmering waves. Brian, Ed and Walt, accompanied only by a flight engineer walked toward the large two-engine aircraft. This was their first solo flight. Solo in a multi-engine aircraft only meant that there was no instructor aboard.

Ed sidled up beside the flight engineer. "Sergeant, you're about to earn your flight pay, with three of the wildest student pilots on base."

"Well, I survived twenty-five missions in a B-seventeen." He surveyed the three students quickly. "You three just may be more dangerous after all." He looked Ed up and down with disdain. "You sure you're cleared for solo?"

Ed dropped back, terminating the conversation.

The four of them ambled out to the waiting aircraft, a headset around their neck, a briefcase full of charts and manuals, and a parachute over one shoulder. The pre-flight inspection was more cursory than usual, due to the oppressive heat and humidity. They climbed into the overheated cockpit, quickly opening side windows for relief. Checklists were called and responded to rapidly. Between wiping sweat from his forehead and cursing the heat, Brian read out the checklist for Walt who occupied the pilot's seat, and in turn responded with the correct reply to each item.

"It's hotter than the hinges of hell in here. Let's get this hunk of metal in the air quick-like. Clear to start number one, Walt." Brian stated.

"Roger. Boost pump on high, mixture full rich, prop full increase RPM, throttle cracked, turning number one. Counting the blades through, one, two, three, four. Priming, and mag switch to both." Walt stated methodically.

The left engine belched, coughed, then roared to life. The same procedure was repeated for the right engine. Walt completed the checklists while Brian received taxi instructions from the tower. He made a thorough run-up with all instruments indicating the aircraft was ready for takeoff. Walt glanced at Brian to signal he was ready for takeoff.

The control tower barked takeoff clearance, as Brian followed Walt through on his takeoff run. His eyes scanned the instruments, waiting for the gear up signal, and flap retraction. Ed, with head set on, was casually observing the events. As the B-25 broke ground and began to ascend, Walt stuck his thumb in the air, called "gear up," then let the nose down slightly to attain 145 knots for minimum single-engine control speed. The aircraft nose moved unexpectedly to the left. Walt countered with right rudder, but at 148 knots, he didn't compensate quickly enough for the immediate pull to the left. The nose moved farther to the left and airspeed dropped to 143 knots.

"You've lost number one, Walt. Feather the damn thing!" Ed yelled at Walt, who seemed dazed by the events. Walt moved sluggishly as he reached for the throttle of the dead engine. Brian turned in his seat and screamed, "Feather number one now, damn it!"

Walt's hand shot forward, as he pushed in the feathering button for number *two* engine. Brian slapped his hand away, pulled the button back out, then hit the feathering button for number one just in time to stop the mistake.

"Good goddamn, you almost feathered the wrong engine." Ed yelled at Walt.

The aircraft, now sixty degrees off to the left, losing airspeed, was spiraling toward the ground, almost out of control. Brian, instinctively, slammed the right engine throttle forward to maximum power, stood hard on the right rudder and lowered the nose to gain airspeed, as the aircraft vibrated and shuddered on the edge of a stall. The B-25 was going through 200 feet in a spiral descent.

There was insufficient time for even a comment from the flight engineer, let alone advice. He had the look of futility that comes when a crash is imminent. Brian fought the controls as he gradually straightened the spiral with straight and level flight at about fifty feet from impact with the ground. He eased the control column back, nursed the lumbering B-25 to one hundred feet, then grudgingly to one hundred fifty feet. "Walt, call the tower, and declare an emergency. Tell 'em we've got one engine feathered, turning on a long down wind, below pattern altitude, and barely holding what we've got."

Walt looked at Brian with a blank stare, fumbling for the tower frequency, then haltingly, made the transmission.

The tower barked back immediately. "Roger, Tango two-one, understand engine out and you're declaring an emergency. Continue on downwind, you're cleared number one for landing, altimeter two-niner-niner-five, wind one hundred eighty degrees at eight knots. Break, break, all Vance traffic clear the traffic pattern we have an emergency in progress. Tango two-one, emergency equipment's moving toward the approach end of runway one-eight. Call turning base leg. We have you in sight now, low, very low on a wide downwind."

Brian's knuckles were white from the pressures he was using on the control column; his hands throbbed as he unconsciously tightened his grip. He was fighting to keep control and gain some altitude. Sweat ran into his eyes but he couldn't wipe it away. Every time he eased back on the control column, fighting for just a few more feet of sky, the aircraft shuddered, and the stall warning horn blared notification.

Ed leaned forward and, for the first time, commented on the situation. "Jesus H Christ, we damn near bought the farm back there. Hold it right there, Brian. Just hold what you've got. To hell with trying to gain any altitude." He reached over and took Brian's checklist and double-checked to see that everything had been accomplished. He mumbled through several items, then hit Walt on the shoulder with his check list. "Clean up the rest of the 'single-engine items'. Turn off the mag and boost pump, if you can find them." He reached over Walt's shoulder, "And give me the damn mike. I'll make the radio calls."

Walt made no visible protest of Ed's taking the microphone from his hand. He continued down the checklist to make sure all emergency items were taken care of, shutting down unnecessary systems.

"Tower, Tango two-one turning base, making a wide pattern and long low final. We'll hold the gear until we've got the field made." Ed's voice indicated anxiety.

"Give me quarter flaps, Walt. Got one fifty knots, but that's all the altitude its gonna' give us. Hold the gear for a while. We can't take the drag. I'll call for the gear later. You understand, Walt?" Brian glanced rapidly at Walt. "Then, Goddamn it, give me a reply."

"Okay, you've got quarter flaps set." He stated angrily. "Call for the gear when you're ready"

"Ed, tell 'em we're turning final now. This damn thing's flying like a Mack truck." Brian glanced at Ed. "Don't tell 'em that though." Ed smiled.

"Okay, gimme the gear now." Brian barked.

"Roger, gear coming down, damn slow, with only one hydraulic pump. It's gettin' there, it's gettin' there. Okay, gear's down, pressure's up, and indicating three in the green." Walt was loosening up a bit.

Ed began the final transmission. "Tower, Tango two-one has gear down and locked, pressure up, and a quarter mile out." He then handed the mike back to Walt.

The B-25 crossed the field boundary with only six feet to spare above the trees. Brian eased back on the controls to reach the overrun portion of the runway. The aircraft hit hard on the initial portion of concrete, bounced back into the air twice as Brian grimaced with the strain. A rough landing, but they were on the ground. The tower notified them to shut down as they turned onto the first available taxiway. Brian hit the brakes as they cleared the runway, and brought the aircraft to a halt. With no comment, or asking for a checklist,

Brian pulled the mixture off, shutting down the remaining engine. He turned toward Walt and just stared at him.

Walt looked straight ahead, expressionless. Ed put his hand on Walt's shoulder. "That mistake damn near caused us to buy the farm."

Walt continued to stare straight ahead, but his attitude was obviously not one of humility. He snapped his head around at Brian. "I had the single engine under control. You sure as hell had no right to take over." A reddened face showed his anger. "Both of you are on an ego trip that won't quit. I should report this to Captain Dodson and let him decide if he needs a piece of your butt."

Ed leaned forward, his face an inch from Walt's. "Why the hell don't you do just that, you stupid bastard."

Brian glanced over his shoulder. "What happened up there is just between us, right, Sergeant?" The Engineer nodded. Brian turned toward Walt, who was still glaring at Ed. "Walt, I know you don't belong in this program but that's not for us to say. I've gotta' fly with you a while longer, but on the ground stay as far away from me as you can."

Walt frowned, shook his head, and swung out of the seat. He bounded down the ladder and stood over to one side, waiting to complete an incident report.

Specifics of the incident were kept among the Group, and never discussed with others. That night at the club, Brian started to explain to Vince and Scott why he took the controls from Walt. Ed took over the explanation. "Hell, he had no choice, we were about to buy it out there because of that stupid sonofabitch. I don't need that bastard to kill me before I get my wings." He ignored the laughter. "What the hell did you expect? Frankly, he can't fly for shit."

"You needed a good scare, Ed. What's that definition of flying a B-25 you use?" Scott asked. "'Hours and hours of boredom, punctuated by moments of stark terror'. Well, you just got your moments of stark terror."

Summer faded gradually into the first signs of fall. The trees were going golden; the rust of an early autumn hue covered the maples. Huge oaks in front of Base Headquarters were russet sentinels. The morning air became crisp. Brian breathed in the cool air and felt a sense of comfort. The mutation of the leaves signaled more than a change of the season. Graduation was six weeks away. The thought of graduation, his wings, buoyed his spirit as he invaded the overcrowded stag bar. The capacity crowd congregated at the end of the bar, merged into a tight throng, with several struggling for a better view. Brian wormed his way through the mass of blue shirts, looked down toward the floor to discover Vince upside down at the end of the bar. "What the hell's he doing?" Brian asked of the guy holding Vince's feet.

"Your buddy here is about to show us how to chug a beer upside down, which is the position that matches his brain." The cadet stated while still holding each leg tightly, so that Vince could maintain his position.

Scott came up unnoticed and leaned forward over Brian's shoulder to whisper in his ear, "Hey, don't look so damn amazed. You never know what to expect from ole' Vince. Our friend down there has ten bucks bet on this, and the guy standing there with the pitcher put a time limit of ten seconds. Want some of the action?"

"Are you serious? I never doubt Vince's talents, but I'm sure as hell not crazy enough to bet on 'em." He glanced back at Scott. "Aint it amazing what you can learn in New Jersey."

"Well, now, he's sorta' celebrating a rumor." Scott took on a sly smile as continued. "If he doesn't drown down there, we've got a piece of news you're gonna' like. And where's Ed?" His head swiveling around, looking for Ed, "He needs to hear this too."

"Hear what?" Brian showed his impatience with the cat and mouse smugness.

The crowd howled encouragement as Vince chugged the beer, a gurgling sound reached out from his throat, as some of the beer ran down his face into his hair. Cheers escalated in tempo as Vince slowly emptied the mug to the countdown of remaining seconds. One large yell signaled he'd made it within the imposed time limit. Vince, looking much worse for the wear, sat upright and wiped beer from his head with the towel dropped on him by the bartender. He glanced up at Brian and Scott and beamed with satisfaction, then let out a satisfied belch. Both were shaking their heads in mock disgust, trying hard not to laugh encouragement to the crumpled wet sight at the end of the bar.

"Hey, Scott, did you ya' tell him yet?" Vince asked, while disbursing another belch.

"Nope, we're waiting to see if you drowned first. Besides, I thought we'd wait for Ed."

"Dammit, what's this hot poop you think you stumbled on? Enough suspense." Brian said.

"What the hell did I just miss?" Ed interrupted by peering between Brian and Scott, looking down at Vince still sitting at the end of the bar. "Forget it." Ed threw his hands up in mock disgust. "I don't even want to know."

"Hey, Ed, come on over here. Vince, get over here and tell 'em the news. Their faces are gonna' light up like a pinball machine." Scott howled.

The Group found a table amid the milling cadets and sat down as Ed and Brian leaned in to hear the latest rumor. Anticipation screened across their face. The buildup had been too effective to seem nonchalant now.

Vince, still wiping at the beer, shoving his hair back from his eyes, began. "This is gospel, fella's. This came from a secretary who actually saw the message." Vince looked back and forth at the three faces. "Hey, Guys, don't gimme that look. Just cool it. She happens to have a thing for Italians." He stopped, looked around the table for emphasis, and then continued. "Listen up. You're gonna' suck this up like an over-speeding Hoover. There's a request on Base, right this minute, lying there on the Colonels' desk. It asks for twenty volunteers from our class, to go to jet transition straight from graduation, then on to a new fighter. The best part to you damn rebels is that the training bases are in Valdosta, Georgia and Panama City, Florida. Now, how does that grab you, you doubting peckerwoods?"

Brian sat paralyzed at the news. He was thinking about jets, flying fighters at last, and being close to Ruston an added attraction. He knew he was going to make sure he was in the twenty selected. He shook the images from his conscious thinking and looked up suddenly. "Are you sure? If you're yanking our chain, your Yankee butt's mud."

"Settle down Ace, this one's for real." Vince added.

At 0730 Monday morning, the Major walked briskly to the front of the room. The only noticeable sounds were heavy breathing, the click of the wall clock's second hand, and someone in the rear drumming their fingers on the table. The rumor had become universal knowledge among the entire class. They sat in silence, eager for details. A "Gentlemen, I've got some good news for some of you pent-up jet jockeys. Your wildest fantasy is here." He looked out at his audience with a grin. "We have a message that asks for twenty volunteers to go to F-94's. This is a brand-new all-weather fighter. Radar equipped for night and weather intercepts and just coming into operational service. Now, before you run over each other to get to me, there'll be a list compiled by the instructors. The initial selection rests strictly with your instructor's recommendation. So, let him know if you want to volunteer. The decision will be quick. We've got to submit names by tomorrow."

"Hot damn, y'all let me find my instructor." Shouted Scott.

"You, and most of this room." Brian said as he scanned the faces, stopping at Walt who sat there unemotionally. "There're some who don't have any desire for fighters." He added.

"Right on." Scott said, as he glanced at Walt.

"We're at the mercy of our instructor to get us in, and I see Wild Bill now." Brian rose quickly to meet Capt. Dodson coming across the room.

Capt. Dodson was wearing his usual smile as Brian approached. "Let me guess, Mister Brannon, you have some idea you wanna' fly jets. Right?"

"Yessir, in the worst way." His anxiety was poorly hidden. "Do I get your recommendation, Sir?"

"Yeah, I'm going to recommend you for the list. I figure you belong in fighters." He paused. "That may not be a compliment Mister Brannon."

Brian didn't care what the meaning was. He was ecstatic just to hear he'd be recommended.

Brian, Ed, Scott and Vince eased up to the bulletin board, trying to get a view of the list. They pushed through the maze of flight suits, as they heard shouts and groans from those looking at the names of the chosen. Scott, as usual, got there first and ran his finger down the list, stopping at one place on the list, thumping the board several times. He let out a rebel yell. Brian, Ed, Scott, and Vince were all listed as "accepted" for the new program. There was backslapping and laughter as they relished their new status. They were *almost* jet jockeys.

That evening in Enid, they celebrated with a steak dinner and several drinks. There was no hiding their garrulous delight at the prospects of being in a jet cockpit in a few weeks. Their demeanor took on a swagger and showed a little more ego than normal. Opportunity had just knocked and they answered. They were about to join the elite, the brotherhood. In the Air Force, fighter pilots are a distinct breed; all others are just pilots.

Two weeks before graduation, they gathered in the main room of the Cadet Club waiting anxiously to hear their assignments. The briefing officer read a variety of orders for those who stayed in multi-engine. Then came eagerly anticipated orders for those going to jets. The Air Force has a habit of changing things on slight notice. Six of the twenty selected for fighters were going to RF-80 aircraft, not F-94's. There was a sudden need for photo reconnaissance pilots in Korea. Brian dropped his head on the table and breathed a sigh of relief when his name wasn't called to fly 'photo reccy' aircraft. Ed, however, was thrilled that he was going to "Reccy" types. The comments began flying from the other three in The Group.

"Hell, Ed, you don't know which end of a camera to point, how you gonna' take a picture of the enemy?" Vince said.

"They knew you'd hit the wrong target if they gave you something with guns on it." Scott added.

Ed smirked and accepted the kidding. The other three stopped the harassment, and listened intently as their orders were read.

Assigned to Moody Air Force Base for a period of eight weeks to attend jet transition and instrument school, then further temporary duty at Tyndall

Air Force Base for a period of six weeks to attend all-weather interceptor training. Reporting to Camp Stoneman, California for processing, transportation and subsequent permanent assignment to Far Eastern Air Forces (FEAF), Headquarters Fifth Air Force. Leave authorized not to exceed 10 days en route to Moody AFB and 30 days leave authorized prior to reporting to Camp Stoneman.

There was no doubt this meant Korea. It only made the assignment more intriguing. After all, combat was what they were ultimately being trained for. There was always excitement and anticipation for those yet to encounter combat. This feeling is usually replaced later by hopeful optimism, and then by stoic resolve, punctuated with fragments of fear. Combat changes one's thought processes dramatically, and fortunately for the Air Force, there are Second Lieutenants who are blissfully ignorant of the process. These four fit that description perfectly.

Brian sat at his desk to read the letter from his mother. She began by saying how proud she was that he was graduating. He read on, digesting the words, looking at their meaning, realizing what he had subconsciously known.

...There are more test to be run, but it appears to be a severe case of viral pneumonia. I'll have to stay in bed for a week or so. They've already got a substitute teacher who says she'll be available that long. You know how I hate the fact I can't be there for your graduation. But it'll still be impossible for me to travel by then. Please know I'll be thinking about you as you get your wings...

He wadded the letter up and tossed it in the waste paper basket. Then took out paper and began a letter to Lori. He wrote a long letter that evening, at least longer than usual. He was anxious to share with her his elation with the orders. He told her he was eagerly looking forward to ten days in Ruston after graduation and then being close enough to spend some weekends there. He wanted to, somehow, convey that life was smiling in his direction, and it was incredible. He told her he appreciated her wish to be there to pin on his wings. He added: *I'll settle for a long talk and a barbecue at The Oaks. I'm looking forward to seeing you...*

Brian walked back and forth in front of the blue Oldsmobile convertible on one of the dealer's lot. It still wasn't sold. He quit resisting the impulse and walked into the office. He dickered back and forth with the salesman, finally getting down to his bottom price. It barely fit into his budget plans but close enough with his advance pay, travel allowances, and flight pay he'd soon be receiving. As he sat there debating the transaction, the salesman never quit talking. Brian held up his hand. "Just show me where to sign." The fighter pilot maxim had begun to set in: *Live today, because tomorrow is always a question mark.* "I'll pick up the car on Friday."

The day before graduation Scott and Brian started loading the car for the trip south. Scott agreed to ride as far as Birmingham, where his brother would meet him.

"My God, Scott, did you ship anything. Looks like you've got everything you own here." Brian moved bags around, rearranging the trunk. "This is gonna' be tight."

Vince, who had been observing the packing attempt diligently, shoved his hat back past the shock of black hair, stuck his hands in his pocket, and strolled around the car, taking in every detail. He stopped, reached over and touched the hood appreciatively, then stroked the hood ornament, tapped the cloth top approvingly, and broke into his rascally smile. "These wheels definitely qualify as officer transportation, Brian. In fact, if you let the top down, put on those new silver wings, new gold bars, and take out a sizeable cash advance, you just might, I say *might*, pick up one of those unsuspecting southern belles down there."

Scott looked at Vince and gave him thumbs up. "Cut the guy a little slack, Vince. He may not even have to let the top down. He could just hold his wings out the window."

Brian's middle finger extended toward the laughing duo. He closed the trunk and walked into the barracks without comment.

Brian flipped the calendar on his desk to the highly circled date: Saturday, November 3, 1951. This was the culmination of thirteen months of comprehensive, and sometimes exhaustive, training for Aviation Cadet Class 51-G. That highly anticipated, and often uncertain, moment was here. At precisely 1000 hours that morning fifty soon to be officers and pilots of the United States Air Force paraded into the auditorium.

Brian knew he'd remember this moment the rest of his life. His heart pounded with the reality that his goal had been reached. This was one of those exceptional moments in his life that should have been shared with someone close. Not today. The personal satisfaction and the significance of this event were more than adequate. He literally inhaled the atmosphere. His hand felt for the crisp one-dollar bill in his pocket to be given to the first enlisted man to salute him after graduation and he beamed.

The ceremony began with the swearing-in of the entire class, followed by the customary speech. The General walked briskly to the rostrum, placed the notes in front of him and began speaking of tradition, of those who had preceded them, of new horizons to conquer, and other pivotal events to come. He postulated about their accomplishment bringing them to this day and indicated that here, sitting in the front three rows of this auditorium, were the very few who could meet all of the prerequisites, the challenges, and the sacrifices demanded of them. They were now officers and pilots in the United States Air Force.

Brian's mind unexpectedly locked upon the word *sacrifices*, and the remainder of the speech was tuned out. He visualized a bench, a beautiful girl, and a crisp autumn night. He could smell the fragrance of her hair as he brushed his face against it. His imagination let him feel the magnetism of her presence, and then the image suddenly vanished. The class stood, bringing the present abruptly back into focus. He crossed the stage, accepting his certificate with the sterling silver wings tied with a small blue ribbon. He rubbed the wings affectionately with his finger, as the ceremony ended with the Chaplain's benediction.

Brian stood and turned to Scott. "Would you do the honors?"

"Glad to, and I'd like you to pin mine on." Scott said.

"Just don't expect a kiss afterward." Brian chuckled.

Scott stepped back and admired his handiwork. "Looks quite good sitting there." He touched the wings lightly. "Did you ever wonder if you'd actually get those?"

Brian scrooched his chin as tried to look down at the silver wings. "I wondered every day if I'd ever see these. I surely never got complacent." He watched Scott looking around at the crowd of smiling visitors and new Second Lieutenants. "I thought your father would be here for this."

"Naw, this's his way of saying 'Scott, you disappointed me.' When I get home, he'll pour us both a drink, talk about the firm, how the town's changed, and how well Misses Carter's hydrangeas are doing this year. He'll never mention the Air Force." He analyzed Brian's expression of surprise at his assertion. "You wish someone would've been here? Your Mom?"

"I wish my father could have been here." Brian said, as he turned away.

Vince sauntered up. "Ed and I'll be waiting for both you hot rocks at Moody. Hey Scott, keep an eye on him. He still thinks he can get a date using a convertible. Explain the facts of life to him." He slapped Brian on the back. "See ya' in ten days."

Ed made the rounds with handshakes. "I'm glad I'll be there at Moody for a quick jet checkout before going over to Shaw Air Force Base. It gives me enough time to watch Vince get court-martialed for some of his crazyness. He wasn't listening when the Colonel said, 'Officer and gentleman'. Vince hasn't been trained in that gentlemen stuff."

"Let's get outta' here Scott. We've got some miles to roll up before tomorrow." Brian said, as he pulled at Scott's sleeve.

Brian and Scott headed the Oldsmobile south. They agreed to swap off driving and go straight through to Birmingham, stopping only for gas and food. Both were anxious to see Vance Air Force Base in the rear view mirror. Night crept up on them as they approached Fort Smith, Arkansas. It was a good time to switch off the driving duties. Brian settled back in the passenger seat, folded his flight jacket as a pillow, and let his thoughts drift to the hypnotic clicking of the highway dividers. He tried to catch some much-needed sleep for his next turn at driving. Instead, he relived the past year with fleeting glimpses of scenes, hazily brought into focus. Restlessly, the discernable images turned to Ruston.

CHAPTER SEVEN

B RIAN TOPPED HOLLOWAY Hill and began the long descending curve toward town. This was the same demarcation point he used when leaving Ruston and arriving. He had left a little over a year ago and, as if living a dream, he was home again. He glanced over his shoulder at the silver wings and gold bars on the officers' blouse hanging in the rear for reassurance. They were real. Enthusiasm at the sight of familiar surroundings replaced the fatigue he felt. Nostalgia crept into his thoughts, as he pressed harder on the accelerator.

He jerked to a stop in front of the large white house, glancing through the windshield at the pale structure. It was home. To him, the house would always be filled with the thoughts and memories of those who had lived there. The porch furniture looked unmoved since the last visit, the shutters still needed a coat of paint, and it looked as inviting as ever. He realized this old house was all of the tangible assets that remained from his grandfather's estate. He smiled as he recalled that at one time his grandfather had owned several thousand acres of land, plantation house, a large herd of white-faced cattle, and a store in Wilcox County. Unfortunately, he became one of the first victims of the great depression, losing everything except a small nest egg for his new start. Brian thought about the story told by his grandfather. He pictured the tall man with the felt hat pulled low, bow tie, and a cameo stickpin centered a few inches below the tie. The image called back a man he remembered for his character, integrity, and unbridled enthusiasm for life. His measured tones made stories of the past unfold vividly before Brian's eyes, as he portrayed events of a bygone era with graphic description.

His grandfather told how he usually shipped his cattle to St. Louis for sale. But due to the lower prices for beef as the depression took hold, the last shipment was only to the Montgomery stockyards, fifty-five miles away. The sale didn't cover the cost of transportation. It was then he knew the inevitability of the economic disaster that surrounded him. When he returned home, he walked into the bank, pulled a chair up close to his friend's desk. He looked the President of The Planters and Stockman's Bank squarely in the eyes and asked how much he was in debt. Reluctantly, his friend pulled out the two mortgages, a secured bank note, and one unsecured note. Right there, without hesitation, his grandfather made an offer. In spite of the encouragement of his friend to "weather this thing out," he signed over the plantation house, the land, the few remaining cattle, and his country store to the bank. He kept only the eight hundred and thirty-two dollars in his savings account for his new start. The new start began and ended in Ruston. He made a modest living in the insurance business, never looked back, but lived as if he had never lost a thing. The only tangible evidence remaining was this large white frame house, with the high gable in front, and shutters that needed a coat of paint. Brian smiled. *His legacy far exceeded material objects.*

Sill looking admiringly at the old house, he jumped from the car, bounded up the steps, and swung open the front door.

"Brian! You scared me half to death." His mother pivoted around at the sound of the door opening. "Come here," she shouted as she regained her composure and ran to meet him. "We didn't expect you to get here this soon. You must've driven like the wind to be here this quick." She was shaking her head in disapproval of his driving. "Go on back to the kitchen and see Aunt Betty and Uncle John. They wanted to be here when you got home." She hugged him as only a mother can.

"You felling better?" Brian asked.

"I'm doing pretty well. Betty's been a godsend these last two weeks. Don't know what I would've done without her."

Brian got a cup of coffee, and pulled a chair close to the kitchen table. Appreciating the aroma of a roast cooking, he breathed in an assortment of other familiar scents as he glanced around the kitchen, reacquainting. His mother was quick to catch him up on all the latest news in Ruston. Aunt Betty interrupted to hear about his future assignment. She frowned and gave a quick glance at Walt when he told them about his orders for Korea. Brian's mother tried not to show concern as she turned her head away to hide the moisture building in the corner of her eyes. "I'd hoped that this fool war would be over by now. When Eisenhower gets sworn in, he'll put an end to it."

"Don't worry about that. It'll probably be over before I get there." Brian rubbed his eyes as if trying to focus. "Guess that drive's getting to me. Think I'll get my things out of the car and take a hot shower. That'll wake me up before dinner. I plan to eat everything in sight tonight." He glanced down at his waist. "Never thought I'd weigh in at only one hundred and fifty-eight pounds."

After dinner, Brian excused himself. He closed his bedroom

door and glanced around the room. The room seemed even less familiar than his last visit. He had a curious feeling it belonged to someone else, even with the memorabilia mounted on the walls and on bookshelves. He was still taking in the subtle features he had always taken for granted as he dialed the phone.

"Ramsay Hall, second floor." A voice answered the phone.

"Could I please speak to Lori Barnes? Room two twelve, I believe."

"Okay, I'll check."

He hated waiting on the dead end of a phone. As he waited, he scanned the pictures on the dresser, reliving moments frozen in time on film. His thoughts were interrupted by her voice.

"Hello."

"Hi there."

"Brian! Oh my gosh, it's really you. I didn't think you'd make it home this quickly. Hey, congratulations, Lieutenant!"

"Thanks, Missy. I'm here to collect on that date for barbecue. Whatcha' got planned for tomorrow night?"

"*You*, is what I've got planned. What time?"

"How 'bout six thirty or so. Could you go for a barbeque at The Oaks?"

"Sounds great. Can't wait to see you!"

"You too. We'll catch up tomorrow night. Bye."

Monday night, Brian entered the lobby and headed for the desk to ask for Lori, but it wasn't necessary. She ran up giving him a hug that lasted an eternity.

"Easy there, I'm gonna' be around for a few days."

"Gosh, it's good seeing you." She grabbed him again in a big hug.

Brian just relaxed and let it happen. She felt soft in his grasp as he held her tightly.

They turned onto Highway twenty-five toward The Oaks. Brian tuned through static and scrambled voices for a radio station. Fine-tuning back and forth, he brought in one that was playing *Blue Moon*. Satisfied, he turned to Lori to continue the conversation.

"You were saying about Don."

"All I was saying was … hey, why the devil can't I squelch your implications of a wild romance here. Don's a great guy. We have fun together, have a lot in common, but it's strictly platonic. And no plans for an immediate change to that condition. Now, aren't you the disappointed one."

Brian looked at Lori with a sly smile. "And what was it that Shakespeare said, *Me thinks ye protest too much?*"

"And Ye are so wrong! Hey, when did you become so enamored with Shakespeare? Certainly not at Auburn."

"No Auburn jokes tonight, Missy. And I'll have to think about all that platonic stuff before I buy it."

"You'd better accept it. That's the way it is." Lori said.

The Oaks appeared ahead in the headlights. Brian swerved into the driveway.

"Look at all the cars." Brian asked, as he glanced at the maze of cars parked at different angles. "It seems the secret of Misses Hestors' great barbecue is out. Who've you been telling about this place?"

"Yeah, it's gotten right popular lately, but not my doing. I figure you must've taken too many other girls here."

Brian laughed. "Lord, I've missed you, gal."

While waiting on their food, Brian listened intently to the news of mutual friends, and looked at the girl sitting across from him. He never realized how Lori's green eyes sparkled, how her hair flew loosely at the toss of her head, or the tilt of her head as she emphasized a point. Her conversations were so animated he'd never really examined the person originating them. He realized, for the first time, just how attractive she was.

She stopped suddenly in mid-sentence. "Why are you staring at me?"

"Just looking at that little piece of lettuce stuck in your front teeth."

"I knew I shouldn't ask. You're in rare form tonight. Just eat your blasted barbecue."

As they caught up on details of the last few months there was a lull in the conversation. Lori looked up at Brian, and seriousness replaced the jocularity. "Anne knew I was meeting you tonight and said to tell you 'hello.' She always asked about you when I got a letter. What I'm trying to tell you is..."

"You know, this conversation was really great until now." Brian's annoyance showed more than he wanted, as he interrupted. He calmed his inflection. "No advice, please. Whatever happens in the future isn't going to be resolved tonight over a barbecue sandwich."

"Okay, I'll wait 'till you bring up the subject next time, and you will, believe me. I know you much better than you give me credit, Lieutenant. Hey, that title sounds quite good, doesn't it?"

"Yeah, but you can just call me *Sir*."

The night ended with a hug, as they agreed to meet for coffee at the Tea House the next morning at ten. Brian leaned back against the door of the car and looked at the front of Ramsay Hall, then back at Lori. "God, it's great being home again. I really enjoyed tonight, Missy."

Morning came too soon. Brian had no idea how tired he'd be from the trip. No real sleep for thirty six-hours had taken its toll.

He blinked his eyes, trying to focus on the clock beside the bed. He reached out, bringing it closer for a look. *Damn, it's almost ten! How did I sleep that long?* He rolled out of the bed, wide-awake.

He jumped in and out of the shower and managed a quick shave. After a quick apology to his mother for not wanting breakfast, he grabbed his flight jacket, bounding through the door.

He turned into the drive next to the Tea House, jumped out of the car on a dead run toward the entrance. He slowed to a deliberate walk as he approached Lori, waiting in a booth.

"Sorry I'm a few minutes late. You see, there was this terrible accident..."

"Just woke up?" She inquired, as she interrupted the statement.

"It shows, huh? I could use some coffee." Brian said, as he looked around the once familiar room.

"I bet you could. But you look pretty tolerable for just gettin' out of bed." Lori stood up. "I'll get the coffee and a couple of donuts. Since your hair's still wet, I reckon you didn't take time for breakfast."

"No, just coffee please." He said.

They finished all of the old business not covered the evening before and most of the gossip about even casual acquaintances. Brian walked Lori back to the dorm. They stopped at the bottom of the circular brick steps.

"Soon as I settle in with Mom and everything, I'll give you a call."

"See ya'."

He watched her run up the steps and turned toward the car. The sun was out. A gentle breeze stirred the few browning leaves clutching tenaciously to the limbs of a dogwood tree. It was one of those typically warm days that prolong the fall seasons in mid-Alabama. The warmth gave him the impulse to let the top down and ignore the cumulus clouds billowing in the southwest. As he began buttoning the cover on the folded top, he looked up, sensing he was being watched. He turned slowly to see Anne standing there, smiling at his effort to get the last snaps closed. The surprise left him momentarily speechless.

"I understand you graduated Saturday." She walked up to the passenger side of the car, placing her hands on the door. "Congratulations. I know how much that meant to you."

The surprise wasn't quick to wear off. Brian was saying "Thank you" mechanically as he stared at Anne. She was more beautiful than his imagination had let him envision the past nine months. Regaining some composure, he tried, only moderately successfully, to react casually. "Where're you going?" He asked.

"To the Post Office. I wanted to get this off today." She held up a pale blue envelope. "The mail on campus doesn't go out 'till tomorrow. You happen to be going by there?"

"Yeah, going right by there. Hop in."

Without hesitation, Anne opened the door and sat down. She looked at the dash and ran her hand over the leather seats. "Like your car. Even though I'm not that fond of convertibles. There's too much wind. But this one's really nice."

They made small talk about school, the warm weather, and the fact that storm clouds were building rapidly in the West. That was the extent of a conversation covering only three blocks to the Post Office. She jumped out and darted up the steps. Brian waited with the engine running, watching the fluid movement of her body as she glided up the second tier of steps. He was equally pleased with the approaching view.

"You have some place to go, or would you like to get a burger?" He asked.

"That would hit the spot. I don't have any classes the rest of the day."

Brian selected his usual booth in The Grill and they slid in to face each other. He fumbled in his pocket for a quarter. Flipping the selection menu around, he picked five songs, and dropped in the coin. He looked around The Grill at the only two occupied booths and the staff preparing the serving line for the noon rush. Turning to Anne, who was just sitting there watching him, "Nothing really changes in Ruston, does it?" He asked.

"No, guess not. Collinwood's the same way. Some of us need that security in our lives."

"How's Justin these days?"

"Justin's fine. We both stay so busy we don't see much of each other. I'll probably see him Thanksgiving."

It was still too early for the noon throng to assemble. He enjoyed the sparse crowd and relative privacy as they ate hamburgers and fries, sipping occasionally on a coke. The songs programmed in the jukebox reached selection number five. *La Vie En Rose* began. Anne stopped eating, glanced at Brian, and smiled. He smiled back.

Gradually, the booths and tables began to fill and Brian sensed the crowd settling in around them.

"How'd you like to go for a ride?" He grimaced. "It's beginning to get a little noisy in here. We can take a few minutes for you to tell me what you've been up to these last few months."

"Okay. There won't be that much to tell. We lead a rather boring life here at A-B."

People were beginning to acknowledge Brian's return with waves, and occasionally a stop at the booth to ask questions, or to give a warm slap on the back. He paid the check, hastily answered a few questions about how he liked the *Army* and excused himself as soon as possible.

A steady light drizzle began, making splatters of wet circles as it hit the pavement around them. They ran for the car as the rain increased in intensity.

"Give me a hand with getting this top back up. If you'd get those snaps on your side." He pointed quickly to the cover on her side. "Damn, I picked a great time to put the top down!" She glanced up, frowning her agreement with the statement, as she rushed to get the snaps off.

Brian brought the top down hard against the windshield, hooked the front fastener with a sigh of relief. Sporadic drops increased to steady rain, as thunder rumbled gently in the distance.

"I'm beginning to have your feelings about convertibles." He chuckled. "Mind if we just ride for a while? The rain may stop after this thunder-bumper moves on through."

"No, I love driving in the rain." She took her usual place with her back right against the passengers' door. It was a familiar site to him. He reached over and tuned in the station with the music he heard from the previous night. The clicking of the wipers combined with the now steady downpour provided a relaxing background to the music. Neither spoke. There was an occasional glance at the other. The silence was in no way disconcerting. It even seemed relevant. The radio continued to put the mood in perspective with *Thinking of You*.

Later, Brian turned into the west gate, but instead of going directly to the dorm, drove past the parking lot. He continued up the long tree lined drive toward the Presidents home and pulled off to the side close to the curb. He reached over, switched off the engine, and left the radio playing softly. The rain pelted the cloth top rhythmically as accompaniment to the music. The rain came down harder, creating a curtain of water outside the windows. The crackle of lightening streaked through the murky sky, followed swiftly by thunder sounding its booming accompaniment. Wind blustered rain across the windshield with each gust, obscuring the outside world. They looked at each other, neither speaking. They sat quietly, immersed in their own thoughts. Slowly, Brian leaned toward Anne. Their lips met. The rain increased in intensity, lightning ripped the sky in bright arcs, followed almost simultaneously by reverberating thunder. She slowly, almost hesitatingly, put her arms around his neck. She pulled him toward her, as he took her in his arms. They held each other without speaking. Their world was confined to that space; nothing existed outside the car. He pulled her close again and kissed her.

Anne pulled back toward the door, smiling softly, looking at Brian as if expecting some explanation. "When we're together, there are always more than a few sparks generated. You've always had that effect on me." She smiled. "But you knew that, didn't you?"

"The last time I saw you, it didn't seem that way." He stated matter-of-factly.

He took her in his arms and they held each other as the rolling, muffled sound of thunder indicated the storm was moving further away. He nuzzled her neck, her ear, then kissed her more passionately than he ever had, and the rest of the world didn't exist. They seemed merged into each other. She pulled back, placed her hands on each side of his face, and looked directly into his eyes. "I didn't expect this to happen."

"Fate went to work on a bench, under a large oak tree over there." He looked over his shoulder toward the front campus, then back at her. "I thought you knew that."

She looked up and frowned. "There are things about me you still don't understand." She sat upright, looked intently at Brian.

"I can wait." He said.

Brian started the engine, as Anne straightened at her dress and ran her fingers through her hair. "I look a mess."

"You look pretty good to me." He said.

"Your mind's somewhat affected, Mister Brannon."

"Can't argue with that assessment." He said.

After parking in front of Ramsay Hall, he opened the door and took her hand. They walked to the front door, both hesitating to leave. "Tonight?" He asked.

"Seven-thirty." She replied.

He called Lori later that afternoon and explained what happened. She said she was pleased but her voice lacked exuberance.

"Something wrong, Lori?"

"You two have common vibrations of the soul. It was just a matter of time." She said.

"Our friendship's never threatened by what happens between Anne and me. We're too close to let that happen."

"Don't worry. We'll always be friends." She stated in a quiet voice.

Tyler leaned back against the back of the booth, watching Brian intently as he described the afternoon. Tyler nodded periodically, paying no attention to the din of noise in The Grill. He was fixed on Brian's story. As Brian finished, Tyler smiled. "I know how you feel about Anne. It's obvious you've had a quick attitude adjustment in the last few hours. I'm glad things are on a different course, and I'd like to apologize for being an ass last Christmas. I shouldn't have said those things about Anne."

Brian slapped him on the arm. "Not necessary. I knew where you were coming from." They rode through familiar territory, glancing at places that evoked memories of earlier times. They laughed at some of their youthful escapades around town. The conversation turned to Ruston as they rehashed some of their favorite remembered experiences, subtly realizing none were current events. Regardless of the direction of their lives, the shared years of growing up in Ruston provided the catalyst for their unique closeness. They were friends.

The final Saturday night of Brian's ten-day leave crept up silently, with no warning, as if it had been stalking him. Brian and Anne strolled over to the bench that had been their reserved place for withdrawing from the rest of the world. They shuffled through the leaves that crunched under foot, as the few lingering leaves on the large oak rustled gently overhead with the wind. They huddled against the chill, merging their bodies as close as possible.

"I'll call you sometime during the week to let you know how it's going at Moody. If they don't have duty for me of some kind, I'll give you a call and see if we can get together."

"Thanksgiving's next week." She said.

"Yeah, but we'll only get the day off. Friday'll be duty as usual."

"What about the Weekend? It's along way, but would you want to come to Collinwood?"

"Is that what *you* want?"

"Of course I do. Mama'll be glad to see you again too. She's asked about you a lot. You two seemed to hit it off real well last Christmas. Maybe this time you won't be dashing off into the night without so much as a 'Goodbye'."

Brian sang to the music as he drove toward Valdosta. He was content with how life was going and enjoying the emotions that were sweeping across his spirit. He relaxed and watched the red-clay hills and piney woods roll past as the pale, fading light began to rob details from the landscape. His thoughts of the last few days ripped him out of the road numbness as he drove through the long straight darkness, watching for the occasional faint flicker of light on the horizon.

He pulled up to the front gate at Moody Air Force Base, slowing to the approaching sentry's hand signal. The sentry saluted, as Brian rolled down the window. "Can I direct you somewhere, Lieutenant?"

"You sure can. Where's Base Headquarters? I need to sign in."

"No need to go there, Sir. Just take a left at the next block. On your right, two blocks down, is the Student Officer Detachment. They'll take care of you right there."

"Thanks."

Brian glanced side to side as the headlights danced against the old buildings. Peeling paint indicated a lack of general housekeeping. Tall Georgia pines, sprouting from every unused plot of dirt, provided a stark background. It altered his mood. He eased into the parking area and went into the office at the 335th Student Officer Training Detachment.

"Evening, Sir. Just reporting in?"

"Unfortunately." Brian responded.

"Oh it ain't that bad, Lieutenant. You'll get used to it down here." He laughed knowingly. "Just keep outta' reach of those 'squitos, don't stop long enough for the soot to settle on you, and definitely stay outta' the Okefenokee."

"Thanks for all that encouragement, Sergeant, but fortunately I won't be here that long." Brian left copies of his orders, medical records, pay records, and it seemed to him, every other military form that was ever generated in the Government printing office. He followed the explicit directions to the BOQ. He muscled his B-4 bag, and a handful of items to the assigned room. Unlocking the door, he moved into the sparsely furnished room. He stopped momentarily, shaking his head. There was a bed, a chest of drawers, and a place to hang clothes. There was no bedside table with a lamp, just a bare overhead light bulb. He dropped the bag and fell back on the bed, looking up at the naked bulb. *So this was it -- the life of a fighter pilot, an officer and gentleman.* The austere environment gave him a sudden feeling of disillusionment. Glancing at his watch, he decided a bite to eat would boost his spirits. The Officers Club would definitely put him in a better mood and he was anxious to see some of the other guys. He rolled off the bed with redefined enthusiasm.

He ambled through the pine trees, as moonlight drifted through the branches, casting a subtle glow on the white structures around him. A large structure loomed in front of him, a sign to the right of the walk announced his destination: *Moody AFB Officers' Club.*

Brian bounded up the steps and eased around the corridor. He spotted several familiar faces down the long hall toward the bar. A few handshakes later, he found Scott sitting alone at a table munching on a sandwich.

"Mind if I have one of those fries?" He asked as he took a chair next to Scott.

"Well! Look who finally made it to *Okefenokee Land*? How'd the leave go?"

"Absolutely perfect."

Scott's head shot up. "My God, what am I hearing?" He laughed and made a sign as if he was pulling the trigger toward Brian. "You can tell me about it later. Sit down and order a sandwich or something, then I'll clue you in on how things work down here." He swiveled in his chair. "Being a native, I love Georgia, but I gotta' tell you, this Base is the damn pits."

"Really? I couldn't detect that at all." Brian added, and then waved his hand toward a fellow with a tray balanced in his hand. "Waiter, could I please see a menu?"

Brian munched on his ham and Swiss while listening to Scott describe the situation in detail. "Basically, this Base was opened for the purpose of putting the jet transition and instrument school in operation. It's bare-bones in amenities, and the BOQ is the best example of that." Scott put down his drink and leaned forward. A frown replaced his usual built-in smile. "Most of the instructors just returned from a combat tour in Korea and aren't too happy with lower Georgia. It's a culture shock that shows in their attitude. They get their kicks by telling us about aircraft bouncing off mountains, running out of sky on a strafing run, or flamed by 'Gook' gunners. They take pure delight in the dazed expressions on us uninitiated."

"Sounds encouraging. What else?" Brian asked.

"I've only been here a week and we've had two major accidents with one fatality. The flying and ground school are being compressed to get us through and out to operational units as fast as possible. Some of us have a really bad feeling it's too frappin' fast."

"Okay, now give me the bad news?" Brian asked.

"Well, there's a spot of good news at that." The frown left, displaced by a sly smile. "The good news is, that flying a jet is the greatest sensation you can imagine. Brian, it's a real kick in the butt." Scott became lost in his description, as he was visibly reliving it. "You put just a little side pressure on the stick and the T-bird rolls effortlessly. The performance puts you in another dimension. Hoss, you're in for one helluva' ride." He became more animated as he talked, complete with hand gestures. "You put this thing on like a tight suit, a flying fuel tank surrounded by a little sheet metal. Kick the tire, light the fire, and blast off through space. You glance out and watch the earth disappear beneath you. God, I can't wait to get up there and poke holes in the sky." He brought his hands down and looked at Brian. "Just wait, when you catch that first smell of JP-four out there on the flight line, you're gonna' know it's definitely a fighter pilot's world. And, Hoss, you're part of it!"

CHAPTER EIGHT

A N ALARM CLOCK wasn't necessary. Brian awoke abruptly to loud, unfamiliar sounds emanating from the flight line. The high-pitched whine of jet engines, followed by a roar of takeoff power, signaled the introduction of this new environment. Anticipation exploded in his head as he rolled out of bed.

He was eager to get the preliminaries taken care of. His first stop was equipment issue. He fingered the newest type equipment as it was issued: Helmet, oxygen mask, bailout bottles, g-suits, and the pilot's handbook for the Lockeed T-33 aircraft. The helmet fit extremely tight as he pulled it on. He adjusted the secure fit, and then lashed the oxygen mask across his face. Fidgeting with the tightness of the mask, he struggled trying to make it comfortable. Glancing in the mirror, he saw the eyes staring back at him, surrounded by strange new apparatus. He smiled behind the mask.

The newest group of virgin jet jockeys at Moody Air Force Base crowded into the small briefing room. Noisily they shuffled into seats among laughter and a buzz of conversation. They snapped to attention automatically as the two officers entered from a side door. "Take your seats, Gentlemen. I'll make this as quick as possible." He stuck with his pronouncement and the briefing was mercifully short. He quickly covered the training schedule and what these fledgling jet jockeys could expect in the next few weeks. When the Colonel announced, "That's all for today. Get settled in. You'll begin training tomorrow in earnest." Brian swung out of his seat and headed for the BOQ.

He zipped his jacket as Scott bounded through the door. "Hey, where're you headed?"

"Thought I'd take in the big metropolis of Valdosta." He waved his arm around the room. "Look at this place. I need to get some stuff to make this poor excuse for a BOQ more livable."

"Yeah, I've seen better flea trap motels than this BOQ." Scott responded. "Hey, I've finished flying for the day. I'll tag along so I can hear more of your antics on leave, not to mention a continuation of my analysis of the 'Muddy Air Patch' situation. You haven't begun to hear the full briefing, Hoss."

"Where are Vince and Ed?"

"Vince is sacked out, gettin' prepared for tonight. Ed and those reccy guys are flying hot 'n heavy every day. Ed's racked up fourteen hours, soloed the F-80, and will be outta' here next week. They'll get the rest of their checkout at Shaw Air Force Base. It's just you and me partner."

Settling comfortably into the seat, Scott pointed toward the turn to Valdosta, then glanced at Brian. "The way you came into the club last night, looking as if you'd just won a lottery, I assumed you had a wing ding time these last few days. I hesitate to ask, but did you see Anne?"

Brian looked straight ahead.

"Well, maybe you met some other enchanting, unsuspecting young thing. Let me guess." Scott scanned his friend's face, watching for a reaction.

Brian continued to look straight ahead, a smile slowly wiped across his face.

"You don't have to answer, Hoss, that silly-ass smile says it all. You're one in-love sonofagun. It's downright pitiful."

Before Brian could respond to Scott, the wailing of sirens and blare of horns came up fast from the rear. Both swiveled to see four emergency vehicles bearing down on them. Brian pulled off the road as quickly as possible, allowing a fire truck, ambulance, and two staff cars to whizz by. Scott pointed after them. "Let's see where they're going. I think another one probably augured in."

"Probably just a drill." Brian asserted.

"They don't need drills at Moody. They get enough of the real thing to train most of the crash crews in the Air Force."

Brian glanced at Scott, disbelief and concern in his eyes, looked back down the highway, and floored the accelerator. They fell in line behind the emergency convoy as it made a left turn, putting them directly north of the base. The vehicles suddenly pulled off the road onto the shoulder. Brian pulled up behind the second staff car.

They walked a short distance toward the gawking crowd and a stream of cars lining both sides of the road. About twenty-five feet from the highway, a raised railroad track that paralleled the highway, was missing a large section bank and track. It looked as if a giant shovel made a swipe at it. Farther out, scattered for hundreds of yards, were bits and pieces of smoldering metal, completely indistinguishable as an aircraft except for one small section of tail. Obviously, there would be no survivor. The five-digit tail number stood like a grave marker above the smoking debris.

"Godamighty, he smacked that track head-on. What the hell was he thinking? Scott asked almost rhetorically. "Why didn't he punch out?"

Brian made no comment. He turned and started walking toward the car.

As the pilots gathered for the evening at the Officer's Club, the topic being discussed around the bar was the latest accident. The discussions always ended with the same conclusion. He made a mistake in judgment. This way it kept accidents in the right perspective; it happened to other pilots. The guys in The Group didn't know this Lieutenant, the latest casualty in a fast-paced training program. He arrived three weeks earlier from Reese AFB and hadn't had time to establish an identity at the bar. This made the verdict of pilot error even more detached.

Vince banged his beer on the bar as he added his analysis to the event. "Flying jets is a helluva' lot different from recip's. You'd better stay ahead of the aircraft or you're going to end up a 'crispy critter'. Everybody wearing wings wasn't meant to fly high performance aircraft. The head nodding showed unanimous agreement at the bar.

"I'll see you guys later." Brian said. "I've got to be at the flight line at o-dark-thirty tomorrow. Then I get to kick the tire and light the fire. Goodnight." Tossing his portion of the bar tab on the bar and grabbing his hat, Brian left to get some sleep in preparation for his first jet ride.

The sun was gradually showing itself through the tall Georgia pines, glistening off the dew that settled on the long needles. It was beginning to provide a little warmth to the morning chill as Brian reached the Ops building. He inhaled deeply. *JP-four does smell differently.* He paused to look at the sleek T-33 aircraft lined up in the usual neat rows, then turned and entered the Ops briefing room. Shortly after he arrived and mingled with the other pilots, the instructors came in from a side door, each looking around for their students.

"Ah, Lieutenant Brannon." The young-looking Major was leaning forward, reading his nametag. "I'm Major Trimble, the flight commander here. We seem to be short a couple of instructors, so I'll be working with you."

Brian put out his hand. "Glad to meet you, Sir. Looks like I've lucked out getting you for an instructor."

"Don't count on it. I may demand a little more and I sure don't have the patience of the junior officers."

As they approached the assigned aircraft, Major Trimble began describing the pre-flight inspection in detail. They threw their chutes and helmets on the wing and the Major never slowed his instruction, pointing out critical items to be checked thoroughly. Brian listened intently, asking questions, feeling, touching, as he moved around the sleek aircraft.

Brian slid into the front cockpit, strapping into the confined space with seat belt and shoulder harness. Putting on his helmet, he fastened the oxygen mask and waited for the first instructions. The wait was short, as the voice on the intercom crackled into his helmet. "I'm going to let you complete your checklist and start the engine."

"Roger. Not sure about all I read last night but I'll give it a try." Brian said.

"Okay, I'll walk you through it the first time. Gang-load the fuel switches. Now show the ground crew you're ready for the auxiliary power." Brian glanced hesitatingly around the unfamiliar cockpit for the right switches, and then pointed to the yellow APU, moving his hand in a rotating circle for power. He was nervous and unsure of his movements, moving switches haltingly. He felt tension invade his body as he fought to relax.

Major Trimble continued, "Ignition switch on. Now hold the start switch until you have about 15 percent RPM, then flip up the fuel sequence switch. That puts ignition and fuel to number seven and number fourteen burner cans. Now, bring the throttle around the horn."

There was a noticeable *thrump,* followed by the roar of the burner cans igniting. It was an impressive sound as the flame shot through all fourteen burners instantaneously.

"Now, slap the fuel sequences switch off with the back of your hand. Glance over and check tailpipe temperature to see if you got a hot start. Looks good. You just made your first engine start. Give the thumbs out signal and a quick salute to let 'em know you're ready to taxi."

The crew chief stepped in front and to the right of the aircraft, both arms extended, motioning them forward. The T-33 bounced clumsily as it taxied over the tarmac with its full fuel load. The wings bounced as the tip tanks bobbed slightly under the stress of almost three thousand pounds of fuel. Brian scanned the unfamiliar instruments; g meter, mach indicator, and oxygen gauges. He grabbed at the tight fit of the oxygen mask, trying unsuccessfully to make it stop cutting into his cheek. He was in a different environment, the world of the jet.

Takeoff was the first noticeable difference. It accelerated slowly then rapidly gained speed. The concrete expansion joints clicked quicker and quicker under the tires until the clicks merged into a staccato. The markers sped by in quick glimpses of remaining runway. The nose came up with very little control pressure, the gear hit the wheel wells with a thump, flaps were milked up slowly and the plane climbed at an angle never before experienced by Brian. He glanced up at bright blue hues of sky, dotted with puffy white clouds. His excitement soared upwards with the climbing jet.

He was astonished at control response, light pressures translated into instant movement of the aircraft. As they shot through a thin level of clouds at 9,000 feet, they popped out of the clouds on top of a valley of snow-like wisps beneath them. The sun took on a new brilliance at these altitudes, and the clouds were radiant puffs of cotton, as if set there for playing tag. Brian banked past a small cumulus cloud as he eased back on the stick, climbing for more altitude. He moved the stick slightly to the right. Just like Scott had described, the jet rolled effortlessly with a small amount of stick pressure.

Brian was experiencing the exhilaration of doing rolls effortlessly through space, lost in another dimension. Major Trimble's voice intruded on his euphoria. "Let's go down, enter the traffic pattern, and shoot a few landings. The fun's just beginning Lieutenant."

Things happened fast at these speeds, requiring split-second response times. Major Trimble talked him through the first landing, assisting considerably, actually taking control of the landing at the last minute. Brian had to accelerate his thinking from reciprocating aircraft quickly. He was pressing to keep his thinking ahead of the aircraft.

He listened intently to the Major casually explaining jet idiosyncrasies that would get you killed in an eye blink. "The first thing you've gotta' realize is that these tight, pitch-up landing patterns increase the possibility of high speed stalls at a low altitude. But most important, sudden forward movement of the throttle from idle could cause a compressor stall. Don't slam the throttle forward and expect to have instant acceleration. Remember, it takes twelve seconds from idle to 100% RPM. Plan ahead for a go-around, or you'll find yourself in the 'toolies'out there."

Brian attempted to assimilate these words of advice as he made landing after landing. Speed accentuated every phase of the landing, working him to keep up with the aircraft. Exhaustion took over as they taxied up and parked at the direction of the hand signals. He was more than ready when the ground crew gave a "cut engine" signal. He stop-cocked the throttle, listening to the engine whine down. His head dropped on his chest, physically drained, and confused at all that was thrown at him. The clammy flight suit, dark with perspiration stains, stuck to him.

Walking back toward the Ops building, he glanced over his shoulder at the sleek machine. He thought about the last hour and thirty minutes. *God help those guys who wear a coat and tie, go to the office every day, and get hemorrhoids.* He was finally in his element.

That night at the club the usual group of pilots gathered for a night of flight talk and drinking. Brian was learning what fighter pilots had always known; they liked to associate with other fighter pilots. There was a common bond and understanding. They talked about flying in a language others would find incomprehensible. The fraternity was already forming at this early stage of their experience. He knew these guys were working with larger-than-life egos, which were becoming more prodigious with increased flying time in jets. He also realized it wasn't an outwardly stated philosophy. It was knowledge within, an example of behavior, understood only by those who experienced it.

Brian closed the door to the phone booth and called Anne in Collinwood. "I wanted to wish you a happy Thanksgiving tomorrow. It's been a long three days since I left. I sorta' miss you."

"I've missed you, too. You're still coming this weekend, aren't you? Aunt Lucy's anxious to meet you and have you stay with her."

"I'll be there. Probably leave early Saturday morning and be there shortly after Noon. Is that all right with you?"

"Sure. I'll save you a piece of turkey." She laughed. "We'll probably be eating leftovers this weekend. Hope you don't mind."

"Cold coon and collards would be fine. Tell your mother not to go to any trouble. Gotta' go now or I won't have enough quarters to feed Ma Bell's phone here. See you in three days."

Early Saturday morning, Brian threw a bag in the car and headed for Collinwood. He watched the town markers glide by: Echo, Climax, Liberty, Pine Apple. Each was different in subtle ways but retained the unmistakable small-town atmosphere so eccentrically Southern. Off to the side, a tractor was plowing under a used-up crop, as red dust swirled behind it. Valleys of kudzu along the countryside seemed to cascade down from engulfed pine trees. Pathetic remnants of a cotton field, bare red clay hills as a backdrop, became part of the panorama. He smiled with appreciation as he looked at an occasional unpainted house, weathered over the years to a dark gray hue, teetering on its foundation of fragile brick pillars. He loved the South, the idiosyncrasies of its people, and its geography. He was brought up on a steady diet of what it truly meant to be a Southerner, and it "took." He was realistic enough to know the South wasn't merely moonlight and magnolias, obvious as he looked over the land. He could separate the economics of the region from its distinct beauty and grace. He had empathy for the area.

Anticipation mounted as the road sign read, "Collinwood 21 miles." The miles clicked by as he sped up toward his destination. He turned sharply at the square, with its pretentious courthouse centered in the rectangle, guarded by its confederate monument. He proceeded down Butler Street, gawking at the white-columned antebellum houses showing years of needed maintenance, their yards filled with camellia bushes. The columned homes held their grace as if time had aged them only to become more distinguished. He pulled up to the large 1920's cottage surrounded by a two-foot high concrete wall, with the number 245 embedded in the entrance. He reached for the ignition switch and sat for a few seconds.

He looked up to see Anne walking rapidly down the walk, between huge blooming camellia bushes, her dark brown hair flowing back as she approached. As she reached the car, she pulled the door open and took his hand, pulling him out of the car. She hugged him, and then quickly led him by the hand toward the house. "I didn't think Saturday would ever get here."

"Well, it made it, and so did I. Let me stretch a minute after that ride."

"You can stretch while you're walking. Come on in, Mama's waiting to see you."

Mrs. Merrill was holding the door open, and took Brian's hand as he entered. "Welcome back, Brian. And we expect you'll be here more than just a few hours this time."

Brian glanced at Anne. She smiled and shrugged her shoulders. "This visit shouldn't have to be cut short. Thanks for having me back."

"Let's go in and sit for a while. That is, unless you two have something planned." She looked back and forth for some indication.

"No, Mama, we don't have anything planned. Let's go into the dining room. Would you like a cup of coffee, some sweet tea, or a coke, Brian?"

"Coffee sounds great." Brian answered.

Brian smiled as he acknowledging the fact Southerners always found the dining room to be the central location for conversations, the comfortable surrounding for important discussions of family matters. The dining room served as a conference table for decisions, problem solving, and most after-dinner discussions. He held the chair for Mrs. Merrill as Anne went to make the coffee. He scanned the flowered wallpaper, his eyes stopping at the darkened walnut breakfront. A large mirror hung precariously over the large top, a bowl of fruit centered below. The two tall windows, framed by lacy white drapes, looked out onto a camellia bush covered in pink blossoms. The room was formal but emanated a homey feeling.

"Brian, tell me about the Air Force and all that's going on in your life since we last talked."

"Well, there's not that much to tell. We're checking-out in jets at Moody, then we'll be in Panama City for about six weeks, and then I have orders for Korea."

"I don't like the sound of you having to go to Korea. Is this a certainty or is there a possibility it could change? The news from over there doesn't seem to get any better at all."

"It's a sure bet. The Air Force doesn't usually change your orders. I'm just glad I could be this near home for now, and ..." His statement was interrupted as Anne swung the door open and entered with the tray of coffee. However, her entrance didn't interrupt Mrs. Merrill's line of questioning. It was apparent that she was getting to some point that she didn't want to broach openly. "It makes decisions quite difficult in planning your future with this hanging over you, don't you think?" She asked.

"Not really. I just don't make plans that wouldn't fit into the ones already made for me. I think you know what I mean, Misses Merrill." Brian put inflection into the comment while looking directly at Mrs. Merrill. Her smile signified she accepted the explanation as stated.

They chatted about Alabama relatives, the weather, lunch plans, and camellias. Brian quickly reestablished the rapport with Mrs. Merrill that he'd enjoyed during his first visit to Collinwood. There was a kindred spirit found in each other. He genuinely liked her, and being Anne's mother just made it an extra benefit.

"Brian, we need to go over to Aunt Lucy's. I told her we'd be by as soon as you got here. She's probably wondering why I haven't called. Let's go."

Aunt Lucy greeted Brian warmly. She had a congenial face, lined delicately by time. Her salt and pepper gray hair was pulled back tightly in a high-riding bun, tortoise shell glasses framed a friendly, but scrutinizing, pair of gray-blue eyes. There was a disarming smile fixed upon a small prim mouth. It was captivating to anyone upon first meeting.

"Have a seat, Brian. I'm sorry I missed you last time, but I understand you were here and gone fairly quickly."

"It was a rather short visit." Brian stated without explanation, while taking a seat beside Anne.

"So I heard," looking at Anne, then back at Brian. "That's okay. You can make up for it this time. Anne tells me you're from Ruston?"

Brian nodded.

"I graduated from Agnes-Baines more years ago than I like to recall. Where do the years go? I suppose there's been lots of changes to Ruston since I went to school there."

"Probably not as many as you might think. Ruston'll always be just a small college town. Believe me, very little changes there. When I go home after being gone for months, I recognize the same news that I got the last time I was there. Sometimes the names even change."

Aunt Lucy laughed so hard she had to catch her side. Brian was glad she had a sense of humor. It was apparent that Anne's family was easygoing, rather lovable people. He sensed that Aunt Lucy was going to be very easy to talk to. It was also quite apparent that she'd be the instigator of any serious discussions. Thirty-eight years as a schoolteacher had made her rather crafty at that skill as well as subtly disarming.

"Look. I'm sure that you two have a lot to do. I'll see you tonight at supper. We still say *supper* down here, Brian. We'll have time to talk more then. Go on now, and enjoy whatever you two planned."

Anne gave directions as he drove. She gave him the complete tour of Collinwood, pointing out every detail of how her life was intertwined with the town. She pointed out the route she took to school every day, where she learned to ride a bike, and the tree she fell out of when she broke her arm. The tour included pointing out the homes of all her friends.

Brian interrupted the nonstop narration. "Excuse me. You haven't shown me Justin's house yet." She looked at him, suspicious of his motive, and then realizing he wasn't being cantankerous, continued. "Turn down that next street to your right. It's about two blocks up on the hill to your right."

"Whew, that's quite a house!" Brian said, as he looked at the large white antebellum house, complete with its massive fluted columns. It was a stately sight, sitting on top of the hill, with two very large and very old magnolias in front, surrounded by a circular brick drive. "Sort of over-built for the neighborhood, don't you think?"

"The McBrides wouldn't see the humor in that. Judge Mc Bride takes personal pride in the gardens. They entertain a lot. I've been to so many parties there, *socials* as Miss Ellie calls them. They were usually held around the gardens in back. As I told you, it's like a second home to me. I'm sort of a member of the family, and that really has nothing to do with Justin and me."

"Somehow, I find that hard to believe but I won't second-guess your relationship with the McBrides." Brian looked up at the large house again. "There's a ready-made life for you up there on that hill. A position in Collinwood society and just about everything a girl dreams of." He nodded in the direction of the house.

She frowned. "That's not what makes people happy. It's certainly not me. When I decide what I want from life, material things won't play a part in the decision."

Aunt Lucy joined them for supper, as she succinctly put it. She wanted to hear more about flying, and the Air Force. Brian reluctantly tried to explain the attraction to flying jet aircraft, the exhilaration of being up in the sky playing tag with the clouds. He also realized that people listen, but never grasp what he's trying to express about flying. It's better to speak in very broad terms, and leave emotion out of the conversation. "As for 'Muddy Air Patch', as Moody is affectionately known, it isn't a very alluring base. The BOQ leaves a lot to be desired in comfort. The first day, I dashed in to get to town to get a few items to make life a little more comfortable. But that was quickly interrupted by the accident..."

"What accident, Brian?" Anne cut into the sentence. "You never mentioned anything about an accident when you called, or today either, for that matter." Anne's tone was surprising.

"A pilot made a mistake in judgment." Brian stated matter-of-factly.

The look that came across Anne's face told him exactly how she accepted such a perfunctory explanation. The old proposition of her regarding his career as too hazardous was raising its ugly head once again. Aunt Lucy's perception of the situation prompted her to quickly ask about the camellias and azaleas in South Georgia.

"The camellias are beautiful, but it's still early for the azaleas," Brian retorted, relieved to be off the hook for further explanations of aircraft and pilot frailties.

After dinner Anne and Brian walked out to the edge of the front yard. They sat on the concrete wall, enjoying being alone at last. He turned to her, pulled her close and kissed her. He continued to hold her in his arms and touched his face against hers. He could never get enough of her. Pressing his face against hers, he wondered if she knew how he felt. She kissed his ear, and whispered, "Just make sure you don't make any of those 'mistakes in judgment'. I'd like to have you around for a while."

"Don't worry. I'm indestructible."

"I'm not." She stated quickly.

Sunday morning Aunt Lucy knocked gently on the guest room door. "I hate to wake you, but it'll soon be time for church and I've got breakfast almost ready."

"Thanks, I'm almost dressed now. I'll only be a minute."

Brian sat down to scrambled eggs, bacon, toast, and coffee, served with a heart-to-heart conversation by Aunt Lucy. She had picked her time and place.

"Brian, I think you have some idea about Anne's relationship with the McBride family. She needed someone to break that cycle of influence. I happen to think you're good for Anne."

"I had the idea their influence was pretty strong last year when I was here. You probably know that's why I left so abruptly. Back then, I just assumed the ties were too strong to break."

"Tommy rot! Don't ever get the idea you can't overcome that hold they think they have on her. I wasn't born yesterday. Now finish your breakfast so you can go to church with Anne." Brian touched her hand. "Thanks, Aunt Lucy. I appreciate you talking to me. Really appreciate it."

The First Baptist Church was packed on the Sunday after Thanksgiving and Brian was sure he got to meet each member of the congregation and the choir too. There was Anne's first Sunday school teacher, the preacher's wife, most of her friends who were home for the holidays, and Judge and Mrs. McBride. The McBrides tried to act nonplused at this intruder who dared venture onto forbidden turf. They moved slowly toward Anne and Brian, Miss Ellie's gaze never leaving Brian. She approached with a fixed smile as she hugged Anne. Judge McBride stood a short distance away, acting as if this formality could be skipped and all would feel better for it. The introductions never erased Miss Ellie's forced smile. It was obviously well practiced over the years. It was a required facade for a Mobile lady indoctrinated in the appropriate way to handle distasteful experiences. She turned toward Brian. "I understand you're from Ruston, Brian?" The words were clipped, distinct, and carried the inference this was asked for a purpose. "I grew up there."

"I'm sure you know Doctor Pearson? He's a very old and dear friend."

"He's been our family doctor for as long as I can remember." Brian answered while assimilating the insinuation that she had already gotten a complete background check on him.

The meeting was pleasant enough outwardly, but Brian could feel the charged air all about him. The Judge said very little, his wife made what little conversation took place. Brian was uncomfortable playing the roll Anne had selected for him. "Nice meeting you."

He closed the door as Anne got into the car, walked around,

unbuttoned his blouse, opened the door, and threw it on the back seat of the car. "I'm glad that's over."

"That's evident in your gestures. Do you think you threw your coat hard enough in the back seat?" She relaxed the frown. "Now, that really wasn't that bad, was it?"

He turned toward her, hesitating to say what he really felt. "Yes, hell, it was. I feel like I just got mentally drawn and quartered back there. I got the meaning of her questions."

"What meaning?"

"I don't care for her getting a background check on me. Not one damn bit."

"What's wrong with them checking on you with a friend of the family? They were just interested because of me."

"My life's none of their damn business"

Come off that indignant attitude. "Believe me, you passed with flying colors and I wanted the McBrides to see that you're really very nice." She punched his shoulder. "When you want to be." She placed her hand on his arm before he could start driving. "I never know what Justin may have told them. I'm sure he had something to say." He glanced over, waiting for the rest of the explanation. "You know –, " Anne grinned broadly, "Miss Ellie did show a little disdain when she first met you. I could tell by the way she squinted her eyes at you. Oh, I know that 'Mobile society' squint very well indeed."

Brian glared at Anne. "It's not one damn bit funny to me. You don't see my point here at all. Do you?

"No, I guess I don't." She spun toward the door.

Anne had already packed and was ready to leave after right after lunch. Mrs. Merrill looked concerned. "That's an awfully long drive for you to Ruston then all the way to Valdosta."

"It's no problem. Another hundred and twenty miles won't be that noticeable. I'm used to it." Brian explained." He moved closer. "I really appreciate you inviting me down."

"Brian, you're welcome any time. I mean that." Mrs. Merrill said as she squeezed his hand.

It was time to relax and enjoy being together. Just the two of them and a lot of highway before being with people again. Brian never liked this time of year. The bareness of the trees became stark sentinels under the gray cirrus clouds. The sun flashed its setting through the naked, silhouetted trees in staccato bursts of light. The sunlight, bursting through the trees, accentuated the starkness of their bare branches. The early setting of the sun always gave the sky a foreboding look. He turned to Anne. "Okay, let's put the McBride's behind us. I don't relish looking at that scowl for the next hundred miles."

"You're the one with the frown. And I think you'd better stay off the subject of the McBrides for a while -- okay?" Brian looked in her direction, then back down the road, making no comment. "By the way, there's something I want to tell you." Brian snapped his head around, reacting to the sudden serious note in her voice. "Oh, don't look so blasted startled. I just wanted you to know I had a long talk with Justin this last week. I explained about seeing you, that I planned to stay friends with him, but he should realize the situation."

"Did he have a problem with that?" Brian asked.

"He was furious. You know, like 'how could you?' Then he turned the conversation around, trying to make me feel guilty. This time I wasn't accepting that guilt trip. I told him to stand on his own two feet and not expect his happiness to always come from me."

"I don't feel sorry for Justin. I think ... never mind what I think."

Anne laughed out loud. "I'm not laughing at you. I'm just thinking about what Justin said. 'I just wish you weren't going out with that *aviator*. I don't trust him. That guy wants to marry you. I told him he was crazy."

He looked at her with a large grin. "I do give ole' Justin credit for one thing; he's very perceptive."

She looked directly at Brian, a little startled, but said nothing. Brian tried to observe her reaction but, whatever she was thinking, it wasn't obvious. A look of apprehension gradually came over her. She placed her hand on his arm. "Remember that first day you were home, and we were parked in the rain? I told you there was something in my past that would help you understand me better?" Brian nodded. "I think now is the time to tell you about a very traumatic time in my life." Brian looked over questioningly, wondering what she was about to say. Tyler's words suddenly rebounded in his brain as he wondered what was about to come.

"My mother remarried when I was twelve..."

Brian interrupted. "I didn't know your mother remarried after your father's death."

"She did. They married a very short time after she met Mister Henson. He moved into our home and everything in my life changed that day. This man made my life a living hell for the five months he was there. He controlled my every move. He picked me up after school and took me straight home. He insisted I eat exactly what he ordered my mother to prepare, and we had asparagus every meal except breakfast. I hate asparagus 'till this very day. He insisted I polish my shoes each night, and he inspected them to see if I had to do it again. My friends weren't allowed to come over, and gradually, he isolated us from the rest of the family. My mother was powerless to help. She was terrified of the man. I felt isolated and alone, and constantly wondered what he was going to do to me. I lived in fear." Tension was building in her voice. She choked back her emotions. "My God, I stayed awake every night, facing my door just in case he came in." She stopped for a moment, regrouping her thoughts. "It came to a head one night as he screamed at me, then he threw me on the bed. He acted insane. I was scared to death. My mother came to the door and told him to stop right that minute. He yelled at her to go to her room, that I needed discipline, then slammed the door and locked it." She stopped and shook her head, as tears began to flow.

Brian pulled over to the side of the road and shut off the engine. He put his arm around her. "It's all right, that's the past. It's over."

"You don't understand. He was touching me all over. I fought as hard as I possibly could. I knew what he was trying to do. The only way I stopped him for a second or two was to tell him I'd be good, just let me get up."

"My God, Anne, did he..."

"No." She interrupted. "When he relaxed his grip, I slid out from under him, bolted through the door, and ran all the way to Aunt Lucy's. She was mortified as I sobbed out what had happened. She called Doctor Parker to come over immediately. He examined me, and then gave me a shot to calm me down. I've never seen Aunt Lucy so furious. She called Judge McBride and told him the story. He issued an immediate warrant and had the sheriff visit Mister Henson. He was told to pack his things, leave that house, and Collinwood immediately. And he did. The important part of this story is the fact Judge McBride made sure I was okay. He came to my rescue. I'll never forget what he did."

"I'm hearing this, but can't believe your mother let it happen."

"Brian, you have to understand how terrified she was. I know that's hard to comprehend but you'd have to know Mister Henson.

He was crazy as a loon, and Mama didn't know it until it was too late." She looked out the window, gathering her thoughts. "We've worked through this over the years. We'll never be as close as most mothers and daughters, but we try to support each other, and have some kind of normalcy in our relationship. She won't, or can't, forgive herself for letting me down when I needed her so desperately. I forgive her, but I can never forget that she wasn't there when I needed her."

"I'm really sorry you had to go through that." He wasn't quite sure what to say to ease the pain. "I'm thankful you got out when you did. What a bastard he must have been." He pulled her close. "I could see some barrier, or a distance, between you and your mother that first time I came to Collinwood. I thought I must be imagining it, and then later it was obvious how close you are to Aunt Lucy. It begins to make a little more sense to me now."

"I didn't sleep well for years, listening for his footsteps, wondering if he was coming through that door again."

"It's a wonder you don't hate all men after that." Brian said.

"I told you I had some hang-ups. I could have easily felt like that about men. I wanted you to know why I have some hesitancy toward making commitments. Why I respond differently to some circumstances than most people." She looked away, as if not wanting to continue, then abruptly turned, as if she had a sudden resolve to explain. "It may give you some insight about how important the people in Collinwood are to me, particularly the McBrides. They got me through a difficult time, and Justin has been the only male in my life until now. He was the only one I trusted. Now you know."

"I'm glad you told me. There's nothing I can say that'll erase that from your memory. All I can do is show you why there's nothing to be afraid of now. You trust me, don't you?"

"Yes. I think I do."

"One other question: Where's that bastard now?"

"I don't know. That's why the fear never leaves completely. He hates me so."

Brian held her close. "No need to be afraid now."

"Brian, we're all afraid of something." She said. "Some don't admit it, some don't even recognize they have fears, but they do. At least I know what mine are."

CHAPTER NINE

THE GATE GUARD stepped out to check identification, and seeing the decal on the windshield, waved Brian through. Brian noticed the clock on the wall in the gatehouse; 0420. *I'll be lucky to get two hours sleep.* His saving grace was the fact that he had classes first, and flying in the afternoon. *Maybe I can catch a nap at lunch.*

During the first class that morning, the First Lieutenant instructor was discussing aircraft systems, with his usual sarcastic responses to questions. He'd just finished going over the necessity for checking the fuselage fuel tank's cap on the pre-flight inspection. Failure to do so, he explained, would allow the fuel to be sucked into the plenum chamber at speeds under 200 knots. A student asked: "Why."

"Because the freakin' airplane will explode into a great big ball of fire. Understand that, Lieutenant?"

This was a typical retort to any question, instilling anything but confidence in those asking or listening. Brian shook his head at the attitude of the instructor but thought better of speaking up. He didn't want be singled out later. Even when Brian asked about the yaw string on the nose of the aircraft, the instructor gave his most sarcastic reply. "If you stall this thing straight up in a hammerhead stall, it'll slide straight down ten thousand feet and you can't kick it off on either wing. So, Lieutenant Brannon, if you see the yaw string go in the opposite direction, I'd suggest you punch out. And by the way, if it's over the Okefenokee, don't even bother opening the chute, an alligator'll get you anyway." The comment brought laughter from the others in the class as Brian stared at him with contempt, anger welling up inside him. But he made no attempt to reject or laugh at his twisted humor. He seethed inside, wondering why he didn't have the guts to speak out. He felt ashamed he let such a comment slide and didn't respond.

That night at the bar, Ed sidled up between Vince and Scott. "You hot rocks can take turns buying me my last drinks at Muddy Air Patch. I pull out tomorrow for Shaw."

Brian moved around toward Ed. "You should be buying us drinks for letting you hang around real fighter pilots this long."

"He's right, Ed." Vince added. "We built your reputation letting you stand here with us at the bar every night."

"Yeah, right. Listen up you hot-rocks. I soloed the F-80 while you guys were trying to find the flight line. Hey, bartender." He slapped his hand down hard on the bar. "Bartender, bring me three martinis. Put 'em on any tab these three might have going."

Two hours later, Brian thought the room was spinning too much for a night before flying. He stood, holding hard to the back of the chair, letting the room stop its rotations. "Try not to auger in the first week over there at Shaw, Ed."

Ed stood, put out his hand around the table. "You guys take it easy. I'll sneak up on you guys again before you know it." He glanced over at Vince, who could hardly focus. "But damn, I'm gonna' miss Vince's nonsense." He sidled between Scott and Brian. "You think there's another fool, somewhere in this Air Force, who can keep me laughing like him?"

Vince broke into a wide grin. "I'm like a rare Picasso, Ed. There aint but one."

Brian knew he was too tired on Mondays to give his best performance in the air. He always muddled through, but by Wednesday he was hitting his peak again. This Wednesday, he taxied out to the active runway for takeoff, feeling good about the flight. As they reached the run-up point, ready to call for takeoff instructions, Brian glanced up. In that split second, he watched an aircraft roll inverted, then go straight into the ground. A mushroom cloud of orange flame mingled with black smoke rose from the crash, rolling skyward in dark boiling testimony of the obvious.

"My God, one just augured in!" Brian yelled into the intercom.

The instructor looked up to see the mushroom shaped fireball rising swiftly. "No, I think someone must have dropped a tip tank out there."

"No way, Major, I saw him go inverted just before impact." Brian insisted. The tower transmitted the message that left no doubt: "All aircraft hold short of the active. We've had an accident. Break, Break. All aircraft in the vicinity of Moody be advised the active runway is closed until further notice. Please advise fuel state. If fuel is low we can find an alternate runway for you."

"Well, looks like you did see one go in after all. We may as well turn around and shut down. It'll take quite a while to clear the crash equipment from the area and the tower has a few birds to try to get back on the ground ASAP."

Brian was still unnerved at seeing the T-33 impact directly in front of him. The foremost question in his mind was: *who the hell was it?* He went through the motions of parking and engine shutdown in robotic fashion. As he walked back to the Ops Building carrying his helmet and chute, his mind replayed the sight of the accident over and over. In the Ops building, he asked if anyone had a name of the pilot yet.

Gradually, the stories filtered in. The Captain, who'd talked to the tower, was telling the other instructors what had happened, "... so he called immediately after takeoff saying his right tip tank was siphoning fuel at a rapid rate. He declared an emergency, saying he was coming right back in to land."

"A siphoning tip tank isn't a goddamn emergency!" An instructor declared loudly.

"We all know that. The tower told him 'Negative, negative, break traffic and burn off some fuel first', and this guy yells: 'Negative, I'm turning final now, gear down and locked.' Well, he just got himself a high-speed stall trying to turn final with that kind of fuel load. He bought it right there."

Brian stepped up and asked, "Do you know his name?" The Captain stopped talking, and looked at Brian emotionlessly. "I don't know for sure, but I was told that the name beside that tail number on the board was Giacano."

Brian felt icy fingers claw at his insides. He heard a roaring in the ears, as nausea engulfed him. He couldn't respond to the answer to his question, but continued staring straight ahead.

"You okay, Lieutenant?"

The others in the group turned to Brian as well. He could hear voices; he saw people looking at him, but he wasn't really cognizant of his surroundings. With questions still posed to him, he turned and walked away, without comment.

He drove to the BOQ. His thoughts spinning with questions he couldn't answer. *This couldn't happen -- not to Vince. He was one of those who had "it." He was the epitome of a jet pilot. There was no way Vince could 'buy the farm.'* He shook his head to clear away the mental haze, but it did no good. He had to find Scott.

Finding Scott's room empty, Brian ran to the club. There at the bar was Scott, drink in hand, moving the glass around in small wet circles on the bar, looking into the drink as if to find an answer there. Brian walked up slowly and stood beside him. Scott turned his head toward Brian, and they looked at each other for several seconds. There was no need to verbalize what they were feeling. They just had part of their gut ripped out. The Group was now two.

The Friday afternoon drive to Ruston seemed much longer to Brian. He had too much time to think with the radio providing only a brief diversion. Finally, he topped Holloway Hill and the College was only two miles ahead. Even though his Friday night arrivals were late, Anne had asked him to come there before going home. It was almost ten when he arrived at Ramsay Hall, and walked into the lobby. Anne was standing there, leaning on the desk. He walked up to her. "You waiting on someone in particular, or can I interest you in going with me?"

"I was waiting on someone but, since he's late, you'll have to do." She took his hand and led him to the door.

It was cold, with a breeze that added to the wind chill as they walked to the Tea House. Brian ambled over to the jukebox, making his selections to add some atmosphere to the over-lit room. The numbers came up as he'd selected them and they had little effect on his disposition. He leaned back, closed his eyes, and tried to relax to the music.

"I do believe you're more attuned to music than anyone I've ever known."

"Music affects everyone at some level they can't explain. It kinda' wraps around your inner soul. Right?"

"Yeah, but ... yeah, I guess it does. That song playing right now says things in just the right way. Listen." *I'll be loving you always – with a love that's true, always – When the things you've planned need a helping hand* . . . Anne said

"I guess it does." Brian stated.

"For some reason, you seem preoccupied tonight. Can't put my finger on it, but something's bothering you." She said.

"Just tired. It's a long drive."

"I've seen you tired before; something's not right. Is it us?"

"No, course not." He looked around the room, wanting to change the subject, but knew he needed to tell her. "I know how you feel about the Air Force, flying, and the way you overreacted Thanksgiving when I mentioned an accident."

"Tell me what happened." She said.

Brian looked toward the door and said nothing for a few seconds, struggling to put it in proper perspective. He realized there was no proper perspective. He looked back at Anne. "Vince was killed Wednesday. He made a bad error in judgment, and it cost him."

"Why is it always 'a bad error in judgment', why not just admit that flying jets can definitely get you killed?" Hostility was evident in her voice. Her facial expression reinforced her verbalization.

"My God, you overreact. Yeah, jets are damn unforgiving for those who shouldn't be flying 'em. There are no accidents, just guys who don't have the reaction time, can't make a split-second decision, or lose their cool. I loved Vince. Loved him like a brother, but he made all of those mistakes, all at one time. And that doesn't have a damn thing to do with me." Brian fired back.

"I'm sorry. I didn't mean to take off on you like that. It's pretty insensitive when I know how you must feel. I know how close you were to Vince." She looked at him with empathy. Did they tell you how it happened?"

"I saw it."

She put her hand to her mouth. "Oh Brian, I'm so sorry." She sucked in a breath. "My God, please forgive me." Her eyes became moist with the apology.

"I know."

Even though nothing could push Vince's accident out of his constant thoughts, his mental state was much improved being in her company. Without warning, however, he would suddenly see the fireball that annihilated his friend. He could see the fire and smoke rolling and billowing straight up, taking on a mushroom shape. The visualization appeared more ominous each time. He'd grit his teeth and tighten his grip on the coke bottle, but presented no other outward indications of his thoughts.

Anne suddenly asked him about the accident, and Brian shook his head indicating he didn't want to talk about it. She slid over, placing her hand on his neck, and gently massaged the back "Don't keep things bottled up inside. It'll eat you from within. Talk to me. Tell me how badly you feel. Let it out."

"It's hard to put into words. I miss him. I just can't believe he won't be there when I get back. I'll miss that easy going sense of humor and that New Jersey accent we made fun of. He was quite a guy ... a true friend. We don't have that many in life that we can lose 'em." He moved his hand self-consciously toward the moisture in his eyes.

"Words don't provide much consolation. They have a hollow ring when you're trying to say 'I know how you feel'– because I don't – I can't. It's too bad we never got to meet. He must've been a special kind of person." She touched his hand. "I feel so bad for you, yet there's nothing I can do to take away the hurt. You'll have to work through it yourself, in your own way, but I'm glad you talked to me about it."

The replaying of the weekend's events made the five-hour drive to Valdosta tolerable and kept him from falling asleep. It also kept his mind off of the accident. The late night drives back to Valdosta were taking their toll. As the miles crept by, sleep beckoned to him, tempting him to close his eyes for just a moment. The road would gradually become a blur, the black asphalt taunting him to close his eyes. Just when he thought he could stay awake no longer, the main gate came into focus, as well as his thoughts back to the reality of the present.

During class that Monday, Brian felt his anger rise to the surface several times as the Lieutenant continued his caustic retort to sporadic questions. Toward the end of the second hour, a question regarding an emergency procedure received short shrift again. Brian felt the blood flow to his brain and pound at his temple. He barely felt the pencil in his hand snap with the pressure.

"Excuse me, Lieutenant. Do you ever stop to wonder about how your answers may kill good pilots, or do you even give a damn?" Brian stated.

Every eye in the room focused quickly on Brian. The silence that followed would make a pin dropping sound like an explosion.

The instructor stiffened and walked to the edge of the platform, looked hard at him. "Do you have a problem, Lieutenant?" He asked.

"No, by God, I believe you've got the problem."

There was a low murmur that flowed across the room. The tension in the air was like static electricity. The two stared at each other, waiting for the other to make the next move. The instructor glanced about the room.

"It's close to time, anyway, that's it for today, gentlemen. I'd like to see you privately, Lieutenant Brannon."

The instructor closed the door and turned to Brian. "Your insubordination could get you out of this program in a damn big hurry."

"Save your breath. Your attitude and half-assed instructing cost a good friend of mine his life. He didn't know diddly about siphoning tip tanks. He had no idea it wasn't a goddamn emergency, because you passed it off with some of your flippant sarcastic comments." Brian moved closer. "You aren't fit to wear the same uniform he wore."

"You don't know when to stop, do you?"

"No, guess I don't. Figure I've only got a few choices: One, just beat the living crap out of you right here. I wish I could, for Vince's sake, but that would get me court-martialed. Two, bring this up to a higher echelon for action against you. Knowing the system, they'd cover your ass, and theirs, too. Three, just let your conscience work on you, knowing you were responsible for at least one good man's death, and probably more. Now, the next move is up to you, Lieutenant."

The instructor stared at Brian. Obviously, contemplating the options. Brian shook his head at the standoff. "You're one pathetic piece of work, and I hope to hell our paths never cross again in this man's Air Force." He turned abruptly and walked away, feeling a burden had been lifted. It was something he had to do, regardless of the consequences. *That one was for you, Vince.* The thought brought a faint smile of satisfaction to his face.

The next day, Major Trimble ambled over and told Brian to get his gear, then turned and started toward the flight line. Brian rushed to catch up with him. As they moved slowly through the door, Major Trimble casually mentioned that this would probably be their last flight together as he was leaving on a long Temporary Duty, and was winding up a few loose ends. "If you do as well today as you did yesterday, I believe you're ready to solo the ole T-Bird tomorrow."

"Is that because I'm one of your loose ends, or do you think I'm really ready?"

Major Trimble never stopped walking toward the door. "You're definitely ready, and probably should go today, but we may as well have one more ride." He stopped at the door, and turned to Brian. "Rumor has it that you teed-off on a certain instructor yesterday. Seems there was something about him being the cause of an accident? In case you're wondering, this is a small base."

"It's sad something didn't happen before Vince went in last week."

A serious look washed across the Major's face. He grabbed Brian's sleeve, pulling him forcefully off the walk, to one side, out of the way of others going to their aircraft. "I want to share something with you. And you should think about it as long as you're in this game. You're going to lose friends in this business. If it didn't have risks, you wouldn't be getting flight pay." He pointed to the crews making their way toward the rows of aircraft. "You, me, and all those guys you see walking out to those planes, do it because of the challenge, and a love of flying. We never say it that way, but that's the real motivation. Those that 'buy the farm' are the ones who make the big mistakes. There's no single factor that kills pilots. It's a chain of events that starts when they begin flight training. Some little flaw builds on itself until he becomes a statistic. The point being: your friend made the big mistake. Nobody did it for him. He made himself a statistic."

Brian looked at the ground, then out to the flight line. He thought for a minute, and then turned back to the Major. "You're the second person to tell me that in so many words. I understand what you mean, Major. Now, I have to accept it."

CHAPTER TEN

S COTT LEFT FOR Tyndall Air Force Base and Brian followed four days later by flying double flights to accelerate his completion of instrument training. Thursday morning Brian threw the last bag into the back seat of the Oldsmobile, and headed toward Florida. The sun highlighted his mood as it gleamed off of the asphalt, creating shimmering mirages ahead. His foot became heavier on the accelerator as he passed the sign, "Welcome to Florida." The sun warmed the day as he sped through Tallahassee and turned right on US 90. He occasionally glanced at the odometer to watch the miles add up. He pulled up to the gate of Tyndall Air Force Base and stopped. The sentry saluted and motioned him through.

The sign-in was as painless as he'd hoped. He got his room assignment, parked the car and began unloading. The long low stucco building was a drastic change from Moody. The elongated screened-in porch along the front served as the entry for the six rooms opening onto it. The palm trees lining the front provided an appealing quality and he felt like he was finally in Bachelor Officer's Quarters worthy of the name. After placing some of his personal items in various places, he went back to the orderly room.

"Sergeant, could you please give me the building and room number for Lieutenant Jeter." The Sergeant scanned his flip file, stopping at the appropriate place.

"Building six twenty-two, room three, sir."

Brian jogged over toward Scott's room, checking his watch to see if he would probably be there. Several knocks later, he took out his pen and left a note stuck in the door frame telling Scott his building and room number, with an additional comment. *"If you don't have other plans let's get a bite later, I need to talk to you."*

He finished straightening his room, and put aside an overnighter already packed to leave first thing the next morning. He read his orders again, making sure there was nothing that required his presence before 0800 Monday morning. He lay back on the bed to rest for a while.

As he reached that twilight zone between consciousness and sleep, the door flew open and Scott was standing at the side of the bed looking at Brian's prone figure. "Geez, you're one lazy SOB. Get up and let's get moving. The oyster and shrimp bar opens in fifteen minutes."

"What the bloody hell are you talking about?" Brian was trying to squint through the sun beaming through the window, trying to focus on the intruder. He rubbed his eyes awake and blinked at Scott. "Just sit down, and take it easy while I get my shirt on."

"Hurry up. You can button it in the car. By the way, where're you parked?"

"It's around back. Let me throw some water on my face and comb my hair."

Scott led the way through the door, Brian still buttoning his shirt and trying to get his hat on. Scott, two steps ahead, was wildly waving his arm, urging him to hurry. Brian dropped into the driver's seat. Scott was already sitting. "Take a hard left out of the lot here. It's about four blocks up on the left. Man, they have the best friggin' oysters on the half-shell you ever tasted. There, just ahead. Take a spot on the side there."

Scott grabbed a table, pushed the chair back with his foot, placed the tray of oysters on the table, pivoted around and headed back for his beer. Brian joined him as Scott returned to the table with mug in one hand and crackers in the other.

"Now that you've loaded the table with food and drink, maybe you can take time between those sliders going down to tell me about the routine here." Brian asserted.

Scott never looked up. He was mixing his cocktail sauce, adding just the right mixture of horseradish and lemon juice, swirling the mixture with a spoon. Brian watched the ritual with amazement "Tell me dude, since these things are still alive, can you feel their little hearts beating on the way down?"

Scott's head snapped up, mouth agape with an oyster poised for eating. "Yeah, right." He wolfed down the oyster. With a smile of pure satisfaction, he sat back and began his briefing, pausing periodically for a swig of beer and another oyster.

"The first thing Monday, you'll meet your RO – Radar Intercept Officer. This is the backseat cat you're gonna' take into combat with you. Think about that one for a while." He frowned as he made the statement, and then continued. "He's fresh out of Navigator/Radar flight school, and I do mean fresh. Let me tell you, I've seen a few of these guys who couldn't find the latrine without some very detailed directions. Magellan they ain't!" Down went another oyster, then a swig of beer. "Damn, I love these things."

"Really, I would've never guessed." Brian stated.

"How's everything going with the old love life these days?" Scott asked.

"Fine. Except I'm beginning to realize, there's not too many weeks left before we leave."

"Brian, ole boy, you knew that all along. Don't expect it to get any easier."

"You always know just what to say to make me feel better. Not to change the subject, but how about the F-ninety four? How's it to fly?

"Like a dream. It's a big T-thirty-three with a bulbous radar nose, nice set of fifty calibers tucked in there, and an afterburner in the back. Let me tell you, that afterburner's a kick in the butt. Light the burner and it'll climb like a homesick angel, with the rate of climb needle buried at six thousand feet a minute."

"Sounds like some bird, can't wait 'till Monday. By the way, where's your RO?"

"He said he felt a little sick after we landed. Well, really, he's a bit hung over. That sonofagun can put it away. Last night I watched him put away five scotch's at the Club after we had a couple beers here." Another oyster went down, followed by a swig of beer. "He drinks scotch on the rocks. I've always been a little suspicious of scotch drinkers."

"I can tell by the way you're talking, you like the guy?"

Scott chuckled. "We make quite a team. Hey, tomorrow night we'll all go out to the beach to ..."

"Hold on!" Brian cut him short. "I'm heading north as soon as I can get out of here."

"I forgot about Miss Anne for a moment. Guess that means we won't be seeing much of you." He leaned back against the chair. "You ever figure out how much of life you're missing by not hanging out with us on the weekend? We could give you a different perspective altogether. You do know she's got your head all screwed around, don't you?"

"Some day I'll explain what *you're* missing." He frowned at Scott. "Finish that last oyster and let's go to the Club. I'm gonna' hit the sack early tonight."

The next morning Brian dressed quickly in a sport shirt and slacks, threw the little bag in the back of the Olds and ambled over to the orderly room. He walked over to the desk and leaned over to let the Sergeant know he was waiting. He didn't look up, but continued talking over the phone. There were a lot of "yessir's" while Brian waited impatiently. Clearing his throat to get some recognition that he was standing there was of no avail. After several more "Yessirs" the Sergeant put the phone down and yelled at the other Sergeant to come over, still ignoring Brian's presence.

"Sergeant, could I speak to you for a minute?"

The Sergeant looked toward Brian, but seemed preoccupied. Then he seemed to take a second look. "Lieutenant, you checked in yesterday, right?"

"Yeah, I did, and I just wanted you to know I'll be gone for the rest of the weekend. Do you need a number where I can be reached?"

"No, Sir, I don't, but I was just going to let you and the other new arrivals know that Colonel Newsome wants all of you at the briefing room, Building six fifty-seven, at oh nine thirty. I just hung up talking with him."

"Well, Sergeant – Sergeant Wills." Brian was straining to read his name tag. "Just pretend you didn't see me here. I'll see what the good Colonel wants first thing Monday."

"I don't think that'd be too good an idea, Lieutenant. I'll tell you straight. The last thing you want to do is piss him off the first day. Life's too short to have that guy on your butt."

Brian held his head down, with both arms extended, resting on the counter, contemplating his next move. His head popped up. "Where th' hell's building six fifty-seven?"

He hurriedly changed into his khaki's and flight jacket, watching his well-laid out plans beginning to unravel. Parking near the large flight operations building, he walked in to see several guys milling about, some standing close, reading the bulletin board. Brian squeezed through to see what everyone was reading. "Damnation! That screws up my plans, but good." He shouted out loud.

Those in earshot were looking at him quizzically. He really didn't care. He looked up to see a Lieutenant, going from person to person, reading name tags. He suddenly stopped in front of Brian, looked up from the name tag, and stuck out his hand. "Hi, I'm Hank Evans, your RO. Looks like we're gonna' be a crew."

Brian was trying to size this guy up as to how astute he looked. It was rather difficult. Hank was average in every department. He was an average height, average build, average sandy colored hair and average smile. "Brian Brannon. Glad to have you in the back seat. Where's home?"

"Des Moines, Iowa. Lived there all my life and graduated from Iowa State. How about you?"

"I'm from Alabama, and that's exactly where I was trying to get to when this damn schedule got posted. I needed to go by Birmingham ..." Brian stopped mid-sentence as if there was really no use in providing further explanation.

"You sound pissed. Listen, if it's that important to you, we can get a move on, right after the briefing. You drop me off to be first in line for drawing flight gear while you park, then do the same thing for personnel, and you can be movin' down the asphalt by noon. How's that sound?"

"We're gonna' make one helluva' team. I like your thinking." Brian exclaimed.

Following the usual "Welcome aboard" briefing, Hank's idea worked perfectly. While Brian parked the car, Hank was already in line for the issue of flight gear, and the same for personnel.

"It's really important to me to get moving and get to Alabama. I'll explain it all to you Monday. Thanks for the help, Hank."

"Hey, negative perspiration. Have a good weekend, and take care of whatever's that important. See ya' Monday."

Brian didn't bother changing clothes or take a chance on being in the proximity of the orderly room again that day. He glanced at his watch as he drove through the gate. It was 1120. He could still make it to Birmingham, and get to Bromberg Jewelers before it closed. He turned up Highway 231 toward Montgomery. He smiled at the thought of Hank. There was something charismatic about his new RO. He took to his personality and easygoing approach to the Air Force.

As he got closer to Birmingham, he kept checking his watch. It was almost 1600 and he was having some regrets about stopping for a sandwich on the outskirts of Greenville. By 1630 he was going down the hill past the statue of Vulcan and soon was parking in the lot next to Brombergs.

He was tired but happy as he parked in front of his house, took his bag inside and said hello to his mother. "Mom, I want to show you something." He flipped open the dark velvet ring box, holding the ring out for her to see. "I wanted you to be the first to know."

She placed her hand over her mouth momentarily. "Brian, it's simply beautiful. Does Anne know?"

"Nope. And she may very well say 'no' when she sees this."

"Not for one minute do you believe that. You know how she feels by now."

"We'll talk about this tomorrow. I'm not gonna' take time to change. It's late, and I want to let Anne know I'm here." He stopped and looked at her for emphasis. "In case you are wondering, I'm not giving her the ring tonight. That calls for a special occasion, like a candlelight dinner. You know the setting." He winked as he spun around for the door.

Anne ran down the steps to meet him in the lobby and hugged him harder than usual.

"Hey, I apologize for the way I look." He said. "I've been on the road in this uniform since this morning and I didn't want to waste time changing."

"You look fine to me. It's late, c'mon, let's just walk for a while." She said it as if there was no choice. "I know a certain bench that just may be unoccupied right now."

He took her hand as he held the door open. She pulled her coat up around her neck as the chill of the night air registered its cool reception. The walk to the bench was invigorating against the bite of the January night. "Tell me about Florida. Is it better than Valdosta and Moody?"

"It's great. Wish you could come down some weekend, and walk the beach and eat some sea food."

"Me too. Who knows, I may make it down for a weekend."

"Now, tell me about school. How's everything going now that the vacation is over? How's Lori these days?"

"Lord knows, it's hard getting back in the grind, and exams are just two weeks away. If you were here more than the weekends, I'd have no hope of passing French, psychology would be a toss up and history would be hopeless. Lori's home this weekend. She'll be sorry she missed you. Now what other questions do you have, Lieutenant?"

Brian laughed. "No more questions – at least for right now. Tell Lori I'm sorry I missed her and maybe I'll see her next weekend. Oh, by the way, I have a message from Scott." He pulled her close and gave her a lingering kiss.

"Scott sends pretty good messages," she said breathlessly. "I'll have to send him one. Speaking of other guys..."

"I wasn't." He quickly injected.

"Oh now, you wait a minute. I wanted to tell you, Jean Glasner got married during the holidays. She told me her husband also flies jets and you might know him. He's leaving for Korea next month and I reckon that's why they decided not to wait. It had to be strictly an impulsive decision, 'cause she never mentioned it before the holidays.'

"Sure, I remember Jean, beautiful girl. Now, as for her husband, it's a big Air Force, but what's his name?"

"Chuck Reynolds. I met him a couple of times here on campus. He seems like such a nice guy. I could see how happy she was."

"All pilots are nice guys. Haven't you noticed?"

"I've noticed one thing. They're definitely different. Maybe that's some of their charm and mystique. But maybe that's why some folks think they're a bit weird." She laughed.

"I know some who fit the last category. Now what does this guy fly? Maybe I'll run across him in Korea."

"My gosh, I don't even know what you fly!"

Brian looked at her with fake disdain. "Well, in the future, if anyone asks, tell them a Lockeed F-ninety-four B, Starfire, with a General Electric J-thirty-three engine and afterburner. Now you know."

"Oh, sure. Got it down pat. I can't tell a Ford from a Chevy."

"Not to change the subject, I want to ask you something about tomorrow night. I made reservations for us at Dale's Cellar, in Birmingham, at eight. I didn't bother asking, so hope that's okay with you."

"Sure that's great, but what's the occasion?" She asked.

"Just had an urge. Something I wanted us to do."

Saturday night he parked in front of Ramsay, sitting there for a moment, wondering how this night would turn out. He ran his fingers over the ring box, flipped it open looking at the ring, then closed it. he slid the ring beside the seat, opened the door of the Olds and bounded up the steps. He opened the front door and stopped as if hit with a bolt of lightning. Anne was waiting in the lobby. She had on a black dress that emphasized every feature of her figure. The black high heels accentuated her well-proportioned legs. He took in the full effect of her and was convinced that there, in front of him, was the most beautiful sight he'd ever seen.

"My God, you look beautiful."

"Thanks, you look good too. Guess we qualify for Dale's Cellar."

He opened the car door and she slid in and turned to rest her back against the passengers' door. He shook his head and laughed at the fact that she always took the same position in a car. His heart beat faster than normal as he started the car and drove through the large metal gates, and afterward turned left toward Birmingham. His mind swirled with impatience. The adrenalin flowed through his body. He drove only a block then, impulsively, slammed on the brakes, pulled to the side of the street, parking next to the curb. The anxiety of knowing what he was going to do later was a too much to endure for the next forty miles. It had to be now.

Anne sat up straight as he turned off the engine. "What's wrong?"

"Nothing's wrong. Not right this minute anyway." He was reaching beside the seat for the ring box, as she watched with a baffled look.

"Brian, what on earth are you doing?"

He pulled up the box, flipped it open quickly, and took out the ring. She leaned toward him trying to see in the dim light. He reached for her left hand and gently placed the ring on her finger. His eyes examined her face. She looked at the ring for several more seconds without saying anything. He swallowed hard, waiting for some indication of what she was thinking.

"I really can't believe this." She held it up toward a small glimmer of light. "It's absolutely beautiful"

She continued to look at the ring for a while, then leaned over and kissed him.

"Yes!" She looked deep into his eyes. "But are *you* sure?"

"Anne, I can't now, or probably never will, be able to explain how much I love you. It goes far beyond such a simple statement. For now, just accept the fact that I do."

"I love you too. But are you really sure you can put the past in proper perspective?"

"You didn't have to ask that." He said.

Cars slowed down to see what was going on. They both laughed. "Just let 'em wonder." Brian announced.

She slid over as close as possibly to him and leaned her head on his shoulder. "This was a complete surprise. It wasn't something I'd really thought about. My gosh, what a shock." She held her hand out in front of her in the dim light, looking at the ring. When you took my hand and put this ring on my finger, a warm feeling came over me. There was absolutely no apprehension, no questioning whatsoever. I just knew. Believe me, that in itself is a bit amazing." Anne straightened. "There'll be some very surprised people tomorrow morning when they see this, not to mention my mother. Lord. I've got to call her first thing in the morning."

"Whatta' you think Justin'll say?"

"You don't want to know what he's going to say, but one thing for sure; he'll say: 'I told you so!' Lord knows, I'm not looking forward to that conversation."

Dale's Cellar was a perfect setting. The table in the corner of the room, the background music playing softly, and the candle flickering on the table added the right atmosphere. Anne occasionally looked at the ring, shaking her head in disbelief. Brian ate sparingly. He was content just to look at the person across from him. He wondered why he was so lucky, why he deserved this. It made him humble to think about his life at that point in time.

They prolonged the night. They stood there on the front portico putting off the inevitable last caress, that last embrace. Neither wanted it to end and it took a long time to say 'goodnight.'

Sunday evening was no easier than all the others. Brian took her in his arms, and held her close as if he could make them blend into one. "This takes too much out of me every blasted Sunday. Knowing that it'll be a week before I see you again."

"It does hurt. And there seems to be no end in sight." She looked out over the campus, a frown indicating her restlessness with the thought. "It would be so nice to have some normalcy in our lives."

"What's normal anyway?" He asked.

"Brian, I've never been one to live on the edge. I still have a lot to deal with when I think about you leaving, and what you do every day."

"Hey, we can deal with these things one at a time. For now let's think about the two and a half months we've got together."

"I hope that's enough. When you're half way around the world, and doing God knows what in Korea, there will be no 'think only of now'. Reality will have set in big-time about then."

"C'mon, we've got each other. That's all that's important." He kissed her several times. "See ya' next week." He spun around and ran for the car before she could respond. He had a five-hour drive waiting and ample time for reminiscing about this weekend.

The alarm rang for a long time before Brian could manage to find the shut off and get his bearings. He wanted to flop back down and close his eyes. He rolled slowly off the bed. He forced himself toward the shower. The warm water ran over him, sedating him farther, as he nodded his head against the wall. His hand found the hot water valve and he quickly twisted it off. The cold water revived him enough to get to the first class. There was no time for breakfast or even a cup of coffee.

Hank slid into the chair next to him in the classroom. "Well, how did it go this weekend?"

Brian slowly turned his face toward Hank but made no reply.

"Jesus, you look beat up. What time did you get in this morning?"

"About four-thirty."

"Well, thank God I'm not flying with you this afternoon."

"Hey, You've been my RO for three days now, and you've already lost faith in me. I'm crushed."

"It ain't faith I need if you fall asleep up there. It's a damn stick in the back seat. I can't fly it with the radar hand control."

"Well, if you ever hear snoring on intercom, just punch out. But don't wake me on the way out."

This wasn't the best way to begin a new crew relationship, or a Monday morning. They were feeling each other out, still not sure of the others personality. Brian did his best to listen to the concept of radar's reflective energy, and what type of objects correlate with various echo returns on the screen. Several times he nodded and caught himself. His head bobbed almost to the top of the desk. He looked at Hank to see if he noticed.

Hank was looking his way. "Hey, don't worry about what he said. It's not really important. Just the whole concept of a radar intercept."

"That's why they gave you to me, so you can explain it all later." Brian retorted.

"How 'bout next Monday I bring you a pillow?" Hank said.

"Thanks, that would be very considerate of you, and you can fluff it periodically." Brian stated softly.

The banter continued through the morning classes until they broke for lunch. "Let's hit the Club for a sandwich. I think I'm awake now." Brian said.

"Your eyes look like a road map. But that 'ole F-94'll get the red out in about two hours." Hank stopped smiling. "Now, tell me what was so important last weekend. You left in a cloud of dust and came back looking like something the hounds drug in."

"I got engaged."

Hank looked at Brian for several seconds as if he wasn't quite sure what he'd just heard. "No wonder you were hell-bent to get to Alabama, and that's not a shabby reason for looking like a pile of dog mess this morning. Congratulations!"

"Thanks."

"Try to stay awake for your orientation flight in a couple of hours. Soon you'll have me in the back seat."

"It'll be the experience of your life, Hank, believe me."

Scott passed by the table with his RO. He slowed beside Brian. "Did ya' do something weird this weekend?"

"Yep." Brian grinned.

"Way to go, Hoss. I'll get details later." Scott's voice fading as he moved on.

At 1300 Brian pulled into a vacant spot in front of the squadrons' operations building. The sight of the sleek F-94's lined up was, as always, an impressive sight. It's bulbous nose housing the radar scope stood out prominently. The rear was enlarged to accommodate the afterburner. As Brian stood there, mesmerized by the aircraft, a large, friendly-looking Captain moved beside him.

"Hi, I'm Doc Blankenship. He pointed toward the F-94's. "Not a bad lookin' bird, is it?" He glanced in Brian's direction for confirmation. Brian nodded. "If you'll go get suited up, we'll go see how it flies." "I'll show you the cockpit, and you'll get your first and last ride in the back seat. After this, you'll have some respect for the cramped quarters your RO has back there. See you in ten minutes." He ambled on toward the operations building.

Brian went through a preflight inspection, taking making careful mental notes of what was important. He walked around the aircraft and examined it in awe. He climbed into the back seat, immediately experiencing the cramped space and limited forward vision for the RO. Sliding on his helmet, he cinched the oxygen mask tight, and adjusted the seat belt and shoulder harness. The console dropped almost in his lap as he released the lever on the side. It was claustrophobic.

Doc explained the start procedure, throwing in a few tricks of the trade as he prepared for take off. "Brian, lean forward and look to your left over the radar console. I want you to watch me engage the afterburner for takeoff. Okay, we're ready to roll. Throttle up to one hundred percent RPM, then move the throttle over to the left into the detent position." The roar of the flame out the tail pipe was thunderous, as the aircraft leaped forward.

"Good God. What a kick in the butt." Brian shouted as the aircraft accelerated rapidly down the runway, and vaulted into the air. The nose came up gracefully, pointing up toward a sapphire horizon, with no reference to the ground below. He felt exhilarated as he looked into a solid panorama of blue.

Doc pulled the throttle out of the detent position and the roar diminished to a low-pitched whir. He lowered the nose to a moderate rate of climb. "You don't want to keep it in burner longer than necessary. Use it to make a 'scramble' takeoff or climb to altitude rapidly. This thing uses about fifty gallons a minute in burner. With eight hundred and sixty gallons of fuel, you see you'd have only twenty minutes of fuel.

Doc cut it short and called for landing as soon as the tip tank fuel was used up. "Tomorrow, take it up, get some air time, then come in and shoot a couple of full stop landings. After your solo flight tomorrow, it'll be intercept training with your RO. That's where the rubber meets the road, Lieutenant."

As they walked away from the flight line, Brian glanced back at the silver aircraft. An idea came upon him. Tomorrow would be the only time he'd ever be alone in an F-94 before leaving the States, and Ruston was only twenty minutes away. The thought was irresistible.

As soon as he opened the door to his room he began planning the big buzz job of Ruston, Alabama. He laid the chart out on the desk, and drew a line directly to Montgomery VOR radio beacon, then drew a second line direct from Montgomery radio to Ruston. He wrote down the heading from Panama City to Montgomery in bold numbers on the chart. He sat back and looked at his planning, including all of the headings, and estimated times en route.

The morning breeze off the Gulf was crisp and invigorating. The sun hung red and clear just above the scrub pines to the east, casting a reddish glow on the horizon. He scanned the sky to the North for clouds. The sky was pure azure. There were only the usual scuddy clouds that hang in over the land area around the Gulf of Mexico. It was an excellent day.

He almost jumped into his flight suit, grabbing his helmet, may west, and parachute as he headed through the door. He threw his chute up on the wing and placed his helmet on the windscreen while he completed the pre-flight inspection. There was a small amount of extra adrenalin flowing as he anticipated this first ride at the controls of an F-94, and the chance to make it a very memorable experience indeed.

Slipping down into the tight cockpit, he buckled up, put on his gloves, and then scanned the unfamiliar instrument panel. He knew the procedures cold, but refreshed his memory of the instrument panel he had only studied in pictures. The start procedure was normal and instrument readings were within limits. Brian called the tower for instructions. "Tyndall tower, Air Force two eight one six, taxi-takeoff."

"Roger, one six, taxi runway three six, altimeter two niner niner four, winds three five zero, ten knots, hold short of active."

"Eight one six, Roger."

Brian pulled out his en route data, clipped it to his knee holder, and double-checked headings. Checking the instrument panel quickly, he performed the "before takeoff" checklist and called the tower. "Tyndall, Air Force two eight one six ready for take off."

"Roger one six, you're cleared for immediate departure, traffic will be your eleven o'clock position, on downwind for landing."

"Roger, one six rolling."

The runway loomed in front of him as he lined up and pushed the throttle forward to 100 percent RPM. The engine began its whine toward maximum power, and his heart rate increased with the drone of the engine. His hand tightened his grip on the stick as he released the brakes. He told himself: *relax; it's a routine flight. No reason to be a little uptight just because you've never been in this type aircraft before, going on an unauthorized cross country flight, navigating totally unfamiliar terrain to make an illegal buzz job.* The release of tension, as the aircraft accelerated, caused him to laugh. Apprehension disappeared with the quickened speed of the aircraft.

His hand reached forward, setting a heading of 347 degrees in the VOR indicator window to intercept the radial of the Montgomery VOR. The aircraft leveled off at 20,000 feet, and the VOR needle settled down dead on the nose of the aircraft. *No sweat, Montgomery in eleven minutes.*

Montgomery loomed on the horizon, with the Alabama River winding around framing Maxwell Air Force Base.

The VOR needle swung indicating station passage. It was time to turn to a heading of 340 degrees, reduce power and begin a descent. A town he knew well shot by under his right wing, and he was only descending through 12,000 feet. His little finger actuated the speed brakes on the throttle handle as he eased the throttle back to twenty-five percent RPM. The altimeter began to unwind as the next small town zipped past his left wing.

Ruston was dead ahead. He glanced at his altimeter as he pushed the throttle back to 100 percent RPM and the airspeed/mach indicator climbed to 400 knots. Lowering the nose slightly, he and the aircraft hurtled along at a few feet above the trees. The campus was sighted dead ahead, as he leveled with Ramsay Hall, putting the gun sight right on the balcony. The airspeed was now going through 460 knots, approaching eight-tenths the speed of sound. Something silver blurred past the right side of the aircraft. Ramsay Hall disappeared under the nose in a blur.

He banked hard left, pulling four G's in a tight turn back to make the last pass. A town six miles from Ruston shot past. Speed was indeed relative and emphasized dramatically when familiar terrain disappeared so quickly. The G forces mashed him into the seat in the tight turn, pulling his facial muscles down until his chin was resting on his chest. He held the pressure on the stick until the compass indicated a ninety-degree heading. He rolled the wings level with the F-94 going down the street in front of Ramsay Hall. Remembering that "something silver" in a blur off of his right wing, he spotted the water tower. *Too frappin' close.*

The aircraft shot past the dormitory and down the road toward the Presidents' home. As the spacious grounds of the President's home zipped past, Brian sucked back on the stick, watching the horizon disappear. When the nose hit a vertical position, he rolled the F-94 twice and rolled out on a heading of 160 degrees, leveling off at 19,000 feet. He eased his helmet back against the headrest and smiled broadly.

Brian adjusted his pillow and lay back on his bed, feeling pleased about how the day turned out, especially the 'great buzz job.' He never told Scott what he did. There was no use taking chances with being grounded. A knock on the door broke his train of thought. He yelled, "C'mon in." Thinking it was Scott.

A young Corporal stuck his head around the door tentatively. "Lieutenant Brannon, you have a person-to-person phone call in the orderly room. They're holding."

"Okay, I'm on my way." Brian rolled off of the bed grabbing for his shirt and cap on a dead run. It alarmed him to be getting a person-to-person call. He ran all across the alley dividing the orderly room and BOQ, and burst through the door. The Sergeant pointed to a receiver lying off of the hook on the next desk. Brian clutched the phone. "Lieutenant Brannon."

"Hi." The softness of her voice was melodic. He cut her off immediately. "What's wrong Anne?"

"Well, I just wanted to ask you what happens when someone writes down your airplane's number and calls the Air Force?"

His heart dropped to his stomach. "Are you telling me that someone got a number off of an aircraft? What for?"

"Don't play dumb with me, Mister. You scared half the student body to death this morning. Do you know how close you came to the water tower?"

"That close, huh? I just wanted to say 'Hi'. You're kidding about somebody calling the Air Force, right?"

"Yes, but I was really embarrassed when the President of the College called me in, and asked me if I knew a Lieutenant Brian Brannon. I told him I never heard of him. He smiled knowingly and said, 'Well if you happen to talk to him, you might tell him that was a spectacular stunt this morning, but if it happens again I'll have no choice but to report it.' He said some of the old maids on campus were highly incensed over the incident and thought it very juvenile. I had to sit in psychology class and listen to Doctor Stennis use that as a prime example of childish, immature behavior. Frankly, it was pretty embarrassing as everyone in class kept turning to look at me. Seriously, that's why I called. Don't do that again." She hesitated. "President Coleman didn't take down your number or report it, but I assure you he will if there's a next time.

"Don't worry, it won't happen again. And tell Doctor Stennis she doesn't have the slightest notion of what she's missing with all that rigid, grown up behavior. By the way, how the hell did President Coleman know who it was?"

"Aw, come on, Brian. This is a small school. Besides, everybody in Ruston knew who it was."

"Well, so much for anonymity. You don't sound too happy. C'mon loosen up. I was just having a little fun."

"Obviously you enjoyed it more than doctor Stennis." She began to laugh.

"That's more like it. But I get the point. I'll try not to make myself the topic of your psych class again. See you this weekend. I love you."

"I love you too. Bye." She said softly.

Brian showered and headed for the Oyster Bar. As was expected, on any given afternoon, there at a table gulping oysters and beer was Scott and Buck. He pulled up a chair and began the usual dialogue of the 'Tyndall Flying Club'. After careful observations, at these afternoon gatherings, Brian began to agree with Scott about Buck's alcohol consumption. Bucks' actions, in this regard, were quite unique. When asked about it, Buck usually made some flippant reply. "I was a professional drinker before coming into the Air Force." or "That's the way I worked my way through the University of Pennsylvania." Occasionally, "It's the only state of mind for flying with Scott."

He was an extremely likeable guy, and if he ever offended anyone, it would be strictly by accident. After talking with Buck for a while, it was obvious he'd grown up with all of the things associated with the higher economic strata. Having a wealthy father, by any standard, probably provided some psychological explanation of Buck's excesses. He was booted out of prep school for inappropriate behavior toward a female teacher. A college record of boozing fraternity weekends, two wrecked cars, and mediocre grades provided enough worry for his father. "My father was pleased and relieved to see me go into the Air Force." He gave his little chuckle. "I reckon my father had hopes the Air Force would change my proclivity for the unconventional. And here I am in the midst of the most curious band of hell-raisers ever gathered together." Taking a long swig of beer, draining the contents, and bouncing the bottle on the table, he glanced up. "He musta' figured it'd do wonders for my drinking too." He slid his chair back and stood unsteadily. "See you guys when you're more sober."

With just Scott and Brian left at the table, Brian pushed back and looked penetratingly at Scott. "Tell me something. I can sorta' figure Buck's reaction to life. With you it gets somewhat harder. It's been on my mind since flight school." Scott looked up from his beer, eyes locked on Brian, waiting for the question.

"With a year of law school under your belt, wasn't it a little drastic to give it all up to go in the Air Force? You got that much love for flying or what?"

Scott rocked back in his chair, swirling the yellow liquid around in his mug. "There was another reason."

"I figured there was something else. It had to be."

Scott finished his beer and pushed the mug away casually. He looked into it as if the question's answer was there in glass. "My father's one damn good attorney, too good, in fact. He had this no-good SOB for a client who was accused of murder. Shot a man in the face with double-ought buck shot right in front of his family." Scott pointed to his face. "There wasn't a whole helluva' lot left above his lower jaw." He lowered his voice that had changed pitch slightly. "The DA had an open and shut case, or so he thought. My father pulled off one brilliant defense. I mean absolutely incredible. The murdering bastard got off on a technicality. Can you believe that? Some small, insignificant, senseless piece of legal mumbo-jumbo got him off. Two weeks later, this depraved piece of garbage killed one of my friends because he felt he'd been insulted by him." His voice tensed again. "For some stupid remark the kid made at a traffic light, he punched him out as he got out of his car. His head hit the concrete like a ripe melon. Never regained consciousness. Later, I stormed into my father's office and told him what he'd done. No, actually I screamed at him. The man had no remorse whatsoever. He calmly said it was his duty to use any legal method he could in the defense of a client. I knew then I couldn't be a part of that. And, in some respects, I guess it was my way of punishing my father." He looked down into the mug and was quiet for a few seconds. Suddenly he looked up. "The answer to your question, Hoss, is: I do love to fly. That's why I'm here, the bottom line, whatever. Now let's get the hell outta' here before I tell you something important in my life."

Every flight was a new learning experience for both Brian and Hank. It forced a fine-tuning of the way their personalities blended. The 'honeymoon' of the first week evaporated with the pressures of flying. Sudden clashes of personality caused flashes of concern. They worked through each one, sometimes only after a complete venting of emotions. It wasn't easy for two strong personalities to blend completely in the confined area of a cockpit, moving through the sky at slightly under the speed of sound. Realization clutched at their thinking: they were completely dependent on each other for survival in this sometimes-unforgiving environment. This was particularly true for Hank. His life depended on Brian's skill as a pilot.

Hank was having a particularly difficult time seeing the scope. The sun slipped through the hooded radar scope, washing out the returns. He solved the problem by taking a up a poncho with him, throwing it over his head to completely darken the scope . . .

"Delta one, climb angels two three, your target is seven zero miles, two o'clock, angels two two."

"Roger, Control"

"Delta one, bogey is now five zero miles, two o'clock position. Bogey will be crossing starboard to port, angels two two."

"Control, Delta one level angels two three."

"Delta one, go buster, and acknowledge."

"Roger, Delta one going buster."

Brian moved the throttle to the detent position, as the aircraft lurched forward as the afterburner roared its answer in the rear. Hank picked up the bogey on his radar and began tracking the target.

"Control, Delta one, Tally-ho" indicating they had radar contact with the target. Hank took over control of the aircraft with his commands.

"Easy port, roll out, and continue easy port. Harder port, and roll out now. I've got lock-on. Bogey is twelve o'clock. Range eight thousand yards." Hank locked onto the target aircraft, which stopped the radar search function, and allowed the radar to point only to that target. Brian immediately got a presentation on the pilot scope as lock-on occurred. He pulled it out of afterburner and concentrated on the scope in front of him.

"Control, Delta one, Judy" indicating target was locked onto by the fighter. Hank called range and overtake as the F-94 bore in for the practice kill. "Three thousand yards, overtake fifty." Then, "two thousand yards overtake fifty, maximum firing range." A few seconds later, "One thousand yards, overtake still fifty, minimum firing range."

Brian squeezed the trigger on the stick, firing his imaginary, fifty caliber rounds from the guns. Hank called out. "Five hundred yards break!" Brian always made a break at the proper time, but this particular day, and for absolutely no reason, he decided to drop down a few feet and fly under the target aircraft.

Hank, however believed Brian had his head buried in the instruments and radar scope, and was about to collide with the target. The poncho over his head prevented him seeing what was taking place outside. Hank was sure he was about to die, that instant, in a midair collision. His last scream, at the top of his lungs, was, "Break, Goddamn it, break." As he flung the poncho off of his head just in time to see the target T-33 zip past over the canopy. Hank sat limp in the seat trying to compose himself enough to respond to the incident. He sat motionless, saying nothing.

After landing, Brian scrambled down the ladder, threw his chute and helmet on the wing, and began completing the aircraft flight log. Hank's hand found Brian's shoulder as he squeezed it in a steel-claw grip. Brian turned instantly to face Hank, looking into eyes that burned into his.

"My butt's in the back seat with only a radar console and no stick. I've got to trust the guy up front. Right now, I don't trust you worth a damn. You scared the holy shit out of me up there, because you like to get your kicks being a 'hot dog.' I've heard about that time when a pilot has just enough hours that he thinks he can do anything. That's when he's dangerous. I guess you're right about at that point, 'cause you're one dangerous sonofabitch." He stared hard at Brian, waiting for an explanation, an apology, or an outburst of some kind. Brian looked back, saying nothing, showing no emotion.

Hank stuck his finger in Brian's face. "Either you fly the intercepts as briefed, and knock off these bullshit, juvenile antics, or we can dissolve this arrangement right now! In fact, say the word and I'll be in the Flight Commander's office before you get the last syllable out."

Brian rubbed his shoulder. He looked at Hank long enough to realize they had found the breaking point. "Look, I'm sorry. I acted like a horse's ass and I should've been thinking about you back there." He fumbled with the pen as he placed it back in his left sleeve. He glanced at Hank with a look of concern. "We've got a lot more flying to do together. I won't do anything stupid like that again. I'll walk the straight and narrow. Now, let's try to finish this thing without any more of this kinda' crap between us."

A smile slowly crept across Hank's face. "Hell, you can't help being a horse's ass and you'll do something stupid again -- probably real soon." Both broke into laughter as Hank continued, "C'mon, let's go get a shower and some oysters. You're damn well buying tonight."

February twenty-second arrived, and it was time to leave Florida. Brian was anxious to have a thirty-day leave and some quality time with Anne. After tossing the last bag in the back seat, he turned and stuck out his hand. "I'll be waiting for you in San Francisco. Let it all hang out for the next thirty days. You need it."

Brian drove through the gates and departed Tyndall Air Force Base in a pensive mood. He would always have a soft spot in his heart for Tyndall. He smiled as he headed the Olds north for the last drive to Ruston.

CHAPTER ELEVEN

BRIAN LEANED BACK lethargically against the chair back beside the phone table. This was the first time he could relax like this in the past fifteen months. The release from responsibility and time-driven obligations made him languish in the perception. He took a deep breath and slowly dialed Anne's number, feeling no need to rush as he usually did when calling her. There was a soft "Hello" on the other end of the phone.

"How 'bout letting me spend a month with you?" Brian asked. "No rushed weekends, no leaving in two days; just some relaxing time."

"That feeling will take a while to soak in. A whole month without you dashing off on Sunday night seems too good to be true. But tell you what, you can rush up here right now. I'll be waiting out front."

"See ya' in ten minutes."

The February wintry cold lingered. The nip from the cold felt invigorating and made them quicken their pace toward their bench.

A formless slate-gray sky was loosing its light, as the muted sun moved toward the horizon. Their breath vaporized in the frosty air, mistily rising in front of them. He took her hand, turning her to him. "I've waited a long time for this leave and God, it feels great. I'm ready to slow the clock down, and stretch it out forever.".

"Give up on that. When we're together, it moves like lightning -- too fast to think about."

"Can't slow it down but I know a way to stretch it some." He moved toward their bench, sat quickly, took her hand and pulled her down beside him. "Come with me to San Francisco. That'll be our last chance to be alone and I want us to have those last few days together."

She frowned as she gazed out across the campus. "I don't know how Mama'll take to that idea." She tensed her jaw. "It doesn't really matter, 'cause I'm going."

"Now that's what I wanted to hear."

"Well, now I've got a little trip for you. Mama's planning on going to Aunt Carolyn's in two weeks. It's down near Destin, Florida. She asked me if you and I would like to go. You'd love it. It's beautiful down there on the Bay, very isolated, sand white as sugar, and the moon reflecting on the water. Very romantic."

"How could I say 'no' to that kind of build up?"

The first two weeks of leave faded away almost unnoticed. It was obvious to Brian that time was becoming a factor to reckon with again as they drove to Florida. Anne was delirious with the anticipation of being in a different environment than Ruston and school. It would be a time to spend hours alone on the beach. He watched her giddiness as they turned off onto the sandy road leading to the cottage. She grabbed his hand, smiling broadly as they pulled to a stop. He was thoroughly enjoying her elation, knowing she was happier than he had ever seen.

The white cottage sitting on a bluff of sand intrigued Brian, looking out over the blue-green water of the bay. Two huge oaks shaded it with Spanish moss clinging to limbs in irregular patterns of gray netting. A screened-in porch sheltered the front of the cottage, wind chimes at each end tinkling with the shifting breeze. The sound of muffled waves attracted his attention to the waters of the bay. He was still glancing back at the white caps as they moved through the gate. Aunt Carolyn stood on the top step waving at the approaching visitors. Brian noticed immediately she was a younger version of Anne's mother. She was exceptionally slim, her dark hair pulled back in a ponytail, chestnut eyes that sparkled, and a broad smile that beckoned.

Aunt Carolyn bounced down the stairs, hugging her sister, then Anne, patting her constantly on the back. Carolyn Walden was Mrs. Merrill's only sister. She was eight years younger than Anne's mother, and was more like an older sister to Anne than an Aunt. She glanced over Anne's shoulder, extending her hand to Brian. "Brian, I'm glad to finally meet you." She took his hand pulling him closer, as she hugged him tightly. She pushed him back, holding his shoulders. "I'm *really* glad you're here. Anne's very special to me." She smiled. "I approve." She continued staring at Brian. "C'mon in and relax. I've got a huge pitcher of cold lemonade that needs drinking. We'll unload the car later."

Walt Walden hitched up his pants as he rose from his chair, ambling toward the group. A smile eased across his face as he put his arm around Anne. "How's my favorite Niece?"

"Uncle Walt, I wish you had another niece so I could find out if I'm really your favorite."

"Of course you are, Annie. I wouldn't give you such a hard time if I didn't love you."

"There it starts again." Anne turned to Brian. "He knows I hate the name 'Annie'. He'd rather aggravate me than eat." His eyes moved up and down Brian as he spoke. "It's great having you down, Brian."

"Thanks, I've looked forward to it. Maybe I'll get to know Villa Tasso like Anne. You could see the anticipation building as we turned off the highway. She could hardly contain herself."

Walt smiled. "She's been like that since she was small. She loves this hunk of beach, the cottage, and especially the Gulf."

After dinner, Anne and Brian excused themselves and moved toward the porch. Brian took her hand as they moved down the steps toward the water. The waves rippled with reflected light, the setting sun casting a swath of orange across the crest of each breaker. The sky meshed with the water in melted tones of scarlet. The sky was furrowed with wispy layers of clouds. The colors arrayed across the horizon from pinkish to deep fiery red. Anne stopped and pointed to the sun as it was beginning its decent, gradually disappearing into the water. "I used to think you'd be able to hear the sizzle as the sun touched the water. I was about nine or so before I stopped listening for the sound."

"Hey, listen. I just heard the sizzle!" Brian said, as he cupped a hand to his ear.

"Okay, smart guy, I'll get you for that one." She grabbed him and pulled him down onto the sand. Holding his arms down she bit his neck playfully.

They sat in the sand with their backs leaning against the dunes and turned their face toward the soft warm sea breeze. Neither spoke as they watched the sun slowly fade into the water and the sky take on darker hews of red. The only sounds were the waves rolling against the sand as the tide began its inevitable march toward the dunes. The soft sea breeze, moist and cold, bathed their faces. She moved close to him, took his arm in both of hers, and rested her head on his shoulder. "What'cha thinking?"

"Oh, guess I was thinking how peaceful this is." He looked down at her. "And how perfect you make it. Contentment's the word. How 'bout you?"

"I looked at the sunset and knew it's sliding toward the other side of the world. And that's where you'll be soon -- halfway 'round the world."

"I'll be close in other ways." Brian said. "But for right now, let's forget about that. I'd rather you bite on my neck again."

Her back arched as she dropped his arm and narrowed her eyes. "How the devil can you be so blasted flippant about it -- Korea, the war, people dying?"

Brian reached out and took back her hand, clutching it tightly. "Easy there. I need to tell you something I believe." He looked directly into her eyes. "You have to take responsibility for making choices. I made one about the Air Force and I made one about you. Sometimes choices come with a little risk." He laughed. "Hey, I took a helluva' risk falling in love with you, and look what happened."

"I don't think that's so funny. I sometimes believe you; Scott and the others, get a kick out of the danger. It's some kind of high you feed on."

A rascally smile crept across his face as if he'd just been caught with his hand in the cookie jar. "C'mon, let's forget about all that. That view out there and this topic don't seem to go together." He kissed her as they lay back in the sand in each other's arms, holding onto each other tightly as if that was their protection from the rest of the world. He wished he could stop time and stay right here. But he knew this was only a temporary sanctuary that would vanish abruptly.

Once back in Ruston, Brian mentally began preparing for the time he would have to leave. He took time to enjoy his surroundings rather than take them for granted as he always had. Slowly drinking another cup of coffee, he would hover around the breakfast table talking to his mother. He was reluctant to interrupt this time spent with her. Even when Aunt Betty came for a visit, he enjoyed the two of them in their non-stop conversations. They reminded each other of past incidents and laughed about the shared experiences. He felt he was establishing ties that had been denied to him, as he soaked up family history and stories of years gone by.

One morning, as he rose from the table, Aunt Betty took his arm without speaking a word and directed him toward the front porch. He made no challenge to her direction. Aunt Betty was his grandmother's sister, but with a fourteen-year difference in their ages, she was more like a sister to Brian's mother than an aunt. Brian's mother had always relied upon Aunt Betty for her strength and patience. She was her confidant in times of anxiety.

Even though her blonde hair was progressively turning to a blend of gray, her appearance was more youthful than her age. She was a strong woman, in stature and personality. She survived the death of her husband and her daughter with stoicism, never evading her role as family matriarch. At the age of fifty-five, she remarried a quiet, gentle man. He was her composed force of support she so well deserved. The family was delighted she found Uncle John to provide her the support she always imparted to her family.

She sat on the swing and put her hand down beside, her emphasizing that was where she wanted him to be seated. "Brian, we never have talked about your father. While Elizabeth is absorbed back in the kitchen for a few minutes, I'd like to talk to you. You'll be leaving soon and there are things you should hear before you leave."

"Why did it take my leaving the country for you to feel it's time to talk to me? Brian asked. "It's something that's bothered me most of my life."

"Frankly, I wasn't sure what your feelings were about your father all these years. You've never been one to open up with your feelings, Brian. This is really the first chance I've had to talk to you about him."

"Is what you're about to tell me gonna' change all those years? One split second later, everything is gonna' be okay?"

"No, quite the contrary, Brian." She frowned at him. "I don't know how you'll react, but at least you would've heard things that could put some closure to your feelings." A seriousness Brian had never seen was mirrored in her face. "Listen to me. It just might make a difference." She hesitated, then softly began, "Your mother was only eighteen when she met your father, who happened to be a very sophisticated twenty-eight. She was swept off her feet by his charm and good looks. It was obvious Ben had a drinking problem but Elizabeth was blinded to it by her infatuation. She'd been sheltered and spoiled all her life, and certainly wasn't emotionally stable enough to deal with this kind of problem. She was convinced everything would be different later. She was in love. Her senior year, in spite of her father's opposition, she accepted a ring right there beside the old cemetery on A-B campus." She smiled. "I must admit, he was one of the most charming men I've ever known. Elizabeth knew her father would never let this wedding take place. Ben was from one of the finest families in Alabama but the age difference and drinking were an absolute no-no to her father. So, the next weekend they eloped." She touched Brian's hand as she continued. "If your father had married anyone with more maturity, things might have turned out differently. Oh, I'm certain both of them loved as much as is humanly possible for two people to share such feelings. It simply wasn't enough." She looked at Brian, searching to see his reaction. He sat there stoically listening, a serious look of inquiry on his face.

"Well, go on. Let's hear it all." Brian said.

She smiled, looked out over the yard, gathering her thoughts to continue. "No matter how hard they tried, they could only struggle with trying to meet the other's needs. Your father was a perfect gentleman, except when he drank. He would go months and never touch a drop. Then, only God knows what made him do it, he would drink for days. There was a personality change that went with the drinking. He had a temper that was astonishing. That's the problem you've never understood. Your mother believed she had no choice in the divorce. I think she believed she was doing it for you as well as herself. Later, his death was such a shock to her. I know now, she'll never get over it. That's why I wanted to talk to you. To try to get you to understand why it's been so difficult for you both. Brian, it's time for you to know something about your father's death. It's going to take some real understanding on your part. This won't be easy for you to ..."

"What in the world is going on with you two? You both look so serious." Brian's mother interrupted as she came out onto the porch, still wiping her hands on her apron. "What were you two talking about?"

"Brian was telling me about how a jet engine actually works. Fascinating. Maybe later we can finish this story." Aunt Betty smiled at Brian.

"Don't stop on my account. Looks as if it was a very interesting topic." Elizabeth gave both a knowing look. The conversation changed abruptly and Brian would have to wait.

Time continued to move inexorably forward on the calendar. Spring announced itself subtly as buds on the pear trees opened slowly, followed by azaleas coming out of hibernation, then the dogwoods dotting the woods with white and pink splotches of color. Their beauty was lost in the realization of the inevitable, the one thing he had forced from his thinking. It was time to leave.

Anne rushed to complete all her assignments so that worrying over some drudgery of classes that hadn't been completed wouldn't distract her. "Brian, I need one full night in the library to finish a term paper for psychology class."

"Okay, that'll give me an opportunity to tell Lori "Goodbye. I feel bad about neglecting our friendship during these last weeks at home. I hope she understands. She always does."

He met Lori in the lobby of Ramsay Hall for a trip to The Oaks. "Hi, Missy. I know we haven't been spending much time together lately, and I accept all the blame."

"Well you should. I'm tired of sharing you with Anne anyway."

"You won't have to tonight. I'm all yours." He said. "How hungry are you?"

"You wouldn't believe it if I told you. I didn't eat lunch, just anticipating that barbeque."

"Then let's get down there." He grabbed her hand and ran for the car.

The drive to The Oaks was short as usual. "Tell me the news with Don these days. It's too bad we didn't have a chance to meet and compare 'Missy notes.' There's probably a volume or two we could fill if we collaborated."

"Now you know why I made sure you two never got together. But since you asked, Don's doing fine. He's flying out of Tachikawa, Japan. He told me he flies to Korea, Okinawa, even the Philippines. He hopes to get a leave in Hawaii before his tour is over."

"Don't be surprised if you get an invitation to meet him there. Would you go?"

"Certainly not! I've told you before, we aren't into that kind of relationship."

"Not yet." He said.

"Brian Brannon, I've wasted all of this time trying to train you, obviously with no success at all. Speaking of trips, Anne told me she's going with you to San Francisco. Very romantic." She gave him a knowing smile.

"I still find it hard to believe, but it worked out after all." Brian reached for the radio to turn up the volume.

"Here, let me do that for you." Lori adjusted the knob to a soft background of music. She turned toward Brian as if she wanted to say something, but wasn't sure of the words to express what she felt. Instead, she turned quickly and looked out of the window.

Brian glanced over. "Lori, what's wrong?"

She snapped her head around, smiling. "What happened to 'Missy.' Now it's 'Lori' all of a sudden."

"Boy, oh boy, if that wasn't a classic bit of misdirection. You can change the subject, toss it right back, and never miss a beat."

"Yeah, it's called 'home court advantage'." She said.

Dinner at The Oaks was delicious, and they continued their talk about ordinary events. Occasionally, they approached topics less mundane, but quickly veered back to the less serious. Brian wiped a bit of barbeque sauce with his napkin, held up the remains of his sandwich. "About two months from now, I'm gonna' be wishing for one of these in a big way."

"That, and *several* other things, fella'."

His smile suddenly disappeared. "Unfortunately, Missy, that's for damn sure."

They chatted, and laughed all the way back to the campus. Brian parked the car and switched off the ignition. Lori reached for the door, and looking back, said, "I'll go see if Anne's back from the library."

"No." Brian grabbed her arm. "She's gonna' be writing that report most of the night. Please sit here with me for a while. It'll be quite a while before we talk again."

"I know." She said in a lowered voice.

Neither said anything for a long time. Brian reached over and turned on the radio again. She took his hand off the knob and turned it off. "We don't need any diversions, do we?"

"No, we don't. I wanted to talk to you about so many things, but now that I've got you here, I don't know how, or where, to begin. You've always been the one person I could talk to. I could always let my hair down with, and here I sit, like a fool, with nothing to say."

"I understand. You've probably bottled up a lot of feelings about the future. I know you've got some apprehensions about where you're going, and leaving Anne."

"This is my job, I asked for it. But I'm going to miss all of you, Ruston, and my mother. Leaving Anne is going to be damn hard." He let his chin rest on his chest.

"I wish I had some magic elixir for what you're feeling. I don't. For whatever it's worth, you're gonna' be missed too." She turned her head away and looked out of the window again. "Damn, I didn't want to do this." Her hand reached toward her eye. "I'm sorry."

"Don't be." He said.

She turned toward him and put her head down on his shoulder. He felt the moisture of a tear against his cheek. Brian put his arm around her and reached with the other into his pocket for a handkerchief. "Here, use this."

"Thanks. Now, say something funny so we can change the subject." She wiped her eyes, sat upright, and smiled at Brian.

"You'll drop me a note once in a while, right?" He asked.

"Sure will. I expect you to do the same. I'll keep an eye on Anne." She leaned over and kissed him on the cheek. "Be careful and hurry back."

"You've got my word on both."

She reached for the door handle and looked back at Brian. "Do me a favor and don't walk me to the door. I think I'll sneak up the side stairs." She patted his hand. "Bye."

"Bye, Missy."

Lori opened the door and began walking toward the side door. Suddenly, Brian swivelled in the seat, jumped out of the other side, and ran after her. "Wait a minute." He grabbed her arm gently and turned her toward him. He took her in his arms and hugged her tightly, holding her in his grip for several seconds. "Now, that's a proper 'Good bye' for us."

She didn't reply. She just looked up at him with a half smile on her face, reached up and touched her hand against his face. He turned, and walked back to the car. As he reached for the door handle, he glanced back. She was still standing there.

CHAPTER TWELVE

T HE PHONE RANG the fourth time, as Brian waited impatiently. "Hello," announced the voice in the receiver.

"Aunt Betty, sorry you couldn't make it up from Selma yesterday, but I understand Uncle John's doing better. It's a wonder he didn't kill himself trying to paint the trim on ceilings that high. He's lucky to have only a couple of cracked ribs."

"Every time he breathes it's my reminder to him he should've listened to me." She laughed that hearty laugh Brian had heard so often. "Now, as for you; take care over there." She hesitated. "Brian, please be careful. We love you. I'm so sorry John and I couldn't be there to tell you 'Goodbye'."

"I'm gonna' miss all of you too. By the way, time just got away from us before we had another chance to finish the conversation we started on the porch that afternoon. You know, when you were about to tell me about my father. What was it you didn't finish that day?"

There was silence on the other end of the phone. "Aunt Betty, you still there?"

"Yes, I'm here. Brian, you're aware of most things I wanted you to think about. Let's not get into more psychological scrutinizing on the phone. Just accept the fact your mother made the best decisions she could at the time. Take my word for that, and don't keep placing your pent-up anger of losing your father at her feet. For right now, try to establish some real communication with your mother before you leave. Will you do that?"

"I don't think we can do in one day what we couldn't do for twenty-one years. Thanks for being for being my favorite Aunt. Let me know about Mom, Okay? See you soon."

Brian slowly lowered the phone onto the receiver as he contemplated the conversation. The mystery created in his thinking about his father should've been resolved. What he'd just been told only made him more inquisitive. Even though he wanted the answers, it wasn't the time to bring this up with his mother. He moved slowly to his room to continue packing.

He felt someone watching, and wheeled around to see his mother standing in the doorway. "You startled me. Come on in and talk while I throw these last few things in the bag. I can see me now, wandering through airports dragging this sixty-pound bag behind me. Just because they say you're allowed that much, doesn't mean you gotta' make sure you've got every ounce of it in there." He laughed as he made conversation, glancing at her for a reaction. She sat on the bed, still looking introspectively at the bag, saying nothing. Suddenly, a forced smile replaced the absorbed look.

"You sure you've got everything? How about me sticking a small thing of cookies in there for you to eat somewhere between here there?"

"I couldn't get a toothpick in here. Thanks anyway." He walked over and sat beside her. "I sure don't have to tell you we've never been able to express our feelings very well. I'm sorry it's been that way over the years but maybe we can begin to do a better job from now on about things that matter." Brian put his hand on her shoulder. "I don't usually do a very good job of saying it, but I love you."

She wiped at the tears that rolled down her cheeks with the handkerchief she held in preparation. "I've always known that. It's been hard for us to verbalize our feelings. But it's really not necessary. We both know how the other feels. Now, please be careful over there. Make sure you come back to me. You're all I've got."

"Don't you worry, I'll be back before you know it. Just take care of yourself." He nervously stood up pulling the bag off to one side. He fidgeted with his uniform he'd left out to wear and tried to force attention away from his tenseness. "Let's go finish off that coffee we left in the pot."

She got up, tucking the handkerchief away in her pocket. "That sounds like a good idea." She smiled broadly, easing the tension of the situation that neither was familiar with. "You might be tempted to finish that last bit of banana pudding in the refrigerator." She added.

The weather in San Francisco was a marked contrast to Ruston where there was a premature heat wave for early spring. The cooler temperature in San Francisco was apparent as they left the plane and walked through the terminal. Anne pulled her collar up around her neck; trying to ward off the moist, cool air that clutched at them. As they stood waiting for a taxi, she gave a shiver, folding her arms around her chest for insulation. The chill in the air added to the invigorating atmosphere of the Bay Area. Both were in awe of the city and its landmarks as they rode to the hotel. Anne leaned forward to get a better look at the buildings. She looked at Brian and smiled. "You had a pretty good idea here, Lieutenant. We're going to enjoy every minute of this place – right?"

"Absolutely."

They strolled through the lobby, taking careful note of their selection of accommodations. Brian approached the desk at the hotel, asking about the reservations for their room. The room was surprisingly large; had a small sitting area, and comfortable bath. Brian tipped the bellhop, then sat and dialed the number he'd written down for the 2349th Personnel Processing Group at Camp Stoneman. He listened, gave a few 'okays," then placed the receiver in the cradle, and walked over to Anne. "The news is good. I've got until 2400 tomorrow to check-in and then I'll be released until Monday morning to begin processing. They estimated four or five days for a flight to Japan."

"Great. We'll make the most of every one of those days."

They walked along Fisherman's Warf with all the excitement of first-time visitors. The lights along the streets and distant sounds of the bay surrounded them. The sea air had a sweet musty aroma. They inhaled deeply, taking in the salty flavor of it.

After dinner and a nightcap at the hotel lounge they went up to room. She moved beside him, looking out the window toward the water, listening to the sounds of boat horns mournfully murmuring in the distance. Brian took her hand, leading her across the room. They fell across the bed, holding each other, talking most of the night, falling asleep occasionally in each other's arms. What initial awkwardness there was at the beginning, the unspoken question of what level of intimacy each expected from the other was soon dispelled. Their mutual concern was to just savor these last moments without complications. Life rushed at them with an onslaught they had never experienced. Brian fought back with an outward calm, while a constant churning of anxiety maintained its tempo in his gut.

Brian and Hank began processing Monday morning. A personnel records check began the day, which ended with all the shots that had ever been conceived for foreign duty. They listened intently at briefings for possible assignments within Fifth Air Force. The mystery would only be solved when they reach Japan. It appeared that Wednesday would be the earliest they would leave. Thursday was more likely. The only requirements were a check-in call at specified times each day and a phone number where he could be reached.

Anne finally met Hank and they hit it off immediately. There was an instant rapport, as if the constant descriptions by Brian had blended their personalities in a familiar way to both. Hank joined them for the next two days of sightseeing and lunch. There was very little of the Bay area that was missed. They rode across the Golden Gate Bridge, then up Knob Hill. They swung awkwardly onto cable cars, walked through China Town, and viewed Alcatraz from the boat tour. Hank was tactful, excusing himself later in the afternoons.

Brian and Anne spent the nights completely engrossed in each other. They were totally happy until momentary flashes of reality punctuated their joy. Even though there were times it felt like ice surging through the veins, the inevitability of leaving each other was never discussed. It was a time to talk of emotions, too long stored, and sensitivities to life not fully acknowledged. Brian talked about his relationship with his mother. He needed to talk about it, to share this with Anne. He started to tell her about the conversation with Aunt Betty, but stopped. There was no use relating something he didn't understand himself. There was a hunger to exchange as much of their life as possible in the few hours remaining. They wanted to reach deep into each other's being, grasping for that which could not be completely revealed – wanting desperately to know that which couldn't be known. They were mildly successful in forcing away maudlin thoughts of what tomorrow would bring. This day, this hour, this moment was to be lived with all their energy. Inwardly, there was the constant disturbing realization he had to leave her. It gnawed at his insides, never retreating, never relinquishing its grip. He hated the specter of time.

Tuesday morning, Brian made his usual check-in call. He hastily jotted down notes as he grunted understanding of the conversation, never changing his facial expression. Anne noted the call took longer than previous days, but even though she observed closely, she couldn't see anything in Brian's demeanor to suggest anything out of the normal. He casually reviewed his notes.

Lv Travis 1045. Commercial to Tokyo. check-in pax desk NLT 0845. ride bus from Stoneman at 0730, or report dir. to dispatcher. 2 bags max. wt. 60 lbs.

He folded the paper and briskly placed it in his pocket. He walked over and grabbed her hand, pulling her to him. "I thought tonight we'd do something special. We'll start with dinner at the Fairmont and then dash across the street to the Mark Hopkins for a drink at the Top of The Mark. How does that sound?"

"Sounds great."

That evening, Brian buttoned his blouse, adjusted his tie, and knocked on the bath room door. As she opened the door he stood there, hypnotized, staring at her. She was a vision of absolute beauty; standing there in the black dress she wore the night they got engaged. He let his brain absorb as much of the image as his senses could digest, wanting to retain the image for as long as possible. "Well, does your stare mean approval or just that I need to adjust my makeup?"

"You're beautiful, absolutely beautiful." He said.

"If this dress meets with your approval, I've got something for you." She walked over to her suitcase, reached into the inside pocket and took out a silver frame containing a five-by-seven picture. "I want to make sure you can remember how I look on very special occasions in San Francisco."

Brian took the picture and looked at it for several minutes. He was speechless as he looked at the picture of Anne wearing the same black dress. He sat down on the bed, cradling the picture between his hands, continuing to look at the picture.

"Hey, you've got the real thing right here. Save that for later."

The Fairmont was impressive, as expected. The dining room was as elegant as the rest of the hotel. Once they were seated, Brian ordered wine, and then reached in his pocket, taking out a small jewelry box. Opening it, he said, "I thought this would remind you of what I constantly try to tell you." He pulled out a small gold square pendant on a chain. "The square contains each of the letters for 'I love you'."

She stared at the square, reading each of the letters ingeniously blended into the design. She looked up and shook her head in disbelief. "Only you would have thought of this. It's absolutely beautiful." She held it out to him. "Here, help me put it on."

He walked behind her and fastened the clasp. She looked over her shoulder, with her hand on the gold square. Her expression suddenly clouded. "Is there any reason why you picked tonight for this?"

"Well, no more so than the picture." His lying was too obvious.

"We'll talk about this after dinner." He glanced at the approaching wine Steward. "Great. Here's the wine."

"Do you have a reporting time? Is that what took you so long to jot down when you were on the phone?" The tone of her voice indicated her anxiety.

Brian tasted the wine, nodding his acceptance to the wine steward.

"Look at me." She said emphatically. "Stop evading the issue, Brian."

He put his glass down, looking into the crystal as if he could find an appropriate answer. The wine steward, sensing the tension, placed the bottle in the ice bucket and left immediately. Brian looked up from his glass. "I was going to tell you after dinner." He cleared his throat. "I'm leaving early tomorrow morning. I have to be at Travis by oh eight forty-five tomorrow."

Anne made no reply. She stared at Brian with a blank expression, as if nothing said had been heard.

"Don't look so shocked." He said. "We both knew this was coming."

"Then why didn't you tell me this afternoon? Why spring it on me now?"

"Would it have sounded any better this afternoon, this morning, or yesterday, for that matter? It's the damn inevitable – no matter when I tell you."

She glanced around the room, as if there was someone there who could undo the situation. "Of course, I knew it was coming. It would've been better if you'd given me a little more warning. Maybe it would've been easier to adjust to the shock of hearing it. I just wasn't ready for it. It's too soon. Just a couple of more days."

"There would never be enough days for us." He stopped her

thought. "Look at it this way. The sooner I leave, the sooner I'll be back."

"That kind of psychology won't make it with me. Not right now."

"Come on, do you want to spend the last few hours arguing about something like this?" He looked at her quizzically.

She shook her head and whispered: "No."

They ordered dinner and said very little. Gradually, the mood eased as they reconciled to the inevitable. Both laughed and joked during dinner, trying to disguise the hollow feeling that nagged at them.

"As soon as we get back to the hotel, I'll call and see if you can get reservations out tomorrow. When you get to Birmingham, give Lori a call. I'm sure she'd be glad to meet you."

Anne was only half-listening to the suggestions but nodded her head in approval. Brian looked up often while eating, trying to absorb the persona that he had to carry in his memory for a long time.

He paid the check and they walked through the lobby, into the crispness of the evening. The night air was refreshing and they inhaled deeply as they crossed the street to the Mark Hopkins. She suddenly threw her hands in the air. "I love San Francisco. This is such a romantic place."

"Yeah, it lives up to its reputation." He looked at her for a long time. "It depends entirely on who you're with." He pulled her close. "San Francisco, Ruston, Collinwood, it doesn't matter, as long as we're together."

She slid her arm around him, looking intently at him. "We should have gotten married the day you started your leave. I'm sorry we didn't."

The panorama from the Top of The Mark was breathtakingly beautiful. Their table by a window, overlooking the Bay, afforded a view of the Golden Gate Bridge, shrouded in the evening mist. The lights of passing ships blurred through the fog, creating a surrealist scene. The barely audible sound of foghorns enunciated the murky exterior. The waiter took their order, a Brandy Alexander for Anne, and a bourbon and seven-up for Brian.

"Excuse me, Lieutenant, but do you want yours from a 'Squadron bottle'?"

"I'm sorry, what's a 'Squadron bottle'?"

"I thought that you ... well, we have a lot of Air Force people coming back. Their squadron maintains a bottle of excellent whiskey, reserved for members of the Squadron who stop here. The last one to empty the bottle buys a new one. Take a look over there behind the bar. All those on the second shelf are 'Squadron bottles.'" Anne glanced around also. "I see the Air Force has a lot of Squadrons over there, or they do a lot of drinking."

"A little of both, ma'am. They've got a lot of tradition, and I reckon they do know how to drink a bit, too."

"I'm sure they do." She said, with a half-smile. "So that's what they call it?"

"I'll have one from that shelf next time." Brian stated. "I happen to be headed the other way right now. Just bar bourbon for me, thanks."

A few minutes later, the waiter brought the drinks, and set them down carefully. "Folks, these are on the bartender. He wishes you luck, and hopes you have a memorable evening." Brian looked up and Anne turned to see the bartender smiling and gave a wave. "Tell him we really appreciate it." Brian held up his glass to the bartender with a silent toast.

There was a small combo playing on the other side of the room. The music added another dimension to the atmosphere as some of their favorite songs garnered their attention between traces of conversation. When the waiter came back to take an order for another round, Brian asked for his pen. He scribbled a note on a napkin and handed it to the waiter along with a folded bill.

When the waiter delivered the note, the bandleader's search followed the pointing of the waiter. The leader grinned broadly in their direction, and gave a thumbs up. The strains of *La Vie En Rose* began.

Anne reached across and placed her hand on his. "It wasn't hard to guess. Don't know if I'll want to hear that song after you're gone. I...." Her voice trailed off. A tear ran down her face as she tried to smile through it. She finally wiped the tear and sat up straight. "Enough of that."

The music continued, and the vocalist joined in for the next refrain, *When you press me to your heart, I'm in a world a part, A world where roses bloom, And Angels sing from above, Ev-'ry day words seem to turn in-to love songs. Give your heart and soul to me And life will always be La Vie en Rose.*

It was impossible for her to completely stop the tears. One would occasionally roll down her cheek. Brian swallowed, having no luck at trying to dislodge the lump in his throat. It had suddenly become a bittersweet night. Leaving her was becoming the hardest thing he'd ever done. It was wrenching his insides. "I know I don't have to say it, but It'll make me feel better if I do. I love you, completely and unconditionally. Don't ever doubt that fact, no matter what happens. You've given me more happiness in the last few months than I believed possible to experience." He looked at her intently. "God, I love you so."

Anne shook her head, tears beginning to flow despite any control she employed to stop them. She slid her chair back suddenly. "Let's go back to the room. Please."

Neither spoke a word during the taxi ride back to the hotel. Each was lost in their own thoughts, as they rode in silence.

"Here we are, sir…"

Brian cut the driver's comments short by handing him the fare and tip and opened the door quickly. They walked rapidly through the lobby to the elevator. Then, at last, opened the door of their room into a sanctuary from the world. Brian threw his jacket on the chair, loosened his tie, and took her in his arms. He nuzzled her neck, kissed her gently on the ear, then her mouth. "It shouldn't be possible to love someone so much you can't tell them, or show them."

"You do it perfectly, in everything you say or do. You're always there to listen, to give me the support I need, and put things in perspective. Like I told you once, you barged into my life like a tornado – and I thank God you did."

The night was spent totally immersed in each other. They held each other the entire night, talking about the future, the past, and how much they were in love. Emotions engulfed them. It was impossible to be this much in love and not express it totally. They made love unconditionally, completely, consumed by their passion for each other. Eventually they slept, waking momentarily, once again making love, caressing each other, and then falling asleep in each other's arms.

The phone ringing pierced their world like a scalpel. Brian, still half asleep, acknowledged the wake-up call from the desk. He sat upright and put his feet on the floor, rubbing his eyes, still trying to wake up. Anne sat beside him. "I want to go with you to the plane. I need to see you off, okay?"

"We've already talked about this. Let's say goodbye here. It'd just make it harder for both of us and prolong the misery of this thing.

Let me just say 'Goodbye' and walk out that door. It's better that way, honestly." She nodded reluctantly, agreeing it was best they not keep stretching one more hour, one more minute. Time, their constant nemesis, had finally won. There was no reprieve, no detainment of this phantom that always pursued them. Now, they were face to face with the inescapable fact that time had evaporated. There was no more.

Brian showered and dressed as quickly as possible. He set the B-4 bag and the small over-nighter near the door. She handed him his blue uniform blouse and patted it gently. He buttoned the uniform while looking intently at her, thinking how beautiful she was.

"I won't know my address for several days but I'll send it as soon as I can." He stood there, looking at her for several minutes, filling his brain with the image of her. "Please tell Mom 'hello', and you might look in on her once in a while. Make sure you tell your mother how much I appreciate her understanding."

Her bottom lip trembled, but no tears. She said nothing.

"I'm gonna' miss you. I love you, Anne Hunter Merrill." He said as his voice quivered slightly.

"I love you, too, and I don't even want to think about how much I'm going to miss you. Please be careful. Please."

He walked to the door, opened it, and put his two bags outside in the hall. He turned and looked at her one more time, then they kissed each other intensely, not wanting to separate this last connection. "I'll be back soon. That's a promise, and you know I never break promises."

"Bye, hurry back to me."

The door closed, and Brian reached down to pick up the bags. He hesitated for a second or two, looking back at the door. He heard Anne's muffled sobbing, as he turned and walked quickly down the hall. He had just done the impossible.

CHAPTER THIRTEEN

FORWARD-LEANING SHAPES IN traditional Asian apparel moved at a shuffling pace, with only an occasional person in European dress mingled into the unfamiliar configuration. The scene provided a panoramic mosaic of color. The houses were small, close together, made unsubstantially of wood, fronted with heavy paper doors. Fish lay in neat rows on open stalls along the way, their pungent smell hung in the air like a cloud. Brian turned his head as if that would escape the stench. A feeling of loneliness swept over him like a gust of icy wind. It was apparent he had entered a different environment, one which he had no understanding or appreciation. Half a world and another culture separated him from home and those he loved. He looked out the window of the bouncing bus, his head bobbing in synchronization with each pot hole. His eyes swept the countryside, watching these strange-looking people at their daily tasks. His morale sank further at the sights from the bus as they entered FEALOGFOR Area "B," Higashi-Fuchu, Japan.

It quickly became apparent that all the guys who had permanent smiles affixed were the ones processing for return to the States. They glanced at the new arrivals briefly, as if embarrassed at their good fortune. The two groups, those arriving and those departing stood out like losers and winners after a football game.

On the afternoon of the second day, the newly arrived crews gathered for their unit assignments. Brian and Hank took a seat near the front, scanning the sparsely furnished room. Paint on the walls was fading, showing light and dark shades of green. The color gave the room a coldness, as if a foreboding for them being there. The mumbling voices of anticipation quieted as the briefing officer began calling off names and assignments. He read assignments methodically, not waiting for comments or questions. Eventually, he called out the names of Lieutenants Brannon and Evans. They glanced at each other nervously, waiting for the assignment about which they had speculated for the last two days. His voice droned on in monotone detachment. "Assigned to the eighty-sixth Fighter Interceptor Squadron, K-13 Korea." The minutia of transportation, departing times, and assembly areas faded, as the reality of their future became a reality. There was no more wondering

"Well, Hank, that answers that one. At least we know where the hell we're gonna' spend the next year. You ready for this?"

"Hell, no. It seemed a long way off when we were doing those intercepts back at Tyndall. We used to joke about it. Now that it's here I can't find a damn thing funny anymore."

"Know what you mean." Brian added. "I just want to get there, get it done, and get the hell back to the States."

The C-119 bounced onto the runway at K-13, and taxied onto the outer taxiway. "I wonder how many landings he's gonna' log after that 'bouncer?'" Brian punched Hank for a reaction, who only looked back blankly, as the engines coughed toward shutdown.

As they stepped off the aircraft, they scanned the boundary of what was known as K-13, Suwon, Korea. The terrain looked as if nothing green had ever grown there. Brown, repulsive dirt was everywhere. Sienna was the primary color of the terrain, producing the impression that the landscape was done as an abstract etching. Hills were faintly visible through the afternoon haze. In the foreground was a tract of scraggy ground where topsoil had been blown away.

The primary structures were Quonset huts, arranged in carefully laid out rows and fondly referred to as "hootches." The conical-shaped metal buildings gave a look of convex symmetry. Their corrugated exterior was cold and uninviting.

The aircraft along the strip were separated by sandbag revetments, a tank periodically placed on top of a sloping mound of dirt, obviously providing some type of protection. On the other side of the field were rows of F-86 Sabre jets, the MiG killers. Between the two areas, dividing the airbase in equal parts was the long 10,000-foot runway. Two F-86's roared down the runway, blending into the shimmering heat waves rising from the scorching concrete. They disappeared into the haze.

A lanky First Lieutenant, walked up to the pair, who stood immobilized by utter disbelief of their new surroundings. "Welcome to Hell," were his words of welcome. The official greeter stuck out his hand. "I'm Chuck Stroud, welcome to the eighty-sixth."

Brian gave him the once-over before responding. "I thought this was referred to as 'Frozen Chosen,' but Hell's more descriptive?" He stated, looking around the barren terrain.

"You got that right the first time. Wait 'till winter, and you'll appreciate that phrase. I was making a reference to our wonderful living conditions here on the back side of the moon."

"Thanks for all of the words of encouragement. Where do we check in?"

"You can start tomorrow. I'm here to help you get situated in your hootch. I believe you two are in six-twenty." He looked at a small note pad. "Yeah, follow me. I've got a jeep and driver to give you a lift to your cozy abode."

Brian and Hank took in their new surroundings as the offensive landscape shot past the jeep. Neither made a comment. The jeep pulled up to a Quonset hut with a black number 620 stenciled on a field of white to the right of the door of the building. They grabbed their bags off the back of the jeep and dropped them on the ground. Dust swirled up beside them.

Chuck took off his hat, wiping at the combination of dust and sweat with the back of his hand. "When you get your gear settled, come on over to the club and meet some of the guys. You're gonna' find you've been assigned to the best squadron in FEAF. We've got a great group of guys. Some weird." He chuckled. "And some even more weird."

"Okay. Oh, by the way, is a Scott Jeter in this squadron by chance?" Brian asked.

"So, you know Scott? Yeah, he's in white flight with me. Been here a couple weeks. Where'd you know ole Scott?"

"I went through flight school with him, basic and advanced, then Moody, and Tyndall. The four of us, Scott, Buck, Hank and I spent a lot of time together in Florida. Right, Hank?"

"Well, three of us anyway, never quite sure whether Buck was with us or not."

"If you see him or Buck, tell 'em that Brian and Hank will see 'em at the club later." Brian added.

"Will do. If you need anything, give a holler. Tomorrow you can start checking in."

They walked through the door of the Quonset hut with little expectation of the creature comforts they'd find inside. They weren't disappointed. The two empty bunks, one in each front corner, didn't exactly beckon to them. Furnishings consisted of two broken down straight chairs, four ammo crates nailed together with a top resembling a desk, and an oil stove prominently positioned toward the back of the hootch. Brian tossed his B-4 bag on the bunk farthest from the door. "Just in case you wanted this bunk, I'll flip you for it."

"No need. This one's fine with me. I can catch a better smell of that sweet aroma that permeates this friggin' place." Hank responded.

After a few silent moments passed, they looked at each other with a blank, questioning stare. Brian glanced casually out the open door with the bare, pockmarked hills as a backdrop. "Have you ever wondered why they can't fight a war in some place like the French Riviera, or Monaco, or any damn place that has decent weather and doesn't stink?"

"Well, I don't think Monaco has invaded one of our allies as of today, but you can always hope." He glanced up with a smirk. "As the fellow once said, 'This aint much of a war, but it's the only one we've got'." They fell back on their bunks laughing.

A tall Lieutenant filled the doorway, placing both hands on the frame; he paused there and looked around the hootch. He held his garrison cap under his left arm while he combed back his black hair with his right hand. "I was just told we've got two new roommates. We needed somebody to fill this thing up. It'll be less room for the rats." He moved quickly toward them with his hand extended. "Hey, guys, I'm Randy Hudson."

Hank introduced himself, then Brian. Hank immediately wanted to know all about K-13 and the squadron. "How long have you been here, Randy?"

"Five weeks, going on five years."

Brian stood up. "I'm damn glad to see everyone here is so frappin' encouraging and upbeat. I feel better already." He slammed his hat onto the mattress.

"Geez, I was just trying to be funny. It aint all bad. We've got a good group of guys here, and the best C.O. in Fifth Air Force." He chuckled. "Hey, wait till you meet Major Don Larson. He's great, different, but great."

The entrance of a gangly, sandy-haired Lieutenant, the fourth occupant of Building 620, interrupted the conversation. Randy introduced his RO, Frank Fisher, who moved briskly toward the two new inhabitants. He had a narrow face that matched his body. He had eyes you noticed. His eyes were a bright greenish-blue, and when he smiled, they were alive. His once-broken nose gave him an unbalanced, rugged look. Frank was an easygoing Texan, who instinctively liked everyone he ever knew. He was either the eternal optimist, or endowed with a personality extremely slow to get upset at anything. Randy was also easy going, but not blessed with the same eternal optimism of his RO. The four Second Lieutenants looked around at each other. Brian was happy considering what chance had dealt in the assignment of occupants to building 620.

Hank prodded the others for some movement toward the Officer's Club. "Let's go over and see if we know any of these characters. Besides, I could use a stiff drink about now." Without additional nudging, the other three grabbed their hats and followed him.

The Officers' Club was composed of several Quonset huts placed together to form a quadraplex. What it lacked in ambience, it made up in service. Conspicuous squadron emblems decorated the sidewalls around the bar, providing most of the color to the room. The camaraderie quickly indicated rank was not taken seriously here. Everyone relaxed together, ate together, played together, and drank together. Sometimes, they died together. Drinking was the primary daily ritual, providing escape from the danger and boredom. Seldom did people find the Club without a poker game in session. The bar had reasonably-priced drinks and tolerable food. Other than the hootch, this was the only place to spend time when not on alert or flying.

Brian scanned the room for Scott and spotted him at a table in the corner of the smoke-filled room with three other guys. He eased up behind Scott. Before he could say anything to startle him, the other guys glanced up, giving away his surprise.

Scott turned to see who, or what, was behind him. "Damnation, look who finally made it to Frozen Chosen. How th' hell are you, Buddy?" He swung around for a complete view. "And look, he brought along his trusty RO. Hi there, Hank."

"And where's *your* trusty RO?" Hank asked.

Scott nodded toward the bar. "You gotta' ask?"

Laughter surrounded the table. Hank shook his head. "Buck's reputation's established rather rapidly wherever he goes. Korea's no exception."

"Excuse me, fellas. I need to give my usual briefing to these guys. They send me out ahead to scout bases for 'em." Scott slid his chair back and began looking for a vacant table. He moved toward one in the corner. "There's a good spot over there. It's far enough away from this mob so we can hear a little conversation."

Settled at the table, Brian and Hank anxiously waited for the news, good and bad. Scott leaned his chair back on the two back legs and began. "Well, I don't reckon you'd classify this a 'garden spot', but I'm sure you can see that for yourself." Heads nodded affirmatively. "The eighty-sixth has a good reputation over here. Most of that's attributable to the C.O. He's one helluva' guy, a wild sonofabitch, but a real fighter pilot, a tiger. The squadron accounted for the first air-to-air kill of the war, the first all-weather squadron in Korea, and several other 'firsts.' The Lightning Lancers are well known around Fifth Air Force. They've kicked some serious butt during this war." Scott scanned the room, then turned back to his audience. "Watch out for the XO. That peckerhead's a card carrying 'yes man'. He'd feed his own to the wolves if he thought it'd further his career. Don't trust the SOB."

"Thanks for the warning, as if there's not enough crap to watch out for here." He paused. "Hey, I saw the eighty-sixes across the field. Those jocks have quite a reputation back in the States." Brian announced.

"Those debased, hot-rocks who fly 'Sabre jets' are on an ego trip that's moronic. You know what these so-called MiG-killers do?" He paused as if he expected a reply, but got none. "They come into the club here and immediately go over and play *Sabre Dance* on that damn juke box, just to bug the hell out of the rest of us. They blow so much smoke about how great they are, they almost believe it themselves." Scott paused and looked around the room to see who might be listening. "We may snatch that record out of the juke one night and stomp it."

"Scott, just tell me if there's some damn way to fly your missions quickly and get the hell out of here. Can you double up?"

"Not likely. For a while we weren't allowed to cross the bomb line unless they had a hot target. Somebody, in their infinite wisdom at FEAF, decided it was taking a chance to let our top-secret radar fall into the wrong hands. Most are combat air patrols just outside of the bomb line, waitin' to protect some stray B-29. Since you gotta' cross the bomb line for a mission, we expend sorties up there that count for nothing. But I heard through 'rumor central' things changed as of yesterday. We're gonna' be free to go up north after the bastards."

"Damn." Brian looked around the smoke filled room. "What a hell hole."

Scott glanced at Hank quizzically. Hank shrugged his shoulders but added no reply.

"Any good news about this friggin' place?" Brian asked.

"C'mon Brian, it could be worse. There's *some* good news. Once in a while, we get to ferry an aircraft back to Itazuke for maintenance. Not only that, you can get one R & R while you're here. Then you can go to Nagoya or Tokyo to get your batteries recharged."

"I've only got one more question. What's our address here? I need to get a letter off tonight so I can get some mail." Brian took out a pen and one of his sets of orders, waiting for Scott's reply.

"Let's see: your name, and serial number, eighty-sixth Fighter Interceptor Squadron, APO nine twenty-nine, Postmaster, San Francisco, California. It seems to take about a week to get a letter from the States."

Brian put the pen and paper in his pocket and looked around the room. "That figures. They must let the Navy bring it over. I'm gonna' get a burger at the snack bar and go back to the hootch. See ya' later."

Scott watched as Brian walked away. He looked back at Hank, rocking forward with his chair. "My God, I've spent a lotta' time with that guy and I've never seen him like this. He's gotta' snap out of that attitude or it'll eat him alive."

"Give him some time. He left Anne in Frisco and it was tough for him."

Scott, in his usual habit, when contemplating something, made little wet circles with the rim of his drink glass. "That'd sho nuff explain it all right. Women can screw with your thinking big time." He looked hard at Hank. "Hoss, this isn't the place for that kind of problem. It'll get you killed." He broke into a grin. "But now I understand what's bending his mind."

"Christ, I didn't leave anybody standing at the gate in Frisco." Hank stated. "And I feel like shit too."

Scott laughed out loud as he contemplated the statement. "You'll get over it."

Brian walked over to the makeshift desk, placed Anne's picture near the back, admiring the girl in the black dress. He laid the stationery on the desk, took out two sheets, and began.

My Dearest Anne,

Hank and I arrived here at K–13 this afternoon. That's Suwon, if you look it up on a map. The area is rather bleak, and I guess that comes from the way I miss you at this moment. The trip over here was long and a stop in Tokyo, for processing, added to the length of the trip.

The few days we had in San Francisco were absolutely great. I'll have each of those nights to think about until I can hold you once again. There's not much to write about now. Maybe I can fill you in later. I wanted to let you know I arrived and give you my address. A letter from you would be so good right about now, but my picture of you will suffice till then. Thanks again! Remember, I love you so very much. Take care of you – for me.

Brian signed the letter and placed it on top of his hat to mail the next day. He lay back on his bunk, closed his eyes, and recalled glimpses of those last few weeks, those last days, and then the last hours with Anne. He finally fell into a disturbed sleep.

The next day, at 0730, Brian and Hank reported to Major Don Larson. They walked briskly up to the desk, saluted smartly, and waited. Brian eyed the walls, covered with pictures of aircraft and people. He glanced at the C.O., his face was older than he had imagined, etched with years not yet lived. His hair was a crisp maple-brown, making an irregular line across a high bony forehead. The Major continued writing on the paper in front of him. Brian looked at Hank, who shrugged his shoulders. Finally, Brian cleared his throat to see if that would get his attention. "No need to do that, Lieutenant. I know you're standing there." His voice was slightly harsh in tonal qualities. He coughed, cleared his throat, and continued to write. After a few more seconds passed, he looked up. There was a distance in his eyes that comes from pressures of command. Slowly, he pushed his chair back and walked around to where they were standing, sizing up the two new Lieutenants. He stuck out his hand rapidly. "I'm Major Larson. Welcome to the eighty-sixth. You're damn fortunate enough to get sent to the best squadron in Fifth Air Force and I know you'll make sure it keeps that reputation. Stand at ease."

He walked back to the chair and sat down again. "I was looking over your records, and writing up your flight assignment when you came in. I've assigned you to Blue Flight. Captain Killian. Woodrow Killian, is the Flight Commander. Damn fine man." He paused again and looked at Brian and Hank as if he was making his evaluation of their potential. "I try to keep the experience fairly equal among the four Flights. We've got some recalled reservists, a few regulars, and a lot of young, new crews here. Your two hootch mates're also in Blue Flight. Right?"

"Yessir." Hank exclaimed.

"Woody'll break you in right. You'll be standing alerts and flying missions in no time. Remember, my door's always open if you have a problem. Good luck."

They saluted, and turned to exit the office. "One more thing," Brian and Hank pivoted around. "I expect each man to be a damn tiger in the air. That doesn't mean you have to be one on the ground. Watch how much hell you raise at the Club. We've got a rowdy group around here already." He added with a twisted half-smile.

Hank, looking back over his shoulder as they left the room and asked: "And just what the hell was that all about?"

"That was the best C.O. in the Fifth Air Force making us feel welcome."

"Brian, I never felt so freakin' welcome in my life. How 'bout you?"

Brian smiled his agreement.

They were fitted with all their flight gear and assigned a locker in the aircrew ready room. Then they set off looking for Woody Killian in the operation shack briefing room. They stepped into the large briefing room with several rows of comfortable chairs, a raised platform in front and a huge map of Korea covering the back wall. Blue Flight was milling around, talking, making jokes, and waiting for the day's mission briefing. Captain Woodrow Killian came through the door like a shot, moving rapidly to the front of the room. He stood at the podium, smiling out at his audience. They quickly took their seats.

Captain Killian, a tall man with an uneven crew-cut, and a jaw line that looked as if it was chiseled from granite, stood in front of the briefing room. He pointed to map references, confidently discussing the day's mission, as if it were a casual training flight. It was to be a combat air patrol, or CAP to aircrews, along the bomb line. Brian and Hank took a seat in the back of the briefing room and listened. He briefed for a six-ship formation, taking off in pairs, call signs to be used, authentication codes, emergency procedures, weather, and escape and evasion procedures. He covered all mission specifics in detail. His thoroughness impressed the two new Lieutenants. While draped casually over chairs, the aircrews took notes as if they were listening to a baseball game. Woody smiled, leaned non-chalantly on the podium. "You got it, let's do it."

Blue flight rose from their seats, as conversations picked where they had been interrupted. Pilots and RO's checked equipment, threw flight gear over their shoulder as they joked about the mission. They ambled through the door as if the were going out with the boys for some fun.

Woody walked to the back of the room and introduced himself, asking all the pertinent questions on home, family, and training. Woody paused, looked at Brian and Hank as if he just thought of something. "You two get suited up and I'll get an aircraft assigned for you to get up and get the feel of flying again after a month-long layoff. Let's go on and get you two back in the saddle again. Tomorrow, we'll do some formation flying, and get you up to speed as quickly as possible. We'll have you standing alert next week."

Brian and Hank dressed in their flight gear, took their helmets, parachutes, dinghies, flares, flashlights, forty-five automatics, then proceeded to the aircraft number that was written on the board. Brian reviewed the various call signs, maps of the area, and their briefing instructions. His finger traced the outline of enemy territory. "Let's hope we stay on the right side of the bomb line, Sport." He handed the maps to Hank. "Look these charts over good, and pick out some terrain features that'll show up on radar. They'll come in handy later."

Hank reluctantly took the maps and radio facility charts. He followed Brian around the aircraft during the preflight inspection instead of getting his gear in place in the cockpit. He stopped Brian with a tug at his sleeve. "Are you comfortable with that short briefing we got?"

"Yeah. I've got a good idea of where everything is on the map, the authentication code for the day, and Ground Control's call sign. Why, what's the matter?"

"Nothing really." He shifted his weight back and forth as he talked. "I guess it's finally hit me where we are, and what we're gonna' be doing here."

"Let me get something across to you right now. I'm as scared as you are. But I'm good at what I do. You were lucky enough to get teamed up with the best damn fighter pilot in the United States Air Force."

A big smile began spreading across Hank's face as he listened.

Brian continued, "I've got some damn good reasons to get back to the States in one piece and I'm gonna' take your raunchy butt with me. Besides, there's the 'big sky, little bullet theory'.

"The what theory?" Hank looked puzzled.

"Look at all the tremendous sky up there." Brian waved his arm. "Think about that little bitsy bullet. What's the chances one'll hit you up there?"

Hank began to chuckle, then broke out in laughter as he thought about the statement. "Okay, Hotshot, let's get this hunk of sheet metal in the air where it belongs."

The next ten days Brian and Hank practiced everything they'd previously learned at Tyndall, and more. Since this was a combat area, there was ample information thrown their way to ensure their survival. It was welcomed and they listened carefully. Ten days of indoctrination and they were finally ready to assume their place in Blue Flight. The first alert was routine, no scramble, and one routine CAP. They stowed their gear and started for the Club.

"Hank, I'm gonna' swing by the orderly room and check for mail, just in case."

The mail clerk looked at Brian as if he should already know by now that there was no mail for him yet. The mail clerk rifled through the stack of mail as if to humor Brian. "Well, well, Lieutenant, you finally hit the jackpot. You've got five letters here."

Brian took the letters as if they were fragile documents, flipping through the stack with a large smile. They were all from Anne. His heart pounded with the anticipation. He tried to sort the letters by date of the postmark but they all were the same. He slid them in his flight suit pocket to read later. He'd savor the anticipation.

Brian settled onto the bunk and took out the first letter. He wanted this to last as long as possible. He began reading.

My Dearest,

I could only think of you going through that hotel door during the trip back. To say that I miss you is such an understatement. My heart literally aches because I miss you so.

I managed to keep some level of composure during the trip back and even while I was with Lori in Birmingham. I told Mama that I hoped everyone was happy that we didn't get married before you left. We should have! She said she wouldn't say one word if I met you at the plane and got married on the spot when you get back. That phrase sounds so good. "When you get back!"

Please hurry home to me and be careful. You're my life. I'm so tired, so

I'll write more later. I'll save these until I get your address. I love you so very much! Anne

Brian folded the letter and placed it back in the envelope, for the next time he'd read it. He took his time reading the other letters, savoring each and every line.

The weather at K-13 warmed up like someone had shot the thermostat to the top setting. Summer was taking the place of spring and the heat only accentuated the barren dusty ground. The indelible scaring of the landscape was mute testimony that a war was taking place over this terrain. Dust swirled everywhere until rain turned it into mud. It was a gooey, reddish mixture of earth and water that clung to boots and clothes tenaciously. Brian settled into a routine as his flying ability became honed to a much finer edge. Several alert scrambles placed him and Hank across the bomb line and over enemy territory. Every scramble increased the adrenalin flow in anticipation of an intercept on a MiG. Once or twice they'd been vectored toward Migs who were trying to intercept B-29's on night bomb runs. Each time the "bogey" broke off before contact. Brian was becoming restless with the routine, eager for a chance to engage a target, and it showed in his pushing the controller for deeper penetrations toward a suspected "bogey."

The night was a murky blackness, with no moon to light the terrain below. Lightening ominously illuminated the ragged edges of thunderstorms as they circled to the southeast. They were too far away to be of any consequence. After a CAP along the bomb line with no target to be vectored toward, Castle control released Brian and Hank to return to K-13. Unexpectedly, Brian spotted a light moving along the ground about 20 miles into hostile territory.

"Hank, let's see if we can light up the countryside with a strafing run on whatever that is down there."

"Negative, Brian. We don't have approval for air-to-ground. Don't be stupid."

"Gooks are Gooks. But I'll give Castle a call and check it out."

"Castle, Roundtree two. We've got a light and movement on the ground. It's approximately twenty miles north. Request permission for an interdiction pass."

"Roundtree two, negative – uh, we don't have authority to modify your mission. You're now released from CAP, cleared to home plate, pigeons 194 degrees, six zero miles. What state fuel?"

"Roger, Control. Fuel well above bingo. Since we're released, be advised we're gonna' make one pass at the ground target."

"Roundtree two, you'll be making this attack at your own discretion. Repeat, at your own discretion."

"Goddamn, Brian, don't do this. We're not cleared for an attack on a ground target."

"Cool it, Hank. I'm rolling in now, let's see if we can do some damage."

Brian flipped on the gun compressor, armed the fifty caliber guns in the nose, reduced power, popped the speed brakes and dove toward the light. He moved his head forward slightly toward the dimly lit display on the gun sight that protruded just in front of the windscreen. He placed the pipper of the manual gun sight right on the moving target and squeezed off a burst of the guns. The aircraft vibrated as the rounds left the gun barrels. He pulled up in a climbing right turn for another pass before the light disappeared.

"One more pass. If we don't hit something, I'll break off."

The aircraft dove again toward the area of moving light. There was a distinct "high" that came from air-to-ground action. The vibration of the fifty-caliber guns rattling away in the nose, and the smell of cordite from the ammo accentuated the experience. Suddenly, little balls of fire were coming up from the ground toward them. The bright tracer rounds from the anti-aircraft weapons didn't particularly alarm Brian. They were off the mark, obviously firing blindly at their unseen enemy. It was hard for Brian not see the beauty in their deadly arc in the sky, as the forty-millimeter rounds curved up. Ignoring the return fire, he tightened his finger over the trigger as the guns rattled away up front. He pulled back on the stick as the sky exploded in front of the aircraft. The blast on the ground lit the horizon as a ball of fire rolled skyward in front of them.

"Hotdamn, I think we hit a fuel truck."

"Hey, this was your wild-ass idea. I don't give a good Goddamn what we hit."

"Okay, okay. We're headed home."

The next morning, as the flight was released from alert status, Hank and Brian ambled toward the club. Woody moved directly into their path. "We've got a problem here. What happened last night ... and don't spare any details?"

Brian glanced over at Hank, who was staring penetratingly at him. His gaze rebounded back at Woody. "Whatta' you mean? Is something wrong?"

"Damn right there's something wrong. You were on a CAP and never vectored to a target according to Castle Control. But the crew chief just showed me a twenty-millimeter hole through the leading edge of your horizontal stabilizer. Now, how the bloody hell did you take a hit on a CAP outside the bomb line?"

"Jesus, I didn't know we picked up a round. Never felt it."

Woody continued glaring at both officers standing in front of him but never said a word. He waited for the explanation.

"Okay, Woody, we saw a light moving on the ground inside the bomb line. You know how seldom you see a gook do something that stupid. We made a couple of passes. Nailed a fuel truck on the second pass. What a fire ball."

"The only one more stupid than that gook was you. You risked an all-weather fighter and crew to hit one cotton-pickin truck. That wasn't your mission." He continued his withering glare at both culprits, waiting for some attempt at an explanation. None came. Woody shook his head. "You two are in such deep kimchee I don't know if even I can help you. I've gotta' report this to the Ops officer and CO. All hell's about to break loose."

"This one was all mine, Woody. Hank told me not to make the strafing run."

"Glad to know one of you might be slightly sane. After you get something to eat, both of you get your butts to the hootch and wait. They'll want a written report of what happened up there last night."

"Damn it, we nailed a truck and maybe hit others in that convoy." Brian stated. "Doesn't that mean something?"

"Save that rah, rah crap for someone else. Don't say another goddamn word right now." Woody barked. They stood there, frozen to the spot, an inscrutable look on their face. Both were speechless as Woody walked away rapidly.

Brian lay on his bunk worrying about the consequences of last night. He turned his head toward Hank. "I'm sorry I got you in this deep." He kicked the end of the bunk. "This is supposed to be a damn war. You'd think *we* were the freakin' enemy."

"Don't tell me about it. I'm stupid enough to be in the back seat with you. Guilt by association." He laughed, breaking the seriousness of the moment.

"Don't stand at ease, you're at attention." Major Larson spoke softly but sternly.

Brian and Hank stiffened instantly into a position of attention, their arms tight against the seam of their pants. Brian focused over the heads of the seated officers in the CO's office. He dared not look directly at the CO or Major Littleton, Squadron Ops Officer, seated to the left of the CO. Instead, he fixed his gaze on the picture of a formation of F-94's on the wall behind the CO. Out of the corner of his eye, Brian could see Woody seated to the left of Major Littleton, staring out the window. His peripheral vision picked up Major Greene, the noted Executive Officer, glaring at them. The tightness in Brian's throat wouldn't go away. He felt his pulse jump in his temples. This was serious. There was no doubt left now.

"I read that bullshit report you called an explanation for your actions last night. Then I took a look at your gun camera film. I can't believe you'd take it upon yourself to attack a ground target across the bomb line with no prior approval. You had no damn justification to go after that target. None. My first thought is to ground both you Hotshots, bury your ass in paper work in the Operation shack, 'till I can transfer both of you to some other Squadron. The reason ..."

Brian interrupted the Major. "Sir, the strafing run was all my idea. Lieutenant..."

"Just stand there and keep your goddamn excuses and explanations to yourself. I've already read your report of this fiasco. Oh, I'm sure it was *your* brilliant idea. I'll give you full credit for the idiotic maneuver. The reason I don't ground you right now, was Woody assuring me you both still have *some* potential. He tells me this type of error in judgment won't happen again." He stared at both officers braced in front of him, looking first at Brian then at Hank. "It better not. If either of you make one mistake, screw up one mission, eat with the wrong hand...in other words, if I hear of one miss-step by either of you two, I'll have you flying a T-6 spotting for the artillery. You understand me?"

"Yessir." They barked in unison.

"Then get the hell outta' here before I change my mind."

They saluted, did an about face, and exited the office as quickly as they could. Woody caught up with them as they walked toward the club. He walked along beside the two without saying anything for a while, and then stopped suddenly. Brian and Hank spun around to face Woody.

"If you're wondering if I saved your hind ends back there. I didn't. Oh sure, I put in a good word for you. That's what I'm expected to do as your flight leader. But it was the 'Old Man' who made the decision. He still has this thing for the 'Tiger instinct'. He was mad as hell, and almost listened to Major Greene tell him to get your butts outta' here before the sun set. But he said 'No' and laughed at the fact that you had the 'balls' to make the attack. He thinks you two have the fighter pilot mind-set. Frankly, with your attitude, I think both of you are gonna' bust your ass, and damn quick. I don't plan on cutting you any slack. Understand where I'm coming from?"

As the weeks passed, the squadron lost three more crews. One was scrambled during night alert and never came back. They just disappeared off the radar scope without even a "mayday" call. The second was making an intercept on a PO-2, known as "Bed Check Charlie," when they collided with the slower moving target. The third was flying a mission when four MiGs surprised them. The

RO, was picked up by rescue after punching out over the Yellow Sea. The pilot was never found. The pilots, who gathered around the bar each evening, accepted these as bad luck or bad decisions on the part of the pilots. RO's seemed to avoid the subject altogether. As pilots discussed these things around the bar, it wasn't callousness, mere acceptance of the price of an air war. The 86th Fighter Interceptor Squadron was, by and large, a cohesive group.

Though never discussed, there was constant measurement of each pilot's ability. He was evaluated by the harshest of critics, his peers. An unwritten, undiscussed hierarchy was formed, not by rank, but by one's skills in the air. Brian was constantly trying to elevate his status in this scheme of the established pecking order. But he also knew what all the others knew; Mike Wycoff was the hottest pilot in the 86th. This fact was further underscored when Mike called the tower for a low pass after a mission when he downed a MiG. Given permission, Mike came down the runway three feet off the ground, exceeding the mach limitations of the F-94. He left pieces of his trim tabs scattered along the runway as he pulled up in a series of vertical rolls. Instead of a royal chewing out, Major Larson beamed to those beside him at the Operations shack, slapped Major Littlcton on the back, and said; "Now there's a tiger."

Woody, the consummate pilot, who believed every word ever written on aircraft limitations, took a different approach toward Mike's exploit. That evening at the Club he sidled up beside Mike at the end of the bar. He stood for a moment waiting for the right time. Mike stopped his conversation and turned toward Woody, who moved directly in front of him. "You're not in my flight, but let me tell you something. Something 'hotdogs' never quite get. Never, repeat, *never* make an airplane do something it's not designed to do.

Not unless you're in combat and have to. Keep it up, and you'll kill yourself like most 'hotdogs do."

Mike eyed Woody suspiciously, but four beers had mellowed his thinking to the point he found no offense at the advice so bluntly given. He slapped Woody on the back and said, "Sure." Then walked casually back to the other end of the bar and ordered another beer.

Brian "pushed the envelope" in the F-94 but always stayed well within his capabilities. Formation was flown just a little closer than required. He liked to see the element leader's anxiousness as he put his tip tank about six feet from his canopy. It was his world up there. He became a different person when he climbed into the cockpit, cold, composed, calculating, but electrified. But the last thing he wanted was the "hotdog" label assigned to him. The impression left by the strafing attack on the truck convoy could easily have tagged him. Great pains were taken to make sure his confidence wasn't translated as a cocky new pilot's bad attitude. He walked a tight rope between flying skills in the air and humility on the ground. He honed his humble skills considerably.

The letters from Anne kept his morale high considering the surroundings and the inability to speed up his missions. He could count on a letter every week or so from Lori, adding considerably to his morale. The days merged into night and week into week as he longed to finish this tour and go home. The constant homesickness never left. It was a persistent ache in the pit of his gut.

As Brian and Hank walked away from the flight line, they heard Woody call out to them. "How would you two like to ferry an aircraft to Itazuke tomorrow? I know it's a day off, but you don't get a chance to get back to Japan that often."

"Great, we'll take it." Hank said instantly.

As they continued walking, Brian looked toward Hank. "Maybe we've redeemed ourselves with ole Woody. Never expected he'd let us take a bird back to Itazuke."

"Don't know about that redemption but it'll be great to relax for a few days. I can use it."

Brian called Itazuke tower for landing instructions as they crossed the Japanese coastline. Japan was noticeably green. Moist land filled with rice paddies and bordered by evergreens stretched out in successive indentations. Off to the left were blue forms of low mountains, covered with dense pines. It looked like they'd emerged from another world. The tires made their usual squeal as they contacted the runway and Brian was feeling the eagerness take over. He was already looking forward to the next two days in a real bed, hot baths, and good food. They checked in with maintenance, and scheduled a departure back with a fresh bird in two days. The next stop was the BOQ. They threw their overnight bags on the floor and fell across the beds. They delighted in the comfort of real beds, with comfortable mattresses, and pillows soft as down.

Hank, still looking at the ceiling, his hands propped under his head, said: "I hear a lot about the Allied Officers' Club on the outskirts of Fukuoka. Wanna' give it a try tonight?"

"Hey, sometimes you think like a pilot, sounds like a winner. I want a long, tall bourbon and a filet about two inches thick." Brian announced, using his fingers for emphasis on the thickness.

Both of them were taking in the sights during the taxi ride to the Officers' Club. There was a glitzy atmosphere in Fukuoka City, a carnival ambience that prevailed along the main route of clubs and bars known to cater to the enlisted. Bright neon blended into a vibrant collage of color. People crowded the streets, mixed with rickshaws and taxis with blaring horns. Suddenly, without notice, the gaudy neon lights disappeared, and the roadside became filled with small houses. They were close together, with little or no yards. Land was a premium, not to be wasted on lawns and shrubs.

The Allied Officers' Club was located farther out toward the bay, away from the main enlisted attraction of bars and bathhouses. The taxi pulled up in front of a large, old Japanese house with a circular drive and formal gardens. Inside, the place was teaming with officers from several allied countries. There were a few Army types, but the majority of the patrons were aircrews from the United Nation countries."

"I think this is the kind of break we needed, and sho' nuff deserve." Brian glanced at Hank for confirmation.

"You better believe it." Hank added enthusiastically. "Let's see if we can elbow our way up to the watering hole."

As they squeezed through the crowd of humanity toward the bar, Brian stopped suddenly, and peered through the smoke obscured room. "My God, can it be?"

"Can it be what?" Hank asked.

"There at the bar – the guy at the end. That looks like ole' Ed Beatty sitting there. He's a good friend of Scott and mine's. He's the other member of 'The Group' from flight training I told you about. Come on, Hank, you gotta' meet this guy."

Brian eased up behind Ed. "Say, fella', that seat's reserved for real fighter pilots."

Ed pivoted around on the bar stool to face whoever issued the insult. "Damn, I might have suspected it was you, or that other idiot, Scott. What're you doing here?"

"Might ask you the same thing. You should be back taking pictures of all those 'gooks' so the real fighter pilots can do 'em in." He hesitated. "Just a minute." He grabbed Hank's sleeve, pulling him closer. "Ed, I want you to meet my RO, Hank Evans."

"Glad to meet ya', Hank, and you have my utmost sympathy flying with this character." Ed took his hand and leaned closer as if he was betraying a confidence. "He got those wings in a box of Cracker Jacks."

"I always suspected that, but reckon it could be worse. I've almost got him broken in now."

They pulled up stools and began reminiscing about flight school and bringing each other up-to-date on what had been happening since they left Vance. Hank decided he'd let them have some time to do their visiting while he excused himself and headed toward two nurses sitting at a table nearby. Ed stopped talking, his eyes following Hank. He punched Brian's arm. "Watch this." Brian turned and scrutinized Hank's approach to the targeted table.

"Poor soul, he doesn't have a prayer with those two." Ed exclaimed. "These nurses don't talk to anyone below the rank of Major."

Brian smiled. "He'll have to learn the hard way. Now tell me about Kimpo. I heard you were up there at K-fourteen."

"What's to tell about K-fourteen? Korea is Korea. One hellhole's the same as the next, but I may not have to be there that much longer. I've already nailed down ninety-one missions. Nine more and I'm on my way to the good ole USA."

Brian's' expression changed. "You mean you could be outta' there in a couple of weeks? Damn, I should have asked for F-eighties and photo reccy. Damn, ninety-one, huh?'

"That's why I'm sitting here nursing my third martini." His expression became reflective, as he turned the martini glass in his hand. "No sweat at first, because you've got a hundred of 'em to do. The end's so far away, you don't even think about going home. But as you begin to get closer to that magic one hundred, your butt begins to 'pucker'. He turned directly toward Brian. "You wonder if fate is going to nail your ass, especially on the last one. Now, wouldn't that be ironic?"

Brian wanted to say something that would modify Ed's mood immediately. "No sweat. You'll knock off those last nine off and be having a drink back at the Top of The Mark before you know it, you lucky sonofabitch. Now, tell me about some of the other guys from fifty-one-G."

Ed looked back at his martini, took a drink, then back at Brian. Tony Szymanski was shot down on his eighty-third mission. Never even got off a Mayday. Brad Shelby. You remember ole Brad?" Brian nodded. Ed continued, "Brad called control that he was hit and losing power. Then he tells 'em he found a sand bar in the middle of the Han river and he was gonna' put that F-eighty down right there. Some of the ROK troops got up there the next day. He must have done a beautiful job of putting it down 'cause the aircraft was intact and his helmet was on the floor, but no Brad. We figure some of the local 'gooks' got to him." He took another swig from the glass. "Bastards." There was a moment neither said anything. Ed glanced around. "I heard Wink Mullin, who was flying an F-eighty, got flamed on a napalm pass. Poor SOB was number four in trail. They had the range by then." He drained the glass. "We've lost a few, but we've been lucky compared to those guys in the class ahead of us that went to F-eighty-fours. Most of 'em are flying 'lead sleds' down at Taegu, in the Ninth Fighter Bomber. Their targets are some kinda' fortified. Forty millimeters throw up a barrage you could walk on. They fly into Hell and look the Devil in the eye every day. Christ, they must know half of 'em won't complete a hundred missions."

Brian stared into his drink. Ed sat there silently, looking intently into a fresh martini just placed in front of him. "You know. I'm ready to leave this war to someone else." His expression became solemn. "There's nobody in the States who gives a happy damn about Korea. I've begun to wonder about 'Duty, Honor, Country' being such a noble calling." He hesitated. "We sure as hell don't have the same number of friends we had last year, Old Sport." He took on a half-smile as he continued. "This war's not really fun anymore." He laughed sarcastically before sipping his martini.

Brian thought for a moment before saying anything. "Remember how we were so full of 'piss and vinegar' back there at Moody? We thought we were the hottest things ever turned loose in the Air Force. It's amazing how combat can warp that perception, and it sho' doesn't take long." Brian chuckled as he took a long drink of bourbon. "I reckon war ages you quick, or kills you quick." He paused a moment. "But you know, Ed, we'd do it again." Brian leaned forward as he continued. "It's that challenge, probably understood only by those who have the curse, a Fighter pilot mentality." Brian took another long swig from his glass. He looked around the room as if he wasn't sure about the next statement. He looked back at Ed. "But that's not to say we don't have our moments. There's always that thought, the one that creeps up on you, and there's no way you can't push it away when it grabs at you. Shit, we all know there's that challenge out there somewhere, waiting, the one that's too big to handle." He slapped Ed on the back and laughed. "Hell, I guess we can't feel invincible every day, can we?"

Ed picked up his martini and turned it slowly in his hand. "Here's to all of our friends, wherever they may be."

"And to you, me and Scott looking back on these times, one day when we're in our nineties, and having one more drink together." Brian brought his glass to Ed's. "One thing's for damn sure ... we won't ever forget this."

Ed smiled and nodded.

CHAPTER FOURTEEN

THE AIRCRAFT LEVELED off at twenty-six thousand feet over the Sea of Japan, heading back to a land consumed by war. Large cumulus clouds, splashed around the sky, blending orange and red hues of reflected sunlight. The sea glistened below as the sun mirrored itself in the illuminating water. Tsu Shima, the small island half way between Japan and Korea, stood out like an emerald set in the shimmering water below. Its beauty almost lost in the fact that it marked the entry back into the combat zone. Both were quiet, lost in their own thoughts.

Hank's voice in the headset snapped the silence. "That was a quick two days, but a nice break from what we're about to go back to."

"Well, at least I'll be getting some mail." Brian replied. "Say, Hank, old buddy, I've got a question. What happened when you moved in on those two females back at the Allied Officers' Club?" Brian smiled behind his oxygen mask as he listened for the answer.

"Who the hell do they think are? Those nurses acted like they didn't have time to talk to a Second Lieutenant. I reckon you gotta' be a doctor, or a field grade officer to get anywhere with those skirts."

Brian laughed into his oxygen mask, in spite of trying to muffle it.

"You laugh, but the worse thing about it was that brunette." Hank stated. "God knows, she had the biggest blue eyes I've ever seen. I committed five of the deadly sins just looking at her."

"You've been over here too long, Sport."

Brian stowed his flight gear and headed straight for the mail room. He stood in front of the small window waiting impatiently as the mail clerk casually sauntered over.

"Yessir, Lieutenant, you got mail. I doubt anybody in the Squadron gets as much as you do."

"That's because I've got a good press agent back in the States."

The startled mail clerk glanced up, laughing. "Here you go, Lieutenant. Five of 'em."

Brian scanned each letter. Two were from Anne, one from his mother, one from Lori, and one from Tyler. He put the letters in his flight jacket to enjoy later. Entering the Club, he decided to get a sandwich and catch up on the latest rumors that usually flowed unchecked. He skirted around several tables and headed toward Mike Wyckoff sitting alone, slumped lethargically in his chair, engrossed in a glass of coke. "Mind if I join you?"

"No, drag up a chair."

"You're in a real talkative mood." Brian commented.

Mike's head jerked up from his coke. "Haven't seen you around the last couple of days."

"Hank and I took a bird over to Itazuke. Just got back. What's been happening here?"

"We lost another crew yesterday." Mike replied.

Brian straightened in the chair and leaned forward, intent on hearing what Mike had to say. "Who was it?"

"Chuck Stroud and Fred Cooper." Mike whispered.

"What th' hell happened?"

"He was flying White Leader's wing. They were in some stinkin' weather, in and outta' the soup. RO wasn't painting anything on the scope but lead thought he saw two 'bogies' through the scud to his left. He signaled for a combat spread formation and broke hard into the targets. It seems Chuck took his eyes off the lead to look back to see what they were going after, just as Conley rolled out. Chuck's bird came up underneath Conley." Mike brought one hand up hard under the other to demonstrate. "Bam! Both went into a flat spin. Conley and his RO punched out and were picked up by one of our choppers, Chuck and Fred didn't get out."

Both of them sat there, saying nothing. Brian thought back to the day they arrived in the C-119 and Chuck meeting them. He recalled his perpetual smile and friendly banter. He was one of the most likeable guys in the Squadron. The worst thing was the fact he was due to go home next month.

Mike, who had been gazing at his coke, finally looked around at Brian. "Well, that's five crews we've lost. Who th' hell's next?"

The words startled Brian. He paused to digest the concern and doubt expressed in the question. They weren't that close and Mike's reputation for hard flying and hard living didn't match up with what he'd just heard. The man had just exposed a vulnerability that shocked Brian. The statement provided some insight into the mentality of a fellow pilot. *Sometimes a man isn't what you think he is. Sometimes, maybe, just maybe, he's not what **he** thinks he is.* He had to stop and consider his own vulnerability. "Who knows who's next, but there'll be others, count on it." Brian thought for a moment. "The difference is you and I don't make those kind of mistakes. Do we?"

With a sudden look of resolve, a smile slowly wiped across Mike's face. "No, by God, I reckon we don't."

Brian settled onto the bunk, adjusted the pillow under his head, and pulled out the letters. He opened each very slowly, making the enjoyment last as long as possible. He unfolded the first letter.

My Dearest Brian:

It seems so long since we said goodbye in San Francisco, and I miss you so very much! It will be an eternity before we're together again, or so it seems on weekends like this one. Excuse my whining. It won't happen again! When I think of your circumstances, it makes me feel ashamed to feel so depressed and lonely. So there, I got it out of my system! Enough of that! Now let me tell you how much you're missed each and every day. A letter from you is all it takes to make me one very happy gal!

Being back in school, where we spent so much time together, makes it harder than when I was in Collinwood this summer. I hesitate when I walk by "the bench." I want to be able to sit down there with you right now -- just for a minute or two -- while you reassure me that everything will be all right. There are so many times I need to talk to you, to have my best friend listen. We did share so much of ourselves those last few months. You've become so important in my life. It's difficult not having you near. That's why I look forward to the day we're together, and that won't be too long now!

I hope everything is fine with you and you're being careful. I read whatever news is available, but it seldom mentions specific units. I do know where Suwon is and I can at least pinpoint you on a map. There seems to be no definite end predicted for this war. Sure hope that Eisenhower will change things when he's elected.

Lori sends her love, and I think she wrote you yesterday, so she probably sent her own. We talk about you often. Do your ears burn? She just stopped by the desk and suggested that we go to The Grill and get a burger. Oh yes, I saw Tyler last weekend, and he sends his regards, and says he'll write soon. He's considering graduate school, Forestry I believe. Ruston is the same. Nothing really changes. It just gets more lonesome here without you. Remember, I love you so very much.

Anne

Brian read the next letter from Anne, then the one from his mother. Her letter made no mention of any physical problems. It was upbeat and newsy. Brian reread the unusual words that were not like his mother and he wondered why. There were few times she didn't relate specific medical problems and the associated recovery. He was puzzled as fitted it back into the envelope.

He pulled Tyler's letter carefully from the envelope. It was short, but for Tyler to write at all was somewhat of a miracle. The letter covered various aspects of fraternity life at Auburn, how poorly the football team was doing, and the latest female in Tyler's life. There was always humor in the way Tyler articulated things and Brian chuckled as he read. As he progressed through the letter, he began to visualize how different their worlds were now. Not too long ago, the next date for the Saturday game would have been significant in his life, as it still was with Tyler. Now, he was concerned with an environment and circumstances Tyler couldn't comprehend.

He saved Lori's letter for last. She was upbeat and filled the pages with all kinds of news. She gave the usual boost to his morale. He tried to make sure he wrote Lori every week, but sometimes was remiss. He could count on her to understand. In fact, she'd never compare the number of letters each sent the other. It wasn't her style. He began reading her letter.

Dear Brian:

Needless to say, I am once again a prisoner of dear old Agnes Baines! Summer was great but we all have to return to reality at some point. If I told you the truth, I am a bit relieved to be back! Made a few dollars playing piano at Vestavia . . . remember the Greek temple restaurant on top of Red Mountain?...during the dinner hour twice a week. The remainder of the time was a bit of a blur.

Hey! Guess what? "Ziggie," Dr. Zighour, gave me the title roll in "Iolanthe," an operetta by Gilbert and Sullivan. He's using some of the senior boys from Ruston High to play some male parts . . . Mark Murphy, his dad's the barber, and Jed Garvin, whose dad has the Coca-Cola franchise. Both are nice kids, but always pestering me to get dates for them with some of the college freshmen! We tell them they are mere "babes in the woods," but they are persistent.

I'm still hearing from Don . . . he's still flying from Tachikawa. How far is k-13 from there? Too bad the two of you couldn't meet . . . you could compare notes on the co-eds at A-B. You, of course couldn't do much comparing because no one captured much of your time except Anne! I don't think Don had much opportunity either for that matter. He just did a lot of bragging on that subject to me.

We have a new physician on campus! Dear Dr. Paul is no longer prescribing her famous "brown liquid" medicine for EVERYTHING! And when you see Dr. Harris, YOU WILL FLIP! She is an extremely good-looking brunette . . . and young! Comes from New Orleans and has a Mardi-Gras mind set.

No more time to bore you. Dinner (ugh!) Bell just rang and then rehearsal for a couple of hours followed by hitting the books. If I want to keep my GPA even close to the Dean's list I'm going to have to get serious about studying, and a little less time drafting letters to lonely servicemen . . . one in particular!

Please take care of yourself . . . we all want you home, safe and sound. I certainly miss having you around to spend time with. Since you're so intrigued by my love life, drop a me a line when you see that you can find a clone of you . . . for me! So far, nothing romantic here on my horizon!

Love,

Lori

The weather began to change, providing relief from the monsoon rains of September. As the Korean Fall became a reality on the calendar, so did the temperature. The horizon was usually lost in the gray mist of the dank coldness that surrounded them. Frank's first act each afternoon was to fire up the oil stove in the Quonset hut as the cold roared in from the north. He would sit next to it warming his hands, mumbling about the bone-chilling cold. The others enjoyed watching to see how close Frank could get to the stove without catching on fire.

Blue flight assumed their night alert, as crews set up their aircraft quickly in the callous wind that whipped the sleet around them. The rain, mixed with ice pellets, rapped a tapping sound on the metal roof of the alert shack as the wind clashed against the windows. Hank turned up the oil stove in the alert hootch and settled in for the night. Two of the alert aircraft had taken off on routine Combat Air Patrol. They returned late that night, moving Brian and Hank up to number one status. They were the next aircraft to scramble, if one was required. Sleep was fitful for Brian when they were number one crew. He dozed, rolled sporadically to another position, then dozed again. At 0213 the penetrating warble of the scramble horn pierced the night as well as Brian and Hank's sleep. Already sleeping in flight suits, boots, and life jackets, they only needed to slip on their forty-five automatics.

Both bounded out of the door, Hank followed Brian as he leaped toward the ladder. The crew chief followed them up the ladder held the harness and parachute straps for Brian as he moved quickly to start the engine. The starter switch began the compressor turning; Brian put on his helmet, then after sliding his arms into the parachute harness, brought the throttle around the horn. The distinct "thrump" indicated ignition. He buckled the shoulder harness, hit the fuel sequence cut off switch, gang-loaded all fuel switches, gave a "thumbs out" sign to disconnect the power cart, and pull the chocks. As the F-94 bounced along the tarmac to the end of the runway, Brian lowered the canopy and called the tower. "Tower, Sierra Bravo Three on a scramble."

"Roger Sierra Bravo Three cleared for a scramble takeoff. There's no other traffic reported, altimeter is two eight six eight, winds down the runway at ten, gusting fifteen, current weather two hundred overcast, less than a mile visibility in rain and sleet. Switch to tactical frequency when airborne."

"Roger, tower. Three rolling." The afterburner lit the surrounding area as the F-94 roared down the runway. The bluish-yellow flame glistened off the wet surface like a thousand flash bulbs going off. Brian lifted the nose, retracted the gear and flaps, watched the rate of climb peg at 6000 feet per minute, and then switched the radio to the TAC frequency. "Castle, Sierra Bravo Three airborne, heading three five zero, climbing through angels niner." They were swallowed by the murky night, as the aircraft climbed toward altitude.

"Roger Bravo Sierra Three, got you on the scope. Turn to a heading of zero one zero, climb to angels two four. Go buster."

"Castle, I'm 'buster' now. Keep the fuel in mind."

"Roger, go 'gait' when you reach altitude. Your bogey is seven zero miles, ten o'clock position. Appears to be angels two two."

"Everything copasetic in the back, Hank?"

"Yeah, got it on search pattern twenty above, ten below. Nothing yet."

"Castle, Sierra Bravo Three, level angels two four. Negative contact."

"Sierra Bravo Three, turn to a heading of zero two five. Your bogey is now four zero miles, crossing port to starboard. It looks like he's about to get into position for a pass on a B-twenty-nine flight twenty miles to his North."

"Hank, we've got us a live one." Brian reached to his left and turned on the gun compressor and armed the fifty caliber guns in the nose.

"Sierra Bravo Three, there are no friendly fighters in that sector. If we make an intercept, you have permission to fire. Repeat. You have permission to fire."

"Roger that, Castle." The adrenalin surged. "Hey, Hank..."

"I got him." Hank shouted. "Turn starboard – roll out now. Hold it right there. I've got lock-on." Hank's voice penetrated the intercom.

"Castle, Sierra Bravo, Tallyho and Judy!"

"Roger, Roger. Understand 'Judy'. He hasn't turned. I don't think he's been alerted that you're closing on him."

"Easy port. Roll out. Bogey is twelve o'clock fourteen miles. I'm painting him good now." Hank almost shouted into the intercom. "We've got a good quartering intercept on him."

"Give me range and overtake." Brian quit flying instruments, focusing solely on the green circle and dot of his pilot's radar scope. He concentrated on only one thing, keeping that dot centered in the circle as it collapsed in size. The attitude of the aircraft was of no importance, just the dot.

"Range two miles, overtake only thirty. He's speeding up, Brian."

Brian pushed the throttle over to the detent position, feeling the instant surge as the afterburner kicked in. He concentrated on the dot in his scope as his hand tightened on the stick, his finger lightly wrapped around the trigger, anticipating the moment to fire. He felt the pulse in his temples. He glanced at the mach indicator approaching .9 mach, maximum allowed airspeed.

"Range three thousand yards, overtake thirty, maximum firing range." Brian held off. He wanted to get in closer before firing.

"Range one thousand yards, overtake now forty." Brian fought to maintain the dot in the center, but didn't fire. The aircraft vibrated its message that he was at maximum airspeed. "Six hundred yards, Brian, damn!" Brian squeezed the trigger as the fifty caliber guns chattered in the nose. There was a slight quiver as each of the fifty caliber guns fired their deadly salvo at the rate of twelve hundred rounds per minute. The smell of cordite from the expended rounds filled the cockpit. He squeezed another burst, then another.

"Minimum firing range, break, break." Instead of breaking, Brian held the trigger down and moved the rudder pedals back and forth to get more coverage.

A massive, blinding, ball of flame lit the sky as the MiG exploded. Debris flew past the right wing and over the top of the canopy. Brian, momentarily blinded by the explosion, snatched the throttle out of afterburner, breaking hard left and down.

"We got him. We got him!" Hank shouted.

Brian keyed his mike. "Castle, scratch one bogey!"

"Roger, Sierra Bravo Three. He's off the scope. Well done, well done! Your pigeons to home plate are one niner six degrees, nine eight miles. What state fuel?"

"Roger that, Castle. We're below bingo fuel. How about a gradual descent and a straight hand-off to GCA? We don't have enough fuel for a standard let-down." He took his thumb off the mike button. "Hank, that last use of the burner put us pretty low on fuel. We're gonna' be on fumes by the time we hit K-thirteen. With a three hundred-foot ceiling, it adds a pucker factor."

"Let's get on the ground before we celebrate. What's the fuel totalizer read now?" Hank inquired.

"You don't wanna' know."

"Sierra Bravo Three, your pigeons now one niner zero, four five miles. GCA standing by for a hand-off. Reported weather now one hundred feet, half a mile visibility in sleet and light rain. GCA'll pick you up on this frequency. There'll be no change in frequency. What state fuel now?"

"Roger, Castle. Fuel's critical. Let's make this one good." Brian continued the decent with reduced power, tensing his muscles in spite of trying to relax. *Damn, this is gonna' be close.* "Castle, we're passing through angels four. Where's GCA? They aren't on frequency yet?" Brian's tone indicated his anxiety.

"Sierra Bravo, this is GCA, continue your descent to two thousand feet. This is your final controller. You need not acknowledge any further instructions. If you hear no transmissions for a period of five seconds, initiate a missed approach, and contact Tower on one twenty-four-point five."

Brian smiled. *Missed approach my ass. There'd be no missed approach. This one's gotta' be good. It's sweaty palms time again!* He made a darting glance up through the windscreen. Solid black. His stomach quivered.

"You'll be intercepting glide slope in thirty seconds. Continue heading. Begin your rate of descent now." The GCA controller barked out commands in staccato tempo. "You're on center line and on glide path. Recheck gear and final flap setting. You're on centerline, now going ten feet low on glide path, adjust your rate of descent. Turn left to one eight zero. You're slightly right of centerline. You're now back on glide slope, continue your rate of decent. You're on centerline, on glide path. You're passing over the outer marker now. You're over the field boundary. If you don't have a visual, initiate an immediate go around."

The runway approach lights seared through the mist as they skimmed over the top and rounded-out for touchdown. The tires squealed their contact with the runway and Brian eased pressure to the brakes. He breathed again. "We had a little luck with us tonight."

"Yeah." Hank, barely audible, replied.

They followed the crew chief's lighted hand signal directions, parked the aircraft, and shut down the engine. Brian took off his helmet, placed it on the windscreen, and sat there with his head in his hands. The previous hour and twenty minutes were soaking in. He felt no elation; he was drained of all emotion.

Hank was standing on the wing, leaning into the cockpit. "How about a cup of coffee. I'm buying."

Brian looked up. "Sounds like a winner."

The rest of the Flight was still asleep. The phone began ringing with congratulatory messages from the controller at the radar sight who directed the intercept. Several crew members began waking up at the commotion. "Hey, hold it down. It's three-damn-thirty in the morning." Brian and Hank went outside with the crew chief and maintenance personnel, who had cut loose in celebrating the downing of the MiG.

Three days later, Brian and Hank christened their newly assigned plane *Mariah*. The words to the song *They Call The Wind Mariah* were a favorite with both of them. It was appropriate. Hank stood on the wing rubbing their name painted on the side of the aircraft, then patted the one red star for the downed aircraft. "How 'bout that." He grinned as Brian snapped his picture. Unlike the emotions felt by ground troops, Brian had no feelings for what may have happened to the downed MiG pilot. This was, after all, a war of machine against machine. Nothing personal.

Brian always went out of the way to avoid giving Anne something to worry about, but he wrote her about the MiG. It was something significant in his life that he had to share with her. His letter made it sound as if it was routine and nothing was mentioned about the twelve gallons of fuel left in the tanks or how close they were to not making it back to K-thirteen.

Randy popped through the door, holding a crumpled piece of paper. "Hey, you lucky sonsabithes. You know someone with enough clout to get all four of us R&R in Japan two days before Thanksgiving." Brian, Hank, and Frank looked up, then at each other. "Hey, don't look so damn dumbfounded. I pulled in one of my markers from the squadron adjutant. We're all going together."

Hank ran over, lifting Randy off the floor. "Godamighty, I won't ever doubt your politicin' butt again. You really pulled one off this time."

Brian leaned back on his bunk thinking of five days of no alerts, no flying, and definitely no trying to stay warm. The concept was exhilarating as it floated through his sensibility.

Randy, since he was the one who pulled off this coup, decided on Tokyo and the R&R center near Mount Fuji.

Four happy Lieutenants grabbed seats on the first courier leaving K-13 for Tachikawa and were in a most jocular mood during the flight over. It was clearly their time to relax, enjoy, and celebrate as the R&R marked the halfway point in their tour. They could see the other end of the gauntlet they'd been running. There was renewed hope that this war was finite after all.

The R&R facility was beautiful. Hank looked out over the formal gardens. "Compare that to what we just left. And take a look at Mount Fuji over there. I love it." They all turned and stared at its snow-capped peak glistening in the sun, rising majestically in the background. Distinctively shaped puffs of fleecy clouds towered behind the peak. .

Their gaze shifted suddenly to three nurses, walking in front of the Aso Kenko. No one commented as Brian smiled at their concentration on the added appraisal of the scenery. He was amused at the swinging of heads as they passed several more females. Two nurses passed through the lobby, as Frank faked a move toward them. "Hey, put your tongue back in. Remember Hank's experience in Fukuoka," Brian cautioned humorlessly.

"Listen, we're now gonna' send in the first team." Frank countered, as he slapped Hank on the back. "Things will be decidedly different now."

"Sure, Randy, we'll see how you make out. I learned the hard way about nurses. You better try some Geisha House. That, and several thousand yen stuffed in both hands, may get you somewhere." Hank added indignantly.

Brian swung in front of the other three, slowing down the entourage. "Wait a minute here. Don't get completely carried away by a few nurses. How 'bout we all meet in the dining room and have a damn good meal together before your raging hormones kick in?"

"Okay, we do need to keep up our strength. But Brian, what'll you be doing while we chase 'round eyes' all around Mount Fuji?" Randy asked.

Hank spoke up before Brian could answer. "He'll be looking for stationery to write a letter to Anne." The three of them enjoyed a laugh at Brian's expense. He smiled good naturedly, letting them have their fun.

Randy summoned the waiter over and ordered more wine. Brian slumped back against the comfortable chair. He was quiet as he sat back to enjoy the conversation and the ambience. His eyes moved up to the tall ceilings, ornately sculptured with Asian designs representing the four seasons. The artist finely conferred the detailed features to each object. He glanced at the walls adorned with murals of oriental scenes painted many years before. Suddenly a word caught his sub consciousness and his mind focused back on the conversation. The subject was now centered on all the things they wanted to do when this tour was over and they were home again.

Frank rocked back in the softness of the chair. His eyes narrowed as he mentally focused on a distant landscape. "I think I'm gonna' go in with Dad on raising some prime beef cattle." His smile expanded. "I've got a totally different opinion now of those prospects than I did back in Childress, Texas." He threw his leg lazily over the chair arm. "You know, I used to look at those cows grazing across that almost-barren pasture, and wonder how long before I could get my butt outta' there. You had to watch every step so's you don't step in cow dung?" Hank almost choked, laughing at Frank's comment. "No, seriously, I'd think up some excuse to get back to school early. Going home was no vacation for me. I was so damn sure I didn't want to spend my life out there in the middle of nowhere, working twelve hours a day. Not me." He shook his head in his own disbelief. "Now, I'd be happy to saddle up and ride 'till my butt ached. I didn't realize how much I really loved that piece of Texas. I do now."

The others listened intently, each visualizing the country in their own way, as Frank described West Texas. His picturesque description of the windswept prairie fixed an image in their mind in such a detailed manner they could almost feel the air and smell the cattle. There was no uncertainty about Frank's feeling for the land.

"I wish I felt that strongly about any place," Hank added. "I'd gladly kick some cow shit if I did, but I don't. I haven't the foggiest idea what I'm gonna' do after I get back, other than kiss the SOB who hands me my discharge."

"We thought you were regular Air Force. Did flying with Brian cool you to that idea?" Randy inquired with a big grin. He turned to Brian. "And what're you gonna' do? That is, after you grab Anne." Everyone at the table chuckled.

"When I get to that point, gang, it really won't matter."

As the others left for their first night on the town, Brian was content to retire to the bar. He chose a stool at the very end of the bar where he had a view of the entire room. Soothing music was coming from the recessed speakers, as the bartender moved in his direction.

"How about a bourbon and seven."

"Any particular brand?"

"No, just as long as it's Southern bourbon."

He drank slowly, focusing on the music and he was alone in his thoughts.

The four gathered together in the bar for their last night of the R&R. The ominous specter of Korea was slinking into their thinking, but remained undiscussed where it couldn't affect the easy nature of the conversation. During the third round of drinks, Randy looked a little perplexed. "Brian, It's a shame you didn't go with us. We felt bad about leaving you alone here."

Brian looked amused. "Don't. It was fine just listening to the music and having a few drinks. It was good to relax for a while. No alerts, no CAPs, no cold hootch, no one shooting at me, and no responsibilities. That's what it's all about."

Frank stood suddenly. "That'll do it for me, gang. I'll meet you in the lobby at 0800 for check out and transportation to "Tachi."

"Hey, wait a minute. I'll go up with you." Hank rose from the chair, dropping a five-dollar bill on the table.

Randy made no move to leave but held up his empty glass. "Brian, how about it? Could we have one more?"

Sensing his friends need to call it a longer night than he himself, Brian settled back in his chair motioning the waitress over. "I guess I could use another snort of bourbon before we go up."

Randy motioned to the waiter. "I'll have a bourbon on the rocks."

They sipped their drinks, each looking into his glass saying nothing. Silence was always in good taste for the two of them. Casually, they made small talk about the room's atmosphere and the ornate carvings on the back bar. Finally, Randy pushed the drink back, leaned back in his chair and asked, "Do you ever get scared up there? You know, sweat it out on some of those missions?" He looked down as if he probably shouldn't have brought the subject up.

"Hell, Randy, there's nobody who doesn't get a few churnings in the belly. The only difference is some don't admit it. Listen, some of those guys, who you think have to carry their balls around in a wheelbarrow, are probably more scared than you. It's natural." Randy chuckled at the analogy, as Brian continued. "Let me assure you, most of us are scared all the time. If someone who does what we do every day says he doesn't feel a little fear gnawing in the gut, they're lying, or very damn stupid."

"You telling me you're scared." Randy looked puzzled.

"Every day." Brian cleared his throat nervously. "But I'm a helluva' lot more afraid of failure. I just push it aside. We've all got our fears, they just come packaged differently."

"No. What I mean, Brian, is being so damn scared you wonder if you're going to be able to get in the aircraft. There're times I think about faking something with the flight surgeon and get grounded for a few days. Just a few days, and I think it'll go away."

Brian didn't answer immediately. He knew this required an answer he may not be able to come up with. He needed to say something that would put Randy's mind at ease. As he sat there looking at his friend, he realized Randy had been staring his dragon in the eye for some time. He also knew not to tinker too much with a man's fear. He needs to do that himself. Brian realized that almost daily, by sheer force of will, Randy had focused every ounce of his being on beating the fear, and never letting it show. He had to attempt an explanation. "Hey, a little fear is a good thing. The guys who go home are the ones make the least mistakes up there. That little fear, gnawing inside you, makes you think, keeps you alert, so you don't make mistakes. Panic, however, will kill you damn quick. Just make sure you use fear the right way." He reached over, slapping Randy on the shoulder. "You won't panic, Buddy, you're a damn good pilot. Don't ever doubt it."

"Thanks, Brian. Just talking about it helps. I'd appreciate it if you kept this just between us. I'd never tell Frank how I feel."

Brian nodded and gave him thumbs up.

Frank made his all-out effort for a touch of the Christmas spirit in hootch 620 with a small Korean pine decorated with bits of tinsel and homemade ornaments. The branches were irregularly shaped, spindly, and sparse. One string of lights, recently shipped from the States, twinkled a buoyant Christmas spirit amid the dreary inside of their hootch. The other three inhabitants were getting into the season spirit only with considerable effort. They were having only moderate success, even with continuous persuasion from Frank.

An arctic gust blew in with Frank as he sauntered through the door and flopped on his bunk. "How's this for luck?" He threw his feet over the end of the bunk. "I just checked the alert schedule and we made out big-time with Christmas Eve and Christmas Day off."

"That's call for a celebration." Hank said. "Not only that, but we're gonna' have us one helluva' time at Blue Flight's Christmas Eve party. I'm gonna' get so damn plastered they'll have to peel me off the overhead." He moved over and looked out onto the snow falling gently on the gravel path. "Maybe then I can forget where the hell I am for a while."

Brian glanced over quickly at Hank. "Well, well, now that doesn't sound like my RO, who's always the eternal optimist. Is Lieutenant 'Pollyanna' a little more pragmatic today? Or is this hell hole gettin' to him too?" Hank gestured back with his middle finger.

Frank rose up and sat on the edge of his bunk. "You two sound like living proof that evolution can go in reverse. Come off that sarcastic, attitude. It's almost Christmas." He leaned forward. "I found out Woody, as a surprise, had his wife make blue silk scarves with the name of each flight member embroidered in gold. He's worked so damn hard keeping those things hidden." He stopped. "You two cynics make damn sure you don't bust his bubble."

"No sweat," Randy added. "I promise they're gonna' act somewhat normal for the next few days."

Brian slammed the briefing room door behind him, blocking out the wind that followed closely. He glanced at the clock in front of the room, making sure he wasn't late for the 0600 briefing. Woody stepped in front of the assembled aircrews. He glanced at the large calendar beside the Korean map. No one had changed the date. He wandered over and flipped it to December twenty-second. "Good day for a mission." Rumblings came up quickly from the audience, as Woody laughed. "Let's get on with why the United States Air Force has allowed us to vacation here in the 'Land of The Morning Calm'." The smile evaporated. "We've gotta' CAP a particularly hot area in this sector." He slapped the map just above Namp'o. Fifth Air Force thought the marginal weather called for F-94's instead of F-86's." Blue Flight listened more intently as Woody concluded the briefing. "Josh and I'll be flying lead, with Randy and Frank on my wing. Walt and Sully, Brian and Hank will lead the second element on his wing.

The briefing was concise, as usual for Woody, and included instructions for a formation takeoff, thirty-second separation between the two elements. Everyone checked their gear carefully, and went to the schedule board to get aircraft assignments. Looking at the board, Randy began laughing. "How 'bout that. I've got *Mariah* today."

Brian's hand found Randy's shoulder. "Hey, I believe you've got my bird there. Somebody made a mistake."

"It shouldn't make that much difference. Besides, it's the Christmas season." He frowned as if deep in thought, then added, "Tell you what, I'll be fair about this thing. I'll flip you for it."

"Damn, I guess it'd be too easy for you just change your name up there." Brian frowned as he took out a quarter. "Call it."

"Tails." Randy shouted.

Brian looked at his coin, put the quarter back in his pocket, and walked away.

"I take that to mean it was a tail." He yelled after Brian. "Hey, Brian, I'll wipe my feet before I get in the cockpit." Brian ignored Randy, continuing out the door rather than giving him the satisfaction of knowing he'd gotten to him.

Once in the air the two elements were given steers to different areas. They occasionally heard radio transmissions directing Woody's element to a lower altitude for a run at a possible bogey, then they were directed to a different tactical frequency. After a few vectors that proved fruitless, they were given pigeons to home plate, and released from the CAP. As Walt was changing through the tactical frequencies, he heard a transmission about an aircraft "down." He rapidly contacted GCI control to ask about the downed bird. "Roger Tango Whiskey One, there is a downed aircraft in the other element."

"Castle, which one?"

"Tango Whiskey One, we have no confirmation on call sign. We've directed Search and Rescue to the spot."

Brian couldn't believe what he was hearing. It had to be Woody or Randy. "Walt, find out the call sign."

"Come on, Two, keep some radio discipline."

They broke over the runway, and took the proper spacing for landing. Brian taxied as fast as possible behind Walt, all the time looking around for *Mariah*. Instead, he spotted Woody, standing beside his aircraft, talking to the C.O. He felt tightness grip his throat as he shut down the engine. He bolted down the ladder, without waiting for Hank, and ran over to Woody and Major Larson.

Woody looked around as Brian approached. "It was Randy and Frank. The SAR rescue boats are out there, but I don't think it's possible..."

"Why don't you think they'll be picked up, Woody?" Brian almost screamed the interruption.

"Easy, easy!" Woody scowled at Brian. "We were at low altitude on the intercept, and the bogeys outran us. I think Randy was hit with ground fire because he yelled out that he had a fire warning light. He immediately headed for the water but, as soon as he crossed the beach, he just stop-cocked the damn engine. He was so worried about that goddamn fire warning light, he wasn't thinking straight. There was no place to go without power, but down. That fire warning light seemed to immobilize his thinking the minute he saw it. He panicked."

Walt and Hank ran up to join the group, eagerly waiting for additional details. Woody continued, "He realized he was going in and they tried to eject. The canopy wouldn't go. Can you believe it, the Goddamn canopy jammed? But he still didn't do a lot of things right. He didn't punch off the tip tanks, he didn't lower flaps, and he didn't even slow his approach. It looked to us like the aircraft broke up on contact with the water. We circled till fuel was bingo, but there was nothing on the water." His voice lowered. "Absolutely nothing."

Major Larson interceded in the conversation. "Well, at least both were single."

Brian dropped his helmet on the asphalt and wheeled on him. The fear and anxiety that he'd been fighting for the last thirty minutes merged with his temper. His anger was uncontrollable as he interrupted the C.O. "I guess bachelors are expendable, you, you ..."

Woody stepped between the two. He grabbed Brian's flight suit with both hands, almost lifting him off the concrete. "What the hell do you think you're saying? You're about to step way over the line here!"

Major Larson took Woody's sleeve. "Take it easy, Woody. I know what he's feeling. I've been there. I'm truly sorry, Lieutenant, truly sorry." The Major's voice lowered. "What I meant was there was no wife and kids I have to explain this to. Mothers and Fathers are hard enough, but letters to wives are damn hard for me to write. I reckon I didn't phrase that too well, did I?"

The explanation calmed Brian's outward anger, inside the rage grabbed at his gut. He reached down and picked up the helmet, turned, and silently walked toward the operations building. Inside the Ops building, he dropped the flight gear in his locker, slid on his flight jacket, acknowledged no one, and left the building with a mixed bag of anger and sadness.

He walked through the door of the hootch and stood there looking at the two bunks on the left side. He looked at family pictures, a hastily tossed jacket lying across a foot locker, a lighter left on the desk, personal effects scattered around the room that represented two vibrant human beings. He glanced down at the few presents Randy and Frank had received from the States. Frank, under the pathetic little Christmas tree, had carefully arranged each one. The sight underscored the grim irony of it all. Despair engulfed him. He sat down on his bunk, placed his head in his hands, and sobbed.

The fact that it was Christmas Eve and a few drinks did little to put gaiety into the gathering at the club. Blue Flight went through the motions of a Christmas party, trying in vain not to talk about their loss. But the topic was unavoidable and it entered conversations like a phantom that crept softly and deftly into any subject.

Blue Flight finished the meal, poured more wine, and lit cigars placed by each plate. They puffed on the cigars and watched as the club manager pulled back a screen to expose the scarves. There, placed carefully in two rows, were scarves for every member. A hush fell on the room. At the end of the top row were two blue scarves, letters embroidered in gold, "Randy" and "Frank." No one told the manager to remove the two scarves.

Woody sensed the tension and quickly pointed to the two scarves. "Hey, Guys, Randy and Frank were a part of us. It's appropriate that they be here with us in everything we do tonight. Those scarves represent two guys we love. They're with us, here tonight."

The words became incoherent as Woody continued. Brian slid his chair back and eased out the side door. He had to get some air. He couldn't breathe. He walked to the edge of the patio and stared into the night, feeling the warmth of tears that ran down his cheeks. He looked up at the star filled sky. It was the quietest night he could remember. Slivers of clouds drifted across the sky in inhuman slowness. He searched the night sky. *Why?*

He couldn't go back inside. Turning his collar up against the wind, he ambled back alone to the hootch. He was overwhelmed with the fact that it was Christmas Eve, as he moved toward his destination. A cold loneliness engulfed him.

The small strand of lights flickering on the tree was mesmerizing. He sat there, watching intently as each bulb glowed and went off, engrossed in the hypnotic effect of the lights. He stared hard into the multi-colored mirage, trying to find solace in the fact that it was Christmas. Scrutinizing the lights, his mind muddled, he wondered what kind of God lets these things happen. The lights merged into a prism-like collage of colors through the moisture in his eyes. He contemplated the remorse God would feel, should feel tonight. Maybe only us mortals feel such pain. Gods don't feel.

He knew this would be one Christmas Eve he'd remember the rest of his life. He took out paper and pen to write Anne. He thought for several minutes how he could possibly say what he was feeling at this moment.

Christmas Eve, 1952

My Dearest Anne,

It's Christmas Eve and I miss you more than I could ever put down on this sheet of paper. Two days ago, we lost Randy and Frank. They were killed as . . .

He wadded up the page and threw it on the floor. He took out another and began again.

Christmas Eve, 1952

My Dearest Anne,

It's Christmas Eve and I miss you more than I could ever express on this paper tonight. I look at the little tree we have here in the hootch and think about last Christmas with you in front of the fire, the big old cedar we decorated reflecting in the window, and you beside me on the sofa. I can almost feel the softness of your hair this very minute, as you put your head on my shoulder. Even though ten thousand miles separate us tonight, you're here with me in my thoughts. Your love sustains me every day. Thank you for being you and for being in my life.

I hope you're having a great Christmas, and that you have the peace that comes from knowing you are loved so very much. It's sobering to think of the true meaning of the season, and we must make sure we remember that in the midst of all the things happening in our lives. It's easy for us to forget, and it's difficult to keep our faith in these difficult times. We do manage to do it in spite of ourselves, however, at least most of the time. The calendar tells me that not only is it Christmas but that there are a lot fewer months before I'm with you again. I don't think there is any force on earth to make me leave you for this long again. The price is way too high to ever be justified.

Until I'm there to tell you, remember I love you more than you could possibly comprehend!

Brian

The New Year was ushered in with little fanfare, except as just one more flip of the calendar. The Korean cold became more assertive in January. It was numbing to the spirit and the body. Outdoors it was like living in a deep freeze and indoors it was impossible to get warm. Two new members of the 86th FIS joined Brian and Hank in hootch 620. They were affable enough, but neither Brian nor Hank made the effort to get close to the new inhabitants. Even though the subject was never discussed, they missed Randy and Frank every day. Daily reminders were everywhere in the hootch of their two friends and their loss. There was a scar on the soul.

January eased into February with little to differentiate the two months. The CO had another letter to write explaining why another crew failed to return from a night mission, and the Korean winter turned brutally cold, showing no mercy to anyone or anything. The cold hung in the air as if daring the sun to warm it. Brian noticed the one thing he looked forward to, the mail, more than anything else was conspicuously missing for several days. This began to disturb him as the days became seven, then ten.

He continued to write Anne faithfully, thinking there must be some glitch in the postal service. However, the fourteenth day came with no letter from Anne, and the reality of the situation became apparent. He had to face the fact that something was wrong, but where were Lori's letters? Normally, she would have provided some explanation, some insight to what was happening. The fact that she couldn't, or wouldn't, make it clear Lori didn't want to discuss it.

On the sixteenth day, a letter arrived from Anne. Brian turned it over and over in his hand, looking at it as if he wished it gone, removed from his sight. Slowly, he placed it in his flight jacket pocket to read later. He was in no hurry to read this letter. Instead, he went to the Club.

Not being in the mood for poker, he declined the invitation to join a game in progress and walked over to the table where Hank and Mike were having a drink. "Mind if I join you?"

"No, we just assumed you'd be at the poker table." Hank nodded in the direction of the smoke-encircled table.

"Not tonight. Thought I'd have a few drinks here."

After Brian's fourth bourbon and seven, Mike put his glass down, and looked squarely at Brian. "Just what the hell's eating at you tonight?"

Brian glared at Mike. "And just what the hell gives you the idea that something's eating at me?"

Before Mike could reply, a group of F-86 pilots wandered up to the jukebox, and began playing *Sabre Dance* for the third consecutive time. Brian swung around for a better view of the culprits. With no further comment to either Hank or Mike, he shoved his chair back, walked directly to the jukebox, and snatched the plug from the wall. The music stopped abruptly, a hush fell across the room, and the quiet echoed around him. Initially, the four F-86 pilots looked surprised but then their mood suddenly changed. A tall blonde Captain stepped forward directly in Brian's line of sight. "Is there any explanation for that last move of yours, or had you rather just bend over and plug it back in?"

Brian moved to within three inches of the guy's face. "I'm rather sick of hearing that idiot song but I guess you goddamn MiG killers have to blow smoke somehow about your wild exploits. Especially since some of you fly a hundred missions and never fire the guns, and then only in daylight, with no clouds in the sky."

Mike was already standing, but Hank continued to sit, shaking his head at what he now knew was the inevitable. Brian was surrounded by all four of the Saber pilots, who were rattling off insults of their own.

Mike jumped between the two opposing ideas in music. "Wait just a minute before we all regret this situation. My friend here has had a few drinks and he has some wide mood swings when he drinks. Besides, you've played that damn song into the ground tonight. How 'bout we all just go back and have a drink and forget the whole thing?"

Brian was smiling as if totally enjoying Mike's negotiating tactics. By then, several members of both units were stepping in to ensure a peaceful conclusion. There was too much to lose in a firestorm such as this, particularly in an Officers' Club. Normally, the charges would begin with "conduct unbecoming an officer and gentleman," and escalate from there. Thanks, in large part to Mike's diplomacy, tempers settled down rapidly, and common sense prevailed.

Back at the table Brian turned to Mike. "What the hell do you mean: 'He has some wild mood swings when he drinks'?"

Mike put his hand on Brian's shoulder, smiled. "Frankly, I don't particularly give a rat's ass what swings your moods! Just don't do something that stupid again. We almost had a bad situation here."

"Alright already." Brian eased a broad grin across his face. "And thanks, Mike, for saving those 'Sabre jocks'."

"Oh sure, I could see they were in imminent danger."

The surrounding laughter continued for several minutes, with occasional stares from the Saber pilots on the other side of the room.

Brian motioned to Hank. "Let's call it an evening and head for the ole' hootch. Whatcha' say? Have I been stupid enough for one night?"

"Good God that requires no answer. See you guys later," Hank announced as he rose to leave. Brian and Hank left the club still laughing about the incident.

After Hank fell asleep, Brian went into the section of the Quonset hootch with the screened area. He pulled the light down low, so as not to disturb the others, and took out the letter from Anne. He opened it slowly, still not wanting to read it, and unfolded the one page.

Dear Brian,

By now you must have realized that something is terribly wrong. I apologize for waiting so long to write you, but I just didn't know how to explain it. I still don't, but I must try. I've shed many tears in trying to figure this thing out and the answers are still not there. You know that I've always had trouble trying to understand the Air Force, and how it would affect our lives. It's a way of life that seems so foreign to my sheltered world. The separation has been horrendous, affecting both of us for these many months. There are disturbing times when I can't remember what you look like, and I have to look at your picture to refresh my memory.

Last week, Jean Glasner was notified that her husband was killed. She's left school and her friends say she's too upset to return. I think about her every day, and wonder how she is coping after being notified he was shot down one month before he was to come home, and after enduring those months of waiting. This has had a devastating effect on me. It was the final straw.

I knew that the feelings I was having weren't fair to either of us. I talked with my pastor about the situation and he told me that I had to write you and tell you these things. It was only fair to you if I do this. I know it seems like I'm not making sense as I read what I'm writing. The thing is, I care for you too much to continue hiding my fears and hoping they'll change. I'll always care for you, and hope everything in your life is

just as you want it. You certainly deserve it. You're one of the most gentle
and honest people I've ever known. I wish you happiness.
I'll place the ring in Mama's safe deposit box until you come home.
Love,
Anne

Brian read the letter a second time, trying to glean some understanding of the words that seared into his brain. He looked over at her picture and thought back to those nights where they shared the most intimate details of their life. He thought about the total happiness they felt just being together. So many thoughts were overwhelming his consciousness. They wandered from Agnes-Baines, Collinwood, the beach at Aunt Carolyn's, and to San Francisco, especially San Francisco.

It defied any explanation he thought of. No two people were more in love or so totally committed to each other. His emotions played games with him, ranging from hurt to rage, and included all those in between. He crumpled the letter in his hand, squeezing it until his hand shook. "Anne, Anne." He whispered to himself, as he turned off the light, and walked over to his bunk. He wondered if a night's sleep would erase these questions of "why" or at least clarify his thinking in the morning.

It didn't. The realization of his loss was more perceptible in the light of day. He'd have to adjust now, to find some way to stop thinking about her.

CHAPTER FIFTEEN

BRIAN REDUCED POWER, popped his speed brakes, and joined in formation with Gaskell. He tucked it in close, placing his tip tank three feet from his element leader's canopy. Gaskell shook his head vigorously, slid out to his left, indicating he wasn't having formation that close. Brian smiled behind the oxygen mask and tucked it in tight again, only a few feet away. He held it there like he was glued to his element leader. Gaskell broke hard left, accelerating into the haze, leaving Brian and Hank behind as the lead aircraft disappeared as if swallowed by the sky.

"Well, well." Brian said. "We lost our leader."

"Amazing, isn't it?" Hank replied. "Maybe if you stuck your tip tank in his lap, you could've made your point better."

As they taxied up and shut down, First Lieutenant Robert J. Gaskell was standing at the bottom of the ladder, waiting. Brian descended the ladder, jumping the last two feet. Gaskell moved up to Brian's nose.

"What th' hell you trying to prove? You're one dangerous sonafabitch in the air. You ever stick your tip tank in my face again and I'll have a piece of your ass."

"Now, don't go lettin' your mouth overload your butt, Hotshot. You might have a punch about like you fly, a bit on the delicate side." Brian fists tensed, waiting for the first blow.

Hank quickly grabbed Brian's arm. "C'mon, let's go get a drink at the club. Don't push it any further." Hank pulled harder on the arm. "C'mon, Brian, let's go."

Brian turned swiftly and followed his friend. Gaskell stood there watching, saying nothing.

As they walked up the gravel path, Hank jumped in front and faced him. "Brian, what th' hell's wrong with you?" He grabbed both sleeves, pulling him closer. "You've got *me* worried now. Some think you've already gone round the bend." Brian pulled loose from Hank's grasp. He walked away, showing no reaction, leaving Hank standing there shaking his head.

Lori wrote within the week. She didn't try to explain Anne's actions, only regret that Brian had to be told when he was so far away. She continued to be a consistent friend, the one known security, where consistency seemed so elusive to him.

Dear Brian:

Where do I begin? I should probably write the type of letter that you seem to enjoy and expect from me...brief, newsy, cheerful, crammed with nonsense and tid-bits, which I hope always, bring a smile to your face. But I just can't do that...not this time. I'm certain that by now you have received Anne's letter, and I know how devastated you must be. I can well understand how caring for and losing someone can hurt deeply. I would

282

give anything if only I had the ability to say or do something to ease that hurt.

I've wanted so much to write to you before now, but I was afraid that my letter might arrive before Anne's ...and I was having difficulty finding the right words to express how I feel. I still can't find those words.

As close as she and I are, you know that she is still a very private person. She has not shared all her reasons with me. I have never been one who asks too many questions, but not having any answers leaves me stunned. I do know that your involvement with the Air Force has always been a stumbling block in your relationship, but I truly thought Anne came to grips with that. I suppose not, and I find it impossible to explain her decision to you. I wish I could – all I can say to to you – have faith in the future.

Brian, I feel so badly for you. I want you to know that my thoughts and prayers are with you always...as are my hopes that you will return safely and find the happiness that you deserve...because you do, you know.

Please write soon and let me know how you're doing.

Always,

Lori

Arctic blasts swept down from Manchuria, accentuated the lingering cold. The callous winds slammed against his body, piercing the spirit as well. Only rarely was relief felt with an intermittent day of some perceptible warmth. Anytime the temperature soared above freezing, it was just enough to tease him that spring was still a possibility. On those days Brian felt the warmth beyond the physical aspects. It momentarily took away part of the virulent outlook that crept insipidly into his spirit. On one of those warmer-than-usual days, Hank bounded through the door of the Club, pulling out a chair in front of Brian, who was munching on a hamburger and a mountain of french fries. Brian hardly looked up as Hank pulled out several sheets of paper. Hank held them at arms length. Shaking the papers playfully, he eased his face around the side. "Want to know what these are?"

"That's a moot point since you're busting a gut to tell me." Brian took a bite of hamburger. Hank sat staring at him, saying nothing. Brian looked up. "Well, go ahead."

"Good God, you're difficult to get in the mood for a little travel to the States. This, my friend, is your preference for stateside assignment. Next come orders for the real world."

Brian put down the hamburger, focusing his attention on Hank. "Now that you brought the subject up, there's something I need to tell you. I'm extending for another tour.

Hank sat expressionless, staring at Brian, his mind groping for words. "What's this bull shit?" Brian looked only at his food, showing no signs he heard the question. Hank continued, "We've been friends a long time. Been through a lot together, good and bad, not to mention that I put my butt on the line with you every day. In other words, I've earned the right to tell you something you aren't gonna' like." He paused for a reaction. None came. He shook his head in disgust. "Godamighty, I wish I could get inside your head and unleash those demons that seem to be raging in there. But, I'll tell you this. No woman in the world is worth what you're doing to yourself." He looked at Brian, hoping for a response. Getting nothing, he leaned closer. "Goddamn it! Are you intent on getting yourself killed? Fella', you need to know which bridges to cross and which ones to burn. Right now you need a great big flame thrower."

Brian gazed out the window then turned back to Hank. "I'm not gonna' justify why I'm doing this, not even to you. And save your trite platitudes for the truly needy."

"Everybody we were close to has gone home, or been killed."

Hank said. "Scott and Buck have orders. Now it's our time to go back. Believe me, it's *time*. For God's sake, Brian, let's go home."

"I didn't say anything about *you* extending." His hands hit the table. "You're going back."

"You've become one cynical, insufferable sonofabitch in the last couple of months, and not just by my calculations. No, oh, hell no. Cynical doesn't even begin to describe your attitude. You're a bitter SOB. If I thought a smack in the mouth would help, I'd try that."

"Well now, Hank, why hold back there. Why don't ya' tell me how you really feel."

"What the hell's the use? You haven't listened to a damn thing I've said. Not a damn thing." There was a pause in the conversation before Hank continued. "Well, if you're hell-bent on doing this stupid thing, then count me in too."

Brian pushed the plate away. "No, hell you won't. I don't want to hear your pissin' and moanin' about what I've done to you. I'd get that speech every morning for breakfast."

"You won't hear any complaints. I don't think anybody else in the squadron would fly with you anyway. They'd have to get some new 'butter bar' Lieutenant in the back seat. I wouldn't do that to some unsuspecting new kid."

"You're just a friend of man. Right?"

There was no talking Hank out of his decision to stay. Later, when Brian brought up the fact that he still had time to change his mind, Hank replied: "You need someone to keep you on the straight and narrow. Nobody's up to that job but me."

A week later, Scott sauntered into the hootch, and plopped on the bunk next to Brian. Hank was standing behind Brian. Scott glanced back and forth, watching them through worried squinted eyes. He leaned forward. "Brian, I've known you a long time, we've been through a lot together since flight training, and shared a chunk of life most people can't even comprehend. Let's finish this thing together and head for the States. We both know it's damn well time."

"Scott, I'd rather not get into this with you. Whatever you're gonna' say won't change a damn thing."

"You're about the craziest sonofabitch I know." Scott grumbled.

"And you're the biggest ass I've seen all day." Brian retorted.

"Then you surely didn't shave today. You have to look in a mirror." Scott said. Then dropped his head appearing to realize all arguments were useless. He looked up suddenly to Hank. "As for you, Hoss, I have a real problem trying to understand. I'm not sure there's that much loyalty left in this old world. So, you my friend are either unique or insane. Since I'll never know the answer to that one, I'll give you the benefit of the doubt."

Three days later, Scott and Buck said their goodbyes, and that they'd be waiting for them in the States. Scott moved toward Brian and put his arms around him. Brian whispered something in his ear, inaudible to the others, as they slapped each other on the back. They stood there for some seconds, looking at each other intently, saying nothing.

Brian squinted as he watched the C-119 courier take off with Scott and Buck on board. A disconcerting and unexpected loneliness swallowed him. He felt desolation slowly replacing the numbness he'd felt for months. He hated it.

The end of April marked the beginning of the second combat tour. They pinned on their first Lieutenant bars, and added another oak leaf cluster to the Air Medal. That afternoon, Hank moved up to the desk and slapped the R&R request on the Adjutant's note pad.

The overweight Captain glanced up. He narrowed his small pale-blue eyes at the intrusion, then casually scanned the paper. "So you want some battery-charging time in Nagoya? So this is where Brian wants to go for his complimentary R&R?"

"It doesn't make a good goddamn to him where he is. I'll just tell him where and when we're going. I made this decision. Ever hear of the number of nurses hanging around the largest hospital in Japan?"

Captain Alfred laughed. "Maybe ole Brian will loosen up a bit."

Hank finished checking into the luxurious Imperial hotel. He looked around admiringly at the lobby. Through the large window at the end he could see the bustling traffic and hear sounds of activity taking place in front of the hotel. The sounds beckoned to him.

"This is fantastic. Soon as you get signed in there, let's shower, change, and head for town. There're some great bars downtown. Let's get crazy."

"Sorry, I'm not interested in oriental women or the bar scene." Brian replied. "You go get crazy enough for both of us. I'll hang around here."

"You finally get here to Nagoya and you're gonna' hibernate in a hotel room?"

"Yep. And the bar, the hot tub, and the restaurant, and..."

"Okay, okay." Hank interrupted quickly. "I get the idea."

Brian was content to relax, to do a little shopping, and enjoy the sights. He particularly enjoyed the Japanese cuisine and Hank found time to join him for several meals. Each pursued their own interests without placing any demands on the other.

The last night in Nagoya, Brian ate dinner and went back to the hotel bar for a couple of drinks before going up to his room. The background music was playing the good old songs he enjoyed. Music had its usual grasp on his emotions. As he listened, toying with his fresh bourbon, he tried to place a particular time and place with each song. He enjoyed the game and the reminiscing. As the next number began playing, Brian's head popped up from his drink. There was no mistaking *La Vie En Rose*.

The bartender moved closer, leaned across the bar, and asked: "What's her name, Lieutenant?"

"Was it that obvious?" Brian snapped.

"You never forget the song you fell in love to." The bartender pressed the issue.

"Well, I have a theory. Love songs are just a hoax to get your imagination in conflict with reason."

"Yeah, she must be really special. Wanna' talk about it?"

"Don't think so." Brian retorted.

The bartender laughed. "Lieutenant, I read somewhere that love's like a spiritual root canal. I believe you'd agree with that." He stopped momentarily, seeing Brian didn't respond to the humor. "Besides, fate usually takes a hand in these matters." He added.

"Sergeant, you're quite a philosopher. I used to believe in fate and all that crap. I reckon we create our own destiny. No, maybe we just stumble blindly along. Like crossing through a long dark room, every step one more surprise."

"C'mon, Lieutenant." The bartender didn't capitulate to Brian's reasoning. "There's gotta' be some master plan, some reason for how and why things happen. You make it sound like life's an infiltration course."

"Not a bad analogy. I could tell you about people who are no longer with us. And believe me, most of 'em had an unadulterated, greedy, appreciation for life. But you think some great 'Master Plan' snuffed them like that?" He snapped his fingers. "What the hell kind of plan is that?"

"Maybe someday you'll understand why." The bartender said.

"No, Sergeant, the more I think about it, the more certain I am that life isn't supposed to be understood. Maybe some things are better left a damn mystery." Brian's inflection terminated the conversation.

The music was good for his soul. He sipped his drink slowly, lost in thought about a distant world. He listened intently to the words of *Smile,* mentally projecting himself to another existence, another time and place.

"Excuse me, mind if I sit here?" Jolted back to the bar in Nagoya, Brian turned to look at an exquisite blonde, wearing First Lieutenant bars on the blue nurse's uniform. "No, sit down." He turned back to his drink, which was almost empty. "Bartender." He pointed to his empty glass, then turned toward the woman sitting next to him. "Can I buy you a drink?"

"No, thanks anyway." She smiled, raising a martini with an empty olive pick, and added, "I noticed you sitting over here alone. You weren't trying to chase down every female in view. That's quite unusual around here. So, I decided to sit here and enjoy my martini. You see, if they think you're with someone, guys aren't hitting on you. I've had enough of that 'eat, drink, and make love, for tomorrow we die' reasoning."

Brian nodded and turned back to wait for his fresh drink. After thinking about what she'd said, he turned suddenly. "I just realized that statement sure wasn't a compliment. In other words, I looked harmless?"

She laughed. "No, I thought you were a gentleman. By the way, my name's Maggie, Maggie Compton." She put out her hand.

"Brian Brannon. Where're you stationed?" He wasn't quick in releasing her hand. She had beautiful face, her short blond hair hung loosely over her forehead. Her hand was smooth and soft, reminding him of the lack of softness in his life this last year.

"I'm assigned to the hospital here in Nagoya." She said. "I took a one-week leave to get away from it for a while. I was tired of standing over an operating table watching some nineteen-year-old lose a body part, knowing he'll never be whole again in any way."

"I know that's tough. He looked around the room. "I certainly recommend this place to put your mind at rest for a while. You can relax here."

The bartender placed Brian's drink in front of him. They said nothing as each played with their drinks and listened to the music. After a few minutes, Maggie touched his arm. "Can I tell you the real reason I decided to sit here?"

"Sure. And what was your *real* reason?" Brian watched her intently, listening to her soft, yet commanding voice. Her eyes came alive when she laughed. The laughter caused her mouth to form small, almost indistinguishable, dimples on each side. It was her extraordinarily sensitive mouth that acquired his rapt attention.

"Call it feminine intuition. I watched you for some time and it was quite apparent you were mentally ten thousand miles from this bar tonight."

"Well, hell, I thought you were a surgical nurse. I'll bet you're really in the psychiatric ward."

Her eyes narrowed. "Are you always this defensive?"

Brian focused on his drink. Neither said anything for minutes.

Finally, Brian swiveled around. "I'm sorry. I must've sounded like an ass. Let's at least be comfortable." He pointed toward a table in a corner of the room. "Let's sit over there at a table." Without a word, she stood and walked over to the table. Brian followed, carrying their nearly-empty glasses. He held a chair for her then pulled his opposite her.

"How'd you decide to be a nurse, in this disaster of a war?"

"A guy I was in love with, back home in Wilmington, Delaware, decided he wasn't."

"A lot of that seems to be going around this year." He said.

"Oh, so that accounts for the far away look at the bar. You were thinking about her."

"Maybe for a fleeting moment there." He smiled. "But back to your case; is that why you joined the Air Force?"

"Probably. It didn't take me long to realize you can't run away from life's problems. You look around and, lo and behold, they're still right there. The only thing that changes is the scenery. What you're running from always comes along for the ride."

Brian nodded. "There're more than a few 'old expressions' about that kind of thing. And like most 'good old expressions', clichés, and sage advice, they never really get around to telling you what to do about it."

"I think I have things under control now. You cope. You adjust." She played nervously with her drink, and then suddenly glanced up. "Besides, I met Stan, a surgeon at the hospital, and we seemed to hit it off from the start. At first, I thought it was the respect I had for his intellect and medical skills, then realized it went beyond that."

"Where's he tonight?"

"He left two weeks ago for the States. It seems like two decades. That's why I took leave. That and the pressures of the hospital made me want to get away."

"Sounds like you're in love with this Stan fellow?"

"I'm not sure. I thought I was. That could be a result of the pressures we were under and the close proximity to each other. Only time'll tell if it was love. I'm more realistic these days, and probably a little cynical to boot." She pulled her chair closer. "He'll be getting out in six weeks and setting up practice in upstate New York. We'll soon know if we hit it off as well back in the States. We may find out we're different people back there." She sipped her martini. "What's your story?"

"It'd sound about the same as yours. Sometimes people change things. Sometimes things change people. Somewhere in there lies a reason for a 'Dear John'." He chuckled. "Oh well, you cope, you adjust – right?"

"Looking at you back there at the bar, I wouldn't say you've adjusted that much."

"There goes that psychoanalysis again."

They talked for the next two and half hours and several more drinks. They easily slipped into conversation about intimate feelings and concerns, exploring thoughts that had never been shared with others. No one had heard the deep emotions, and inner thoughts that Brian, for some unforeseen reason, felt so easy to convey to Maggie. He could never remember feeling such an emotional release. It was if the pressure of pent-up feelings was about to explode and here was the relief valve. As they talked he felt as though his mind and Maggie's were one. Their thoughts meshed, woven together in mutual understanding and acceptance. His melancholy feelings were soon replaced with a buoyancy of spirit.

As they examined their lives, sharing feelings, Brian couldn't stop looking into her riveting blue eyes, watching her full lips, and winsome smile. This, along with the tilting of her head when she laughed, had begun to be unsettling. He was relieved to see a slight amount of nervousness on her part when she glanced at her watch. "I think I should get some sleep. It's been a very long day."

Brian stood up and slid her chair back. "You've brightened my evening immensely, and I appreciate it, Lieutenant Maggie Compton. Thanks." She turned quickly. "We're both pretty vulnerable right now. If things were different..."

He took her hand before she could finish her statement and led her out into the brightly-lit lobby. She stopped and looked up at him. "I'd ask you to walk me up to my room, but that'd be a mistake. Wouldn't it?"

"We both know it would, but there's absolutely nothing I'd rather do at this very moment." He took her hand as they walked to the elevator. Looking intently at each other, they rode in silence to the fourth floor, then walked down the long hall to her room. Maggie opened the door and moved quickly across the room. She turned on the lamp beside the sofa, and then pointed to the small refrigerator. "Care for a drink?"

"No thanks."

She sat beside him on the sofa, kicked off her shoes, and tucked her feet up under her. He moved closer. Her mouth lifted to his. The intensity surprised Brian.

Maggie stood quickly. Reaching down for his hand, she pulled him toward her. He followed her to the bedroom. There was no surprise. They knew what was going to happen.

They spent the rest of the evening engulfed in emotions that neither had any desire to control. They made love well into the night before falling asleep in each other's arms. It was a night of pure passion and absolute abandonment of all inhibitions.

Brian woke and eased out of the bed where Maggie lay sleeping, a vision of perfect beauty to him. As he buttoned his shirt, he watched admiringly as a small wisp of hair moved intermittently with each breath. She awoke, trying to focus on the figure standing beside her. She smiled, holding her arms outstretched to him. Brian bent down and kissed her tenderly. She held onto his hand. "Can't we have breakfast?"

"My RO'll wonder what happened to me. We've got to catch the courier back to Korea in two hours." Brian rechecked his watch as he spoke.

Maggie's eyes met Brian's. She smiled and shook her head. "I have a distinct feeling that when you leave this room, we'll never see each other again, and I think you know that, too."

"Don't be ridiculous. You'll see me again before you know it. This was an evening I'll remember for a long time. Who knows what the future holds, but I'll tell you this; you're one, very special lady." He looked away nervously. "I left my address on the table."

She walked him to the door, put her arms around him, touched her face to his, and whispered, "Be careful back there in Korea."

"Sure." He turned and left without looking back.

Back in his room, Brian showered and quickly packed his bag. The door flew open as Hank bounded into the room, hurriedly grabbing things to place in his B-4 bag startled him. "I know I'm pushing the time factor." He never stopped packing. "I'm sorry, Brian, but my God, last night was something else! And I'm really sorry I bailed out on you and left you alone at the bar. I hope you weren't too bored, Buddy."

Brian looked at Hank with a large smile. "Hey, don't worry about it. I needed the rest."

CHAPTER SIXTEEN

THEY STEPPED OFF the courier, looking around at a panorama of desolate terrain. The change from what they had just left was abrupt and depressing. The mid-day sun illuminated a world of uneven ground, of treeless hills and baked brown earth. Reluctantly, they walked toward their hootch, lost in individual memories of the past few days.

It took little time getting back into the pattern of alerts, flying and whatever diversity they could discover to make Korea and the war seem less pervasive in their lives. Time was measurable only by events, and in the absence of anything other than the mundane, the next month moved faster than either anticipated. They were either getting used to their environment or impervious to its requirements.

Hank lazily reached over and answered the buzzing field phone in the alert shack. He paused momentarily and turned to Brian with a quizzical look. "Hey, it's for you, a Lieutenant Compton." He held his hand over the receiver. "Sounds like a female."

Brian reached over and took the phone without commenting. "Hi Maggie, where in the world are you? Geez, it's hard enough to talk to other bases here in Korea, much less Japan."

"I'm here in Korea, at K-2, Taegu. I filled in at the last minute for one of the flight nurses who was sick. I thought if I got this close, maybe there'd be a remote possibility of seeing you. There was a slim chance the flight would RON 'till tomorrow but the aircraft commander just told me we'd be departing within the hour. They have all of the patients ready to leave, and unfortunately, no need to stay over." She explained.

"Damn, with a little planning, I could have flown a bird down there and spent a few hours with you. We're always catching each other just as we're leaving some place."

"I'm as disappointed as you." she said. "Do you think it's possible to get a few days in Nagoya soon? That night back at the Imperial was a bit incredible. I can't forget that night."

"Neither can I." He glanced at Hank, who was taking in the conversation with a look of incredulity. "It'll be tough, but I'll give a shot at getting a few days off next month. If I get lucky, I'll catch a courier going in that direction. There are a few things ..."

"Sorry, gotta' go. The ambulances are already on the ramp. Hurry to Nagoya. Bye."

There was only a steady buzz on the other end. Their conversation was left there, suspended, unfinished. Brian thought how analogous it was to their relationship.

"Excuse me, but just who the hell's Lieutenant Compton? Maggie to be precise?" Hank asked. Brian still holding the phone, looking blankly at the wall, didn't respond. Hank touched his arm. "Where the hell have I been that I could have missed *that* chapter? By the sound of the conversation, something heavy happened between you two. Where the bloody hell was I?"

Brian slowly placed the phone on top of the olive drab case and looked over at Hank. "It's a subject for another time, another place, and should only be discussed over a drink." He winked. "If the time's ever right, I may tell you about Maggie."

Hank knew it was time to change the subject.

"Hey, just thirty more minutes 'till we get off alert. I hate being number one the last hour of alert. It's about this time of the day that I get those bad feelings about this place."

Brian glanced around the sky at the billowy rain clouds to the North, light barely visible through breaks in the stratocumulus layers. Clouds massed to the West were like a formless gray sheet, from which may come drizzle. "The F-eighty-sixes could have pulled alert today. The weather isn't that marginal, even for those..." The warbling sound of the scramble horn terminated his statement. Both leaped off the bench, running toward the aircraft. Brian bounded up the ladder, followed closely by Hank. Straps were snapped in place, engine started, canopy lowered, as they exited the alert pad for a scramble takeoff. They rounded the turn to the active runway without any checks. Scramble takeoffs left no time for such luxuries. The glow of the afterburner glistened off the wet runway, reflecting in the tip tanks, as the aircraft lunged forward on its takeoff roll.

"Just our shitty luck to be scrambled with only twenty-five minutes to go before the Club. Let's make this quick so we can get some chow." Hank grumbled into his oxygen mask.

"No sweat, this'll probably turn out to be a couple of F-eighties who forgot to authenticate the correct code."

"Victor One, your bogies are seven-eight miles, twelve o'clock, angels three zero."

"Well hell, what did I tell you, Hank. There's a pair of 'em we need to identify fast and get on home."

They were skimming through the top edge of the overcast, darting in and out of the turbid clouds, as sky and earth merged into gray murkiness around them. Hank looked up from the scope long enough to notice the broken, intermittent layer of clouds. "Brian, if we jump *two* MiGs in this kind of weather we could end up in with more than we bargained for. We'd be in very deep kimchee."

"Negative on the kimchee, Sport, we're gonna' make sure they're the ones in a world of hurt. Just keep the radar in search mode."

"I got 'em. Two bogies twenty degrees port – oh, shit – the targets split. Jesus, Brian, they know we're here."

"Get lock-on for one of 'em and just give me range and overtake." Brian asserted in the intercom, as he eased the throttle to 100%, and flipped the gun compressor on.

"Lock-on." Fifteen hundred yards."

"Castle, Victor One, Judy"

"Roger on the Judy."

"Brian we're closing fast. One thousand yards; maximum firing range. Fire!"

Brian held his finger over the trigger but held off on firing. He knew he'd have to save some ammo for the wingman.

"Five-hundred yards." Hank yelled in the intercom.

Brian squeezed off a burst of the fifty calibers. They popped out of the clouds into bright blue sky. Brian kept the dot centered in the scope and held the trigger down. He could see the tracers biting into the MiG, as pieces of the right wing flew into the air. The MiG pilot broke hard left and Brian pulled back on the stick, breaking with him, trying to keep in position on his tail. He fired another burst, and another, as the G forces mashed them into the seat. They scored a couple of added hits, but not enough for the kill, and the MiG was pulling away. The G-forces almost caused both to black out, as Brian pulled tighter in the turn, the F-94 vibrating on verge of a high-speed stall.

"Brian, let's get the hell out of here." Hanks voice strained with the G forces. Brian was too busy pulling the nose up for another shot. "Damn." He grunted through the G forces pulling at his body. "Just one more burst." It was obvious the MiG was turning inside of them and they were no longer in cloud cover. The F-94 vibrated laboriously as Brian pulled tighter in the turn, indicating they were on the edge of a high-speed stall. Brian squeezed the trigger in a long burst from the fifty caliber guns. Smoke and flame poured from the belly of the MiG as it rolled inverted. Brian broke hard right. "Damn, we nailed him but I wanted no doubt on the gun camera film. But we got him! Let's get outta' of here."

The aircraft lurched hard right, banging helmets into the canopy, as holes appeared in the left wing. The second MiG had rolled upside down, and pulled through in a half loop, to come in behind Brian and Hank. Brian rammed the throttle to afterburner and broke hard left. The F-94 bucked as the MiG's thirty-seven millimeter cannon shredded metal. Pieces of the left wing disappeared as cannon fire continued to rip into the aircraft. Brian knew speed is everything in a fighter, but this required something drastic, and instantly.

"We've only got one chance. Here goes." Brian snatched the nose straight up, pulled the throttle from afterburner to idle, and deployed the speed brakes simultaneously. The F-94 decelerated instantly in a near vertical attitude. The MiG, caught by surprise, shot past the top of the canopy. Brian rolled the F-94 and pulled the nose straight through, diving into the clouds below. The altimeter wound down as the F-94 screamed toward the ground. Brian leveled-off at ten thousand feet in the midst of solid clouds. The aircraft vibrated the stick in his hand, telling him immediately the damage wasn't confined to the wing. His flight suit was clammy from perspiration and he felt drained as he eased the throttled back to eighty-five percent RPM. The vibration increased even at a reduced power setting.

"That was close, Hank." Brian glanced at the left wing. "Damn, he made some hits on us but good."

"Hey, Brian, take another look at the damage out there. We're losing fuel out of both wing tanks on the left side. Those are some good-sized holes over there. The back of the tip tank's completely gone." Hank's voice indicated his anxiety.

Brian looked over his left shoulder again to see fuel pouring out of the shredded metal that was once a wing. "That's not the worst of it." He knew the aircraft vibrating violently indicated a damaged compressor. "It's gonna be tight, Hank. We're not gonna' make K-thirteen. We'd better head for the water and punch out there."

"Negative!" Hank shouted. "Keep it heading south and try cross the bomb line. You know the odds of getting rescue to come up there to look for us."

"You're right. It's gonna' be dark soon, and I don't like the thought of spending the night in the drink. We're heading south." He flipped the radio frequency to the emergency channel of 121.5 MHZ, keyed the mike button on the throttle: "Mayday, Mayday, Mayday, Victor One."

"Roger, Victor One. We have your transponder on radar and acknowledge your Mayday. Your pigeons to friendly territory are one eight-niner degrees, four-zero miles. Can you make it?"

"I doubt it, Castle. Get a chopper in the air if you can. Well hell, that answers that. Castle, we've flamed out at angels niner. Looks like we're gonna' be a little short."

Brian secured the fuel switches and reduced the rate of descent to five hundred feet per minute. "Hank, we're gonna' have to punch out at about four thousand. That'll get us as close as possible and still give us time to eject."

"Damn, let's wait till at least three thousand feet. That'll get us a little closer. I don't wanna' be over the north if it's possible. Wait as long as we can."

"Okay, I'll blow the canopy at three thousand. When it goes, don't hesitate."

"Roger, roger!" Hank answered.

"Castle control, Victor One going through angels five. Do you still have us?"

"Roger, Victor One, but you're still two-one miles north of the bomb line. We've got a chopper in the air."

"Roger, Castle. We're punching at angels three, going through four now."

"Good luck, Victor One."

As the dying aircraft went through three thousand feet, Brian eased the nose up to reduce the air speed, and yanked the canopy eject handle. Even with his visor down, the wind slapped at his face. A loud explosion announced that Hank's seat left the aircraft. Brian placed his head against the headrest, squeezing the trigger under the right armrest. Pilot and seat exploded into a blast of air. The force ripped away his oxygen mask and helmet. Instinctively, he released the lap belt and grabbed at the ripcord. Earth and sky spun wildly, blending together in a surrealist blending of indistinguishable colors, as he tumbled through space. He yanked harder on the rip cord and his body snapped straight to an upright position with the sudden shock of the canopy opening. The jolt was welcomed, as the canopy billowed above him. He looked around for Hank, then down at the bleak terrain beneath his boots, wondering how far they were from any friendly troops. Hank's oscillating chute, was barely visible on the distant horizon. Glancing down again, he tried to maneuver the chute toward a rice paddy, but was having little luck turning into the wind. He felt the warm trickle of blood run down his cheek. The helmet visor cut a three-inch gash in his forehead as it ripped away. He felt a throbbing in his head but he was too happy to be out of the aircraft and a good chute overhead to care.

As the ground accelerated toward him, he spotted a small earthen dike between rice paddies, and tried to lift his legs to hit on the other side. He glanced up quickly for a last glimpse of Hank's position in relation to his. He focused on a small clump of trees in Hank's direction to use later as a point of reference. The wind was carrying him against the dike in spite of his efforts to miss it. Pulling hard on the right risers did no good. He hit going backwards, crushing the wind from his lungs, as his back slammed against the mound of dirt. The shock of the impact was excruciating as the piercing pain radiated down his back.

He slowly rolled over on his stomach, sucking hard to get air. The pain in his back was almost intolerable. He gradually lifted his head, looking for someone who may have seen their descent. When he realized no one was approaching, he slid down low in the rice paddy, pulling the parachute down into the mud with him. A few feet away was a pipe, about ten inches in diameter, used to equalized the water between the two rice paddies. Brian fought the searing pain as he stuffed the chute into the pipe. He realized he was still wearing the bright yellow Mae West, and wasted no time unhooking the straps, pushing the life jacket into the pipe with the parachute. He lay there trying to get his breath back, fighting the pain.

Slowly, he pulled himself to the top of the dirt mound and looked again for the clump of trees. The sun was barely visible on the top of the hills. He knew he'd have to find Hank soon. Slowly, he made progress toward the trees about two hundred yards away. Darkness was approaching fast as he dropped down and crawled closer toward the trees. Periodically, he stopped to listen, afraid to call out to Hank. There was no sign of his RO. It was almost dark and the panic about finding Hank was building. He called out softly, then a little louder. "Hank." He waited. "Hank can you hear me?"

A voice startled him. It was no more than ten feet away in a slight depression in the ground. "Shh! I'm over here."

Brian crawled over to find Hank propped up on one elbow. "I think I broke my damn ankle. I couldn't walk so I pulled myself down in this little ditch." He looked closer at Brian. "Damn, that's a nasty looking gash over your eye."

Brian leaned over the left leg and looked at the ankle. Hank had unlaced his boot and propped his swollen foot up on his jacket. The bone was pushing against skin, bulging at a contorted angle. "Well, ole Buddy looks like you did your usual good job. It's broken. No doubt about that." Brian glanced around the ground. "I'm gonna' get something to splint it and see if you can walk."

Brian pulled Hank's chute into a ball and cut several of the nylon lines to use in tying the ankle. He stopped momentarily, gritting his teeth against the pain in his back.

"You're hurt, too. It's not just that cut there. What happened?"

"I hit a damn dike going in backwards. Hurt my back, but I'll be okay." He continued to look for sticks to place on either side of Hank's ankle. Finally, he found two that were suitable and wrapped the ankle with the parachute cord. He cinched the cord tight as he stabilized the ankle as best he could. Hank yelled out. "Damn, go easy man, that hurts like hell!"

"I knew you'd start to bellyache right away. Just can't take you anywhere."

Hank smiled and lay back, looking up through the trees at the darkening sky. "How th' hell do you think we're gonna' get out of this?" He closed his eyes momentarily. "You've got a busted back and me with a broken ankle." He turned toward Brian. "We both know we're not gonna' get outta' here, don't we?"

"No, by God, I don't know that. Once before, I told you I was going home and I was going to take your raunchy butt with me. We're going to get our asses out of here! Don't pull any of that negative, I-give-up, bull shit with me."

Hank laughed out loud, letting his head fall back against the ground. "Guess I got your motivation up. Just a few weeks ago, you acted as if you didn't give a rat's ass whether you went back or not."

"Well, let's say I'm motivated now, more scared than I thought possible, but motivated." He grabbed Hank's sleeve. "I'm not about to end up in some damn POW camp. We've heard enough stories of what goes on there. I wouldn't make it as a prisoner." He shook his head from side to side as he conjectured the possibility. "By the way, did you get any kind of a fix before we punched out?"

"The best I can figure is we're about fifteen miles north of the friendlies, more or less. There's got be one whole helluva' lot of 'gooks' between them and us. Of course, we could be non-chalant and tell 'em we're just passing through." Hank's sense of humor returned momentarily. "We could tell them – hey, listen. There's a chopper over there at treetop level." Hank reached for a flare, as Brian grabbed his hand.

"No way." Brian said. "We don't know who's watching that chopper. We can't take a chance."

The rattle of small arms fire, punctuated with heavier machine gun fire broke through the stillness. It was obviously directed at the chopper, who quickly terminated the rescue attempt. There was no doubt left with the dismayed inhabitants of the rice paddy that their chutes had been spotted by the North Koreans as they came down. They were searching for them when the chopper confirmed the area. Now they would be swarming all over the area.

Hank grimaced in pain. The realization they were all alone sank in as the last sounds of the helicopter gradually disappeared. The disconcerting quiet settled in like a mist, as they listened intently to hear if the troops that fired on the chopper were coming their way.

Hank turned to Brian. "We might have a chance of making it out of here if we travel at night and hide out during daylight."

"It's worth a try. Can you walk?" Brian asked.

"I reckon so. You laced this sonofabitch tight enough to hold anything together. Any tighter and my voice would've changed. I'm gonna' tie my boot to my flight suit."

"Forget the friggin' boot. You won't need it on this trip. No more conversation." "Okay, if we hear something, just pull the other off the road." Hank whispered.

Brian looked at Hank quizzically. "Do you still have that little compass you always kept for good luck?"

Hank rolled over, feeling in his pocket, pulled out the small compass on the end of a key chain. "What the hell do you expect me to do with this? This is supposed to be a good luck charm, not something you navigate with."

"Well, Magellan, would you rather take a fix on the stars with your sextant?"

"All right, I get the point! South's that way, or close to it." He glanced up from the small compass and pointed toward a clump of trees in the bend of a small road. The rutted trail wasn't much bigger than a path.

"Check your forty-five." Brian held up his weapon. "I hope you have at least one extra clip."

Hank looked around in disbelief. "You plan to shoot your way out of here, Sport?"

"Right now I don't know what I'm gonna' do. Let's get moving."

"First, lean down here and let me clean that cut with some of this chute you cut up." Hank grimaced at the sight of the gaping wound. "Geez, you could use some stitches in that thing."

"Don't reach for your sewing kit." Brian chuckled, "It'll be okay for now, I'll keep a piece of the chute tied around my head until it stops bleeding."

The walking was slow and tedious. With each step he took Brian could hardly stand the pain and Hank was struggling to put as little weight as possible on his left ankle. They listened for strange sounds. The noises of the North Korean countryside were mixed, presenting bizarre sounds they'd never heard before. They stopped every hour to rest and each time it seemed harder to get back on their feet. Their progress continued at a tediously slow rate but the important thing was the fact they were heading south. It was enough of a boost to their sagging morale that they were moving, hopefully in the right direction.

Hank sank slowly to the ground. "I can't walk one more step on this thing. You go on."

"Don't be such a damn martyr. I couldn't find the next tree without you." He glanced around, taking in the area to see what would serve as a hiding place. "There's a new moon. It'll make it harder for them to see us. Give me your hand. Right up ahead is a ditch. Just a few more steps and we'll hold up there."

"Okay, pull me up. I can make that."

They settled into the lowest part of the ditch, about ten yards off the small road. The earth underneath them was wet spongy ground, soaking into their flight suits. The dankness of the marshy land beside the ditch smelled of human waste. Pain took their minds off the wet discomfort and kept them from sleeping any longer than small naps. The never-ceasing pain would overcome their exhaustion and awaken them to try a different position. Thoughts of water permeated their thinking, as they moved their tongue against the dryness.

Slowly, the sun began to cast a soft glow to their left, indicating dawn's approach. Deflected light rays gave a distorted image to the scrubby trees. As the sun provided illumination of the area, Hank eased his head up to see what was happening. Three peasants were beginning work in a field of turnips about fifty yards to their right, and two more were drawing water out of a well near a small hut off to the left. "Tonight we need to get some water from that well before we start moving." He whispered. "I never knew how thirst could work on you."

"It's tough to lie here hurting, and not move." Brian whispered. That's better than some Gook walking up on us."

Hank eased up occasionally to see what the peasants were doing. He watched as they took their break to eat rice and kimchee out of small oblong metal cans. He punched Brian and pointed their way. Brian eased up, his eyes barely clearing the edge of the ditch. "I always hated their pickled-rotted cabbage.' He turned up his nose. "The pungent smell's nauseating to get a whiff of. But right now the thought of that kimchee seems tempting." Hank nodded and sunk back into the wetness.

Finally, the sun began to sink toward the horizon to their right, and shadows of the trees grew longer. The sunlight streamed through the trees, casting hard shadows, as it dropped slowly into the horizon. Darkness crept tediously over the countryside. The workers flung their primitive tools over their shoulder and sauntered down the road. They listened intently for any signs of human activity. Except for the barking of a dog off in the distance, and cicadas vocalizing in the trees, they heard nothing. It was difficult to stand after being immobile for so many hours. The pain hit with a vengeance as Brian stood erect. He whispered to Hank. "Let's make our way to that well. That okay with you?"

"Yeah, I'm for that."

Brian reached down and picked up a heavy stick with a bend at the end. Handing it to Hank, he motioned how he could use it as a cane. They again began their tedious trek south.

They walked all that night, stopping every hour for a short rest. At the first glow of light in the east, they began looking for a place to hide. It was getting more difficult to find cover from the peasants working the fields. Almost hidden in a clump of tall grass was an abandoned shed. "That looks as if it might provide a place to spend the daylight hours." Hank said, moving off in that direction. He bent down, checking it out cautiously. It amounted to a pile of boards, with one section of a wall still standing. Brian kneeled down beside him, and both pulled at the loose boards. They fashioned a makeshift wall about two feet high. This left a space of about five feet between the existing wall and the stacked boards.

With the approaching dawn, clouds were building toward

the southeast. By noon, the billowing clouds blossomed into full-blown cumulus thunderstorms. The cool winds ahead of the storm clouds were welcomed as they swept over them. They could hear the muttering thunder in the distance, as the trees began to sway with the approaching gusts. The first drops of rain splattered onto the boards, then increased in intensity as the rain lashed over them in moving sheets of water. The thunder boomed in response to the flashes of lightning as the thunderstorm passed directly overhead. They rolled onto their backs, letting the rain fall into their mouths. The downpour pelted the ground hard enough to beat the dirt into mud, splattering onto their faces. As the storm passed toward the northwest, Hank turned toward Brian and tried to squelch his laughter.

"What the hell's so funny?" Brian whispered.

"If you could see yourself, unshaved, wet, mud and blood all over your face. We must look like shit." Hank continued to be amused by their state of dishevelment. It broke the monotony of trying to lie still while the pain monopolized his thoughts. They listened carefully to see if someone could hear Hank's laughing. It was surprisingly quiet as they listened for signs of activity.

"What day is it?" Hank inquired.

Brian thought for a moment, trying to clear the cobwebs. "We went down Tuesday. It must be Thursday. Why? You got a date tonight?"

Hank just shook his head, indicating mock disgust. Then smiled ear to ear. "I was thinking of the schedule. These are our two days off. Do you think they'll make it up to us when we get back?"

Hank's infrequent humor rescued their bowed spirits at the most critical of times. It was becoming increasingly obvious that the odds were against rescue. The alternatives were never talked about. Sagging morale, as well as their physical conditions, was taking its toll. It was more difficult each time to get on their feet and begin moving. Hank's foot was swollen more than the first day; the bulging wrappings indicated the weight placed on it was doing more damage. Brian could barely tolerate the pain in his back. He was emotionally drained and physically exhausted, but the alternative was unthinkable.

They watched the sun setting slowly. An hour later, light drained from the sky and it was dark enough to come out of hiding and make more progress toward the south. They were mustering that last bit of energy and determination to begin walking again. Hank rose on his good knee, using the makeshift cane, and brought himself to an upright position. "Well, I believe south is still down that road. Let's do it."

Brian struggled to get to his feet, but slumped back down and grunted with the pain.

Hank leaned down toward Brian. "C'mon, get up and let's hit the road. We've got places to see and things to do. C'mon, Brian, get your ass up!"

Brian made one more attempt and was on his feet. "If you're waiting on me, you're backing up." He stopped cold in his tracks. "Hank, what the hell's that up ahead? I saw a light."

Hank peered through the darkness, looking across the horizon. "Hell, I don't see ... get down!" He grabbed Brian's sleeve, yanking him down, rolling into the mud-filled irrigation ditch beside the road. "It's a patrol." He murmured.

"Aw shit." Brian answered, as he pushed his body deeper into the muck.

"Lay still. Don't move a muscle." Hank whispered.

The sound of footsteps grinding into the dirt of the small road came closer. The light from several flashlights swept across the paddies and into the tree line. The sound of unintelligible voices became louder as the patrol came closer, finally standing right above them. Brian held his breath, making almost no movement of his chest as he slowly eased out some of the air bursting at his lungs. His muscles tensed as his heart beat faster. He could feel the pulsating, pounding cadence in his temples, fearing it must sound like a drum beat to the troops four feet above his head. He couldn't hear or feel Hank's presence even though he was inches away. He knew this was his last moments of freedom, or life itself. *God, help us now. Whatever happens, let it be over quick.* He prayed silently.

The voices seemed to grow louder as they obviously were having a difference of opinion. The burst of automatic weapon fire was no more than five feet away, as the sound of bullets splintered the darkness, splattering into the mud close by. A second burst cut through the night, crashing into the vegetation beside them. Brian's heart beat as if were coming out of his chest. There was a shout by one of the soldiers and a sudden shuffling of feet, as the patrol moved rapidly down the road. Something had gotten their attention further north of where Hank and Brian lay in the mud. They listened as the sounds disappeared into the stillness of the night.

Slowly Brian moved his legs, and then turned over on his back, wiping muck out of his eyes and mouth. Hank reached over, touching him on the shoulder. "I don't hear anything. Do you?"

"Don't think so. Let's ease up to the edge of the road and take a look."

Tediously they eased up the side of the roadbed, making almost no sound except their still pounding hearts. Each looked in both directions, peering into the blackness for signs of a light. Hank smiled as he squeezed Brain's arm. "We just got damn lucky." He frowned. "At least till next time."

Their energy and stamina were draining rapidly and they had to make progress this night or face the inevitable. Sheer determination was all that kept them moving into the early hours of dawn. They both stopped at the same time and looked at each other. It was ample indication they needed to take a break. They were exhausted.

Brian dropped down, resting his forehead on the soft earth. He was tempted to just stay there and never get back up. His body was weary, too tired to keep playing out this charade of getting back. He knew he was never going home again. His thoughts centered on Ruston, and days of growing up. He thought of days when he sat on his father's lap, playfully tugging at his tie. He remembered how he loved being with him. His thoughts turned to his mother and how he disappointed her with his decision to go to flight training. There were times he could have been a better son. He hoped she forgave him for some of the things he said and those not said. Fleeting glimpses of his past dashed through his brain. He realized he was going to die here in the dirt of some Godforsaken piece of real estate that nobody cared about, and the people he loved would never know. He dropped his head. *So this is where it ends?*

Hank rose up on one elbow. "What were you thinking?"

"Just thinking about Ruston."

"There's nothing unique about Des Moines. Just the same, I'd like to get back there. I'd ..." His voice trailed off as he turned his head toward Brian. "I don't think we're going to get out of here and you damn well know it too."

Brian looked him in the eyes. "I'm sorry for getting you in this mess. If it hadn't been for me, you'd already be back there relaxing at home. God, I'm really sorry, Hank"

"Don't be so quick to take credit for me being here. I made that decision." He sat silently, his head bowed. He rose up abruptly. "No, damn it. I'm not going out this way. Get your butt up and let's get moving. Get up Brian. Get up!"

"It's no use, Hank."

"Get your ass up." He punched Brian with the stick. "Now."

Brian glared at him, as he mustered every bit of remaining energy, got to his feet, and preceded down the small road.

Two hours into the misery, there seemed to be thunderstorms or heat lightning on the horizon. Brian grabbed Hank's sleeve to stop him. "Look over there! That's not lightning. That, by God, is artillery fire. Damnation, that's the front line over there!"

"Great. But that means there's probably a regiment between the friendlies and us. Got any ideas for this one?"

"Not really." Brian looked across the horizon, trying to fully grasp the situation. "It's getting lighter. That hill over there might give us some cover until we figure out who's out there ahead of us. Can you make it that far?"

"Hell, I reckon." Hank replied

As they approached the edge of the hill, there on the edge was an outcropping of rocks. They found enough room to wedge behind the rocks and still be able to have some view of the area. With the sun barely distinguishable over the mountains, the sound of artillery increased in intensity. Small flashes, followed by numerous, familiar "thrumps" as artillery impacted earth. Abundant flashes of light indicated the magnitude of the artillery barrage. Suddenly, in the distance they could see vehicles moving in their direction, then with more light, the outline of troops came into focus. The situation was obviously bleak as the troops came closer to their hiding place. Brian chambered a round in the forty-five automatic.

Hank reached over and touched his hand. "Are you stupid enough to fire on 'em?"

"I don't know. Hell, I just don't know anymore" Brian whispered.

The figures became clearer as they darted ahead in groups of three or four, covering each other. Brian placed the pistol on the ledge in front of him and waited. As the figures moved into focus, advancing no more than thirty yards in front of their position, his hand closed around the butt of the automatic. A soldier looked in their direction, giving a hand signal to those near him. It was obvious they'd been seen. Hank tugged on Brian's sleeve. "It's no use to kill one or two of 'em. Not now."

The conversation was cut short by the sound of Korean speech, and several of the troops aiming their rifles toward them. Brian dropped the automatic, stood up and raised his hands. Hank managed to pull himself up and raise one hand, as he held the stick with the other. The soldiers ran toward them, still shouting commands that were totally unintelligible to Brian and Hank.

Hank looked closer at the uniforms, squinting at the sight of the two who were closest. "My God, Brian, they're South Korean. They're ROK troops, not North Korean or Chinese!"

Brian sank back down on his knees and dropped his head. The discovery that these were South Korean troops was overwhelming. His reserve of strength was gone and he was in no way embarrassed about it.

The ROK soldiers kneeled down beside Brian and took out a

canteen. One of the others offered Hank his canteen, as he yelled back incoherent comments to his comrades.

Finally, a Captain who spoke very broken English came forward. "You two Air Force?" His finger touched Hanks' wings. "How long you here?"

"Yes, Air Force. I think we've been here four days." Hank answered.

The Korean officer continued. "Jeep come soon. Take you back American sector. Big offensive. Very big." He moved his arm in a wide arc, indicating the scope of the operation. "No medical here. Wait American medics, okay?"

"Yeah, sure. I feel fine already," Hank said.

The jeep pulled alongside an American Lt. Colonel, who looked over at the dirty, ragtag pair of American airmen. He walked quickly to the jeep. "Well, looks like you two joined the infantry the hard way. I'm Colonel Hawkins." He watched as they laboriously eased out of the jeep. "Hey, I'm sorry for the joke. I didn't realize you were injured."

"Quite all right, Sir." Hank announced as he pulled himself to attention as best he could, and saluted the officer.

Brian eased off the jeep, pulled himself almost erect as he saluted. The Colonel returned their salute, and apologetically told them they'd have to wait for the next truck of med-evac wounded to go back. "In the mean time, let my men get you some chow. It's C-rations, but it's probably a lot better than you've had recently and my medics'll get you some painkiller."

By nightfall, they were back in an American field hospital. After a rudimentary bath, and several x-rays, they were placed on a cot. An orthopedic doctor approached Brian with a handful of x-rays. "Well, we've taken a few stitches in your forehead and the x-rays show some fractures. It'd be an extra move to send you back to your Base, so I'm sending both of you out on the next air-evac to the hospital in Nagoya. We'll notify your unit. I know you want to make sure the word gets back to your family that you're all right."

"Thanks, Doc. We'd appreciate it if you could make sure word gets back to the Eighty-sixth Fighter Squadron at K-thirteen." There was a pause. "Today," Brian added.

The doctor smiled knowingly. "Consider it done."

The comfort of a major hospital, the thought of being back in Japan, coupled with enough painkillers, made the tests and procedures quite tolerable. A nurse brought a phone for both of them to call home. Brian's mother was ecstatic that he was back and very happy he wasn't hurt badly. Her voice cracked through the tears of pure joy and relief.

It took another day of probing, x-rays, and questions for a definite diagnosis. The doctor moved beside Hank. You've got a severe break in that ankle and the bone had been displaced by the constant walking on it. It's almost a compound fracture. We've got you scheduled for surgery tomorrow morning." He touched hank's arm. "Got any questions about the surgery?"

Hank shook his head. "Let's just get it done."

The doctor swapped charts as he approached Brian. "You've got two cracked vertebrae. It appears to be hairline fractures that we can stabilize with traction." We'll take a look at it later to decide if surgery is required." He scraped the bottom of Brian's foot. "Feel that?"

"Yeah." Brian answered.

"You might have some nerve damage. We'll do some more test in a couple of days." He pulled around on the traction rig. "This should take some pressure off, help the pain, and prevent any further nerve damage. I'll see you tomorrow."

As they loaded Hank onto the gurney for surgery, Brian laughed. "Hank I'll save a pillow or two for you. You'll need it under that leg when they get through making a pin cushion outta' your ankle." Hank was too groggy to come back with his usual humorous retort. Brian watched Hank disappear through the door of the ward, then layback and waited for the painkillers to intervene once again. His eyes felt heavy as he waited. Sleep was welcomed as the only escape from the pain.

The murmur of voices surrounded him as he opened his eyes. There was a radiant face looking down at him.

"Hey, fly-boy, heard you could use a little TLC."

"Maggie! What're you doing here?" He murmured groggily.

"Did you forget? I happen to work here when I'm not R & R'ing with a handsome Lieutenant." She winked and squeezed his hand. "I saw your name on the admittance list and wondered if it could possibly be you. The doctor filled me in on the details. I was doing my damndest to get you back here to Nagoya, but this wasn't exactly what I had in mind. How're you feeling?"

"Not too bad for being hog-tied to this contraption. Lord, Maggie you look good. What a way to wake up." He reached for her hand. "How 'bout dinner at the Imperial tonight?"

"You're a bit tied up right now." She laughed. "But I appreciate the thought. Tell you what. Hurry and get better, 'cause I'm taking *you* to dinner as soon as you're released from here." She squeezed his hand. "Brian, I was hoping to see you again, but certainly not this way and we..."

"Excuse me, Lieutenant Brannon, there's someone here to see you." The charge nurse interrupted, "Your Squadron Commander."

Brian looked at Maggie and she quickly took command of the situation, "Look, I'll come back later. Take care." And with that she turned and told the nurse, "I was just leaving. You can send him in."

Lt. Colonel Kellog strolled up to the bed. "Welcome back, Brian." He took his hand in both of his. "We just about gave up on seeing you and Hank again. The whole squadron's damn glad you made it back. I'd hoped both of you would be here, however, I'll give Hank his later." He opened a long blue box, reached over and a Purple Heart on Brian's robe. "The guys back at the squadron still don't believe it." He laughed. "They were about ready to carve your names in the bar too." He was enjoying the idea of it as he told the story. "By the way, I wrote you both up for a DFC but you realize they it probably won't get through those 'weeny's at Fifth Air Force Headquarters. Well, anyway, it was a way for you to know my personal feelings. Not everybody would have walked out of there like you two did. Now get some rest and I'll see you later." He gripped Brian's shoulder, and leaned closer for emphasis. Their eyes met. "This war is over for you, Brian."

Brian watched the C.O. walk down the long row of beds toward the door. There was an emotional release as he realized his war was finally over, physically and mentally. It *was* time to go home. He rolled over toward the wall and closed his eyes.

A few days later Hank stood by Brian's bed wearing his walking boot, still on crutches, his uniform on, and a small bag packed. Tucked under his arm were orders for going home on convalescent leave, then later to the hospital at Fort Leavenworth for follow-up treatment and therapy. He stood there, rubbing the foot of the bed nervously. "When you get a glimpse of death making a close pass, it's not easy to forget who you shared the view with." He chuckled as he moved closer. "You said you'd make sure my raunchy butt went home ... and you did just that." His hand found Brian's shoulder. "Thanks for the privilege of being your RO."

"I didn't have anything to do with you going home. *You* got us out of there. I'd never have made it without you." There was a long pause. "Thanks for being a damn good friend. Not many people would have stayed behind like you did. And don't ever think I don't know why. I won't forget it."

"Where else could I have had so much fun?" Hank tried to ease the tension.

Brian cleared his throat, trying to put thoughts into words. "It was one helluva' privilege to have you in the back seat." He stopped for a second, cleared his throat again, "I don't know if having you back there made me a better pilot. I do know it made me a better person." He grabbed Hank's hand. "Let me know your address soon as you get there. Take care."

"Sure will, Buddy. Hey, we'll probably be together again. After all, we're the best cotton-pickin team in the Air Force."

"Right on." Brian said.

Hank swung around and hobbled out the door without looking back, before either saw the tears in the other's eyes.

When Maggie didn't return to visit during the next few days, Brian began to wonder what was wrong. He called for the charge nurse at the main nurse's station down the corridor. Within a few minutes she appeared in the doorway. She cautiously approached the bed. "You need something Lieutenant?"

"I need to know which ward Lieutenant Compton is assigned to and information on how to reach her."

The nurse turned toward the door as if she expected someone to come answer the question for her. She looked back at Brian, a concerned expression on her face. "Lieutenant, I know Maggie was your friend. She asked about you several times when you first came in." She clutched the folder she was holding to her chest, as if to use it as a shield. "The day after she came to see you, she was hit by a taxi, right down the street from the hospital. She was in a comma for three days." She shook her head. "Maggie died without regaining consciousness."

Brian rolled slowly toward the wall, straining against the traction, and buried his head in his hands.

"I'm so sorry. None of us wanted to tell you. You were groggy from the pain killers and we just ..." She realized her attempt to ameliorate the situation was useless. "Is there anything I can do for you, Lieutenant?"

Brian turned back and shook his head. He stared at the ceiling, saying nothing. The nurse's face showed sadness for Brian as she turned slowly and left the room.

For the next few days Brian's thoughts were confused and unfocused. His mind was in turmoil attempting to reconcile Maggie's death. He could make no sense of it. He and Hank had just survived combat, ejection over hostile territory, and escaping the enemy against all odds. Maggie couldn't survive walking across the street. Fate was a contradiction of all logic, an ambush of reasoning.

The doctor stood at the foot of Brian's bed, holding a thick folder of medical records. He read a few seconds, took out his pen and began to write. He clicked the pen, stuck it in his shirt, and leaned on the foot of the bed.

"You're about ready to leave here. We'll try to get you on a medevac aircraft to the States in the next day or two. I'll check which hospital and let you know."

Brian pulled himself up as far as he could. "Look, Major, I'm not about to go home on a damn gurney. Give me a few more days and I'll be able to walk fine."

The doctor looked at him emotionless, as he considered the request. "If it means that much, we'll take off the traction in two more days and let you start walking to see how the pain is." His tone was unconvincing. "You might be damn glad to get back in that harness after you've been up a while"

Two days later, Brian was painfully on his feet. He gritted his teeth as he walked up and down the corridor, pushing harder than the doctor ordered. There was considerable pain but it was tolerable. He could do it.

Four days later, Brian dressed slowly, pulling his shirt on, then with a delicate balance, managed to get his pants on. An orderly helped him with his shoes. He pressed gingerly on each foot, trying not to stand to get the shoes on. The orderly tied each shoe and looked up to see if he was grimacing during the ordeal. The discomfort was bearable. He wasn't about to show any indication of pain that would change the orders. Nothing was going to stop him from leaving.

It had been weeks since he had on anything except hospital issued pajamas and the uniform was uncomfortable. He looked in the mirror at the stranger looking back. The image he saw wasn't an impressive sight. Combing his hair, he hardly recognized the sallow likeness as he examined his face.

The nurse barged in quickly with his records and orders. "Major Hargess doesn't feel too good about this move, he thinks he made a mistake going along with you on this, but here's your paperwork. You'll be discharged as a patient when the aircraft lands at Travis Air Force Base. After a thirty-day leave, report to the hospital at Maxwell Air Force Base for reevaluation and subsequent assignment." She smiled. "Good luck, Lieutenant.

Brian looked out the window as the C-124 taxied out for takeoff. The aircraft lifted off the runway at Tachikawa, climbing laboriously toward the East. He leaned forward, looking out the window. He watched the jagged Japanese coastline slowly disappear as the aircraft climbed out over the Pacific. The irregular green shoreline, dotted with buildings, diminished to a delicate fringe beside the darker waters of ocean. The Pacific finally became detached from the land. He leaned his head back and closed his eyes. *Yes, it was time to go home.*

CHAPTER SEVENTEEN

AS THE C-124 taxied tediously toward the terminal at Travis Air Force Base, medical personnel began stirring about in a bevy of activity, preparing patients for exiting the aircraft. Brian kept his seat as stretcher after stretcher of the seriously injured was taken off. Ambulatory patients were last. He was in no hurry as he sat back, looking at the activity outside the aircraft, and contemplating the fact he was actually back in the States. As the last patient moved slowly down the isle, Brian stood up and immediately grabbed the armrest. The pain clutched at him. He needed a few steps toward the doorway to be able to walk without a noticeable limp. As he reached the door, he stopped and inhaled the air. It was a fresh smell, pleasantly familiar scents he'd missed for a long time. Closing his eyes, he breathed deeply.

The Sergeant on duty at the travel section was helpful in arranging his flight to Birmingham, telling him that the next available flight was at 0135 hours the next morning. Brian glanced at the terminal clock. It was 1400 hours. There were eleven and a half hours available to do something he'd thought about for the last few days. Glancing again at the clock, he calculated there was sufficient time to do this and still be at the terminal just after midnight for the Delta flight. He scribbled a telegram to his mother, telling her of his arrival in Birmingham the next afternoon. The operator assured its delivery. He lowered the receiver on the hook and slowly, he ambled out to the taxi station.

"Where to?" asked the driver.

"Fairmont Hotel."

Brian was pleased the driver was considerate enough not to make conversation during the trip to San Francisco. Instead of having to make conversation, he took the opportunity to examine the landscape he'd missed the last time. The Bay Bridge gleamed in the sunlight reflecting the pale reddish tone of the steel. The water below rippled with the effect of the wind and current. In the distance, buildings provided a backdrop of iridescence formations, as the sun washed them with a radiant glow. He felt he was traveling in a time warp, as he recalled the shabby landscape, and flimsy, crowded, low structures he had become so familiar with.

The driver pulled up to the hotel and quickly opened the door. Brian paid him and glanced about at the tall, massive buildings surrounding him. They seemed strange, abstract renditions of his dreams. Not quite like he remembered at all. Yet this was the brick and stone that appeared in his musings, when he let his mind drift to the nights and days there that held such intrinsic memories for him.

Walking slowly through the hotel lobby, alive with sounds of people and activity, he observed the marble entry, the massive mahogany counters, and the surroundings suddenly registered in his thoughts. The familiarity was vague and somewhat ill defined at first. He stood at the desk, still looking around, as a voice asked, "Can I help you, Sir?"

"I'd like a room for just a few hours." He glanced at his watch. "I'll check out about eleven-thirty."

The desk clerk handed him a key. "Room three forty-two. Do you have luggage?"

"No, just the one small bag."

Brian dropped the bag, walked to the window, and looked out over the bay. Visions of that last night here with Anne shot through his brain in rapid-fire snapshots. His stomach heaved as he caught a sensation of the helpless feeling of having to leave her. Bits and pieces of emotions he felt those last few hours emerged from his subconscious. He turned suddenly from the window and the perceptions evaporated.

He showered for almost thirty minutes, letting the spray run over his body as he relaxed in its warmth. The soothing water washed away some of the dark emotions he'd been unable to completely bring to the surface a few minutes before. He basked in the feeling of calming warmth that caressed his body and spirit. Wrapping himself in a large towel, he fell back across the bed, letting sleep come as exhaustion overtook him.

The alarm startled him as he focused on unaccustomed surroundings, and then waited several seconds to realize where he was. Dressing slowly, he brushed at the few wrinkles in his trousers. Looking into the mirror, he adjusted his tie and smiled at the slightly curious countenance staring back. He took a pain pill from his pocket, popped it in his mouth, and sipped a handful of water from the faucet to make it go down.

The elevator ride to the Top of The Mark swiftly took him toward the promise he made to himself. The doors opened to a room that flaunted its image in his memory. He felt the atmosphere of the room glide over him, as he glanced toward a certain table. Haltingly, he turned and walked to the bar. Pausing to glance around the room, he noticed everything was exactly as he remembered. Lifting himself cautiously onto the bar stool, he glanced up at the shelf of bottles. The bartender leaned partway across the bar, placing a cocktail napkin in front of him. "What can I get ya', Lieutenant?"

"I'd like a bourbon and seven from the Eighty-Sixth Fighter Squadron Bottle."

The bartender turned toward the rows of bottles, looking back and forth on the shelf, finally finding the requested bottle. Pouring generously into the glass, he commented on the activity with the bottles. "It's been busy lately with these Squadron bottles. Lots of you guys are coming home and it looks like they're going to finally sign that peace thing."

Brian nodded in agreement. Then, with glass in hand, walked over to the window, looked out over the harbor. He observed the thick gray mist rolling in like a shroud, slowly being pulled over the face of the bay. His hand motioned toward the window with the glass. He summoned his feelings as he thought about friends. *Here's to you, Randy, Frank, Chuck, and all of you who didn't make the trip back.* His mind suddenly caught a fleeting vision of a beautiful blond. *And Maggie. Why Maggie?* Abruptly, his capacity to reason couldn't comprehend that loss. He would never be able to grasp the reason providence made its decision to snatch Maggie from this world. *Where's the reasoning behind such capricious acts of outrage?* Reflecting on their faces, he could hear their laughter, feel their energy. He took a long drink from the glass. *I hope those who flew with you, those*

*whose lives you touched, remember all you guys years from now. I know
I will. Count on it.* Slowly, reluctantly, he turned toward the table by
the window, the one he and Anne had occupied that last night. He
pulled out the chair, sat down, and glanced across the table, looking
intently at the empty space. His mind beckoned her presence, looking
beautiful in the black dress, her hair reflecting in the soft light. With
the illusion there in front of him, he could almost hear the refrain of
La Vie En Rose.

His awareness snapped back to the reality of the moment. It was
apparent that was a long time ago. Things change. People change.
He stared out into the misty darkness of the harbor, thinking about
how life takes so many unpredictable turns. A smile found its way
across his face. *Fate does have a very queer sense of humor.*

"Excuse me, Lieutenant, could I get you another drink?" The
bartender, unnoticed, was standing at his side. Brian looked up at
the bartender who was waiting for an answer.

"No, thanks, I just wanted to have that one."

"I understand, Lieutenant."

Brian left a ten-dollar bill on the table and walked to the door.
He stopped, turned around and his eyes made a scan of the room
one more time. He knew he wouldn't come back again. This closed
a chapter of his life.

He crossed the street to the Fairmont, and checked out. He
picked up his bag, walked out front and signaled a taxi. As the cab
pulled alongside the main entrance, he looked back at the Mark
Hopkins and contemplated how this moment was imagined back at
K-13. He shrugged at his reflection, leaned over and got into the taxi.

After changing planes in Dallas, he was on the final leg of the
journey home. There were no doubts in his mind that he was a

different person than the one who left almost a year and a half ago. He hoped it wouldn't be a disappointment to everyone. Views of Ruston and the large old house flashed in his mind. He knew once he got home, he could relax for a while. Other thoughts built quickly. He remembered the people in Ruston who had always been part of his life. Mentally, there were his mother, Aunt Betty, Lori, and Tyler as sharp as a picture. It helped pass the time as the flight made its way across the Southern states. Periodically, he checked his watch as the anticipation of getting home mingled with unexplained nervousness. The pilot made a straight-in approach to the Birmingham Municipal Airport. Brian glanced out the window at the skyline outlined on the horizon, smiling at how good it looked after all of those months. The wheels contacted the runway, braked hard to turn off onto an approaching taxiway, and bounced lazily to the terminal. Brian strained to see who he could recognize. There, in the small crowd, were his mother, Aunt Betty and Uncle John waiting patiently for the airplane to park.

It took a long time for the ground handlers to move the stairway into position. The impatient passengers were standing in the isle, gathering their belongings, and leaning down to get a glimpse of those waiting to greet them. The door finally opened and the Que of passengers made their way down the steps, walking hurriedly to those waiting. Brian scanned the crowd again, spotting his mother. She had her hand over her mouth muffling sounds of joy. She strained at the small fence separating them. Brian walked faster. As he got closer, he realized how thin and pale she was. She threw her arms around his neck. "You're home. You're home!"

He tried not to grimace in pain as she held onto him and continued to squeeze. He looked over her shoulder and greeted the other two until she released her grip. Then he kissed his Aunt, who was wiping a tear, and shook hands with his Uncle. "It's good to be home again. Sure did miss all of you."

Uncle John inquired about Brian's bag, and started off to retrieve it. They all walked slowly to the car, his mother still holding onto his arm, continuing the nonstop news accounts of Ruston. Brian smiled and nodded as the events and happenings were carefully detailed for him. Mercifully, they didn't deluge him with questions that required painful explanations. His mother would occasionally pat his hand and smile, indicating her pleasure in having him back. He glanced at her occasionally, trying to register the changes he saw without being obvious. She squeezed his hand and announced, "We're going to have your favorite meal tonight. How'd you like country-fried steak, potatoes in cream sauce, butter beans, sliced tomatoes, and cornbread? Oh, and yes, Aunt Betty made you a chocolate pie."

"That's about as close to heaven as I could imagine. I've waited a long time for some of your cooking." He leaned back in the seat smiling at the thought.

He felt brief nostalgia as they topped Holloway Hill and descended into Ruston. When the car pulled up to the large white frame house, Brian stepped out of the car, paused and scrutinized the home where he grew up. His mind abruptly flashed back to a desolate piece of Korean real estate on a dark night, when he wondered if he'd ever be home again. He shook off the thought and reached for the bag.

"No, Brian, I've got it. You go on up and take a seat on the porch," said his Uncle.

Brian continued past the porch down the hall to his room. He stood in the doorway and looked around at the affable surroundings, his eyes stopping at several objects of a distant past. There was only an obscure familiarity with the room. Rubbing the foot of the bed, gently running his hand over the smooth surface of the rounded foot, he was making sure this was the right place. A smile slowly spread across his face as he tossed his hat on the pillow. He was home. Turning quickly, he eased the door shut behind him and went back to the porch. They sat and visited as his mother brought iced tea to everyone.

Brian heard someone calling his name. He leaned forward to see Lori racing up the steps and rose and to meet her at the top. She grabbed him around his neck and hugged. She pushed him away to arms length, wiping embarrassingly at a tear. "Oh, I'm so glad you're home!" She hugged him again. The pain in his back was worth the outward expression.

"Let me tell you. It's good being back. How'd you know I was home, Missy?"

Lori looked around Brian and smiled at his mother. He glanced back at his mother then continued his questioning. "What the devil are you still doing in Ruston in July? Didn't you graduate last month?"

"I did, but I needed one more course to get a teacher's certification, and it was only offered in the summer. So, here I am."

"What've you been doing with all your extra time in Ruston? There's not a lot going on around here in the summer, as I remember it." Brian continued the questioning.

"That's a different story and it'll take some time in the telling. Later, I'll tell you all about it. I left some friends at The Grill and I should get back. I told them I'd only be a minute."

Brian walked down the steps with her. "I'll call you tomorrow, or better still, are you free to go to The Oaks for a barbeque tomorrow night? I've thought about one of those for a long time."

"That sounds great. About sevenish?" She reached over and

hugged him again. "I can't tell you how happy I am to see you back." She bounded down the last step.

"See you tomorrow night. Sevenish." He stopped her. "Hey wait. Are you staying in Old Main?"

"Sure am. I'll see you in the lobby." She yelled back as she walked down the street.

After dinner, while his mother was resting, he took Aunt Betty's arm and motioned toward the door. "Let's go for a walk."

As they walked slowly down the street, Brian glanced at homes he had passed unnoticed every day as a boy. Now he found particulars never before observed, subtle designs in architecture, different hues of paint, and the way the sidewalk buckled from encroaching roots of an oak tree. He turned toward his aunt, "What's the story you never finished in the swing that day?"

"Brian, it can wait. You just got home and¼"

"I've waited a long time to hear what you never finished." Brian interrupted. "I tried to get you to tell me on the phone the day I left. It's definitely time now. Let's have it."

"It's difficult to tell you, knowing how you felt about your father, the divorce, and some question about placing blame." She paused, looking hard at Brian. "I think you should have time to adjust to this before you talk with your mother." She stopped, squared away in front of him, and took his other hand. "Brian, this is going to require you to call up all the understanding you have. It's going to put you to the test how you react to your mother." She squeezed hard. "Brian, as the years pass, she needs you more than ever. Think about this after I tell you."

"For God's sake just tell me, Aunt Betty." He pleaded.

"Brian, your father didn't die of a heart attack. He took his own life."

There was a stunned look on Brian's face. Mentally he just had the wind knocked out him. The memories he conjured up over the years suddenly weren't real. He needed some time to completely digest this thing, thrown at him like a fist to the gut.

"Welcome home." Brian exclaimed sarcastically.

"I know it's not easy to hear. And I wish to heaven they had told you when you were nine. But your grandmother was emphatic in asking that you not be told."

"How did it happen?" He asked calmly.

"Apparently, it was an overdose of the prescription medication he was taking. In case you're wondering, no, it was no accident. He started a note, but never finished it."

"What did it say?" Brian asked, needing more information.

"He said he loved you very much, and he would always be in love with your mother."

"Damn! Damn!" Brian hit the oak tree with his hand.

She put her hands on his shoulders and gripped him firmly. "Whatever you do, don't dare blame your mother. It was the alcohol that killed him, not the divorce. Life was more than he could handle because the drinking had cost him the two people he loved most. Life dealt both of them a cruel blow. She never forgave herself for his death. She's lived with the thought that somehow she should have tried harder. And the worst thing was believing that you thought so too."

"I can't tell you how I feel about this but I'll work through it."

He took her arm and they started back home. She glanced at him occasionally to see his reaction. There was none. He was alone in his thoughts.

The next afternoon, Brian borrowed his mother's car and drove up to Old Main, parking out front. He leaned against the car and looked around the campus, absorbing the view. It was beautiful in the summer. The trees were leafed out providing their acres of shade as a relief from the summer sun. The landscaping gave emphasis to the architecture. An array of muted colors blended with the brick streets and walks for a refreshing effect on Brian. He viewed the last remnants of the wisteria blooming across the front arches of Old Main. The grape-like clusters, hanging loosely across the wide, arched porch always fascinated him as a boy. There would always be many memories connected with the campus of Agnes-Baines College. Smiling at the sensation, he started toward the wide front steps. Lori bounded through the door, waving as she ran down the steps. He laughed to himself. *Missy, you never do anything slowly.*

"Hi there!" She shouted.

"Well, Missy, you sure as hell never change."

She took his arm, holding tightly, as they moved toward the car. Brian flinched as he stepped off the curb too fast. Lori noticed his expression. "Your mother told me you had a fracture in two vertebrae. How bad is it?"

"Not too bad. It only hurts when people disagree with me, so be careful 'bout that."

She hit his shoulder playfully. "You haven't changed either."

The conversation was as relaxed as it had always been between the two of them as Lori explained what had happened with some of their mutual friends and brought Brian up-to-date on the happenings on campus and around Ruston.

"Now tell me about Lori. What's new in her life?" Brian inquired.

She began to laugh. "There's not much to tell. Just school and very little socializing."

Brian didn't let it rest with the brief explanation. "How about getting down to specifics, beginning with Don."

"Oh, very well, since you're so blasted inquisitive. Don's gotten serious, or so he thinks. He never comes right out with something so definite as a proposal. He hints at things, hoping I'll pick it up from there. But, before you make one of your smart remarks, let me tell you; I've made no commitments." She stopped for a second or two, then sheepishly continued. "I've had a date or two with someone in Ruston." She looked embarrassed. "Strictly platonic, of course."

"Well now, that sounds interesting. I should know him since I probably know everyone in town. Who was the object of your charms this summer?"

"Well, he's slightly younger than I..." She paused. "It was Jed Garvin."

Brian turned around to look at Lori. "He *is* younger. I believe he's still in college, right?"

"Well yes. He'll graduate early and be starting med. school after next year. We were both bored, and just had some fun together. C'mon now, don't make a big deal out of it."

Brian made no reply; he just shook his head in disbelief. "How'd Don accept that?"

"We've never discussed it."

"Now, that really makes it clear. You've had an active summer, Miss Barnes."

They pulled up beside the large oak trees that gave the place its name. Brian directed Lori to his usual spot and they took a seat. There was only one other couple in the place. Lori explained that, during the week, especially in the summer, it wasn't crowded. They placed their order with the waitress, then sat and looked at each other for several seconds.

"You haven't asked the obvious; 'How's Anne?' It's something you need to talk about."

Brian looked out the window, thinking how he should react to her comment. Before he could formulate a response, Lori intervened, "Look at me. I'm your friend. I wish I could tell you some things I'm not at liberty to discuss. There's more to this than you know, but for now, just tell me what you're feeling."

"There's not much to say. Why engage in maudlin, sentimental bullshit about life's might-have-beens? It ended. It took a little time to accept it. I mean the timing of it. I used to laugh about 'Dear John' letters. They didn't seem quite so funny after that."

"Brian, there may be reasons for decisions people make that you don't begin to understand. Don't be so damn unsympathetic to that thought. You don't really know why Anne wrote you that letter. She might still care – more than you know."

"It's a wee bit late for that."

"Obviously you've built up too damn much hostility for us to talk about it. But don't say something that's better left unsaid. You're being an obstinate ass about the subject, so let's let it drop."

"Fine. That's exactly what I had in mind."

There was along period of silence before the warmth of their previous rapport returned. Finally, Lori hit his shoulder in her playful manner. "Hey, I'm sorry. We don't need this."

"Right." He grinned. "It was a little strange for us to go at it like that. I'm sorry for my piss-poor attitude. It pops out sometimes."

"It sure does, Lieutenant. It sure does." She nudged him and laughed. "But most of the time you're tolerably lovable."

Brian parked in front of the dormitory and they sat talking until after midnight. They enjoyed the lack of interruptions as they talked.

Lori explained to him how worried they'd been after receiving news that he and Hank had been shot down.

"Yeah, Hank and I were damn lucky." He still didn't feel comfortable talking about Korea, the friends he lost, or things he couldn't resolve himself. The experiences of those months still played over and over in his brain, unwilling to be displaced by the events he tried to push into their place. He would have to leave them there, transitorily churning in the recesses of his reason, but he certainly didn't have to verbalize them. Instead, he'd mention some humorous event, avoiding those things too deeply placed in his thoughts to reveal, even to Lori.

The next morning at breakfast, he sat looking at his mother, wondering when she would bring up this specter that was haunting both of them. They ate and made small talk about the changes in Ruston. Brian, unable to keep his patience in check any longer, asked the question plaguing him. "I know about my father. Aunt Betty told me."

She put her fork down and smiled. "We've always had our most serious discussions at the breakfast table. There must be some symbolism in that." She looked at him penetratingly. "Brian, I wanted to tell you a thousand times. But I knew how you idolized the image of your father. The last thing I wanted to do was destroy that image

"Damn!" Brian exclaimed, showing his frustration and hurt. He smiled. "I know you did what you thought was best. I won't second guess that."

"Brian, don't let the fact that life and people aren't perfect; aren't what you expect them to be, cloud your perspective. You're back. Be thankful for that." Her face almost glowed. "That alone makes my world right. I hope you think of those things now and let the past go.

Just let it go." She leaned across the table. "Now let's see some 'happy' on that face. C'mon, do it for me."

He rose from the chair, walked behind her and placed his arms around her. "I'm sorry for not assuming you always did what was best. I was an ass. Forgive me?"

She placed her hands over his. "Of course I forgive you. I understood your hurt at not having him, yet not really knowing why."

Brian and Lori enjoyed each other's company for the next few days. He shared the pain he felt about his father. Lori offered no advice but made him aware that she was there in every sense of the word. Sharing this with her diluted the anguish he built up about a situation he had absolutely no control over. There was solace in the touch of her hand and the look that indicated she understood.

They took in movies, broiled steaks on the grill in Reynolds Hall, grabbed an occasional milk shake at The Grill, and even relished a swim at "Bull Dog Bend."

He took time to buy a new car. It was a maroon Buick two-door hardtop. The top painted a bright white. The mobility was very welcomed, and provided hours of pleasure driving around familiar scenes of Ruston. There was enjoyment in looking at familiar places, recalling the years growing up in Ruston, and dwelling on the happy events of a youth that seemed so long ago. The feeling of belonging here was beginning to have a relaxing affect and Korea was finally becoming his "past" instead of the "present." He told Lori she was responsible for the way he felt and his quick attitude adjustment.

They parked in front of the dorm, and admired the stillness of the campus on a cool summer evening. He became quiet, looking at the person beside him. She looked back as their eyes met. He pulled her close, kissing her cheek. His hand touched her face, turning it toward him, then kissed her with growing intensity. She instinctively drew back, unnerved by the suddenness of the incident. He placed his arms around her, pulling her back to him, their lips meeting passionately as she kissed him back. She sat motionless, silently, her eyes searching for answers. She quickly opened the car door and turned toward him. "I think we'd better cool it for tonight. We took ourselves by surprise just now."

"Maybe it wasn't a surprise." Brian replied as he got out the other side of the car.

"Oh, I definitely think it was. Don't make me a surrogate for someone else, while you sort through your emotions." The tone of her voice indicated resentment. She quickly forced a smile. "Now, to change the subject; there's something I want to ask you about tomorrow night."

"Sure, whatcha' got in mind?" Brian asked, still concerned about her previous response.

"I have a favor to ask. Could you be right here at eight tomorrow night, no questions?'

"Sure, I'll be here. Now, let me walk you to the door." He didn't follow up with questions he wanted to ask. He'd play along with her request.

The next evening, Brian slid slowly out of the car, sauntering quickly toward the familiar arched porch of the building. Lori was waiting in the lobby. He took her hand as they strolled down the large steps onto the walk. Lori stopped suddenly, looking down the long brick drive, then turned to Brian. "I'm waiting for someone I want you to meet. Let's sit here and wait. They'll be here any minute now."

Brian obliged by sitting on the front bench with her. He looked inquiringly at her but said nothing of the unusual request. His curiosity was getting the best of his not wanting to ask. As his resolve weakened and he was about to ask the inevitable question, the lights of a car shined up the street.

"I think this may be them." Lori exclaimed.

For some unexplained reason, he had no desire to meet these people. He impulsively wanted to be alone. Brian jumped up. "Look, I'll meet 'em later. I'm gonna' walk over there for a minute while you visit with them. I'll be right over there." He pointed to the big grassy area in front of the campus and began walking before an exasperated Lori could stop him.

Brian walked over to the large oak tree he'd remembered scores of times before. He glanced over to the bench he'd shared so many nights with Anne. This was the first time he'd been back to this spot. Walking up to the bench, he rubbed his hand along the back, glanced up at the sprawling branches of the old oak tree, and a smile crossed his face as memories streamed through his reflections of nights spent here. Breaking the momentary spell, he glanced back at Lori greeting the two people who'd gotten out of the car. It seemed she was telling the girl something, when the girl abruptly turned and began moving toward Brian.

He strained to see the outline of a girl walking in his direction. His heart skipped a beat as she got closer. The silhouetted walk was all too familiar. It was Anne. His body tingled with anticipation and shock. Butterflies danced uncontrollably in his stomach. She slowed down as she approached; the glow of the nearby lamp reflected a luster to her chestnut hair. She stopped, the light illuminating her face in a strange way. They both stood riveted to the spot looking intently at each other. Brian's thoughts were spinning wildly, uninhibited, indefinite.

She moved closer, taking his hands in hers. "Brian, thank God you're home." She held his hands tightly, her eyes fixed on his. Gradually, he put his arms around her. It was a good feeling to hold her, yet strange to sense her body against his. The feeling was no longer familiar.

"I think we've a lot to talk about." She whispered in his ear.

He nodded in the direction of the parked car. "I believe you have a date waiting for you over there."

"Oh no, we're just good friends." She glanced over toward the bench. "Would you like to sit for a few minutes? That ole' bench is rather familiar, isn't it?"

Brian followed her to the bench and sat beside her, staring at the beauty he had tried so hard to dispel from his consciousness. They sat there looking into each other's eyes, saying nothing. Anne again took the initiative, and placed her hand on his. "Brian it's hard to find the right words. There're feelings I need to express but the words just don't seem to come." She paused. "Lori called me the minute she heard you were missing. Those were the longest days of my life. It was horrible, not knowing. I prayed a lot. The news you were back was unbelievable and my prayers were answered."

"Thanks. I appreciate the fact people cared."

Anne looked at him penetratingly. "You just aren't going to make this easy, are you?"

"I didn't realize I was being difficult. Anne, it's been a long time, and ..."

She didn't let him finish. "I know you were hurt when you got my letter." She took his hand again. "I'm so very sorry I hurt you. It was the last thing in the world I wanted to do. But I felt I had to do it." She hesitated, looking out into the darkness, then back at Brian. "At that particular time, I was a very confused person. Everything overwhelmed me. I know that's not going to change what you felt.

Or even what you might be feeling now." She paused and looked at him, expecting some indication of approval. "I'm trying my best to explain myself but not doing a very good job of it. I think I need some time to explain things, to tell you about¼" she stopped suddenly as if she couldn't find the right words. She looked perplexed, waiting for some indication of what was going on in his head.

"What do you expect me to say? Everything's okay now, 'cause I understand there was a problem with your thinking. That I understand how you felt?' People don't respond that way. At least I don't. It'll take me some time to adjust to these feelings, whatever they are. Hell, putting it very plainly, Anne, I just don't have any answers right now."

She forced a smile. "Listen, I'm going to Aunt Carolyn's this weekend. She'd love to have you come down and I would too. We definitely need some time to talk. I owe you an explanation – or at least a try at one."

Brian looked back at the couple standing in front of Old Main, then back at Anne, as if gathering his thoughts. "Sure. Why not? I'd love to see them again and we obviously need to talk. I'll leave Saturday morning and be there about the middle of the afternoon, if that's okay?"

"Sure. That's fine. I'll call her first thing tomorrow. They'll be thrilled to hear you're coming." She grabbed his hand, turning toward the people who were waiting in front of Old Main. "Walk me back to the car."

As the car's taillights disappeared down the tree-lined street, Brian turned toward Lori. "That was quite a stunt you pulled tonight, Missy. Now just what the hell gave you the bright idea to do this without telling me?"

"If I'd told you Anne was coming tonight, that I knew she really wanted to see you, you'd have made sure you were nowhere around this campus. I know your stubborn, intractable disposition, Lieutenant Brannon. The only one way I could get you two together was if *neither* of you knew. And I have absolutely no regrets." She grabbed his arm. "Don't you think it's about time you faced your feelings instead of staying in denial?" Lori's eyes flashed as she became more animated. "Now, come off of that hurt expression you're trying so damn hard to maintain. I know you were glad to see her." She stood on her tiptoes, looking him right in the eyes. "I'm right you know."

"I wonder why I even try to get mad at you. It's just no use." He began to laugh. "Missy, you're incredible!"

"And when are you two getting together?" Lori inquired sheepishly.

"Oh, don't worry. Since this was all your doing, I'm gonna' be sure you get all the details. I'm going down to her Aunt Carolyn's Saturday. Who knows what happens then. We have to *talk,* and that's the way we left it. But let me assure you, Missy, you'll be the first to know the dialogue."

"I've a rather good picture in my mind how that *talk* will go. Just don't let your pride get between you and what you really want in life. There may just be things you haven't yet faced. Sorry, Chum, couldn't help throwing that in." She hugged him, holding on longer than usual. She pulled back, still holding both his hands. "Now, go make things right in your life. Fate doesn't always give you another chance."

CHAPTER EIGHTEEN

THE SUN SHOWED itself over the tops of the trees, penetrating the morning haze, its orange glow already beginning to heat the day. Brian turned right at the badge-shaped sign proclaiming U.S. Highway Thirty One. He was filled with anticipation and a reasonable degree of anxiety. Leaning back, he contemplated the next two hundred miles of highway between him and the Gulf. His thoughts churned around the possibilities of what might be said, felt, or perceived when he saw Anne again. His mind toyed with him as he tried to focus on what he would say, what he would do, diverting into different scenarios of possibilities. He smiled as he realized these things couldn't be programmed. They have to be played out as they take place.

As he crossed into Butler County, he observed the Spanish moss beginning to drape from the trees. The gray webs of netting, hanging subtly from the low-slung bows of oaks and sweet gums, distinguished south Alabama from the rest of the state. Their presence announced, ever so discretely, he was entering the Black Belt. The color of the soil was not the only distinguishing feature of the region. Brian felt he was going back in time when he entered this leveling of the earth as it became rich in color, taking on a charcoal hue. The people here were as different as the soil. They were gentle in expression, warm in acceptance of people, embodied a uniqueness of character, and had complete disdain for its lack. This unwavering spirit and zest for life survived a Civil War, Reconstruction, two World Wars, the boll weevil, and the great depression, still retaining its dignity. He loved this part of the south because it had yet to be completely consumed by the twentieth century. It was not yet "gone with the wind."

A shower had passed over the highway ahead, leaving misty steam currents rising from the hot concrete. Brian stared hypnotically into the mist as if there in the haze were answers to his questions. He chuckled to himself as he broke the momentary trance. *Looking into the future is about like trying to see into a fog.* He reached down, twisting the dial to turn on the radio. The silence was too inviting to unbridled musings.

Scrubby pines and sandy composition of the road's shoulders acknowledged he was approaching the Gulf. Suddenly, he came to the intersection where he had to turn one way or the other on the panhandle stretch of Florida. Left would take him to Panama City. Right would take him toward Pensacola and his destination. He accelerated, anticipating the turnoff to Villa Tasso, just before Fort Walton Beach.

He began slowing down, scanning the area for the small sign that would tell him which of the nondescript sandy roads to turn onto. It was difficult to see the sign from the highway, since its sole objective was to let friends and families know the destination of the road, but not announce it to the world. It was easy to miss the small sandy road almost hidden in the palmettos, which led to the six houses that comprised the small analogous community. The cottages were built in the late 1920's, simple in design, and each a unique expression of its owner. The original settlement was composed of friends who shared a love for art, music, the humanities, and above all, a yearning for a retreat from the rest of the world.

Anne's Uncle Walt and Aunt Carolyn had been given the house as a wedding present by his father, who designed and built it. Only two of the original owners still lived in Villa Tasso, but the newer inhabitants still retained a passion for privacy.

The small green sign, aged with time, its chalky white letters barely distinguishing themselves, came up abruptly on the left side of the road. Brian braked hard to make the turn. The sandy roadbed was well packed from use; only the grassy section dividing the two ruts remained undisturbed. He drove cautiously, threading his way around the turns, watching for the fork in the small road marking the edge of the drop-off to the beach. As he eased around the last curve, he saw the white two-story cottage ahead on the left. It beckoned him with its warmth as the afternoon sun bathed the front with an incandescence. The afternoon sun touched it gently. Spanish moss, hanging gray tendrils, oozed from the large oak. They moved casually with the breeze, displaying their frailty with gracefulness. In front stretched an unlimited expanse of blue-green water, small whitecaps dancing toward shore.

He stopped just off the road, on the brink of the high sea wall. He got out, stretching his legs to ameliorate the pain in his back. He walked to the edge of the steep sandy drop that formed a slowly decaying wall that gave way to the sea in measureless bits. The breeze was cool against his face as he turned toward it and listened to the sound of the constant pounding waves. Clouds were drifting across in measured slowness, shifting their position gradually across an indigo-blue sky. He stood a minute, taking a deep breath, inhaling the salty air. Quickly, he turned toward the house, walked deliberately toward the gate of the fenced yard, disregarding the churning in his gut.

As he opened the gate latch, the door at the end of the long screened porch screeched as it opened. He looked up instantly. Anne stood there on the top step smiling, wearing navy blue shorts and a white halter top, her hair moving gently with each slight gust of the on shore breeze. He slowed as he looked at her. She appeared thinner than he remembered, but still her beauty carried a sense of incredulity for him. She stepped down, walking quickly to meet him in the path. She reached out, taking his hand. "Glad you got here early, come on in and speak to Aunt Carolyn. We've been looking forward to this all day." She held his arm with both hands as they moved toward the porch. "How was the trip down?"

"Fine. A little rain, but it was nice driving." He stopped and looked back at Choctawhatchee Bay. "It hasn't changed a bit from the way I remembered it. This has got to be one of the most beautiful sights anywhere." He looked back at her. "Yep, quite a view."

She smiled embarrassingly at the offhand compliment. "And how was your mother?"

"Mom's doing okay but I'll tell you more about that later. She said to tell you hello."

Aunt Carolyn, standing on the porch, drying her hands on an apron, motioned them to come in. She held the screen door open as wide as it would go against the spring that would snap it back into place as protection against the mosquitoes and sand flies. "Hi, Brian. We're glad you decided to come down for a visit." She took his hand in both of hers. "I bet you've enjoyed your leave so far. And while you're down here, I want you to do nothing but some plain ole' relaxing."

"Thanks. You've got the perfect place for doing that. You know, I pictured this place in my mind several times during the last year and a half. I really enjoyed those few days here last time. Thanks for the invitation to come back." He looked past her. "Where's Walt?"

"He's in Pensacola at a meeting and won't be back 'till late. By the way, we're only having cold cuts and potato salad for supper, so we can eat anytime you two decide. You two go relax while I finish a few things here. We'll have time to visit later." Aunt Carolyn turned and went back inside.

"The tide is out. How about a walk on the beach before supper?" Anne asked as she kicked of her sandals and ran toward the surf.

"Looks like we're definitely gonna' take that walk on the beach." Brian Laughed.

"Well, take off your shoes and let's go." Anne spun around and ran down the sloping path at the edge of the drop to the beach. Brian was still fumbling with his laces, hopping awkwardly toward the path. He dropped his shoes on the sand and took off running after her.

"Hey, wait a minute." He shouted as he chased after her, trying his best to run against the pain. He followed, watching the graceful movement of her body as she ran through the sand. She slowed quickly and darted into an alcove on the sea wall, washed away by time and water. As he finally caught up with her, she was breathing very hard, holding her chest. Looking up at him, she patting the sand beside her. "What kept you?"

He fell in a heap beside her, panting from the run. "My God,

I got out of shape fast, lying around doing nothing for too many weeks."

She still clutched her chest as she fell back against the dune, breathing hard. "I just got a¼" she gulped in air, "a head start on you."

Brian looked at her lying there, hair flowing in disarray, eyes as penetrating as ever, and a faint smile that was too inviting. He leaned over and almost kissed her, but stopped for reasons he couldn't explain. He rolled back onto the sand, surprised at the conflict of feelings that engulfed him. She lay there, motionless, gazing into his eyes, studying his reaction. She raised up on one elbow, still looking intently at him, her face a few inches away.

"I know you're still bothered by the letter."

He shook his head side to side

"Oh yes, you are. At least be honest." She sat straight up. "I'm sorry, but at the time there were some compelling reasons. I wish we could just forget that happened; but we can't. We may as well face it and this seems like a good time." She cocked her head, lowering her voice. "Brian, I thought our wolds were too different. That you would actually be relieved. We were together for such a short period of time, always feeling the pressure of time. I believe we needed some breathing room to think things through."

"Why didn't you share that with me instead of that damn letter? That explanation, however, fell a little short and doesn't really explain anything to me."

"You had no doubts?" She asked.

"No. Hell no. And sitting here, I'm amazed you told me that you did. Frankly, I had rather have heard that you met someone and were madly in love."

They just looked at each other, both reluctant to continue the conversation. Anne rose slowly to her feet and dusted the sand from her shorts. "We can talk about this later. A cold glass of lemonade would probably help both of our dispositions right about now. Sure as hell couldn't hurt. C'mon let's go to the house."

He leaned over, his arms resting on his knees. He tried to formulate what he wanted to say. Strong feelings were whirling about in his head, disorganized, and confusing. He needed more time to work through this, to put things in their proper place. It had to be confronted sooner or later, but not at this moment.

She reached down, taking his hand to pull him up. "Now tell me about those last few months in Korea. How you felt and what made you extend. Did I have anything to do with that? Was it my letter?" Anne scanned his face for the answer. She searched his eyes as if she could find the answer was there.

"I can't really explain it to you. It's not something I want to talk about right now. I'll tell you this though: I never forgave myself for Hank staying over there with me. I damn nearly got him killed."

She put her hands on his shoulder. "It's over. Don't keep beating on yourself for something in the past. I don't know your reasons, or what happened, but you need to let it go. Just let it go."

"Good idea. Let's walk down the beach."

They strolled slowly along the water's edge, letting the waves wash over their feet. The placid rolling of the waves, and a shrill cry of a gull was a backdrop to their thoughts. They walked in silence, both locked into their thoughts. The sun made it's move toward the water, casting a glow on the breakers.

"Are you hungry?" Anne broke the silence.

"Matter of fact I am. Let's go."

The cups were filled and refilled as the conversation extended past the meal. Brian laughed at Aunt Carolyn's explanation of the repairs over the years to keep the cottage in operating order. "You know these houses were originally designed and built as vacation homes and luxuries weren't considered essential. Over the years, Walt's mastered everything from plumbing to carpentry, and a generous exposure to the care and cleaning of septic tanks. Necessity has certainly been the mother of invention around here." She continued her stories of misadventures, learning experiences, and threw in a few hilarious hurricane stories to keep them in stitches.

Walt came in late, walked over and slapped Brian on the back. "It's about time you got back here. You look great." He stuck out his hand. "It's good that you could come down here and visit a while." He chuckled. "I needed someone to keep Annie occupied so she doesn't drive me up the wall."

Anne glared her false indignation at their ongoing contest of wills, as Walt pulled up a chair beside Brian and quickly joined in the conversation. They laughed and talked for the next hour. Anne casually glanced at her watch, then at her aunt.

Carolyn smiled, glanced down at her watch. "It's late. I'm an early riser and if I don't get my eight hours I'm grumpy all day."

"I believe I'd call it cantankerous." Walt injected, while pushing away from the table. "However, you two stay up 'till whenever. We'll see you in the morning."

Anne and Brian meandered down the path toward the sea wall. Brian stopped at the edge, leaned back against the front of his car, and gazed out across the bay. The night was dark, accented only by a sprinkling of stars and an occasional shrimp trawler's lights moving sluggishly across the horizon. The breeze was refreshing as it moved steadily across the sand with slight hints of a gust. Anne walked up and stood close to him, looking into his eyes. He slowly raised his arms around her, pulling her closer. She stroked the back of his neck, playing with the nape of his hair. He scrutinized her face in the shadowy light, searching her eyes as they held each other in silence. The softness of her was comfortable against his body. He made no effort to move her hair as the gulf breeze blew it across his face. It had a familiar smell as he let it envelope him.

She looked up at him. "What do we do now?"

They were frozen there, holding each other as the waves continued their muffled crashing against the shore in the background. Brian glanced up at the wheeling stars in their inexorable path. Destiny, providence, fate or whatever that enigmatic force might be, made its claim on their lives. He knew there was nothing either do to change its course now, any more than they could alter the path of the stars.

"Almost three years ago, a night I'll never forget, you walked into The Grill and a bomb went off in my head. During those next three weeks I fell hopelessly in love with you." He took her hands in his. "Later, when we became engaged, I knew it was forever. I never had a doubt it was forever. And that last night in San Francisco was something else. My God, there was a passion so deep and sharp that few men ever experience that." He took a deep breath. "But I'm not the same person who left you back in San Francisco. I..."

She squeezed his hand, stopping his statement. "No, Brian, we're not different people. We've just experienced more of life. And so far we've both managed to survive whatever it tossed our way." She squeezed his hand extremely hard, looking intently in his eyes. "It's totally beyond our control to change things back to that time we were so naive, when we had each other and our innocence. That was an illusion we tried to hang onto too long. We really only have right now. That's all."

"Let's admit it; time, that enigmatic force we fought so hard took its toll on our relationship." He touched her face. "We just make the best of what it deals us."

The only sound was the crashing of the waves as they collided with the shore and retreated. He pulled her close. "I agree; we only have right now. There's no way we can go back to those feelings we shared before I left. We may as well be realistic." He held her tightly.

"I know." she said.

But, Anne, you never forget your first love. It's a special part of your life forever."

"I'm sorry the way things turned out, Brian." She held his hands tightly in hers. "Remember this: Wherever you are, and whatever you are doing, you'll always have a special place in my heart"

"I know." He kissed her cheek, and turned quickly.

The drive back to Ruston was bittersweet as the burden he had been unable to shake was gone. It had been carried away with the tide he had watched so mysteriously last night. There remained a hollow feeling in the pit of his stomach as he remembered how close he and Anne had come to the magic that people search for so diligently. His thoughts were maudlin as he reached for the radio dial.

The music was soothing, and he settled back relaxing to the melody. He thought of Lori. Those thoughts centered around the shared friendship, closeness, and her unswerving loyalty. He couldn't help contrasting emotions felt between Anne and Lori, and the contrast was illuminating. He knew that talking to Lori would bring things into proper perspective. It always did. He smiled as his foot came down harder on the gas pedal accelerating him toward his destination.

He braked to a stop in front of Main dormitory, tired but

exhilarated. There was a gnawing need to talk with Lori. To bring these unbridled emotions to some kind of acceptable resolution. Sharing his thoughts with the one person who would understand was necessary.

He leaned over the large desk, covered with papers and keys being fussed over by the harried receptionist. "Excuse me" Failing to get a response he repeated his request; this time successfully. She looked up from her frantic note taking as she moved papers. "Can I help you."

"Could you please page Lori Barnes?"

She blew at a shock of hair as she pointed with her left hand. "Lori left for the library about an hour ago. You can probably still catch her there." She immediately resumed her shuffling of papers.

Brian pivoted and shot through the door, down the steps, turning toward the library. He walked briskly along he uneven brick walk. He was deep in thought as he heard his name. He glanced up to see Lori coming his way. She stopped dead in her tracks, dropping her hands to her side. A frown, and the cock of her head, outwardly indicated her foreboding that Brian was back in Ruston. She regained her composure as she continued walking toward him, visibly shaking her head for emphasis.

He waited for her, not moving, only watching her intently. She stopped directly in front of him, still frowning. "What may I ask is the meaning of your presence back here in Ruston so soon."

"Let's sit over here on this bench. Maybe I can explain it to you. And again, maybe I can't." He stated.

Lori sat down, placing the notebook on the bench beside her. She swung around to look him directly in the eyes. "Don't tell me you ent down there with a chip on your shoulder and screwed this thing up again. You know, Mister Brannon there is just so much I can do on your behalf. Even I can't work miracles." She cocked her head at the usual angle for emphasis, her green eyes flashing. "Okay, let's hear what happened."

Her examining gaze never left as he took her hand. She winced at the tightness of his grip. He cleared his throat. "I want this to come out the right way and that's not going to be easy for me". He squeezed her hand harder. "Anne and I had something special at one time. But there are different kinds of love. There is the kind that burns brightly like a Nova, blinding you to anything else by its brilliance. It goes out the same way, leaving you with only the memory of that powerful light as the darkness surrounds you." He moved closer, continuing to talk. "Then there is the kind of love that grows slowly, steadily, consistently, always building on itself, increasing in its intensity." His eyes never left hers, his gaze as strong as his grasp of her hand. "Last night, as I watched the tide against the beach, I looked into that ink black night, and and reasoning suddenly told me what I had subconsciously known for way too long."

Shock washed across her face. "That's impossible. You'll never love anyone other than Anne. Don't you sit there and tell me, that out of a clear blue sky, You've changed how you feel. No. Never. I can't accept that and I don't know why you even bother..." Her voice became softer, then stopped completely.

He said nothing. The look in his eyes said it all, but she was hesitant in accepting their message, refusing to acknowledge what she must have realized at that moment. She sensed a change in Brian, in his words, his expression, his touch. But it was still too new, too different, too tenuous to believe. Lori wouldn't acknowledge the indications she was watching and feeling. Instead, she withdrew slightly and began to fidget with her necklace. "Brian just look around you. Look at all those things that remind you of Anne. There are ghosts of the past drifting all about you as you sit there. How can you be sure of your feelings right now?" She hesitated. "Whatever you do, don't say something that's only a reflex from last night" Her voice trembled. "Be careful what you say right now...very careful."

He pulled her close, putting his face next to hers. He could hear her breathing as he whispered. "It's funny how fortune lets you fumble around, thinking you're in control of your life. Then suddenly one day the fates let you know there are other forces at work." He held her closer. "I love you Missy". She buried her head against his face. He felt the warmth of her tears touch his cheek. Suddenly, he felt a contentment he had never experienced, a tranquility he had never known.